The Plot To Kill The Pope

Anonymous

Books by Anonymous –

The Book With No Name
The Eye of the Moon
The Devil's Graveyard
The Book of Death
The Red Mohawk
Sanchez: A Christmas Carol
The Plot to Kill the Pope

The author can be found on Facebook and Twitter as Bourbon Kid.

Contents

"Self awareness is knowing everyone else thinks you're an idiot." – Anonymous.

The Late Night Drive

Damn this rain!
Diane Crawford had been on the same long, winding country road for over forty miles with no sign of any civilisation. And the rain was coming down like nothing she'd ever seen back home. It felt like an invisible man was standing on the hood of her car constantly throwing buckets of water onto her windscreen. Visibility was at an absolute minimum. If she crashed and died on this horrible road out in the middle of nowhere, no one would find her until morning. And it would be her own bloody fault. Only a crazy person would drive in weather like this. Or a person like Diane who was more scared of pulling over by the side of the road in a backwoods country with zero streetlights. What she needed was a hotel or gas station, just somewhere that she could stop and take stock of things while the weather calmed down. It was 2am when she finally saw an old gas station up ahead. There was a big bright yellow signpost outside that was probably quite garish to look at during the daylight hours, but at night it was a blessing to see something so colourful at the side of the road. The red lettering on the yellow background was easy to read.

Barney's Gas and Goods Store.
Open All Hours.

Diane steered her Audi A3 off the road and onto the gas station forecourt. Even though the signpost had said the place was "OPEN ALL HOURS" it certainly didn't look that way. There were no lights on inside the shop and the place looked deserted.

She pulled up alongside one of the gas pumps and killed the engine. The lights on her dashboard died with the exception of the digital clock that read 2:02am. Diane didn't desperately need fuel, but her desire to get off the road meant she was willing to stick thirty dollars' worth in, just to stay out of the rain for a while. And she was in the middle of a very unfamiliar and barren stretch of country so there was a high chance she wouldn't see another gas station for a long time.

An old guy in the last town had given her directions for a short cut, but she was beginning to suspect he'd sent her on a detour to the set of a Stephen King movie. This whole place was creepy, badly lit and surrounded by tall trees and thick bushes.

She grabbed her raincoat from the passenger seat and fought with it in an effort to get it on before she opened the car door to get out.

It was a crinkly thin yellow plastic anorak, which didn't offer a lot of warmth, but it did keep the rain out and it was easily visible. She pulled the hood up over her head and tugged at the laces to tighten it around her neck, ensuring that the rain wouldn't be able to get at her hair. Just before she climbed out of the car she caught sight of her reflection in the rear view mirror. The yellow anorak made her look like she was about to cook up some crystal meth with Walter White. She pushed the door open, fighting against the weather as she climbed out. A huge gust of wind blew the door shut for her, saving her a job.

The gas pump she had parked alongside was switched off, so she hurried over to the shop to look for an attendant. On the glass entrance door was a sign –

AFTER 10 PM RING THE BELL FOR ASSISTANCE.

She looked around the doorframe and spotted a plastic grey buzzer. It was crusty and old with a cobweb on the bottom of it that glistened in the rain. She pressed it hard and held her finger on it. She heard no sound of a bell ringing inside but it did vibrate a little beneath her finger. After about five seconds she let go of the buzzer and pressed her face up against the window, framing her hands around her face to get a clear look inside. Almost immediately a light flickered on inside the store.

She backed away a little and looked for any signs of movement. At the other end of the front window of the store was a sales counter that looked onto the forecourt. A young man appeared through a strip curtain next to the shelves of cigarettes behind the counter.

He peered out through the window to see who had pressed the buzzer on the door. Diane guessed that he was little more than sixteen or seventeen years old. He had messy brown hair. It crossed her mind that she might have woken him up, but then again, he was a teenager so it was entirely likely that his hair was meant to look shitty. Diane had two teenage sons of her own and they both insisted on dodgy *"birds nest"* haircuts that she had no doubt they would regret when they were older. This kid looked the same, only slightly grubbier than her sons, who were fairly hygienic as teenage boys go.

The attendant spotted Diane and waved at her. He came out from behind the counter and walked over to the door. He unbolted it in three different places before pulling it open.

'Come on in before you get blown away!' he said with a smile.

'Thank you,' said Diane, stepping inside and lowering the hood on her coat. 'I was wondering if I could get some gas? I've been

6

driving all night and I've got a feeling if I don't fill up now I'm going to regret it in about fifty miles time.'

'Wise move,' said the boy. 'There's not another station for at least fifty miles. I can promise you it's not worth the risk. I ran out of gas down that way once,' he pointed in the direction she was headed. 'Worst mistake I ever made.'

'I hope the weather wasn't as bad as this,' said Diane.

'Fortunately not, but I'll never make that mistake again.' The boy closed the door behind her. Diane noticed he had the name Steven sewn into his denim dungarees.

'Is that your name? Steven?' she asked.

He looked down at his dungarees. 'Yeah. My dad's a dick who can't remember the names of his kids if we don't have our name sewn into our clothes.'

'Your dad is Barney who runs the place?'

'Yeah. Don't let my mom catch you saying he runs the place though!' he joked. 'I think Dad's only input is the name badges.'

Diane laughed politely.

'I'll go get the keys for the pumps,' Steven said, heading back to the counter. 'Would you like a coffee? I've just brewed a pot.'

The thought of drinking coffee at 2am would normally be an absolute no-go, but Diane was desperate for some caffeine to keep her going. 'That would be great, thanks,' she said.

There was a selection of chocolate bars for sale on the counter and a pot of coffee on a hot plate next to the till. Steven ducked down beneath the counter and reappeared a moment later with a plastic white coffee cup. He placed it down on the counter and started pouring a very dark blend of coffee from the jug into the cup. 'Milk and sugar?' he asked.

'Just some sugar would be great, thanks,' said Diane. 'How much do I owe you?'

'The coffee's on the house. A lot of people need it this time of night, if only to get them through the next fifty miles of road.' He spotted Diane inspecting the quality of the coffee he was pouring. 'Don't worry,' he said, reassuring her, 'this is pretty fresh. I only brewed it about twenty minutes ago.'

'It looks fine.'

Steven finished pouring the coffee and replaced the jug on the hot plate. 'I'll just go and get you some sugar,' he said. He vanished through the strip curtain behind the counter, only to poke his head back through it a second later. 'I won't be a minute,' he said. 'I've just got to get the keys for the gas pumps as well.'

Diane looked around the shop floor. The place was more of a DIY store than an everyday convenience outlet. Gardening tools and fertiliser bags were more prevalent than the usual displays of groceries and oversized junk food products one would normally associate with such a store.

After making a fair bit of noise out back Steven eventually returned from the back room with a set of keys and four sachets of sugar. He handed the sachets to her. 'Is that enough?' he asked.

'I'll only need two, thanks.'

'Cool. Just leave the others on the counter. I'll go fill your car with petrol for you. How much would you like?'

'Oh, you don't have to fill the car for me,' said Diane. 'I can do that myself.'

'I'm sure you can. Unfortunately it's actually a policy here. We fill all the cars. We used to let customers do it themselves, but we had way too many drive offs. And out here, there ain't a whole lot we can do about it, so we fill all the cars ourselves. I can see you're not the type to do a drive off, but policy is policy, you know?'

Diane nodded. 'That's fine. I'll take thirty dollars of unleaded please.'

'No problem ma'am. Will I need your car keys?'

Diane reached into her coat pocket for her keys and handed them over to him. He took them and walked back to the entrance. As soon as he opened the door the sound of the wind and rain rushed into the store. Steven fought his way out and pulled the door shut behind him to stop it from swinging back open. He switched on an outside light and hurried over to Diane's car, crouching to keep the rain out of his eyes. Neither the wind nor rain was showing any sign of easing so the poor lad's hair was getting even messier as it blew around all over the place.

Diane took a big sip of the coffee. It was divine. Probably cheap crap really, but in the current scenario it tasted like heaven. If the petrol had a similar effect on her car it would be well worth the money. The rush from the caffeine kicked in instantly and reinvigorated her, ready for the rest of the journey to her sister's home in the countryside.

Steven finished filling up her car and fought his way through the wind and rain to get back to the shop. His dungarees were soaked right through. His dark red jumper probably was too but it was hard to tell. He pushed the door open and practically jumped back into the shop before fighting to close it again.

'It's pretty mental out there,' he said, running his hand through his wet hair.

'You don't need to tell me,' said Diane. I've been driving in that all night!'

'You got much further to go?'

'Heading to my sister's for a week. If I don't take any more wrong turns I should be there in about two hours.'

'Two hours you say?' said Steven as he walked back behind the counter. 'Where abouts does she live?'

'A place called Knots County. According to my car's computer it's about fifty miles from here.'

'More like seventy.'

Diane took another sip of coffee. 'Good job I've had this coffee then. It'll keep me awake just long enough to get there if I'm lucky.'

Steven smiled at her but said nothing. It reminded her that he probably had other things to be doing.

'Thirty bucks right?' she said, placing the empty coffee cup down on the counter.

'Actually it's only twenty-eight dollars. I tried to put another two dollars in but there just wasn't room in your tank. You're filled up now, miss.'

Diane reached inside her coat pocket for her purse. 'You can have thirty anyway for being honest about it,' she said, 'because I wouldn't have checked.'

She pulled out her Visa card and held it out to him. He was standing by the till with a set of keys in his hand, looking like he was considering opening it.

'There you go,' she said.

To her surprise he didn't take the card from her. He was staring over her shoulder at something outside on the forecourt. He had a confused look on his face.

'What the hell is that?' he muttered under his breath, just loud enough for Diane to hear it. His eyes were following something that was moving across the forecourt. Diane felt a little embarrassed that she was standing there with her hand outstretched offering him her Visa card and he was ignoring her.

And then behind her she heard the wind and rain rush into the store once again as the door at the entrance opened. Someone had walked into the shop. Steven's confused look rapidly changed to a wide-eyed look of shock at the sight of what had come through the door behind Diane. She turned around to see who it was and realised right away why Steven looked so spooked.

The man who had entered the store was tall and almost as wide as a door. The most noticeable thing about him was that he was wearing a bright red leather jacket and a yellow skull mask with a stripe of red hair on the top and a hideous grin across its face. He had some weapons or gardening tools strapped across his back too. It was hard to tell what they were, but Diane could see a metal handle protruding over each of his shoulders. She knew who this man was from an article she'd seen in the news recently. It was *The Red Mohawk.*

She backed away until her feet connected with a display of compost bags in the hardware area of the store. The Red Mohawk ignored her and walked up to the counter where Steven was staring at him, dumbfounded. As the Mohawk passed Diane she got a good look at the two items he had strapped across the back of his red jacket. In a cross formation he had a baseball bat and a silver sword, both secured within brown leather sheaths.

He reached across the counter and grabbed Steven by his hair. He dragged the dumbstruck young man halfway across the counter until his head was hanging over the end. His stomach was laid flat out on the counter with his legs dangling over the other side, kicking out at the shelves of cigarettes as he struggled to free himself from the Red Mohawk's grip.

There wasn't much else Steven could do other than yell at the top of his voice, "WHAT THE FUCK!'

The Red Mohawk offered no explanation for his actions. He reached back over his shoulder and unsheathed the sword. He held Steven down with one hand and brandished the two-foot long blade over his head.

Stupid though it might seem, Diane considered the possibility that she might be witnessing a prank of some kind for a cable TV show. There was just no way this could be real. The reality didn't kick in until the Red Mohawk thrust the sword down, piercing the middle of Steven's back. It made a gut-wrenching squelching noise as the steel blade delved into his flesh. It went in deep, right through his back, not stopping until it was wedged firmly into the counter beneath him. A fountain of blood briefly squirted up from his back where the blade had entered.

And Steven screamed.

Diane had never heard anyone scream like that before. The sound of it burned into her ears and frazzled her nerves. She was hearing the sound of a boy close to death, fighting to stay alive, desperate for someone to hear him and come to his rescue. But Diane wasn't that person. She wasn't that brave. But then again, who was?

10

When Steven ran out of breath and stopped screaming, which happened very quickly, he sucked in what little oxygen he could and screamed again.

The Red Mohawk had paid no attention to Diane at first, but as he waited for Steven to finish hollering he turned his head slowly and looked across at her. In the eyeholes of the yellow skull mask she saw a pair of eyes that she would never forget, eyes that signified the very incarnate of evil. She stood frozen to the spot, paralysed with shock and fear, even though deep down she knew that she should be running as far away from this man as she could.

But fortunately for Diane, the Red Mohawk had no interest in her. He turned his attention back to his stricken victim. Steven was desperately struggling in a vain attempt to free himself, reaching out with grasping hands hoping to grab onto something, *anything* that might help him. The blade pinning him to the counter made it impossible for him to reach back for anything that could be of use to him. A Snickers bar was the only thing within his reach and Diane was certain that it wouldn't help him in his current predicament, even if the guy in the mask happened to be allergic to nuts.

The Red Mohawk reached over to a radio behind the candy rack on the counter and switched it on. Diane recognised the song that came blaring out. It was *Rush Hour* by Jane Weidlin. For reasons she couldn't quite explain, it was the trigger that finally snapped her out of the trance that had left her gawping at the events unfolding in front of her. She came to her senses and sprinted for the exit, knocking over a garden gnome as she went.

When she reached the door she wondered for a second if there was anything she could do to help Steven. The thought left her head almost as soon as it entered. She was in no position to stand up to a masked killer with a sword. She yanked the door open and immediately a gale force wind hit her in the face, accompanied by specks of rainwater and a cold chill. It knocked her off balance and twisted her around giving her a perfect view of what was going on back at the counter. The Red Mohawk had unsheathed his baseball bat and taken up a position beside Steven, wielding the bat above the boy's head. Steven was in no state to fight back and his futile attempts to free himself had ceased. He was sobbing, but he no longer had the strength to even look up at his tormenter. His head drooped down over the counter, blood trickling out of his mouth onto the floor. The counter was covered in a puddle of blood too, that was only getting bigger as it rushed out of the entry wound in his back. Diane winced and closed her eyes as the Red Mohawk smashed the baseball bat down onto Steven's skull. But even with her eyes closed it felt like she saw the impact. A small amount of vomit squirted into her mouth. She'd seen enough. She raced out of the store into the wind and rain.

She was only inches from her car when she realised she had a problem. *Steven still had her car keys.* She was going nowhere in that car. She wasn't even getting *into* that car. She grabbed at the handle on the door but it wouldn't open. Steven had locked it again after filling the car up.

A feeling of despair wrenched at her heart, squeezing every ounce of hope out of her. Her head began to feel heavy, then dizzy as she was gripped by anxiety and the very real fear of death. The dizziness rushed through her veins like a supercharged virus. She dropped to her knees, panting for breath.

"GET UP!" her inner-self screamed at her. *"GET UP AND RUN!"*

She pressed the palms of her hands into the ground and pushed herself up. The ground was soaked in rain and littered with small stones that pressed into her fingers, the sharpness at least providing her with confirmation that she was still alive. But the harder she pushed down in her attempts to stand herself up, the weaker she felt. The strength in her arms and legs evaporated, exiting her body through her lungs every time she exhaled. She remembered fainting on two previous occasions in her life. If this became the third time then she feared it would be the last.

She reached out and planted her hand against the back of the car to steady herself. But the strength in her arms had vanished completely. She slid back to the ground, managing to twist herself around into a sitting position, propped up with her back against the car. The rain on the ground soaked into her skirt and through to her buttocks, turning them ice cold.

Through the window of the store she watched the Red Mohawk repeatedly beat Steven over the head with his baseball bat. Over the sound of the wind and rain she could even hear the bat connecting with its target.

As her vision became blurred, her hearing also faded. After the fourth clank of bat against bone inside the store, her head fell back against the car. She slid down to one side, her spine no longer strong enough to keep her upright. And by the time her face splashed into a puddle on the ground she was unconscious.

The Closet

The boy would never forget the sound of the car screeching to a halt on the driveway in front of the house. He and his father had been building a Lego village, but at the sound of the screeching tyres his father jumped up and raced to the window. He peered through the blinds. And at that moment the whole world changed.

The boy's father stepped back from the window. The colour drained from his face. Even though the boy was only five years old, he could tell that something was wrong. His father rushed over to him and hauled him up from the floor. He held the boy tightly against his chest and carried him down the hall and into the main bedroom. He placed him down on the floor by the closet. Then he pulled the closet doors open and ordered his son to step inside.

'What's wrong, Daddy?'

'Nothing. We're going to play a game of hide and seek. You stay in here until your mother finds you, you understand?'

'Okay.'

His father seemed frantic, flustered by something, but the boy could not understand what. Next to the boy's feet was an old portable CD player and a set of headphones. His father reached down and grabbed them.

'I want you to stay in the closet and listen to the music. Don't make a sound, okay?'

'Okay, Dad.'

His father's hair was flopping around his face but he made no attempt to brush it back. He placed his hands on the boy's shoulders and looked him in the eye. 'No matter what happens,' he said, 'no matter what you see or hear, keep listening to the music, concentrate on the music, nothing else. And do not come out of this closet until I say so, okay?'

'What's happening, Dad?'

His father slipped the headphones over his ears. 'Just listen to the music son. Concentrate on the music. The Lord will protect you.' He kissed the boy on the forehead and whispered, 'I love you son, and so does your mother. Always.'

The boy's father pressed a button on the Walkman and closed the closet door. It was dark inside the closet. The only light afforded to the boy came through in thin stripes from the panelled wooden slats on the closet door.

Concentrate on the music.

The boy did as his father instructed, even though the phrase "The Lord will protect you" was playing on his mind. *Protect him from what?* He only asked himself the question once before he was distracted by the music on the tape. His mother played it all the time. It was a compilation of her favourite Catholic hymns performed by the local church choir. The track that filtered through the headphones and into his psyche was *Silent Night*. The boy liked the song because it was his mother's favourite. She always sang it to him before bedtime as Christmas drew near. He was seven years old now though, and the days of sitting on his mother's lap and listening to her beautiful voice were a thing of the past. Lego and toy guns were his world now.

Halfway through *Silent Night* he heard a loud bang. It made him jump. A bang usually meant the end of something, like a balloon popping, or a tyre bursting. The boy had heard both of those things before, but neither of them was as loud as the bang that now had him trembling inside the closet.

Concentrate on the music.

He remembered his father's words. He tried hard to listen and understand the lyrics and block out all other thoughts. Some of the words didn't make sense to him, and never had. It had always been the soothing voices of the singers that gave the song its beauty, not the lyrics. During quieter moments of the song, he heard screams coming from the living room. A woman's screams. Had his mother come home early from work?

Concentrate on the music, son.

A tear slid down his cheek. He wasn't entirely sure what had made him cry but he knew he was scared. The game he was playing with his father didn't have the same appeal as the usual antics they got up to. The air in the closet was thick and musty. The slivers of light coming in through the slats in the door highlighted the specks of dusting floating all around him. He was alone and all he had to keep him company was the voices of the church choir.

When *Silent Night* came to an end, there was a two-second silence before the next song commenced. During those two seconds the boy heard a man's voice screaming out in the next room. He couldn't tell if it was his father's voice or not.

The next song on the CD was *Amazing Grace*. It was a song he wouldn't hear again for several years. But it would always remind him of the day his parents were murdered. And of the moment he looked into the eyes of their killer.

A short, stocky man in a blue tracksuit wearing a black balaclava over his face entered the bedroom. In his hand was a long sharp knife, covered in thick splashes of red blood. The blood of the boy's parents.

The piercing green eyes of the man in the balaclava scoured the room until they settled on the closet door. His eyes were staring right through the slats at the boy. He took one step towards the closet before something distracted him. The boy would later realise that it was the sound of a police siren a few blocks away. The man in the balaclava took one last look at the closet door, then turned and vanished from the room, like a shadow, dissolving into the darkness.

The boy remained in the closet *concentrating on the music* for ten more minutes until another man entered the bedroom. The boy recognised him. It was Devon Pincent, a friend of his father. He was carrying a gun and taking careful steps in case the intruder was still in the house. But he wasn't. He was long gone.

Devon looked around the bedroom, pointing his gun at everything he stared at. Eventually, much like the man in the balaclava had done before, his eyes settled on the closet. He tentatively approached it with his gun pointed and ready to fire. He reached out with his free hand and pulled the closet door open. At the sight of the boy, he tucked his gun into a holster inside his jacket. He reached out and took the headphones off the boy's head.

'Hello Joey,' he said. 'I need you to come with me. But you have to keep your eyes closed, okay?'

Devon picked him up and carried him out of the house to a waiting ambulance. But Joey didn't close his eyes. He saw everything.

The Nun

Sister Claudia walked into *The Orient Express* on a cold morning in September expecting little more than a quick breakfast with her old friend Pete. It had been exactly six months since she'd seen him, a timescale that had become a regular routine since she had relocated to Boston three years earlier.

The Orient Express was one of those gimmicky diners that had sprung up all over town in the mid-nineties for reasons no one could quite remember. The hook of this place was that from the outside it looked like a train. And when you stepped inside you had a choice of seating in two train carriages situated on either side of the counter. But as anyone who's ever tried to eat dinner in the economy section of a train will tell you, it's a shitty and uncomfortable form of dining. The only thing that made *The Orient Express* better than eating on a real train was the fact that it didn't move at a hundred miles an hour while you were trying to digest your food.

Claudia hadn't been into *The Orient Express* since the last time she'd met up with Pete. She didn't like the place because it was always busy and noisy. Today was no exception. Half the tables in each carriage were taken, there was an offensive amount of chatter from the other customers and the CD player on the counter was playing the song, *Fast Train* by Solomon Burke. One of the most irritating things about this place was the music. They only played songs with the word *train* in the title, which meant the same few songs playing over and over. Claudia had heard *Fast Train* many times before. *But today would be the last.*

She spotted Pete sitting at a table at the back of one of the carriages. He was wearing the same old tight-fitting brown leather jacket he'd lived in for the last ten years and a cloth cap, which was a new addition to his regular look. He saw her and waved her over. Even from a distance it was obvious that he'd lost weight, around his face at least. Six months earlier he'd had a swollen red face, brought on by drinking beer for breakfast, lunch and dinner. Today he was a healthy looking little fellow in his early fifties. There were plenty of things about him that hadn't changed though. His shifty mannerisms, unkempt eyebrows and yellow, gappy teeth made him look like the kind of guy that would rob an old lady at knifepoint if he thought he'd get away with it.

Claudia manoeuvred herself into the seat opposite him, which is no easy feat when you're wearing a long black holy habit. Legroom at the table was minimal and by sitting opposite Pete, Claudia found her knees knocking against his.

'Good morning Pete, nice to see you,' she said.

'Yeah, yeah, you look well too,' said Pete, inadvertently reminding her that he was shit at small talk.

'Have you got something for me?' Claudia asked.

Pete reached into his jacket and pulled out a thick yellow envelope. He slid it across the table to Claudia. The envelope wasn't sealed so the contents were easy to see. And it was what Claudia was hoping for, a wad of dirty fifty-dollar bills.

'Twenty thousand,' said Pete. 'You don't need to count it.'

Claudia picked up the envelope and started flicking through the notes, not to count them, more to check that they were all fifties. It looked like they were, and there was almost certainly twenty-thousand dollars there, give or take a few hundred.

'You staying for a drink today?' Pete asked her.

'Of course.'

Claudia slipped the envelope into a pocket in the slit of her habit, while Pete beckoned the waitress over. A short, curvy lady soon appeared at Claudia's shoulder.

'Coffee for my friend please, Trudie,' said Pete.

'Anything else?' Trudie asked.

Claudia would have liked to take a long look at the menu, but she knew from previous visits that Trudie had little patience for people who took time to make their order.

'I had a nice lemon cake last time I was here,' she said. 'I'll have another slice of that if you've got any, please.'

Trudie wrote down the order on her notepad, stuck her pencil behind her ear and headed back behind the counter. Pete peered over Claudia's shoulder to watch Trudie walking away, checking out her ass without so much as a hint of discretion.

'She's married,' said Claudia, 'to a local hood.'

Pete didn't appear to hear her. 'That woman has a lovely ass,' he said.

'Like I said, she's married.'

Pete looked back at Claudia. 'That doesn't matter,' he said.

'Maybe not to you, but it matters to her. You've got no chance. Besides, she's thirty-four. Way too young for you.'

'Doesn't stop me from looking.'

'Any news from back home?'

Pete looked surprised by the question. 'Like what?'

'How is my brother?'

'No idea. I don't see him.'

'You hear anything about him?'

'Only that he travels around a lot. Mostly in Europe.'

'Has he met anyone?'

'I should think he's met lots of people. What kind of question is that?'

'I mean has he met a woman. I always thought he would have settled down by now.'

Pete frowned. 'Is this what you want to ask me about?'

'I guess not. I just wanted to know if there was, you know, anything you think I need to know about? Like, has he made any money on that property I gave him.'

'I don't know *shit*. I'm not the man they give information to. I'm the man that delivers packages.'

'I know, but...' In the reflection of a nearby window Claudia spotted Trudie returning. The waitress was carrying a tray with a mug of coffee and a slice of lemon sponge cake on it. She stopped at their table and placed the tray down in front of Claudia. She picked up the mug of coffee and placed it down on the table.

'Thanks Trudie,' said Claudia.

'No problem.' Trudie placed the plate with the cake on it down on the table next to the coffee. 'Frank says the lemon cake is on the house today,' she added.

Upon hearing that it might be free, Pete suddenly took an interest in the cake. 'Can you get me a slice of that too?' he inquired.

'Sorry,' said Trudie. 'That was the last slice. We were ten minutes away from throwing it out. It should be okay, but if it's a bit chewy, feel free to leave it.'

Claudia smiled. 'I'm sure it will be fine, thanks.'

Trudie picked up some napkins from the tray and placed them on the table. Claudia noticed a small white envelope on the tray, which had previously been hidden beneath the napkins. It had two words written on it in blue ink. The words jumped out at her.

Sister Claudia.

'Is that for me?' she asked, pointing at it.

Trudie looked as surprised to see the envelope as Claudia did. She picked it up and took an age to read the two words on it.

'It's got your name on it,' she declared eventually. 'I don't know where it came from, though.'

She handed it to Claudia.

18

Pete looked across curiously at the envelope. 'What's that then?' he asked.

'It's an envelope,' said Claudia. 'What did you think it was? A spoon?'

Trudie picked up the tray and turned to walk back to the counter. Pete reached out and grabbed her arm, stopping her in her tracks.

'Who's it from?' he asked.

Trudie pulled her arm away from him, making it clear she didn't appreciate being touched by a customer.

'Your guess is as good as mine,' she said defensively. 'Someone must have slipped it on there when I wasn't looking. I'll ask Frank, see if it's from him.'

She walked back to the counter area while Pete admired her ass again for a few seconds before Claudia cleared her throat and broke his concentration.

'This is weird, don't you think?' she said.

'Secret admirer, maybe?' Pete suggested.

'Only one way to find out.'

Claudia tore open the envelope. There was a slip of white paper inside, folded in two. She took it out and unfolded it, her fingers trembling. On the paper was a short handwritten message. It read:

One of the customers in this diner is about to kill you.
Guess who?

The Plot to Kill the Pope

'The Pope will be assassinated in one week's time.'

Rodeo Rex slammed his bottle of *Shitting Monkey* beer down on the bar top. 'Oh come on!' he barked. 'You're making this shit up! You can't possibly expect me to believe this?'

He balled his fists in an attempt to keep himself from taking a swipe at the woman sitting next to him. If it had been anyone else or any other situation, he would have. "This is horse shit," he muttered under his breath.

Rex was a Hell's Angel. Or rather, he was *THE Hell's Angel*. His identity among biker gangs was the stuff of legend. Many Hell's Angels claimed to have met him or even ridden with him, but many others scarcely believed he existed. He was a deadly biker-cum-bounty hunter in his mid-thirties, equipped with a permanent bad mood. And this lady seemed not to understand who she was peddling this horse shit to.

The bar he was drinking in was called PURGATORY, conveniently located in an area of the desert known as *The Devil's Graveyard*. With the exception of a shitty gas station a few miles down the road, it was the only place in The Devil's Graveyard where you could get a drink.

The woman in question, the one whom Rex believed was *"making this shit up!"* was Annabel de Frugyn, or as she preferred to be known, *The Mystic Lady*. It was hard to tell exactly how old she was, but at a guess Rex would have said she was in her seventies. The cobwebs hanging from her lanky, grey hair weren't doing her any favours and her clothes didn't help matters either. She wore a musty blue cardigan over a long brown dress that might not always have been that colour.

Much like Rex, The Mystic Lady had a bit of legend about her. The rumour was that her hair had gone grey when she was a teenager and that as a consequence, she'd achieved her life ambition at seventeen when she became a smelly old fortune-teller with dodgy personal hygiene. She was notorious for her ability to predict the future, the only problem was, her predictions were never one hundred percent correct. She'd always get one or two crucial details completely wrong. It annoyed the shit out of Rex, but the fact people still took her seriously annoyed him even more.

'I've seen a vision of the Pope's killer,' she croaked.

Rex looked across at the bartender. 'I can't believe you called me here to listen to this useless old bitch prattle on about her visions. You know how unreliable she is! She's the worst fortune teller ever.'

'Actually I'm a medium,' Annabel said defensively.

'You look more like a large,' said Rex.

The bartender intervened to calm things down. 'Rex if I thought she was making this up, I wouldn't have brought you in on this.'

Rex had to take into consideration that he was more irritable than usual. He'd been riding through the desert on his Harley for most of the morning and the heat had really gotten to him. He took off his Stetson hat and placed it down on the bar top. His thick shoulder length brown hair was sticking to his head and he had sweat dripping down onto a set of bulging biceps worthy of a WWE wrestler. Rex always wore a sleeveless blue denim jacket these days, partly to show off his muscles and partly to make sure everyone saw the name emblazoned across the back of the jacket in Gold lettering. *Dead Hunter.* Rex was part of a small team of "killers for hire" known as *The Dead Hunters*. He was proud of it and wanted everyone to know.

'Does she know who is going to kill the Pope?' he asked. 'That would be a start.'

The bartender, a big black dude who always wore a red suit no matter what the occasion slid a newspaper across the bar top to Rex. 'She thinks it's this guy,' he said, pointing at a face on the front page.

Rex studied the main article. The headline said "THE RED MOHAWK STRIKES AGAIN". Beneath it was a picture of a yellow skull mask with a red crest on the top.

'The Red Mohawk?' said Rex. 'Who's that?'

'That's the demon who's going to kill the Pope,' said Annabel.

'Demon? What the fuck do you mean by demon? Do you even know what a demon is?'

The Mystic Lady wrapped her woolly blue cardigan around herself as if she was feeling the cold and leaned in close as she continued her story. 'That demon killed hundreds of people in a town called B Movie Hell.'

'B Movie Hell? She really *is* making this shit up, isn't she!' Rex complained. 'Can't you send her back downstairs where she belongs?'

His complaint was aimed at the bartender, a man often referred to simply as *The Man In Red*, although Rex had come to know him better by his nickname, Scratch.

Scratch grinned but gave Rex a gentle nod as if to say *"Go on, indulge the old cow"*. Scratch had that rare ability to say a thousand words with a simple nod or smirk, his mind was easy to read, when he wanted it to be. So Rex took another sip of *Shitting Monkey* and let the Mystic Lady carry on.

'I had a vision,' she said, waving her arms around for absolutely no reason other than to create some kind of other worldly atmosphere, which naturally annoyed Rex immensely.

'What vision?' he snapped, hoping it would hurry her up.

'I saw the Pope murdered by a demon who hid behind a mask. And I saw the mask as clear as day. It was the Red Mohawk. It's up to you to stop him!' she wailed.

Rex glanced across at Scratch. 'Why are you taking this seriously?'

'Because I believe her,' Scratch replied.

'What? Why?'

'The Pope was admitted to a private hospital last week,' Scratch said. He picked up the newspaper and turned it to page seven. He pointed at an article about the Pope. It confirmed that the holy man had been admitted to the *Hospital of the Pointless Miracle* in Switzerland for a lifesaving operation to rid him of skin cancer.

'What is this telling me exactly?' Rex asked.

'I happen to know that the Pope was sneaked out of that hospital before this article even hit the newspapers,' he said. 'He arrived in America last night. If anyone was ever planning on assassinating the Pope, now is the best time to do it. He is attending a secret event next week where he is going to pay the US government five million dollars for a new treatment to cure his cancer. He's coming to the US in secret because if word got out that he was spending five million dollars of the Catholic church's money on a cure for his own cancer, it might not go down too well.'

'How do you know all this?'

'I have a lot of friends in the church,' Scratch replied with an evil glint in his eye.

Rex took a deep breath as he processed the information. 'Why would you want to save the Pope?' he asked.

Scratch maintained his perpetual grin. 'Like I said, I have friends in the church. And one of them is the Pope.'

'*You're friends* with the Pope?'

'We go way back.'

The whole thing had the feel of a practical joke about it, but Rex decided to play along anyway. 'Okay, so where is this assassination taking place? And when?' he asked, plonking his Stetson back on his head.

'Unfortunately my visions don't work like that,' said Annabel. 'I can't give you a location.'

'Of course you can't,' said Rex, his sarcasm going into overdrive, 'because you'd get it wrong. That's the kind of thing you can't guess isn't it?'

'She can tell you the exact time though,' said Scratch.

'Right, go on,' said Rex. 'I could use a good laugh.'

Annabel put a cheap silver wristwatch down on the bar and slid it over to Rex. He picked it up and took a good look at it. It had a digital display that was counting backwards by the second.

'What's this for?' he asked.

'That watch is set to reach zero at the exact moment the Pope will be murdered,' said Annabel.

'Bullshit!'

Scratch stepped in again to offer a better explanation than Annabel had provided. 'What she's trying to say is, that according to her vision, the Pope will be assassinated at exactly 12:12 p.m. on Christmas Eve. I set that watch up to count down to the precise second, but, if you manage to intercept the assassin before he gets to the Pope, Annabel's vision will change and the watch will stop counting down. That's when you'll know that your mission has been successful.'

'You're trying to tell me that this watch is in tune with her vision of the future?'

'Not exactly,' said Scratch. 'Annabel has an identical watch that is counting down. As soon as her vision changes and she sees that the Pope is saved, she will stop her watch. Yours will then also stop automatically. It will beep three times to signify that your mission has been a success. But until you hear it beep, the Pope is not safe.'

Rex clenched his fists and took slow breaths to stay calm. 'I'm not even convinced she knows how to tell the time, let alone predict the future!' he grumbled through gritted teeth.

'Well I trust her,' said Scratch. 'She's sees the future as it is planned. It's up to you to change it. Stop the Red Mohawk and the Pope will live, but only because Annabel has forewarned us. Without her warning and your intervention, the Pope will surely die.'

The Mystic Lady looked increasingly smug now that she had the backing of Scratch. 'See,' she said triumphantly. 'You can save the Pope. You'll be a hero and it'll be all thanks to me and my vision. Unless you get killed, of course.'

Rex slipped the cheap digital watch onto his wrist and downed the rest of his bottle of beer. 'I'm not going to argue anymore,' he said. 'But please tell me we've got some leads, because Christmas Eve is only eight days away and that's not a lot of time. You've got somewhere for us to start this wild goose chase, right?'

Scratch nodded. 'The three of you will fly to Romania tonight.'

'The three of us? What do you mean, the *three of us?*'

'You'll be doing this job with Elvis and the Bourbon Kid.'

Rex was furious. 'The Kid is a homicidal maniac! One sip of bourbon and he starts killing innocent people for absolutely no reason!'

'That's why I like him.'

Unfortunately for Rex he was in no position to argue. He'd made a deal with Scratch some years earlier. In exchange for Scratch breaking him out of an eternal hellhole, he had agreed to work for him hunting down people that Scratch referred to as *Hell dodgers*, namely people who belonged in hell, but had somehow managed to avoid it one way or another.

'Don't make me work with the Kid again,' Rex pleaded. 'Every time I turn my back I feel like he's gonna shoot me in the back of the head.'

Scratch reached down under the bar and pulled out a whisky glass and a bottle of bourbon. 'Well he's been behind you ever since you came in,' he said as he filled the glass with bourbon. 'And he hasn't tried to kill you yet.'

Rex spun around on his barstool. He stared around the bar looking for a sign of the Bourbon Kid, wondering if Scratch was playing a joke or not. Eventually his eyes settled on a dark corner of the bar. Sitting in the shadows, dressed all in black with a hood pulled over his head, concealing most of his face was an unshaven man in his mid-thirties who Rex knew only too well. It was the Bourbon Kid. He wasn't quite as big as Rex, but he was deceptively strong. Rex had learned that the hard way. The black glove on Rex's right hand was a permanent reminder of an incident when the Kid had crushed all his fingers and metacarpals after Rex triumphed over him at arm-wrestling.

Rex turned back to Scratch, who had placed another bottle of *Shitting Monkey* down on the bar next to the glass of bourbon.

'Why don't the two of you share a drink while we wait for Elvis to show up?' he said.

Right on cue, the double doors at the bar entrance swung open and in walked the coolest man on the planet. Dressed in a pale blue suit with the jacket unbuttoned almost all the way down was a man known by just one name, *Elvis*. He was a dead ringer for a thirty-five-year-old Elvis Presley. But this Elvis was a renowned killer, known to many of his associates as the *Hitman from Hell*. He could sing a bit (and he often did) but his real talent was hunting down and killing folks. And like Rex he had signed a contract with Scratch that required him to hunt down *Hell dodgers*.

'Hey Rex, watcha doin' here?' he asked, clocking the giant biker as soon as he walked in.

Rex took a pull on his new bottle of *Shitting Monkey* before replying. 'Me, you and the Bourbon Kid got a job to do. We gotta kill a guy called the Red Mohawk to stop him from killing the Pope.'

'Cool,' said Elvis. 'I'm in.'

Scratch tossed a bottle of *Shitting Monkey* across the room to Elvis. He caught it, took a sip then spotted the Bourbon Kid in the corner. 'Hey Kid, wassup?' he said, strolling over to join him.

Rex watched on enviously, seething at the fact he hadn't noticed the Kid sitting in the corner, yet Elvis clocked him straight away.

Scratch tapped him on the shoulder. 'Rex, be a sport and take the Kid's drink over to him, will you?' he said.

Rex picked up the Kid's glass of bourbon and was about to walk over and join the others for a drink, when something crossed his mind. 'Say, Scratch, this Red Mohawk guy, has he got a motive for wanting to kill the Pope?'

'I don't know,' Scratch replied. 'But he once ended up in a mental asylum because he murdered a nun, so it's possible he's got issues with religious folks.'

'He murdered a nun, huh? I'm gonna enjoy hunting this asshole.'

One

General Alexis Calhoon had a headache. A really bad one. Six years in charge of the top-secret government agency known as Phantom Operations had given her more than her fair share of headaches. Most of the problems had come from what she often referred to as *"The Old Boys Network",* a group of middle-aged male agents who reported into her. She had inherited them from her predecessor, General Drebbin who was every bit as incompetent as his surname suggested.

Even now, the Old Boys Network still occasionally worked under the misguided belief that Calhoon was best off not knowing what they were up to. To a degree they were right. If she knew half of what they got up to, and didn't prosecute them for it, she'd one day end up in prison with them.

During the early days of her tenure she'd been paranoid that the *"old boys"* might not accept her because she was a black woman in a department of white middle aged men, but if any of them had ever had a problem with it, they hadn't said anything. So she soon came to the conclusion that none of the guys gave a shit as long as they could keep their little secrets and informants to themselves. At times it did piss her off that they kept her in the dark, but no amount of rollickings would make them change their ways. And the worst agent of the lot, the one with the most secrets was sitting right in front of her, on the other side of her desk. He was a balding grey-haired fifty-year-old white fellow who should have been forced to retire long ago. His latest indiscretion had made the front pages of the national newspapers too. The bastard. Hence the very, very bad headache.

Calhoon had been looking at the picture on the front page of the newspaper for much of the morning, cussing to herself and inwardly cursing the man in the silver suit who was sitting opposite her. The newspaper cover story featured a huge picture of a yellow skull mask with a red crest on the top of it and the headline -

THE RED MOHAWK STRIKES AGAIN

She folded the newspaper up and threw it across the desk at Devon Pincent. It hit him in the chest and fell into his lap. He brushed away some fluff from his jacket and then picked the paper up. He took a look at the front page, shrugged and then placed the paper back down on the desk. Sitting next to Pincent was Blake Jackson, Calhoon's second in command. Jackson was a high flyer, in his early forties and destined for great things after picking up several medals for bravery during his time in the US Marines. His cause was helped no end by the fact he looked like Denzel Washington, which for some reason meant everyone liked him the minute they saw him. He wasn't one for hiding his feelings, and Calhoon could tell he was every bit as angry as she was, simply from the way he was staring at Pincent.

'Well?' said Jackson. 'What have you got to say for yourself?'

Devon shrugged. 'What do you mean?'

'You told us this guy was gone and would never show up again. If he gets caught and identified as your boy Joey Conrad, we're fucked.'

Calhoon sighed. 'Blake, calm down. Devon is about to tell us that he knows nothing about who this Red Mohawk character is, because if God forbid, Devon did know anything about this, he'd be going to prison.'

Devon took another look at the photo on the newspaper. 'There must be thousands of masks like that,' he said. 'How could I possibly know who's behind every Halloween mask in the country?'

Jackson snatched the newspaper off the desk and held it up, showing the picture to Calhoon again, as if she hadn't seen it enough already. 'General, this is Joey Conrad!' he said tapping the picture of the Red Mohawk to unnecessarily emphasise who he was referring to. 'He beat a teenage boy to death with a baseball bat, then chopped up the rest of his family with a fucking sword. We've only just finished covering up what went down in B Movie Hell last year and now we've got this gas station massacre! It can't go on! This asshole will singlehandedly bring down Phantom Ops if we don't find him and eliminate him.'

Devon cleared his throat, which was always an indication that a smug comment was forthcoming. 'Maybe the woman who saw him, what's her name, Diane Crawford? Maybe she made the whole thing up? Her story is rather muddled and she claims she fainted and missed most of it. I think more will come to light about this case over the coming weeks. If the Red Mohawk is such a psychopath, why did he leave Ms Crawford alive?'

'Thank you for the compelling insight,' Calhoon interjected sarcastically. 'But everything this guy does has your fingerprints on it Devon. If the day ever comes when I can prove you helped him escape from that asylum so he could go on a murder rampage in B Movie Hell to rescue your daughter, you're going to prison.'

Devon remained calm, as always. 'General, I think you're putting two and two together and coming up with twenty-two.'

'If that's a joke I don't get it,' said Calhoon tersely. 'And frankly I'm tired of your attitude. So in the interests of protecting this department and the jobs of everyone in it, I have no choice but to suspend you. Some day soon the police or the press are going to put the pieces together and realise, as I do, that Joey Conrad is the man behind the Red Mohawk mask and that you're the one who set him free. And when that day comes I want this department distanced as far from this shit-storm as possible. Therefore, from this moment on, you are to have absolutely no contact with anyone in this department. Your access to the building and all of your passwords and User ID's have been revoked. And before long, any evidence that you ever worked here will be erased.'

'But General…'

'Devon, thank you for your many years of service, now please leave.'

'But General, I'm working on something big right now.'

'No you're not. You don't work here.'

'But I've found our old friend Solomon Bennett! He's hiding out in Romania.'

The mention of the name Solomon Bennett was a sure-fire way to grab Calhoon's attention. She visibly stiffened for a moment, before regaining her composure and dismissing the information.

'If he's in Romania then good for him. Unless he sets foot in America, I don't want to hear that man's name again.'

'That's the thing,' Devon said, with pleading eyes. 'I think he's planning to come back here, and I suspect it might have something to do with your Christmas Miracle event and the Pope's visit.'

'You mean Bennett wants to get his hands on the cancer cure?' Calhoon sneered. 'He wouldn't have the guts, or the firepower.'

'Maybe not,' Devon agreed. 'But he still thinks that cure belongs to him. So until I know for sure what his plans are, it's imperative that I keep you informed of his whereabouts. And maybe you should postpone the event?'

Calhoon didn't deliberate the offer for long, particularly the suggestion that the Pope's visit should be postponed. That visit was to be the highlight of her career.

'Solomon Bennett is a dinosaur,' she snapped. 'He's been AWOL for five years. If he shows up in this country he won't get past customs without me knowing about it.'

'But if he does get past customs, I've got five bucks that says he comes looking for you, General.'

'Devon, I want you *and your five bucks* out of my office right now.'

Blake Jackson placed his hand on Devon's shoulder. 'Just go, otherwise you're only going to make things worse for yourself. If you forget anything or leave your coat behind, give me a call. I'll sort everything out for you.'

Devon got up and made his way over to the door. For a moment it looked like he might turn back and say something else, but he thought better of it and let himself out. When he was gone and the door was closed behind him, Calhoon brought another matter to Jackson's attention.

'Blake there's something else,' she said. She reached into her desk drawer and pulled out a brown envelope. She slid it across the desk.

'What's this?' Jackson asked.

'Open it.'

The envelope had Alexis Calhoon's name written on it in black felt pen. Jackson held the envelope up by its end and emptied the contents out onto the desk. An A4 size photo of the Pope fell out along with a playing card. He picked them up and studied them closely, one after the other, checking them again and again, back and forth.

'I sure hope that's a joke,' he said.

Written across the photo of the Pope in black felt pen was a message. It read –

THE POPE DIES NEXT
YOURS TRULY,
THE RED MOHAWK

The small playing card was a hand made Top Trump card with a picture of the Red Mohawk on it. Beneath the picture were four Trump categories, that read as such –

PHYSICAL STRENGTH 92
FEAR FACTOR   96
KILLING POWER   99
HORROR RATING   94

'My first thought was that it was a joke,' Calhoon agreed. 'But then I asked myself, who would think this was funny?'

'No one,' said Jackson.

'Right. And with the Pope attending my Christmas Miracle event next Saturday only a brainless idiot would send me this and think I'd find it funny.'

'Do you know any brainless idiots?'

'No. So I did some digging.' Calhoon reached into her desk drawer again and pulled out a VHS tape and slid it across the desk to Jackson. It was a copy of a Robbie Coltrane movie with the rather bizarre title *The Pope Must Die*.

Jackson looked bemused. '*The Pope Must Die?* There's a film called The Pope Must Die?'

'This is the British version,' said Calhoon. 'Believe it or not, when this came out in the early nineties, the US version was renamed *The Pope Must Diet* in order to avoid offending the Catholic Church.'

'Imagine if that happened today,' said Jackson, studying the back cover of the video case. 'Twitter would go into meltdown with people protesting that it's offensive to imply that the Pope is fat.'

The mere mention of Twitter shortened Calhoon's temper. 'Well that's by the by,' she continued. 'The reason I'm showing you this is because it's one of the items that were taken from Joey Conrad's room at Grimwald's Asylum after the B Movie Hell massacre last year. You may recall he had a bunch of DVD's of films like *Halloween* and *The Texas Chainsaw Massacre*. Films that we believed influenced his murder spree. Well he had one video tape too, *this one*.'

'I remember now,' said Jackson. 'He's obsessed with copying stuff from movies isn't he?'

'Yes, so I am worried that after receiving this threat to kill the Pope I then find this videotape in Joey Conrad's storage file.'

'This is bad,' said Jackson, sliding the video back across the desk. 'The timing of this is all wrong. I mean how could the Red Mohawk know about the Pope's visit? Only a handful of people are aware of what we're planning.'

'Yes,' said Calhoon. 'And unfortunately, Devon is one of them.'

'Devon wouldn't have anything to do with this though, surely?'

'I agree. But he just tried to get me to postpone my Christmas Miracle event by telling me that Solomon Bennett might hijack it. I bet Devon knows what the Red Mohawk is up to, even if he's not behind it.'

Jackson scowled and waved his hand dismissively. 'I don't care how good this Red Mohawk is, he'll never get to the Pope. And besides, the Pope gets hundreds of death threats every year. If you cancelled events every time he was threatened, he'd never be seen in public!'

Calhoon leaned back in her chair. 'True. But because Devon was at one time linked to the Red Mohawk, it makes this a legitimate threat, which could be an enormous embarrassment to this department if anything happens.'

'You're not seriously considering postponing?' Jackson picked up the poster of the Pope containing the threat and took another look at it. 'Based on this feeble, schoolboy threat?'

'No, I'm not,' said Calhoon. 'Not a chance, but what I will do is get our people in the press to run a story about how the Red Mohawk has threatened to kill the Pope. I'll inform the Pope that the threat is being taken seriously and that we will change the location at the last minute as an added precaution. But I'm not cancelling. We need the five million dollar donation from the Papal House and above all else we need the Pope to appear at the event to show our investors that we've cured his skin cancer.'

Jackson looked surprised. 'It sounds like you've got things all worked out. Are you sure we need to change the venue though? I mean it's already secret.'

'True. But protocol demands that in the case of a legitimate threat we have to move to our Contingency venue.'

'Which is?'

'I'll let you know after I've spoken with His Holiness.'

'Okay.'

Calhoon was pleased to see that Jackson was on board with her plan. The two of them had worked well together since she had brought him into the department. He had no love for the Old Boys Network either, and he liked the way she worked. He was an ideal number two. Some might say he was a "Yes man" but that's exactly what Calhoon wanted.

'So what are you planning to do about Devon?' he asked, knowing she would have something up her sleeve.

'I'm glad you asked.' Calhoon smiled. 'I want you to have him followed, have his personal phone calls monitored and check his recent emails for anything suspicious. If he's still in contact with Joey Conrad, I want to know about it.'

'Yes ma'am.'

'Good, that will be all.'

Jackson made no attempt to get up from his seat. 'By the way,' he said coyly. 'Who is Solomon Bennett? And why would he want your cancer cure?'

Calhoon let out a deep sigh. 'He was a member of this department before you joined. And he's also one of the main reasons Joey Conrad ended up in a mental hospital.'

Two

Romania was one of the few countries in Europe that Mozart had never planned to visit. But circumstances change and Mozart's circumstances had changed significantly in the last seventy-two hours. He'd spent four months locked up in a Turkish prison with no hope for parole. But then suddenly with no explanation, a man he'd never met before had broken him out of the prison. A man of very few words with metal bolts protruding from either side of his neck, just like Frankenstein's monster. And so Mozart ended up in Romania with even more people he'd never met before, one of whom was Solomon Bennett, the man who had arranged the daring prison break.

Solomon Bennett was short and stocky with a flattop of salt and pepper hair, and lines on his face that held deep secrets. But for the eye-patch covering his right eye, he wouldn't have been terribly noticeable. Mozart guessed that Bennett preferred it like that.

Bennett didn't talk much about himself. He never explained what happened to his eye but he was quick to inform Mozart of his reasons for breaking him out of prison. And Mozart liked what he heard. Bennett had assembled a small army of brainwashed followers who were going to follow him to the USA to carry out a daring mission that would involve a lot of killing. Bennett had the muscle in his giant sidekick Frankenstein, and he had a chemical weapons expert who he was taking Mozart to meet right now. But what he didn't have was a psychopath, someone like Mozart who could think outside the box, a man with the flair to leave a permanent mental or physical scar on every one of his victims. And Mozart had plenty of victims.

Solomon Bennett's passion and attention to detail impressed Mozart straight away. He was brutally honest and for a man of his age, he was in impeccable shape. And the eye-patch gave him that classic "comic book villain" look that really appealed to Mozart.

When it came to his own appearance, Mozart made a point of looking very average, which had helped him evade the authorities during a ten-year killing spree. He was a thirty-six year old man of average height and build who dressed conservatively, usually in jeans and a shirt, although his clothing of choice right now was "grey prison boiler suit". He had thick black hair with a few silver streaks on the sides that he was intending to get rid of pretty soon, depending on what hair products he could get his hands on in Romania.

They arrived at a warehouse in Bucharest just before midnight. A party of burly men and scantily-clad women drinking and dancing to loud Romanian pop music was in full swing inside.

'These are your men?' Mozart shouted over the music as Bennett led him through the crowd towards a door at the far end of the room.

'Yeah. They're all ex-military,' said Bennett. 'But none of them has much in the way of initiative. They follow orders without question, which is great, but I need you to provide a touch of brainpower to all the muscle.'

'That guy who broke me out of prison, the one who looked like Frankenstein. He seemed kind of robot-like, what's the deal with him?'

'It's a long story,' said Bennett. 'An experiment went awry some years back. It left him with what you might call a thick skin. He's all muscle, but no brains. You and him will work together once we get to America. I need to stay in the shadows.'

'I assume you're paying me for this?'

Bennett stopped and eyeballed Mozart with his good eye. 'Consider your prison breakout as a down payment. The rest will be waiting for you when you acquire my new premises in the States.'

'Sounds great,' said Mozart, looking around. 'But if you don't mind, I'd really like to get laid. Haven't seen a woman in quite a while if you know what I mean.'

'I've already arranged it. Follow me.'

Mozart made eye contact with a dark skinned woman, wearing little more than her underwear. She was dancing nearby on her own, a few feet away from all the other partygoers. She smiled at him and winked.

'I'll take that one,' Mozart said, nudging Bennett and pointing at her.

'That's Jasmine,' said Bennett. 'She's licked every guy's butt in here.'

'She sounds like my kind of girl.'

'Have patience,' said Bennett. 'I think what I have lined up for you will appeal to your sociopathic tendencies.'

They arrived at the door at the far end of the room. Standing guard outside it was a muscular woman in her mid-twenties, dressed in military combat gear. She had a flat-top haircut similar to Bennett's and she was holding a tray with a bottle of champagne and two flute glasses on it. Bennett took the tray from her.

'Mozart, this is Denise,' he said. 'You'll be working with her a lot in the next few weeks. She's our female muscle. She hates other women so she's useful if you need to beat any women up in public. She can do it without anyone interfering.'

Denise held out her hand. 'Pleased to meet you Mozart,' she said in a husky voice. 'I'm a big fan of your work.'

Mozart shook her hand. She maintained eye contact with him throughout. He had a feeling they'd be fucking before the night was through, unless he could get to Jasmine first.

Denise opened the door and Bennett led Mozart through it into his private lounge. It wasn't a fancy place by any means, but it had two sofas and a television. In the middle of the floor was a white polar bear rug. Draped across each sofa was a female hooker. One was a slim blonde in a bright red dress, which Mozart considered was a clever ruse to distract from the fact that she was cross-eyed. The other was built like a wrestler and when she smiled it became apparent that she probably *was* a wrestler, because she was missing quite a few teeth. She had short brown hair and smudged lipstick that wouldn't look out of place in a circus. And she was wearing nothing more than a black bra and panties with stockings and a suspender belt.

Bennett kicked the door shut and placed the tray with the champagne down on a coffee table near the door. 'Meet Dorina and Nicoleta,' he said, nodding at the two hookers.

Both women smiled and waved at Mozart. The cross-eyed one might have been waving at something else, but Mozart had a hunch she was looking at him, so he politely waved back at both of them.

'Before we get started, let's have some champagne,' said Bennett. He cracked open the bottle that Denise had handed to him and poured it into the two glasses. Dorina and Nicoleta jumped up and bounded over to him. He held out a glass of champagne for each of them. 'Ladies,' he said with a smile. 'This is the finest champagne anywhere in the world today. Drink up and let's get this party started.'

Dorina and Nicoleta gratefully accepted the drinks. Dorina, the skinny blonde necked hers in one go. It was hard to tell if it had any effect on her because she remained cross-eyed. Nicoleta took a few sips and made some approving noises, as if she was some kind of champagne connoisseur.

'Ooh, that's nice,' said Dorina, before unleashing a loud burp.

'Quite,' said Bennett,' Now why don't you both get naked and we'll come join you on the sofas in a second.'

Mozart wasn't especially enamoured with Bennett's choice of female company. He was about to say something about it, when Bennett slapped him across the shoulder.

'So which one do you want?' he asked. 'Dorina or Nicoleta?'

Both women had retaken their positions sprawled cross the sofas and were smiling enthusiastically at Mozart, hoping he would choose them. It was a tough choice, slim and cross-eyed, or curvy and toothless?

But to Mozart's surprise, before he made his choice, Dorina slid off her sofa and onto the floor. Out cold. No quivering, no moaning, just a loud thud as she landed on the polar bear rug.

Nicoleta stared open-mouthed at her fallen friend. 'Did your hip give out again?' she asked. 'Oh well, looks like I've got both guys to myself.'

She stood up and began a striptease. She got halfway through unclasping her bra when without warning she too collapsed, falling on top of Dorina with a thud and rolling onto her back, staring up at the ceiling.

Mozart had never been so relieved to see two women pass out. He looked over at Bennett. 'Did you drug them?' he asked.

'Worked perfectly didn't it?' said Bennett, triumphantly.

'But they were hookers, right? You don't need to drug hookers, trust me.'

'I know,' said Bennett, 'but this champagne is the key to my plan.'

'What plan?'

'I'll explain later. I just wanted to show you how it works.'

The door to the lounge opened and Denise walked in with another man who was wearing a long white coat. He had a wiry frame and crazy ginger perm that made it look like he'd had an electric shock and was permanently stuck with the after-effects.

'It worked then,' he said, grinning at Bennett and Mozart.

'Less than thirty seconds,' said Bennett.

'Who the fuck is this asshole?' said Mozart, not enjoying the feeling that a prank was being played and he wasn't part of it.

'This is Dr Henry Jekyll,' said Bennett. 'Or as I like to call him, *The Mad Doctor*.'

'Did you say Dr Jekyll?'

Bennett smiled, but didn't answer the question. 'Denise, take our new friend out for a drink please, would you?' he said.

Denise grabbed Mozart's butt cheeks in a firm grip. She whispered in his ear. 'Come with me soldier. I'll fill you in on all of this.' She took Mozart's hand and led him back out to the party area.

Some crazy Romanian dance music was blaring out and the lights had dimmed. The party was absolutely rocking now.

'What's going on?' Mozart asked. 'First of all Frankenstein breaks me out of prison and now Dr Jekyll is drugging hookers for me!'

Denise handed him a bottle of beer. 'Drink this. Let's get drunk and then I'll give you the monster fuck of your life. When we're done I'll tell you all about Frankenstein and Dr Jekyll.'

Mozart liked the idea of fucking Denise, certainly a lot more than he fancied fucking either of the two hookers. He hadn't been with a woman for quite some time, and it crossed his mind that one might not be enough to satisfy is sexual appetite, so he looked around the room until he spotted Jasmine the dark skinned girl again. She was still on her own.

'What say we make this a threesome?' he suggested to Denise.

'With who?'

'The Indian looking girl over there.'

Denise knew who he meant straight away. 'You mean Jasmine? She's actually American.'

'American? What the hell is she doing working as a hooker in Romania?'

'Do you want her or not?'

Mozart took a sip of his beer. It tasted good. He grabbed Denise by the back of her head and planted a kiss on her lips. 'Let's go get her,' he said.

In the back room, Dr Jekyll was ecstatic that his champagne drug had worked so well. Solomon Bennett wasn't quite so pleased.

'I need it to take at least a minute before they pass out,' he said, grabbing Dr Jekyll by the throat and squeezing hard. 'At least one minute, no more than two, got it?'

'Yes boss, of course.'

'Good, because these two skanks were out cold within thirty seconds. It needs to be longer than that.'

Bennett released his grip on Jekyll's throat and patted him on the cheek. 'Get back to work, doctor. I'm going to join the party.'

As soon as Bennett had left the room, Jekyll hurried over to the two unconscious hookers. The skinnier one of the two was stirring. He could see a change in her face. Something was happening to her that he hadn't told Bennett about. It was supposed to be a surprise, but seeing as how Bennett had grabbed him around the throat, Jekyll decided it would remain a surprise. He pulled a knife out of his pocket and slit the two hookers throats before they could regain consciousness.

Three

Jack Munson's assignment in Romania required him to locate and provide evidence of the existence of his former friend and colleague, Solomon Bennett. It should have been a tedious job but it had turned into the most fun assignment he'd ever had. The thing that had made it so much fun was his travelling companion, the delightful and ever-so-slightly-bonkers former hooker, Jasmine. He hadn't expected to get on so well with her, but she'd wrapped herself around his heart far easier than he believed was possible.

Initially he'd been reluctant to take her with him, but she'd given him so much shit about burning her home down and leaving her homeless, that he'd felt obliged to let her tag along. How she ever thought of the Beaver Palace as home though, was beyond him. It had been a horrible place, full of young women held against their will and forced into sexual service. Burning it to the ground was the best thing that had happened to it, and to Jasmine. And besides, she'd promised him that she would wake him up with a blowjob and the world's best breakfast every morning if he took her to Romania with him. She'd lied about the breakfast though, unless you considered burnt toast to be a delicacy.

For several years prior to taking on the Romania job given to him by Devon Pincent, Munson had lived alone with just a bottle of rum for company most nights. As a result he'd forgotten just how much he enjoyed female company. And Jasmine, in spite of the burnt breakfasts was without doubt the most fun person he'd ever met. She had boundless energy and a child-like enthusiasm for *everything*.

Because she had spent almost her entire life as a hooker in B Movie Hell, she'd missed out on so many of life's great things. So now she was lapping up all the new experiences that Romania had to offer.

The thing she was enjoying most was working as an undercover spy. Munson had given her a few tips and trained her to defend herself if she was in trouble. But one thing he hadn't taught her, that she had an incredible gift for, was how to get information from men. She was a deft hand at infiltrating all-male establishments and extracting information. She had started off simple, usually interrogating the drunkest or ugliest man in a place to find out if he'd heard anything about Solomon Bennett. But over time she had mastered her technique to the point where five minutes in a room with a politician would be all she needed to gather enough information to bring down a government.

But since infiltrating Solomon Bennett's hideout, Jasmine had been spending more and more time there, meaning Jack was often on his own watching Romanian television in their rented apartment. And Romanian television is not good. Not good at all. There wasn't a single show on any of the stations that could take his mind off the fact that Jasmine was working alone, dishing out sexual favours to Solomon Bennett's men in exchange for information. The more she was away, the more Jack missed her. And the more he thought about her doing sexual favours for other men, the more jealous he became. She didn't mind doing it, she loved guys and loved watching the expression on their faces when she made them come. And initially, Jack didn't mind her doing it either. But that was before he fell head-over-heels for her.

Her influence on him had been so positive too. He'd even managed to control his drinking and no longer touched a drop when he was on his own. He would happily get drunk with Jasmine because it was so much damn fun. But he knew if he started polishing off bottles of rum to compensate for the loneliness when she wasn't around, she would soon see him for what he used to be, a lousy self-pitying drunk.

Tonight was to be their last night in Romania. Jasmine had learned that Solomon Bennett and his men were heading for the USA the very next day, so that was their cue to leave too.

It was 2am when she arrived back from the big send-off party Bennett had thrown for his men. Jack was slouched in front of the television in his gold *Rocky Balboa* dressing gown, with his feet up on the coffee table. The sound of her key in the door made him jump up and rush over to the door. Every time she arrived home he feared the worst, dreading the possibility she might have been hurt, but not once had she ever come back with a single scratch or bruise on her. Tonight was no different.

She walked through the door wearing a long brown raincoat, black leather boots and a big grin on her face.

'Hello soldier!' she said planting a big smacker on him. Jack slipped his arms around her waist and pulled her in close. Jasmine always smelled good, no matter what she'd been up to. Her long dark hair smelt like peaches, whether it was first thing in the morning or last thing at night.

'What's with the raincoat?' he asked.

Jasmine untied a cloth belt that was wrapped around her waist. Her coat fell open and Munson saw his most favourite thing. She was completely naked underneath the coat. Apart from her knee high leather boots.

'How the hell did this happen?' he asked, knowing that the story would be good but not necessarily the sort of thing he would want to know every detail of.

'Seeing as how it was the last time they were ever going to see me, a bunch of Bennett's henchmen asked if they could keep all my clothes as a souvenir.'

'Damn.'

'Yeah. Lucky someone gave me a coat at the end of the night.' She reached into the one of the coat pockets and pulled out a bottle of rum. 'I thought we should celebrate.'

Munson looked at the bottle. 'I fuckin' love you, Jaz.'

She kissed him again, then took off her coat and hung it up on a peg on the wall. Munson watched her ass wiggle from side to side as she made her way into the lounge. He was still transfixed by it as if it was the first time he'd seen it. She plonked herself down on the couch in front of the television and started unzipping her boots. Jack considered grabbing a couple of glasses from the kitchen, but decided against it. Instead he headed straight for the sofa and sat down next to Jasmine.

'So what did you find out tonight?' he asked. 'Anything?'

Jasmine tossed one of her boots across the room. 'I'll tell you what,' she said. 'It's a good job this assignment's over because tonight, for the first time, I started to think they were onto me.'

'How come?'

'A new guy showed up and he was bothering me with questions all the time.'

'Like what?'

'Like why an American girl is working as a hooker in Romania.'

'What did you tell him?'

'Nothing, I just sucked his dick, only for about five seconds though. Man, that guy needed to get laid.'

'Five seconds?'

'Yeah. He'd been in prison for ages, but Bennett's people broke him out. They wanted him to help with something big that they're planning. He's gonna be Bennett's right hand man for something.'

'And what was the name of this guy?'

'Mozart.'

'Mozart?'

'Yeah, just Mozart. He didn't have a second name. I did ask.'

Jack knew who Mozart was and what he'd been in prison for. Hearing that Jasmine had just been with him sent a shiver down his spine. 'He didn't do anything to you, did he?'

'Nothing out of the ordinary, why?'

'No reason. Was Solomon's big bodyguard there tonight?'

Jasmine shook her head. 'No, he's rarely there and even when he is, he barely says anything. And from what I can tell, he doesn't fuck either. No one's got near him, and a few have tried I can assure you.'

She threw her second boot across the room and picked up the bottle of rum she had stuck down the side of the couch. She unscrewed the lid and offered it to Jack. He refused.

'You should have the first sip?' he said. 'I think you've earned it.'

Jasmine snuggled up to him, pulling her feet up onto the sofa. 'I'm okay,' she said. 'I had a few drinks earlier. You can go first, baby.'

Jack took the bottle from her and downed a mouthful of rum. It was cheap stuff, but rum is rum and it went down smoothly all the same. 'So what else happened tonight?' he asked.

'There was this bottle of champagne and no one was allowed any of it. But then Dorina and Nicoleta were taken off to Bennett's private room. The champagne went in a while later. I noticed because I was watching what this Mozart guy was doing and he went in with it. When I asked him about it later, that's when he got kind of weird with me. But a woman called Denise told me the champagne was poisoned. Apparently they're going to poison a bunch of rich people with this champagne when they get to America.'

'Poisoned champagne, huh? Did you get the name of it?'

'No. But it was made by the creepy doctor guy. I'd never seen him before either.'

'What creepy doctor guy?'

'Don't laugh, but his name is Dr Jekyll.'

Jack frowned and thought for a moment. 'Did he have curly ginger hair?'

Jasmine reached over and grabbed the bottle of rum from him. She took a swig from it. 'He's as ginger as they come,' she said. 'And apparently he told one of the girls he's a descendant of the real Dr Jekyll.'

'I don't think the *real* Dr Jekyll was actually real.'

'I'm just telling you what I heard.' Jasmine put the bottle of rum down on the coffee table. She climbed up onto Munson's lap, wrapping her long brown legs around him. 'He's Dr Jekyll's great, great, great, great grandson,' she said, pulling Jack's dressing gown open.

'He might think he is,' said Jack. 'But he's not. I know the man you're talking about and he's a deluded nutcase.'

'Let's not talk about him any more then,' said Jasmine, sliding her hand down towards his cock. 'The guy's got a ginger perm and he reminds me of that girl who played Annie in the musical.'

Munson ran his hand down her back and stared down at her breasts. Her skin was so smooth. And her tits were fucking awesome.

'You're right,' he said. 'I don't wanna think about Annie either.'

Jasmine wrapped her hand around the shaft of his cock and started caressing it, in a way that made him close his eyes and take a sharp intake of breath. She was slowly building up a head of steam when she stopped suddenly.

'Why didn't you reply to my text earlier?' she said.

Jack opened his eyes. 'What text?'

'I got a photo of the Frankenstein guy. I sent it to you with a funny message.'

Jack was notoriously bad at checking his phone for text messages. Usually because he couldn't remember where he'd left the phone.

'Where the hell is my phone?' he muttered for the tenth time that week.

Jasmine spotted it, where it so often was, stuck down the side of the sofa. She reached down with her free hand and grabbed it. Jack closed his eyes again while Jasmine carried on stroking his cock with one hand and flicking through his text messages with the other.

'Here it is,' she said excitedly.

Jack opened his eyes. Jasmine was holding his cell phone up in front of his face. The photo on the phone had a picture of a man with bolts protruding from either side of his neck. Underneath it, Jasmine's witty text said *This guy looks like you in the morning xxx."*

Jack snatched the phone from her and studied the face on the man in the picture. 'That's Frank Grealish!'

'Do you know him?' Jasmine asked.

'Where did you get this picture?'

'One of the other girls took it a couple of days ago. I got her to send it on to me.'

'That's impossible,' said Jack, staring at the photo. 'This man's been dead for five years.'

Four

When Alexis Calhoon made her way down to the Technology laboratory to witness the unveiling of Solomon Bennett's newly designed bulletproof suit she wasn't expecting anything particularly ground-breaking. She'd only assigned herself a thirty-minute window in her day for the unveiling because she had no idea just how significant this minor experiment was going to turn out to be.

She arrived at the lab at just after three o'clock. Devon Pincent and Solomon Bennett were already there. They were both wearing long white lab coats and plastic safety glasses. The glasses looked odd on Solomon Bennett because he had a black eye-patch over his right eye.

Behind Pincent and Bennett was a large window that looked into the laboratory where the man they had chosen for the experiment was being prepared for the suit fitting by a lab technician who Calhoon had never met before. Solomon Bennett greeted her with a forced smile and offered her a lab coat.

'Fuck off I'm not wearing that,' she said, walking up to the window.

Bennett put the spare lab coat down on a table by the window. 'Would you like some safety glasses?' he inquired.

'Do I need them?'

'We'll be observing the experiment through the window,' said Bennett, 'so you're probably okay, but I don't like to take chances.' Seeing as he only had one eye, it was understandable that he might want to protect it.

'I've only got half an hour to spare,' said Calhoon as she put on the safety glasses, 'so let's just get on with it.'

'Yes ma'am.'

Calhoon walked up to the window and stood alongside Devon Pincent. She tried to get a good look at the lab technician who was busy fussing around inside the laboratory. He had a head of curly ginger hair, big enough to be called an afro, and he was wearing a pair of tinted red safety glasses. He was standing in front of a large glass cylinder that stretched from the floor to the ceiling. Another man was in the room with him, sitting in a chair with his back to everyone. He was wearing a black dressing gown with the hood pulled up over his head.

Calhoon nudged Devon in the ribs. 'Do you know this lab technician?' she asked.

Devon shook his head. 'I'm the same as you, General. This is the first time I'm seeing any of this.'

'Who is he?'

Solomon Bennett answered. 'His name is Doctor Henry Jekyll.'

'I beg your pardon?'

'Henry Jekyll.'

Major Bennett wasn't renowned for his sense of humour, in fact Calhoon couldn't remember him ever saying anything funny, or playing any pranks. But Dr Jekyll? That sounded like a really poor attempt at humour.

'What's his real name?' she asked.

'Henry Jekyll is his real name.'

'That doesn't inspire confidence,' said Calhoon. 'What's he a doctor in anyway?'

Bennett scratched his head. 'I'm not actually sure. I've never asked him.'

Devon whispered in Calhoon's ear. 'It's not too late to back out of this, you know.'

Calhoon ignored him even though she had her doubts about what was about to happen. She had sanctioned the experiment and backing out of it now would look like she'd made a mistake. She could live with that, but not with Devon being smug about it for the next ten years.

'Let's get started then,' she said, nodding at Bennett.

Bennett rapped his knuckles on the window to grab Dr Jekyll's attention. Jekyll looked up and gave Bennett a "thumbs-up" sign. He then mouthed some words at Bennett who made a "get on with it" gesture with his hand.

'Dr Jekyll hasn't quite grasped that the lab is soundproof,' he said apologetically to Calhoon.

Calhoon ignored him and carried on staring through the window. Dr Jekyll was leaning down and whispering something in the ear of the man seated beside him. A moment later the man stood up and lowered the hood on his gown. His head was completely shaved, as smooth as a billiard ball. And he had two metal bolts protruding from his neck, one on either side.

'What the hell are those bolts on his neck for?' Calhoon asked.

'Breathing apparatus,' said Bennett.

Before she could query further, the man took off his gown and dropped it to the floor. He was completely naked, much to Calhoon's surprise. When he turned around to face the window she recognised him as Frank Grealish. On the last occasion that she had seen him he'd had dark cropped hair. Now he had a pasty white scalp. She glanced down and saw that didn't have a single hair on his chest, stomach, pubic area or legs. For a moment, Calhoon didn't know where to look. Devon Pincent said out loud exactly what she was thinking.

'Where the fuck is all his hair?'

'He had to be completely hairless for this to work,' said Bennett.

'And is it necessary for him to be naked?' asked Calhoon.

'We're making his entire body bulletproof,' said Bennett. 'Therefore he has to be naked.'

'Can't the suit go over his underpants?'

'It could but it wouldn't make them bulletproof.'

Calhoon looked puzzled. 'Are you planning on firing bullets at his dick, then?'

'No ma'am. We're not firing any bullets at him just yet. This is just the part where we fit the suit to him. It's imperative that he's in this condition.'

Devon interrupted. 'I still don't understand why he has those bolts in his neck.'

'I told you already. Breathing apparatus.'

Calhoon looked Bennett in the eye. 'Do those bolts penetrate his skin?'

'Yes.'

'How far?'

'They're connected to his lungs so that he can breathe during the implementation of the suit.'

Devon reacted angrily. 'You mean that's why you needed him for two weeks? So you could stick metal tubes into him?'

'He had to be prepared properly for the process.'

Devon grabbed Calhoon by the arm. 'General did you know about this?'

Calhoon glanced down at her arm and Devon wisely removed his hand. 'No Devon I did not know about this,' she said, her nostrils flaring as she struggled to maintain calm. 'Because if Major Bennett had told me about this, he knows full well I would have wanted to know more. Major, what exactly are you about to do to that young man in there?'

'Dr Jekyll can explain it better,' said Bennett.

'Yes, but Dr Jekyll is in there and he can't hear us, so why don't you explain it in a manner that you think I will understand?'

Solomon Bennett pointed through the window into the lab again. Frank Grealish had stepped inside the cylindrical glass chamber. He stood up straight with his shoulders back, facing the window while Dr Jekyll secured two lengths of tube onto the metal bolts on either side of his neck. The tubes were attached to holes on the side of the chamber.

'See those tubes,' said Bennett. 'They're allowing oxygen into the chamber during the process. The oxygen will flow into the bolt on the left side of Frank's neck and once it's passed through his lungs it will be exhaled through the right side.'

'Why?' Calhoon asked, firmly.

'Because without them Frank will suffocate during the installation of the suit.'

'What suit? Where's the suit?' Calhoon asked, scouring the lab for any sign of anything resembling a suit.

'The suit will be sprayed onto him.'

'Come again?'

'It will be sprayed on to him.'

Calhoon wasn't sure she was hearing correctly. 'You mean to tell me you're spray tanning a bulletproof suit onto this soldier?'

'Yes ma'am. That's exactly what we're doing.'

Calhoon looked back through the window. Dr Jekyll slipped a pair of black goggles over Frank Grealish's eyes in order to protect him from the forthcoming spray.

'Pardon me,' said Devon. 'But what exactly is in this bulletproof spray?'

'I don't remember what the technical name is. It's something beginning with *Mist,* I know that because the substance we're using starts off as a mist before it attaches itself to its host and becomes a solid form.'

'All right,' said Calhoon. 'But what's *in* it? What's it *made* of?'

Bennett ignored them both and instead signalled through the window to Dr Jekyll.

'START THE REACTOR!' he shouted. Even though the room was soundproof, Bennett was one of those people who believed if he shouted he would still be heard. Either way, Dr Jekyll knew what he meant.

The three of them watched with more than a little trepidation as Dr Jekyll pressed a button on the side of the glass chamber. He stepped back away from it and seconds later, steam started filling up the chamber, rising up from the bottom.

They were supposed to be watching the creation of a bulletproof soldier. What they actually witnessed was the creation of a monster.

Five

Sneaking illegally out of a country on a cargo plane was best done at night in order to attract less attention. Unfortunately for Jack, Jasmine loved a bit of danger so he'd had to convince her that it was actually the *most dangerous* time to leave. Much of their time in Romania had been spent with Jack convincing her they were in constant danger, even when they weren't. He could usually keep her on edge by telling her about dangerous situations he had encountered in his time working for Phantom Ops.

During their cab drive to the airbase he regaled her with a tale of the time he caught a late night flight out of Bangkok and was attacked by a one armed man. Jasmine loved the story. Basically if it sounded like anything from a James Bond movie it turned her on. The story about the one armed man was true and had occurred when Jack was fairly new in the agency. When he told the story to Jasmine it sounded exciting and dangerous, whereas the reality of it was, Jack had beaten up a one armed man who was old enough to be his grandfather. Of course, he left the man's age out of the story when he told it to Jasmine.

Their cab arrived at the private airbase on the outskirts of Bucharest just after midnight. The cab driver was familiar with the procedure. He dropped them next to a twenty-foot high fence not far from the main entrance, waited for them to take their luggage from the trunk and then sped off into the night.

Jack's luggage consisted of a rucksack containing all his personal items. Jasmine had somehow accumulated enough possessions to fill a large suitcase, in spite of arriving in Romania with nothing but the clothes on her back.

'What do we do now?' Jasmine asked. She was shivering in the cold. Jack had suggested she wear dark colours in order to blend into the night. To Jasmine that meant a black top that was almost small enough to be called a bra and a pair of barely visible hotpants, plus her trademark knee high boots and a black purse over her shoulder. Jack had wrapped up warm in a thick brown sweater and dark pants.

'Jack Munson?' said a man's voice. It came from the woodland on the opposite side of the road.

A burly, bald-headed man in a green military uniform approached them. He was smoking a rolled-up cigarette.

'That's me,' said Jack, putting down Jasmine's suitcase and shaking the man's hand. 'And this is Jasmine.'

Jasmine walked up to the man and stood on tiptoe so that she could kiss him on the cheek. Even though it was dark, Jack could tell it took the man by surprise. Kissing the "hired criminal" wasn't usually part of the deal. This man was their arranger, hired by Devon Pincent to escort them onto their illegal flight with little or no fuss.

'I am Andrei,' the man said. 'I will take you to your plane.'

He pointed through the fence to an ancient looking warplane on a runway a hundred yards away. 'Zis is your plane,' he said.

'That's a plane?' Jasmine asked. 'It looks like a boat with wings!'

'That's because it's old,' said Jack. 'It's probably a death trap. That's why it's not costing us much.'

'Brilliant!'

Andrei took one last drag on his cigarette and tossed it to the floor by his feet. He ground it into the dirt with one of his large black boots. 'Follow me,' he said.

They followed Andrei along the perimeter of the fence for a while until he stopped and yanked open a section of it that looked like it had been vandalised. He gestured for them to go through it. Jasmine ducked her head and squeezed through. Andrei took a moment to check out her ass, not caring if it bothered Jack. Once they were inside the grounds of the airbase, Andrei rearranged the fence and concealed the gap.

As they headed towards the plane Jack saw two men preparing it for take-off. One was checking the propellers while the other was leaning against it smoking a cigarette.

'Can I smoke on this plane?' Jasmine asked.

Andrei marched past her. 'We must hurry, quickly!' he said.

The man who was leaning against the plane threw away his cigarette and began walking towards them. He was wearing a long dark coat with a hood pulled up over his head.

'Is there a buffet on the plane?' Jasmine asked Andrei.

Jack was struggling to keep up with them due to the strain of carrying Jasmine's suitcase. 'Honey, stop asking the man questions,' he whispered.

Jasmine looked back at him. 'I'm just being friendly,' she said.

Jack grabbed her by the arm, stopping her in her tracks. 'I know, angel, it's just that it's important that we stay low key. Andrei doesn't want to remember anything about us in case anyone asks him about this flight later.'

Jasmine nodded to show she understood. 'Top secret, right? Part of our undercover mission?'

'Yeah.'

Andrei had walked on ahead. He turned and shouted back to them. 'Wait there a moment, yes?'

While Andrei approached the man in the long black coat, possibly to arrange payment, Jack took the opportunity to put down Jasmine's suitcase.

'What's going on now?' Jasmine asked.

'Just formalities,' said Jack. 'Nothing to worry about.'

Unfortunately there was something to worry about. The man checking the propeller suddenly started sprinting towards them, trying to catch up with his friend in the long hooded coat who was discussing something with Andrei.

Jasmine whispered in Jack's ear. 'Something's wrong.'

She was right. She'd figured it out half a second before Jack. Kudos to her, she had a talent for sensing when something was amiss.

'Stay close to me,' Jack whispered in her ear. Inconsequentially he noticed how great her hair smelled.

His thoughts about her hair didn't last long. Jasmine screamed out sharply and pointed up ahead. Andrei had dropped to his knees in front of the guy in the hood. Jack looked for any sign of a weapon in the hooded man's hands. There was nothing. But he had definitely done something to Andrei because the Romanian fell forwards and landed face down on the concrete. Jack felt a rush of adrenaline. He'd seen men fall that way before.

Dead men fall like that.

He grabbed Jasmine by the arm. 'Let's get out of here!'

'What about my suitcase!'

'Fuck the suitcase.'

He dragged her away from the approaching men and pushed her back towards the gap in the fence they had come through. But now they had a bigger problem.

A much bigger problem.

From out of nowhere a giant of a man had crept up behind them. He stood between them and their escape route. The moonlight lit him up just enough for them to get a good look at him. He was dressed from head to toe in blue denim, with a big brown Stetson hat on his head.

'You must be Jack Munson,' he said in a deep southern accent.

Jack stepped in front of Jasmine. 'Just let the girl go,' he said.

The big man smiled. 'We're your flight crew, Mr Munson. My name is Rex. We're escorting you back to America.'

In all his years of taking illegal flights, Jack hadn't had an encounter like this one.

'Why should I trust you?' said Jack. 'Your guy just killed my contact.'

Rex peered over Jack's shoulder and saw Andrei splayed out on the ground. He shook his head. 'For fucks sake,' he grumbled.

The hooded man arrived at Jack's side. He smelled of alcohol and cigarettes.

Rex glared at him. 'Did you kill Andrei?'

The man replied in a husky, gravelly tone. 'Yeah.'

'Why?'

'I felt like it.'

The other man, the one who had been checking the propeller was leaning over Andrei looking for any signs of life. He had a thick head of dark hair and looked oddly familiar.

'Is that Elvis?' Jasmine asked, pointing at him.

Rex took his Stetson off and bowed down before her as if she was royalty. 'Yes it is ma'am,' he said. 'And my other friend here is the Bourbon Kid. We'll be escorting you home. There's nothing to worry about.'

Elvis jogged over to them. From up close it was apparent that he was wearing a dark red jumpsuit and a pair of gold-rimmed sunglasses, even though it was the middle of the night.

'That dude's dead,' he said.

'Your mate killed him,' said Jasmine.

'No shit,' said Elvis. He looked Jasmine up and down. 'You know you are *unbelievably* cute.'

Jack figured that they weren't about to be killed by these men, and also that Rex was the only one worth talking to. 'What the fuck is going on?' he demanded. 'Who are *you guys?*'

'We're the Dead Hunters,' said Rex.

'Dead Hunters? What's that mean?'

'We hunt people. Then we make 'em dead.'

'What's that got to do with us?'

'We're looking for the Red Mohawk. And word on the street is, you were tracking him last year in B Movie Hell, but when it all went to shit, you skipped the country.'

'I don't know what you're talking about.'

'Don't worry,' said Rex. 'It'll all come back to you while we're on the flight home.'

Six

The lyrics to *Hopelessly Devoted To You* by Olivia Newton John summed up exactly how Baby felt about Joey Conrad. Crazy though it might seem to anyone else, she was hopelessly devoted to the Red Mohawk, the man who had rescued her from the horrors of life as a hooker in B Movie Hell.

Singing the song out loud for an audience was nerve wracking to say the least. This wasn't a big audience, but it was an important one. Baby was performing for the producers of the local theatre production of *Grease*. Her father Devon Pincent was sitting with the producers in the front row of seats below the stage. He'd arranged for her to have a private audition while all the other girls who wanted the part of Sandy were still queuing around the block outside.

In the build-up to her performance her stomach had been in knots brought on by the fear of hitting a bum note, but once she started singing, all the nerves and the knots in her stomach faded away. Baby was in a world of her own, standing on stage in her new pink dress, singing the song and feeling like it was written just for her.

As she sang the first verse she reminisced about her first meeting with Joey. She'd been sitting at the counter in a diner waiting to order a milkshake when he appeared behind Arnold, the man who had accompanied her there. His yellow skull mask had scared the bejesus out of her at first. Watching him chop Arnold's fingers off with a meat cleaver had scared her even more. She'd raced out of the diner and run as far away from him as she could, thinking he was going to kill her next. Silly really, but she'd had no way of knowing at the time that she was destined to fall in love with that masked lunatic.

He had later admitted to her that he dragged Arnold into the washroom before killing him because he didn't want to create a bad impression on his first meeting with her. Baby loved how thoughtful that was. Other serial killers might just have gone ahead and ripped Arnold's innards out right in front of her, but not the Red Mohawk, he was the considerate type. And he'd killed almost a hundred people, *just for her*.

It was so romantic.

When she finished singing *Hopelessly Devoted* the three producers leapt to their feet and applauded. Her father stayed in his seat, but he was clapping too and Baby had a feeling he was welling up with pride because he was blinking a heck of a lot.

The chief producer, Camberwick Bender was the senior judge on the panel. He was a colourful character renowned for his flamboyant dress sense and a love of hats. His hat of choice on this occasion was a grey-green fedora made from sea grass. It didn't exactly go with the bright orange shirt and green sweater he had wrapped around his shoulders, but no one was about to tell him.

When the applause ended Camberwick exchanged a few quick looks with his two female colleagues. No words were exchanged, but it was obvious they had a telepathic understanding of each other because all three of them nodded in unison. Camberwick looked up at Baby and smiled, showing off a shiny white set of expensive teeth.

'Congratulations Baby,' he said. 'You've just landed the part of Sandy. Welcome to Grease!'

It seemed unusual that they had made a decision so quickly, particularly when there were still a few hundred girls waiting to audition, but Baby quickly forgot about the other girls and jumped for joy at the news she was in the show.

'Rehearsals start tomorrow at ten o'clock,' said Camberwick. 'I look forward to working with you.'

'Thank you so much,' said Baby. 'I won't let you down, I promise.'

She didn't get a chance to hang around and chat with the producers because they had plenty of other people to audition for the other parts in the show. But that didn't matter because Devon had already planned a celebratory lunch for her.

He took her out to Bambino's Italian restaurant. The owner was a friend of his and had reserved them a decent sized table next to a window that provided a view across the city. Devon, ever the proud father, made a point of telling their waiter all about how his daughter had just landed the lead role in Grease. It wasn't lost on Baby that she'd landed the part rather easily though.

'Did you know that Camberwick guy on the judges panel?' she asked as she flicked through the menu looking for a vegetarian option.

'I'm a well-respected member of the community, Baby. I know everyone who's anyone in this town.'

'Did you fix it so I got the part?'

'No.'

'Are you sure? I got the feeling they were intimidated by you in there.'

Devon loosened his tie. He'd put on his favourite silver suit to take her to the audition and done everything possible to make the day special, even driving her there in his Aston Martin, the car he normally left in the garage back home because he said it was only for special occasions.

'I made Camberwick an offer he couldn't refuse,' he said as casually as he could.

'You mean you bribed him?'

'Blackmail is probably a better way to describe it.'

'Oh my God. Blackmailed him? How?'

'Nothing major really, but Camberwick is a happily married man.'

Baby was surprised to hear that. 'I thought he was gay, you know from the way he dressed.'

'He's in the closet sweetheart. And he wants to stay that way for the sake of his marriage.'

'But surely everyone knows he's gay. There must be loads of people that could blackmail him with that information?'

'Yes, but I doubt any of them could make it front page news that he had an affair with a Hollywood A list actor.'

Baby had no idea that her father was privileged with such amazing gossip. 'Oh my God you have to tell me who!' she said.

'So you're okay with me blackmailing him to get you the part?'

'I will be if you tell me the name of the actor he had an affair with!'

'I can't do that Baby, it's confidential. That's what my job is all about, confidentiality.'

'In that case, I'm not sure I'm happy about you blackmailing him to get me the part. I wanted to get it off my own back,' Baby said, not entirely truthfully.

Devon put his menu down and looked her in the eye. 'Baby, you're all I have left in the world. For fifteen years I thought I would never hear your voice again. When you sing, you have the voice of an angel. You're good enough to be the star of any show that this school puts on, do you understand?'

'Of course I do, Dad. But I feel bad for all those other girls who were queuing down the street to audition.'

'If you like, we can go back and I'll tell the producers that you want to audition again along with all the other hopefuls. Do you want me to do that? I will if that's what you want?'

Baby didn't want to go through the trauma of the audition again, or more importantly have to admit to anyone that her father had tried to fix it for her the first time round. 'I guess not,' she said. 'I mean, I am *Sandy in Grease* and that is the coolest thing ever!'

'Good. Now let's order. I'm starving.'

Devon called their waiter back over and ordered himself a steak. Baby chose a salad. Once the waiter was gone, she decided the time was right to take advantage of her father's good mood to ask a question that might prove somewhat sensitive.

'Dad, do you think you might be able to get word to Joey Conrad about the show, so he could come and watch?'

Devon rolled his eyes and let out a deep sigh. 'I doubt it honey. I've no idea where he is these days.'

'But he was in the news again the other day for that gas station thing. You must be in touch with him still.'

Devon went back to avoiding eye contact. He stared out of the window behind Baby pretending to be interested in something outside. 'Joey's got some serious mental health issues, Baby,' he said. 'He's a dangerous person to be around.'

'That didn't stop you sending him to come and find me in B Movie Hell.'

'He was the best man for that job. He owed me a favour.'

'Why? What did you do for him?'

'I did lots for him, Baby. But let's not talk about it.'

Baby looked away in a huff, hoping her father would notice and soften when he saw that he had upset her. But while she was looking away, she caught sight of a newspaper on the next table. It was folded in two but she saw a picture of the Red Mohawk's mask on the front page. She pushed her chair back. It made an awful scratching noise as it scraped along the floor. She got up and reached over to the next table, grabbing the newspaper and opening it up.

'What's that?' said Devon, taking a sudden interest and reaching out for the paper.

Baby sat down but kept the newspaper for herself. The headline was a real eye-catcher.

RED MOHAWK THREATENS TO KILL THE POPE

Baby's face dropped. 'This must be a lie!' she said, showing Devon the front page.

He looked surprised to see the article, but sat back in his chair and made no further attempt to grab the paper.

'See,' he said smugly. 'I told you he was dangerous.'

'But why would he want to kill the Pope?'

'Like I told you before, Baby, he's insane.'

Baby lowered her voice to a whisper. 'The Joey I knew wouldn't want to kill the Pope.'

'You only knew him for one day.'

'That was long enough to know he wouldn't kill the Pope.'

'Really?' Devon raised his eyebrows. 'And how many people did he kill in the one day you knew him?'

'I don't know. I lost count.'

'Exactly.'

Baby folded the paper up and put it down on the table. 'Please daddy, you could at least tell me a bit about him, like how he ended up in an asylum.'

'It's not a pleasant story.'

'I don't care.'

'Fine. One day your Prince Charming walked into a diner in Boston and stabbed a nun to death. Are you happy now?'

Baby felt her veins turn to ice. The revelation that Joey had stabbed a nun to death rammed home the reality of what he really was, a cold-blooded killer.

'That's horrible,' she said, her heart sinking. 'Why would he do that?'

Devon tapped the headline on the newspaper several times with his index finger. 'Probably for the same reason he wants to kill the Pope.'

'He doesn't like religious people?'

'Something like that. Let's not talk about it any more. Our food will be here in a minute.'

Seven

'What kind of plane is this?' Jasmine asked.

'It's a military cargo plane,' said Jack.

Jasmine had never been on a nice plane. The one they'd flown to Romania in was a rust-bucket. This one wasn't much better. And it was full of weirdoes.

She was sitting next to Jack on a bench on one side of the plane. Directly opposite her was the Bourbon Kid. He had his legs stretched out and the hood of his coat still pulled up over his head, which was annoying because Jasmine wanted to get a better look at his face. All she could see was that he was unshaven and was probably in his thirties, far too old to be referred to as *Kid*, surely?

Rodeo Rex was sitting opposite Jack. He was even weirder than the Kid because he was wearing a black glove on his right hand but no glove on his left. Jasmine was itching to ask him about it. Had they been in Romania so long that she'd fallen behind in what was fashionable? Or had Rex maybe lost his other glove? Judging by the oversized Stetson he was wearing and his wavy brown mullet haircut, she decided that he was probably behind the times rather than cutting edge when it came to fashion. In spite of the dodgy fashion though, Rex still had sex appeal. His sleeveless blue denim jacket showed off a set of biceps bigger than any Jasmine had ever seen, and she'd seen some big muscles in her time. He had some crazy tattoos on his arms too, featuring skulls, snakes and words like DEATH and CHOSEN.

The other guy, Elvis was in the cockpit flying the plane. His fashion sense was quirky too, but a lot more predictable. He was clearly an Elvis impersonator of sorts.

'Is your friend a good pilot?' Jasmine asked Rex.

'He's the best pilot in this plane,' Rex replied, earnestly.

Jasmine's excitement was beginning to get the better of her so she reached into her purse and pulled out a pack of cigarettes. She had six left, which meant she would have to pace herself, because right now she felt like smoking them all one after the other.

Rex leant across. 'No smoking on the plane,' he said softly.

'Fuck you. I'm bored.'

She took a cigarette out of the pack and put it between her lips. Then she pulled her zippo lighter from her bag and flicked it open. She was just about to light her cigarette with it when it inexplicably flew out of her hand as if someone had caught it on the end of an invisible fishing rod. It zipped across the walkway and into Rex's gloved hand then vanished as he closed his fist around it.

Jack said aloud what Jasmine was thinking. 'What the fuck happened there?'

Rex slipped the lighter into a pocket on his jeans. 'I told her no smoking, that's what happened,' he said.

'Yeah, but how the fuck did you get the lighter to fly into your hand?' Jack inquired.

'I used *the force*.'

Rex sat back, looking extremely pleased with himself.

The Bourbon Kid leant forward and gestured to Jasmine. 'Give me your cigarettes,' he said.

There was something about this guy. When he spoke his voice had a gravelly quality to it, and with his face barely visible underneath his hood, he looked a bit like the Grim Reaper. And Jasmine was afraid of the Reaper, so she did as he said and tossed her pack of cigarettes over to him. Throwing wasn't a strong point of hers though and the pack of cigarettes went up past his shoulder. Nonetheless the Kid plucked them out of the air with his left hand. He then put the pack up to his mouth and pulled one of the cigarettes out with his teeth.

Rex grabbed the Kid's arm. 'You'd better not light that,' he said.

The Kid sucked on the unlit cigarette. To Jasmine's surprise the end of the cigarette lit up all by itself when he inhaled. He took the cigarette out of his mouth, twisted it round between his fingers and held it out to Jasmine, inviting her to take it. She tentatively reached across and accepted the cigarette from him, while Rex glowered at her. She put it between her lips and took a drag. It felt so good to be sucking in a lungful of smoke. She exhaled and smiled at the Kid. He didn't reciprocate. He just tossed the pack of cigarettes back to her.

'Thanks,' she said.

Rex shook his head and elbowed the Kid. 'Why have you got to be such a dick all the time?'

The Kid didn't reply. He closed his eyes and put his head back against the side of the plane.

Jasmine took another puff on the cigarette. She suddenly felt far more comfortable and relaxed than she had just thirty seconds earlier. She took four or five more puffs until she plucked up the courage to ask the Kid a question.

'How did you do that?'

He didn't open his eyes but answered her anyway. 'It's a secret. I only show my friends.'

'Great! Can we be friends?' Jasmine asked, enthusiastically.

Jack reached across and rubbed her back. He whispered in her ear. 'Jaz, I think he's saying he doesn't want to show you.'

'But I want to know. That's so cool. I want to be able to do it!'

Rodeo Rex stamped his foot on the floor, which grabbed everyone's attention. 'What the fuck is wrong with you?' he said, glaring at Jasmine. 'I just made your zippo lighter fly across the plane into my hand, and all you wanna know is, how does he light his fucking cigarette!'

'Fine,' said Jasmine. 'Tell us about your weird trick.'

The Bourbon Kid answered on Rex's behalf. 'He's got a magnetic hand.'

Jasmine stared at Rex's gloved hand and cringed. 'Ooh, that's creepy!'

Jack leant over towards Rex. 'Can I see it?' he asked.

Rex loosened the glove one finger at a time and then yanked it off. Underneath was a shiny fist made of steel. He showed off a few grasping gestures with it to prove that it worked just like a normal hand.

'How the hell did you end up with a metal hand?' Jack asked.

'Is it your wanking hand?' Jasmine inquired.

Rex ignored her and chose to answer Jack's question instead. 'My real hand had to be amputated, so I had a new one built, and just recently I've had it magnetised.'

Jack frowned. 'Doesn't the magnet cause you problems though? Surely it makes your hand stick to stuff all the time?'

Rex shook his head. 'The magnet is like the rest of the hand. It works when I want it to work.'

'How?'

'How do you make your fingers move?' Rex asked.

'I just wiggle them like this,' said Jack, wiggling his fingers.

'Exactly. Your mind controls your hand. Just like mine does.'

Jasmine grimaced. 'Ewww, that's so freaky. Do you wipe your butt with that hand?'

'It's not freaky!' Rex bellowed. He sat back against the wall, looking like a child in a huff.

'What happened to your original hand?' Jack asked. 'Why did it have to be amputated?'

Rex slipped his glove back on. 'I don't wanna talk about this anymore,' he grumbled. 'Let's talk about the Red Mohawk. I wanna know everything you know about him. You can start by telling me why you were the only man the government sent to try and stop him.'

A waft of smoke from Jasmine's cigarette floated across the walkway and passed under Rex's nose. He waved it away with his gloved hand and glared at her.

'If you're gonna smoke you're gonna have to go and sit in the cockpit,' he snapped. 'Me and Jack have got shit to talk about.'

Jasmine blew some more smoke at Rex and stood up. She leaned over and kissed Jack on the cheek. 'I'll be back in a minute, sweetie,' she said.

She got up and walked over to the cockpit door. There was a red cape hanging on it, one that looked like it matched Elvis's red suit. *"Capes are pretty cool,"* Jasmine thought to herself. *"I must get one."*

She turned the handle on the cockpit door and pulled it open. Inside the cockpit Elvis was sitting in one of two seats, steering the plane with some kind of joystick. He looked back at her and smiled. 'Hey honey,' he said. 'What can I do for ya?'

'Your friend said I could smoke in here.'

Elvis patted the co-pilot seat next to him. 'So come on in.'

Jasmine closed the door behind her and sat down in the co-pilot seat. Through the cockpit window she could see the night sky and the clouds up ahead. 'Wow this is so cool,' she said.

'I like it too,' said Elvis. 'Did you get bored of the conversation back there?'

'It was getting a bit too macho for my liking.'

'Yeah. That happens.'

'So is it just the three of you in the Dead Hunters?' Jasmine asked.

'The Dead Hunters?' said Elvis, looking confused.

'Rex said you were called the Dead Hunters. You hunt killers and then make 'em dead. That's what he said.'

Elvis smiled. 'Ha. He's always trying to come up with a name for us. Unfortunately all the names he comes up with are fuckin' awful.'

'I thought the Dead Hunters was a really cool name!'

Elvis shrugged. 'Maybe we'll keep it then.'

'So what do you guys actually do? And what do you want with the Red Mohawk?'

'Can I have a drag on that smoke?'

'Sure, honey.' Jasmine handed him her cigarette. He took a puff on it and handed it back.

'We hunt down anything and anyone who we think should be in Hell. Then we make sure that's where they end up.'

'Wow. So you think the Red Mohawk should be in Hell?'

'Rex thinks so. Word is, he's got a problem with the Catholic Church so he's gonna try to assassinate the Pope.'

'Who's the Pope?'

'He's like a figurehead for the church.'

'I know that,' said Jasmine. 'But what's his real name?'

'Fucked if I know,' Elvis replied. 'He's like Batman or James Bond, they change the actor every few years. It's hard to keep up.'

'Is that why the Red Mohawk wants to kill him? Does he want to be Pope?'

Elvis laughed. 'That's one possibility.'

'I met the Red Mohawk once,' said Jasmine. 'He didn't try to kill me. He killed all the men that ran the whorehouse I worked in.'

'You worked in a whorehouse?'

'Yeah.'

'You don't look like a whore.'

'I'm not any more. Jack has taught me how to be an undercover agent.'

Elvis peered over his sunglasses at her, his eyes lingering mostly on her cleavage. 'You're an undercover agent?'

'Yeah. I'm really good at it too.'

Elvis didn't look convinced. 'You must be pretty smart then. Working undercover is a dangerous business.'

'I'm a lot cleverer than people realise,' said Jasmine proudly. 'Jack told me, people look at me and think I'm an airhead because of the clothes I wear and the way I talk and stuff, so no one ever realises how clever I am.'

Elvis smiled. 'So how do you get information out of people then? What's your big move?'

'I only get information from men, or sometimes lesbians. Most guys will tell me all their secrets if they think it will impress me. I mean look at you, you've just told me all about what you guys do.'

'I haven't even scratched the surface of what we do, honey.'

Jasmine took one last drag on her cigarette. 'Mind if I throw this out the window?' she said.

Elvis reached down to the dashboard and pulled out an ashtray. 'Probably safer if you just stub it out in here,' he said.

'Oh, okay.' Jasmine stubbed her cigarette out in the ashtray. She looked around at all the other knobs and levers in the cockpit. 'So where do you keep the auto-pilot?' she asked.

'What?'

'You know, *the auto-pilot*, the inflatable guy who flies the plane if you get food poisoning.'

Elvis peered over the top of his sunglasses at her again. 'Are you pretending to be stupid now?' he asked.

Jasmine grinned. 'Sometimes even I don't know.'

Eight

Jack Munson burst through the doors into the laboratory. Devon Pincent and Solomon Bennett were already there inside the laboratory watching Dr Jekyll attempting to resuscitate the lifeless body of Frank Grealish. Grealish was on his back on the floor and Jekyll was administering shock treatment with a pair of electric paddles. It didn't seem to be having any effect.

'Is he dead?' Munson asked.

Devon's face gave him his answer. He looked grim and troubled. Only minutes earlier Devon had called Munson in a panic, telling him that Frank Grealish was having some kind of heart attack. Munson had rushed down from his office to see for himself. It looked like the heart attack was well and truly over. And so was Frank's life.

Dr Jekyll stopped trying to shock the corpse back into life and put the electric paddles down. He looked up at the others. 'He's gone,' he said, wiping the sweat from his brow.

Solomon Bennett lashed out at the nearest thing to him, which happened to be the plastic chair Frank Grealish had been sitting in before the ill-fated experiment. He kicked it halfway across the room and then as if he felt that wasn't sufficient enough to show how upset he was, he ran after it, picked it up and threw it against the window. The window was made of stern stuff, so the chair simply bounced off it straight back at Bennett. He held his hands up to protect his face and deflected it away. It landed on the floor and he kicked it again, this time spooning it up in the air.

'Are you having fun there?' Devon asked him, sarcastically.

'FUCK OFF!'

It didn't look like Bennett was going to calm down any time soon so Munson got straight to the point. 'What the hell were you doing here?' he asked. 'I just saw Calhoon in the corridor. She looks really pissed.'

Bennett was too angry to reply, which was kind of ironic because Munson was furious too, but he was holding his anger in until he'd worked out who was to blame.

Devon walked over to the beaten up plastic chair and set it upright as he responded to Munson's question. 'They were fitting a bulletproof skin to him. It seemed to be going well but then he started struggling for breath. We pulled him out of the chamber but he had this God awful seizure.'

'Bulletproof *skin?* '

'Yeah.'

'Is that just a clever name for the bulletproof suit we've been talking about for the last three days? Or has this fuckwit,' he pointed at Bennett, 'done something fucking stupid?'

'It's an accident, a setback that's all,' said Bennett.

Munson took a closer look at the body on the floor. 'Why has he got bolts in his neck? Is that why this is called the Frankenstein project? And why does his skin look like rubber? What in God's name have you done?'

Dr Jekyll stood up, gingerly. 'That's the Mistralyte,' he said. 'It melded itself perfectly to his skin just like we'd hoped, but it looks like his heart couldn't cope with the procedure. I think he's had a massive coronary.'

'What the fuck is Mistralyte?' Munson raged.

'Well,' Jekyll replied, calmly. 'It's a *liquid-rubber-skin* hybrid. At the right temperature, when it comes into contact with human skin it solidifies like elastic and attaches itself to the skin, using it as a host. And it's completely impenetrable. If Frank hadn't had a heart attack, we'd now be looking at the first ever bullet proof soldier.'

'You fucking assholes!' Munson yelled, venting his anger at both Bennett and Jekyll.

'Jack, calm down, for fucks sake!' Devon yelled. 'What's done is done!'

Munson grabbed Dr Jekyll by the collar of his coat and pulled him in close. 'Can you get this suit off of him?' he growled.

The doctor shook his head. 'No.'

Munson took a deep breath. 'Let me get this straight in my head. If Frank had survived this experiment, this *dog shit experiment*, would he have been able to take the suit off?'

'No, it's permanent,' said Jekyll.

Munson turned back to Solomon Bennett. 'If I was in your shoes I'd be halfway to Brazil about now,' he said.

'Don't be so dramatic,' Bennett muttered.

'Where do you think Calhoon is right now?' Munson snapped. 'She's gone to get the MP's. You're about to be arrested Solomon.' He turned back to Dr Jekyll. 'And that goes for you too you little weirdo.'

'She wouldn't do that,' said Bennett. 'She commissioned this whole experiment. If I go down, she goes down with me.'

Right on cue Alexis Calhoon came storming down the corridor towards the lab, accompanied by two armed officers from the Military Police. She walked in, pointed at Bennett and Dr Jekyll.

'Him and him!' she said.

If ever there had been any doubt about how tough Alexis Calhoon could be, what followed was an example of a ruthless streak that had served her well and would continue to do so for many more years. Bennett and Jekyll were handcuffed and marched out of the building, despite their protests and Bennett's claims that proper procedures for arrest weren't being carried out.

'I hope they're going to be court marshalled,' said Munson. 'The pair of them should be suspended at the very least. Fucking disgrace what's happened here today.'

'Court marshalled?' Calhoon raised her eyebrows. 'That's not how I work, Jack. They're going to be shot and buried in the desert.'

Munson started to laugh politely even though he didn't think it was an appropriate time for Calhoon to be making jokes. But he stopped himself when it occurred to him that she might not be joking.

Calhoon pointed at the dead body of Frank Grealish. 'This young man has no family, *correct?'*

'That's right,' said Devon. 'None of the Blackwash recruits have any family.'

'Well that's something I suppose. He'll have to go down as *Missing in Action*. Devon you can draft up the report. And Jack, I want you to get Frank Grealish zipped up in a body bag before anyone else sees this. He can be buried in the desert along with Bennett and that fucking Dr Jekyll idiot. And tomorrow we can discuss how we make your Operation Blackwash go the same way.'

Nine

It felt good to be back on American soil. Elvis had safely crash-landed the Romanian plane in a remote forest clearing. No one had suffered any significant injuries, which meant he kept up his track record of never having killed a passenger in all his years of crash-landing planes of all sizes in forests, rivers and from time to time, runways. He really had turned crash-landing (or as Rex preferred to call it, *"crashing"*) into an art form.

Rex stood by the plane, puffing on a cigar while he watched Jack and Jasmine head off into the night hoping to find a cab to take them home. Elvis and the Bourbon Kid had been rummaging around in the cargo hold while Rex gave Jack directions back to civilisation. Eventually Elvis hopped off the plane with a rucksack full of stuff that he'd found in the cargo hold of the plane. The Bourbon Kid was still in there, making a fair amount of noise as he helped himself to some of the gear.

'Did you find anything any good back there?' Rex asked.

'They were smuggling some very diverse stuff on that plane,' Elvis said. 'I got a few boxes of cigarettes, but there's explosives on there, cigars, spirits and chocolate eggs.'

'I'll grab myself some cigars in a minute then,' said Rex. He tossed his rather burnt tasting cigar over his shoulder and into some dirt.

'Jack Munson tell you anything?' Elvis asked.

'Not much. Did you get anything out of Jasmine when she was in the cockpit with you?'

'Like what? A phone number?'

'No. Like stuff about the Red Mohawk.'

Elvis rubbed his chin, which was usually a sign that he was confused about something. 'She said she met the Red Mohawk when she was working in a whorehouse. Said he killed everyone apart from the girls who worked there.'

'In B Movie Hell?'

'Yeah.'

'Did she say anything else?'

'Yeah, she said she was an undercover agent.'

Rex checked to see if Elvis was kidding, but it looked like he was deadly serious. 'An undercover agent? Doing what?'

'She infiltrated a military base where she says she saw Frankenstein, Dr Jekyll and Mozart. And the base was run by a dude called Eye-patch Bennett who had one eye.'

'So she was talking shit then?'

'I guess so. Did any of that tie up with what Munson said?'

Rex shook his head. 'Jack said he was looking for the Red Mohawk but never found him. Reckons he has no idea who was underneath the mask.'

'You believe him?'

'I dunno.'

The Bourbon Kid jumped out of the plane behind them. He had a cigarette hanging from the corner of his mouth and he was carrying a rucksack over his shoulder, filled with items he'd pilfered from the cargo hold.

'Been helping yourself to chocolate eggs?' said Rex, scornfully.

'Yeah, you want one?' The Kid tossed an oval shaped object at Rex. Rex caught it in the palm of his human hand.

'A Kinder egg? What the fuck do I want with a Kinder egg?' he sneered. He threw the egg back to the Kid who caught it and slipped it back into his rucksack.

'Don't say I never give you anything,' the Kid said dryly.

Elvis stepped in and moved the conversation on before Rex had a chance to launch into a rant about how stupid chocolate eggs were. 'Hey Kid, what did you make of Jack Munson? Was he tellin' the truth?'

'Nope.'

'So what's your theory?' said Rex. 'Why's he lying?'

The Kid pulled a half bottle of bourbon out of his rucksack and unscrewed the lid before replying. 'Because he knows who the Red Mohawk is. He'll warn him we're coming for him.'

'You think?'

'You should follow him,' said the Kid. He took a swig from his bottle of bourbon before adding, 'and Elvis should follow his girlfriend.'

'I'm up for that,' said Elvis.

Rex slapped Elvis across the chest with the back of his hand. 'Don't get too close to her,' he said. 'Follow her, *don't fuck her.*'

'Hey cool it, man,' said Elvis. 'I'll keep my distance, but you know, if fate plays a hand....'

Rex nodded at the Kid. 'What are *you* gonna do?'

'I'm gonna get drunk, then I'm gonna find the Red Mohawk.'

'And how are you gonna do that?'

The Kid reached inside his jacket and pulled out a pack of cigarettes. He took one out with his teeth and sucked hard on it. It lit up and he blew some smoke out through his nostrils before replying to Rex.

'The Red Mohawk killed all the men who ran the whorehouse in B Movie Hell.'

'Yeah, so?'

'So my guess is he did it for a woman. Once I find her, I'll find him.'

Ten

Solomon Bennett and Dr Jekyll were sitting on a bench in the back of a military prison truck. Sitting opposite them was an armed prison guard, a stern forty-something black guy with a bushy moustache who was ready to shoot them if they made any attempt to escape. And on the floor in the middle of the truck was a zipped up black body bag containing the corpse of Frank Grealish.

The ride was a bumpy one and for the first few minutes there was an uncomfortable lack of conversation. Bennett knew what was about to happen. He and Jekyll were going to be disposed of. He had to try and talk his way out of it.

'Do you know who I am?' he asked the guard.

The guard stared straight ahead and ignored him. Bennett had to consider the fact that if the roles were reversed he would do the same thing. It's a lot harder to kill someone if you've gotten to know them.

'I'm Major Solomon Bennett. If you let us out of the truck, I can make sure we disappear. No one will ever see us again. And I can also see to it that a suitcase full of money arrives at your door.'

The guard continued to ignore him.

'A million bucks,' Bennett said, hoping to generate at least a flicker of interest. 'Okay, two million, for you and your buddy driving the truck.'

Finally, the guard's eyes lit up at the mention of the two million. *"Everyone has their price,"* Bennett thought, inwardly smirking to himself.

The guard beckoned him to lean across the aisle so he could whisper into his ear. Bennett's hands were cuffed behind his back, which made it almost impossible to stand up in a moving truck, so he stuck his neck out across the aisle and offered the guard his ear.

All Bennett got for his troubles was a smack across the back of his head from the butt of the guard's pistol. The blow hurt like hell so it was probably a blessing that he lost consciousness almost immediately. The last thing he remembered was the sensation of his face landing on the black body bag that Frank Grealish was zipped up in.

He remained unconscious for just short of twenty minutes. During that time he had occasional moments where he heard a lot of the noise going on around him. The sensation was similar to being drunk and dozing off in front of the television in the middle of a John Woo film. His deep sleep was punctuated by sounds of gunfire, people shouting, and something that sounded suspiciously like a car crash.

When he eventually woke up his head was pounding. It felt like a giant pulse was squashed between his skull and his scalp, throbbing incessantly. And when he opened his eyes he saw that the situation in the back of the prison truck had changed completely. He was back in his spot on the bench with his back pressed up against the side of the truck, but he was no longer in handcuffs and the man sitting opposite him was now Henry Jekyll, not the miserable bastard guard who'd smashed him over the head.

'What the hell happened?' he asked.

The truck bounced up on the road, shaking Bennett right to his bones and sending his headache to stratospheric levels of agonising pain.

'We're in the back of the prison truck,' Jekyll replied. 'Don't you remember?'

'Don't be smug, it doesn't suit you,' said Bennett, rubbing the back of his head.

He glanced down at the floor and noticed that Frank Grealish's body bag was empty. 'What's going on?' he asked, wincing in pain as the head throbbing became ever more real.

Henry Jekyll was grinning, which although not a pleasant sight was a good sign that things were not as desperate as they had been twenty minutes earlier. 'It worked, Solomon,' he said. 'It bloody well worked!'

'What worked?'

'Guess who's driving the truck?'

'What?'

'The truck. Guess who's driving it right now?'

'Henry, I've got the headache from hell. Just tell me what the fuck is going on.'

Jekyll reached down and picked up the body bag. 'Look,' he said, beaming. 'See, our experiment worked. Frank Grealish is alive and he's driving the truck.'

It wasn't possible to see the driver from the back of the truck, which was supposed to be a portable prison cell.

'What happened to the guards?'

'You should have seen it Solomon. It was everything we hoped it would be.'

'Stop talking in riddles. What's happened?'

'Frank woke up. He wasn't dead. When the guard saw the body bag moving he unzipped it. Frank was alive.'

'How?'

'Never mind that. I ordered him to kill the guards. Oh Solomon, it was beautiful. You should have seen it. He grabbed that guy who hit you, grabbed him by the throat and, well, that's when the best thing happened.'

Bennett forgot about his headache for a moment. 'Where are the guards now?' he asked.

'They tried to shoot him,' said Jekyll, clapping his hands together like a happy seal. 'He took four bullets in the chest, and they all bounced off him. Our experiment worked. He's bulletproof!'

'And the guards?'

'He killed them both. Crushed the first one's throat even though he shot him once in the chest. The driver slammed on the brakes and the next thing you know, he's swung the back doors open and fired three more shots at Frank. Frank just shrugged them off and picked up the first guard's gun. Then BANG! Both guards are dead. And you and me, we've got the bulletproof soldier we always wanted.'

'What did you do with the bodies?'

'We just dumped them by the road and I got Frank to drive us the hell out of here!'

Bennett rubbed his head again. 'Okay, back up a second,' he said. 'An hour ago Frank didn't have a pulse or a heartbeat. I mean, he was dead, we all saw it.'

'He wasn't dead. He just passed out during the skin grafting process. He still has a pulse, but you can't feel it through his bulletproof skin. And he's able to breathe through those bolts on his neck, so not only is he invincible but he can also play dead.'

Bennett couldn't help but smile for once. 'This is incredible,' he said. 'We've got ourselves a real life Frankenstein.'

'This is my best invention yet,' said Jekyll. 'If we can get ourselves some more Mistralyte we can make more of them. This is the greatest military invention in history. An invincible assassin!'

'Let's not get ahead of ourselves,' said Bennett. 'For now, let's just get out of the country before Calhoon finds out we've escaped.'

Eleven

Baby arrived home from rehearsal and was greeted by the smell of a roast dinner wafting into the hallway from the kitchen. She called out to her father but got no response so she followed the scent of food into the kitchen where she found him bent over with his head in the oven.

'Hi dad, what are you doing?' she asked.

Devon pulled his head back out of the oven. His face was red and covered in sweat. 'Hey Baby,' he said, smiling. 'Just making dinner.'

A few drops of sweat trickled off his face and onto a blue apron he was wearing. The apron was covered in food stains, some of which looked fresh. One of the things Baby had learned about her father since they'd been living together was that he was a messy cook.

The kitchen table had four places set, and there were three saucepans on the stove, two of which were on the verge of bubbling over.

'What are we having exactly?' Baby asked.

'Roast beef. We've got guests for dinner. How was your rehearsal?'

'It was okay.'

She was about to ask who the guests were when Devon asked her another question. 'Have you made many friends in the show?'

'I got asked out on a date.'

Devon wiped some sweat off his brow. 'By one of the cast?'

'Yeah. The guy playing Danny Zuco invited me to go rehearse some lines with him on Friday night.'

'You like him?'

Baby pressed her hands down on the back of one of the chairs at the kitchen table. 'He's no Ryan Gosling,' she said, 'but all the other girls seem to like him.'

'I didn't ask if the other girls like him. I asked if you do.'

Before Baby could respond to her father's direct questioning, the doorbell rang indicating that their guests had arrived.

'Can you get that?' said Devon. He pulled one of the chairs out from under the table and sat down on it, looking exhausted from the heat.

Baby left the kitchen and walked through the hallway to the front door. Through the window she could see two figures standing outside. She opened the door and was delighted to discover that she recognised both of them. It was her father's old colleague Jack Munson and his new girlfriend Jasmine, who had been one of Baby's best friends during her time as a hooker in B Movie Hell.

'Oh My God. Jack, Jasmine? What are you doing here?' she beamed.

Jack looked a lot healthier than when she had last seen him in B Movie Hell. He looked years younger, he wasn't bleary eyed and he was well dressed in smart black trousers and a blue shirt with a trendy black leather jacket. Jasmine had obviously given him a makeover.

He smiled at Baby. 'Your father invited us over for dinner. Did he not tell you?'

'No. I mean, he said we had guests, but...'

Jasmine barged Jack aside and stepped into the hall. She threw her arms around Baby. 'Baby!' she squealed. 'It's so good to see you again. You look great!'

'You too.'

Jasmine was wearing a pair of leopard skin leggings and a low cut black top. It was a style she'd been carrying off for years. Her long dark hair was a little windswept but Jasmine had a way about her that meant she could carry it off like it was meant to be that way.

Munson cleared his throat. 'So you got a hug for your uncle Jack too, or what?'

'Of course.'

Baby pulled herself away from Jasmine and gave Munson a hug and a kiss on the cheek. 'You look really well, Jack,' she said.

'Of course I do, and so do you. You've got your mother's good looks. Now where's that old fart you call your father?'

'I'm right here!'

Devon appeared in the hallway behind Baby. He and Jack embraced in a warm hug. It was obvious that their friendship was deep.

'Good to see you Devon,' said Jack. 'You look fuckin' old though.'

'Yeah, having a teenage daughter will do that to you.' He glanced over at Jack's date. 'So this is the wonderful Jasmine that I've heard so much about,' he said. He looked her up and down and then threw an envious glance at Jack. Quite what he made of her leopard print pants was anyone's guess. Like all men though, he warmed to Jasmine immediately, particularly when she slid her hands onto his shoulders and planted a kiss on his cheek.

'Lovely to meet you,' she said.

Baby knew all about the effect a kiss on the cheek from Jasmine could have on a man, so she grabbed her by the hand and dragged her into the lounge.

Baby had changed a few things around in her new home since she'd been there, but the lounge was still very much a gentleman's room. Her father's sporting trophies adorned the shelves on the walls and there was a huge widescreen television hanging on the wall opposite a large black leather sofa. Baby jumped onto the sofa and switched on the television with a remote control. A country music channel came on. Neither Baby nor Jasmine was interested in the music but at least it would drown out their voices so that Devon and Jack wouldn't be able to hear what they were talking about.

'Have you seen any of the other girls?' Baby asked.

Jasmine shook her head. 'Nope. I've not seen anyone. I've been in Romania with Jack ever since he burned down the Beaver Palace.'

'Doing what? Are you and him a real item?'

'Yeah. I tell you Baby there's a lot to be said for older guys. Beneath that miserable, gruff exterior he's....' She paused for thought. 'He's grumpy. Yeah he's usually grumpy but it's kind of sweet, you know? I have more fun with him than I had giving Silvio Mellencamp blow jobs all day.'

Baby shuddered at the mention of the name Silvio Mellencamp. Her old boss at the Beaver Palace had been beheaded by the Red Mohawk. It was a grim way for anyone to die, but he'd deserved it, kind of. The memories of Mellencamp's sleazy antics would live with her forever.

'So what were you doing in Romania all this time?' Baby asked, changing the subject quickly.

'I've been helping Jack track down some bad guys.'

'Bad guys? Like who?'

'Frankenstein, Mozart, Dr Jekyll...'

'Those aren't real people though, *are they?'* Baby asked, failing to hide her confusion.

'That's not even the half of it,' said Jasmine. 'On the plane home we ran into Elvis, Rodeo Rex and the Bourbon Kid. And those guys are looking for your friend the Red Mohawk.'

In the kitchen Devon and Jack Munson were having a remarkably similar conversation.

'Rodeo Rex and Elvis?' said Devon. 'But those fellas are supposed to be dead. I remember it from years ago. Miles Jensen confirmed they were dead right before he vanished.'

'Well they were definitely alive when I saw them last night,' Munson replied. 'And the other guy with them was the Bourbon Kid. I'm only telling you what I saw.'

'The Bourbon Kid? I didn't think he was real.'

'Well they seemed real enough, and they're after your friend, the Red Mohawk. The good news is, from what I can tell they don't know his real identity.'

'What the hell do they want with him?'

'They want to kill him.'

'But why? He hasn't done anything to them, has he?'

Munson sighed. 'These guys were total crackpots. The big one, Rex, he said some shit about how they were trying to stop him from killing the Pope.'

'How the hell do they know about that?'

'You mean it's true?'

'No, at least, I don't *think* it is, but it's front page news.'

'How the hell is it front page news?'

'A death threat was sent to Calhoon's office and it's being taken seriously.'

Munson walked over to the kitchen door and pushed it to, leaving only a small gap, but making it harder for Jasmine or Baby to listen into their conversation.

'Have you contacted Joey and asked him about it?' he asked.

'I can't,' said Devon. 'I'm pretty sure all my phone calls and emails are being monitored.'

'Are you being followed too?'

'I think so.' He lowered his voice to a whisper. 'For all I know the house is bugged too,' he half-joked, before changing the subject entirely. 'So let's get down to the serious business. How are you really getting on with Jasmine? She looks like she could seriously wear you out.'

'She makes great burnt toast. But she's got real talent too. She was a big help in Romania.'

'You lucky bastard.'

Munson laughed. 'Don't let your imagination run away with you. What I mean is, she's a pretty decent undercover agent, a real natural.'

'What?'

'I'm not kidding, that girl can get information out of just about anyone. Half the reason I've come back with any news from Romania is because of her.'

Devon walked over to the door and peered around it into the lounge. He saw Jasmine on the sofa with her left leg hooked behind her head as she was telling Baby some kind of story. He frowned and stepped back inside the kitchen. 'You're messing with me, surely?'

'No. That girl is gifted.'

'You gave her some training then?'

'A little, not much, but it's her acting skills, they're worthy of an *Academy Award*. You see, she knows people from all walks of life and she's got a gift for making folks open up to her and tell her stuff. And, although she's got no common sense at all, she's an expert in some really unusual stuff. She learnt a lot by watching cable TV apparently.'

Devon had to accept that Munson was so smitten with Jasmine that he would defend her all night, so he got down to the serious matter at hand. 'So come on, what did you find out about Solomon Bennett?'

Munson's demeanour switched from jokey to serious in an instant. 'It's really disturbing stuff.'

'What is?'

'The peas are bubbling over.'

'Eh?'

Munson pointed at a saucepan on the hob behind him. Devon spun around and saw the lid on the pan bouncing up and down as the boiling water escaped from it. He lifted the pan and held it away from the stove while he turned down the heat a little before he placed the pan back down again.

When he turned around Munson handed him a cell phone. 'Take a look at this,' he said.

There was a photo of Solomon Bennett on the phone's display. He hadn't changed since the last time Devon had seen him.

'How did you get this?' Devon asked.

'Jasmine took it. I didn't believe it was him until she got me a photo.'

'And did you find out what he's up to?'

'Jasmine says he's formed a small cult, or as she likes to call it, an army of henchmen.'

Devon handed the cell phone back. 'This is what I'd heard. But what's he need an army for? What's he planning?'

'A big robbery, or heist of some kind. All the henchmen believe it's going to make them rich. And whatever this job is, they're coming over here to do it.'

'I bet it's Calhoon's Christmas Miracle event. The one the Pope is attending.'

Munson perched his butt against the kitchen table and then hopped up onto it. He had notoriously bad knees and standing around for too long chatting tended to make them turn blue so he was always looking for something to sit on.

'It must be serious,' he said, grabbing an orange from a bowl of fruit on the table. 'Because he's got some specialists working with him.'

'What kind of specialists?'

'One is our old friend the *mad doctor*.'

'Dr Jekyll, *that clown?*' Devon scoffed. 'I'm not worried about him. Who else?'

'You heard of Mozart?'

'The composer?'

'No. The *other* guy.'

Devon frowned. 'The man of many faces?'

'Yeah.'

'But he's in a high security military prison in Turkey,' he paused. 'Isn't he?'

Munson had grabbed three oranges from the fruit bowl on the table and was now juggling them. It didn't impress Devon, in fact it annoyed him because he could visualise Munson dropping one onto the floor at any moment.

'No he's not,' said Munson. 'He broke out. The Turks are keeping quiet about it though. I guess they're hoping they can catch him before anyone finds out about his escape.'

'How the hell did he break out? No one's ever broken out of that prison?'

Munson dropped all three oranges, just as Devon had predicted. They bounced onto the floor and started rolling off in different directions. It didn't bother Munson. He reached into his pocket and pulled out his phone again.

'He had help,' he said, flicking through the photos on his phone. 'According to Jasmine, a man broke him out of prison single handedly, at least, that's what Mozart told her.'

'Jasmine *met* Mozart?'

'Yeah, but she also met this guy.'

Munson held up his phone so Devon could see it. The photo on screen was of a man he recognised, a former test subject on Operation Blackwash. Devon's jaw dropped open.

'That's Frank Grealish!'

Munson nodded. 'These days he's just called Frankenstein.'

'Jasmine took this photo?'

'One of her friends did.'

'He's still got the bolts in his neck!'

'Yeah. And if he's capable of single-handedly breaking Mozart out of a military prison, imagine what else he's capable of.'

Devon kept staring at the photo. 'I knew it!' he said. 'That's why they're coming back to hijack the Christmas Miracle event. They want the Mistralyte to create more Frankensteins!'

'You mean there's more of that stuff?'

'It's what they're using to cure the Pope's skin cancer. Once the Pope has shown that it works and given his endorsement, Alexis Calhoon is selling the rest of it off to a bunch of Pharmaceutical companies. Bennett is going to want to hijack that event and steal the Mistralyte.'

'Let me get this straight in my head,' said Munson. 'Solomon Bennett is going to use Frankenstein, Dr Jekyll and Mozart, and an army of henchmen, to steal a cancer cure, but at the same event, the Red Mohawk is going to try to kill the Pope?'

'It's a crazy world isn't it?'

Twelve

The T & T Brewery had been up and running for three years. Except it wasn't really a brewery. It was a pretend brewery. If the cops or the feds ever stepped inside the building they would have found a highly illegal drug manufacturing operation going on. On an average day there would be twenty men operating on the ground floor, creating, packaging and arranging distribution of massive amounts of Class A drugs.

In a corner on the top floor was a small office, which was home to LeBron, a twenty-one year old black man who in the space of four years had gone from a street dealer to the biggest drug baron in the state. LeBron was usually busy counting money with his girlfriend Tina, a punky white girl with blonde dreadlocks and an ass that could chew walnuts.

It was a cold morning in the week leading up to Christmas, and LeBron was sitting behind his desk watching Sesame Street while he counted a pile of money that had been emptied onto the desk. Tina was sitting on a creamy white sofa on the other side of the room. The pair of them were wearing matching "his and hers" gold tracksuits. The tackiest, shittiest tracksuits in existence, but because they were expensive and gold coloured, Tina just had to buy them. And then she had to insist that LeBron wore his whenever she wore hers, which was practically every fucking day.

It was ten o'clock when Tina's phone buzzed. She picked it up and saw that it was Boney Pete calling. Boney usually only called her when they had visitors. He was the unofficial secretary in their fake brewery.

She answered the call with a "Yeah".

'Is LeBron there? I need to speak to LeBron!' Boney sounded desperate. And there was also a heck of a lot of background noise, which made it sound like he was at a party.

'Where are you?' Tina asked.

'I'm downstairs!'

A loud bang followed and Tina had to hold the phone away from her ear. She put it on speaker so that LeBron could hear. LeBron muted Sesame Street.

'What was that?' he asked.

'Boney Pete,' said Tina, holding up the phone. 'He says he wants to talk to you.'

LeBron shouted at the phone. 'Yo Boney, hurry up man, I'm watching Sesame Street.'

Boney Pete didn't reply. Instead the sound of gunfire bellowed out of the phone. It was coming from downstairs and now that Bert and Ernie weren't singing the Alphabet Song any more, Tina and LeBron could hear it loud and clear in their office upstairs.

LeBron jumped up from the desk and rushed over to the door in the corner. As soon as he opened it the sound of chaos on the floor below flooded into the office.

Tina sprung into action. She raced over to a cupboard in the corner of the office and pulled it open. Inside were two handguns, stored there just in case of an incident such as this one. She grabbed one and tossed it across to LeBron. He caught it and checked it was loaded. Tina took the other handgun for herself. The gunfire from downstairs was relentless, interspersed with the sound of men screaming and objects being knocked over.

LeBron peered out through the door, his gun pointed and ready for action.

'You see anything?' Tina asked.

'Yeah. Everyone's coming up the stairs! Jesus, Tina take a look at this motherfucker!'

Tina bounded over to the door and peered over his shoulder to get a look at what he was seeing. Three of their guards were standing at the top of the stairs at the far end of the room. They were all armed and were firing nonstop at someone who was walking up the stairs towards them.

All three of them were gunned down in quick succession and a moment later, their killer came into view on the stairs. He had cropped black hair and he was wearing combat pants and a skin-tight black T-shirt. He paused on the stairs to reload his gun. When he looked back up, Tina spotted a pair of metal bolts sticking out of his neck and a pair of black goggles covering his eyes.

'He looks like fucking Frankenstein!' said LeBron.

Tina backed away. 'Lock the fucking door!' she said.

LeBron didn't need to be told twice. He slammed the door shut and turned the key in the lock. Tina dived under LeBron's desk and he was quick to join her. The two of them sat there snuggled together like a couple of kids hiding from thunder and lightning.

'I think we're fucked,' LeBron whispered in her ear.

The gunfire outside had temporarily stopped. They listened carefully, waiting for the awful moment when Frankenstein arrived at the door.

Clunk.

Clunk.

Clunk.

Even the sound of him walking was terrifying. The clunking came to a halt right outside the door. The door rattled, but remained shut.

'What are we gonna do?' Tina whispered.

'Just shoot at anyone who comes through that door.'

CRASH!

The door was knocked off its hinges. It toppled over onto the floor inside the office with an almighty thud. Frankenstein walked in. He stood on the broken door and looked around the room.

LeBron didn't hesitate. He rolled out from under the desk and opened fire on the intruder. Tina laid flat on her belly under the desk and started shooting at Frankenstein's legs. For the next ten seconds the two of them peppered the giant brute with every bullet they had. Every once in a while a bullet would hit Frankenstein in the face and jar his head back a little, but it didn't seem to bother him. Bullets bounced off this guy. He was big, ugly and impervious to pain.

Frankenstein had a gun in his hand but at no point did he attempt to use it. He just stood there, presumably waiting for them to stop shooting at him.

Eventually when they both ran out of bullets, the terrifying realisation that they had been shooting at something not quite human hit them both like a wave of ice water. Frankenstein pointed his gun at LeBron.

'LeBron Raven?' he said.

'Yes,' LeBron replied, his voice trembling.

Frankenstein grabbed LeBron by his arm and hauled him out of the office.

'Baby wait for me!' Tina yelled.

She ran to the hole where the door had once been and ran through it. Frankenstein had shoved LeBron to the floor in the main hall outside. Another man was coming up the stairs. When he reached the top Tina realised that she recognised him. He'd been in the news some time ago. His name was Mozart and he was one of the world's most notorious psychopaths, known for a particularly sick method of murdering couples. Her heart sank. As he walked towards LeBron, Tina dropped to her knees in despair. Mozart looked at her and smiled.

'Frankenstein,' he said. 'Take the bitch back into the office and keep her there while I speak with her boyfriend.'

Frankenstein hauled Tina up off the floor and forcefully ushered her back into the office. As soon as she was inside she dashed over to the sofa and cowered on it. Outside in the warehouse hall she heard Mozart introduce himself to LeBron.

'My name is Mozart,' he said. 'And I'm going to take your office. Your time in charge of this warehouse is over.'

LeBron replied. 'Okay, just let me and Tina go. Take whatever you want. We've got money in there, hundreds of thousands of dollars. You can have it all.'

Frankenstein was blocking Tina's route out of the office and also making it difficult for her to hear what was being said outside.

The last thing she heard LeBron say was, *'What are you doing with that?'*

For the next fifteen minutes or so, Tina heard LeBron, the love of her life, screaming in unbearable agony. It was enough to break her, to make her want to rip her own ears off. She sobbed and wailed and cried until her throat burned. When her lover, LeBron finally stopped screaming, she knew deep down in her heart that he was dead. She sobbed and wailed, knowing that she was soon to be dead too. She prayed that it would be a quick death, abrupt and painless.

But then came the real horror. The rumours about Mozart were true, not just an awful folklore or urban legend.

Frankenstein stepped aside and allowed Mozart to enter the office. He had a bloodied machete in his hand. LeBron's blood was dripping from it onto the floor.

Tina felt a fountain of drool pour from her mouth as she looked up at the disgusting sight in front of her. Mozart had used the machete to cut off LeBron's face.

And he was now wearing LeBron's face as a mask.

It was secured to his head by two elastic bands, one wrapped around his forehead and another around his chin.

LeBron's blood was dripping out from under the chin and seeping out of the gaping eyeholes that were now filled with the hateful, laughing eyes of Mozart, the man of many faces. Tina had read all about his horrific crimes, even thinking that they would make good source material for a film. But now she was to be one of the victims. Now it didn't seem so cool.

She screamed louder than she had ever screamed before. The burning in her throat no longer bothered her. The pain of seeing someone else's eyes looking down upon her through her decimated lover's face was unbearable.

For the next thirty minutes Tina screamed and cried, begging Mozart to kill her. But Mozart loved to hear his victims scream. And there was no depth he wouldn't stoop to in order to make that happen. Tina suffered more than any person should.

Finally when she could scream no more and had not an ounce of fight left in her, Mozart cut her face off too, so that he could add it to his collection.

Thirteen

Getting dressed for a date wasn't something Baby had ever had to do before. It was surprisingly difficult too, particularly when she wasn't sure if Jason Moxy had asked her out purely to rehearse their lines for *Grease*, or because he liked her. All of a sudden every outfit she owned seemed to be giving off a message. Some said, *"Look at me I'm easy",* others screamed, *"Keep your hands off!".* What she needed was something in between, so after an hour of trying out different things she eventually plumped for a pair of three quarter length jeans and a white blouse. Casual and not too slutty.

Jason showed up at her door at eight o'clock. Before he had any chance to get her out of the house to his car, Devon invited him in for a friendly father to *"potential-dead-man-if-you-hurt-my-daughter"* interrogation.

Baby was impressed at how adept her father was at extracting information from her date. It took him less than two minutes to establish that Jason was from a wealthy family, loved sports and desperately hoped to one day become a singer on Broadway. And if his Broadway dream didn't come true he had a backup plan, which went down extremely well with Devon who was a lover of contingency. Jason's father owned a car rental company which his son would take over one day if he didn't become a Broadway star. So all in all he seemed like a fairly good egg.

Baby still couldn't figure out if they were going on a date or not though because Jason had turned up in his Danny Zuco costume. He was wearing blue jeans, a white T-shirt and a black leather jacket with the *T-Birds* logo on the back. *Rehearsal or date?* She still didn't know.

Eventually when Devon was satisfied that Jason wasn't a total shit, he allowed them to leave. Jason led Baby down the driveway to his car, which was one of the coolest cars she'd seen, bettered only by the Red Mohawk's red and yellow stock car. Jason's ride was an exact replica of the white Ford convertible that Danny Zuco drove in *Grease*, complete with silver and red lightning stripes down the sides.

'This is the coolest car I've ever been in,' Baby said, pretending for a moment to forget the existence of the Red Mohawk's car.

'My dad lent it to me for the evening,' said Jason. 'He's got replicas of every famous movie car ever made. I thought you'd like this one though.'

'I love it. What others does he have?'

'He's got all the good ones. The car from *Back To the Future*, the one from *Knight Rider*, the *General Lee, Herbie, A Team van, Batmobile....*'

'Wow.'

'Yeah. Maybe if we go out again, I'll bring a different car each time?'

Baby loved the idea of being seen around town in all kinds of cool, famous cars. It would almost be reason enough to go out with Jason every night of the week. While they cruised around town with the top down everyone stopped to stare. Baby felt like a rock star.

'Where are we going anyway?' she asked.

'There's a really cool spot on the outskirts of town,' said Jason. 'It's the perfect place for us to rehearse the scene at the *Drive In* where Danny gives Sandy his ring.'

'Why are we doing that scene?'

'It's one of the only scenes with no other characters in. We can work through the whole thing together without any interruptions. It'll be good for building up chemistry between us. There's nothing worse than a show where the two lead actors look like they've never met before.'

'Oh, yeah, I know what you mean.'

Jason pointed at the glove box. 'I've got the script in there if you want to start memorising your lines before we get there.'

'Okay.'

Baby opened the glove box. There was a rolled up copy of the script for the show. She pulled it out and opened it up. Jason had certainly come prepared to rehearse. She started reading through the scene, but in her head she was preoccupied by something that the other girls in the show had said to her. They had been adamant that she would be going on a date, but this really was starting to look like Jason was concerned only with rehearsing.

She was halfway through reading the scene when he steered the car off the road and down an unlit gravel track. They cruised down it for about half a mile before they arrived in an area of open grass on a cliff top that overlooked the outskirts of the city. Jason stopped the car five yards short of the cliff edge.

'Where are we?' Baby asked, looking out through the front windscreen.

'Dead Man's Drop,' said Jason.

'It feels like we're miles away from anywhere.'

Jason laughed. 'I promise you, it's not nearly as bad as it looks. We're only a mile away from the centre of town.'

'Do many people come here?'

'I would expect to see a few more cars pull up later. This place is known to the local kids as a place to make out. Give it an hour or two and there will be a bunch of cars here.'

'Is this really the best place to rehearse?'

Jason shrugged. 'There's no drive-in cinema in town so this is the next best thing. Look up at the sky,' he said, pointing up through the open roof. 'Isn't that just the most beautiful sight?'

He had a point. There was a full moon up above them, glowing brightly in the night sky. There were no clouds, just the moon and stars surrounding it.

'See that big star up there?' said Jason, pointing into a large cluster of shining stars.

Baby had no fucking clue which one he was pointing at but she played along anyway. 'Oh yeah. That one's real nice,' she agreed.

'That's Mars.'

'Oh wow, really?'

'Yeah, I mean, technically it's a planet of course, but all stars are planets in reality. They just look like stars from a distance.'

'I didn't know that.'

'I learned about it in second grade. I suppose you missed out on a lot of education while you were stuck in that whorehouse.'

'Uh yeah, I suppose so.'

Baby hadn't expected him to mention her time in B Movie Hell. She had hoped he wouldn't even know about it, but it seemed that the story had obviously gotten around.

'I'm kind of trying to forget about that time in my life,' she said.

'Oh,' said Jason. 'That might be difficult because the girl playing Rizzo's been spreading rumours about you.'

Baby felt a cold flush wash over her. She hadn't ever felt embarrassed about working at the Beaver Palace while she was there, but now that she was back in the real world it felt like something she should be ashamed of.

'What's Rizzo been saying?' she asked.

'She says you won an award for best blow job in the whorehouse.'

'Oh God no. That's not true!'

It sure as hell wasn't true. Jasmine had won that award every year. But that's another story. For a fleeting moment Jason looked disappointed. He tried to change the subject by pulling a pack of cigarettes out of his jacket pocket.

'You wanna smoke?' he asked.

Baby shook her head. Jason pulled out a cigarette and lit it with a cheap disposable lighter. He took a drag and held his breath for a couple of seconds before exhaling loudly.

'I didn't believe anything Rizzo was saying,' he said. 'She's just jealous that you got the role of Sandy. She thinks your dad used some influence to get you the part.'

Baby cringed. 'Oh, what? Why?'

Jason took another drag on his cigarette. When he smoked he looked just like John Travolta, although more like the Travolta from the movie *Broken Arrow* rather than *Grease*.

'It doesn't matter if your dad had anything to do with it,' he said. 'My pop got me the part as Danny. That's just how things work in this business.'

'Really?'

'Yeah. I don't know what the big deal is, I really don't.'

'So lots of people have done it then?'

'Oh yeah. The School of Performing Arts doesn't get a lot of Government funding so when kids with wealthy parents come along and make big donations, they get the best parts. If you think about it, it's only fair. If it wasn't for people like your dad and mine, that school would be broke and there wouldn't be any shows for anyone to appear in.'

Baby breathed a sigh of relief. 'That makes me feel a little better,' she said. 'I've been feeling really guilty about the whole thing.'

'You shouldn't, Baby. You're a great singer and you're way prettier than the other girls who were up for your part. You'd have gotten it anyway, with or without your father's input.'

'Thanks. I think you make a great Danny too. Your hair looks really great in the quiff and the jacket looks really cool on you.'

Jason smiled. In spite of being a smoker he had perfect white teeth. Baby couldn't help but smile back.

'Shall we get started on this script?' he said.

'Yeah, let's do it. Shall we start from the top?'

Jason took one last puff on his cigarette and flicked it over the windscreen onto the trunk of the car even though he'd barely smoked half of it. 'Let's start at the part where Danny has just given Sandy his ring to wear, and he's nervous about how to put his arm around her.

'Okay.'

Jason sat back and pressed a button on the dashboard. The roof of the car started rolling up, blocking out the moonlight. Baby looked at the script. Without the faint light from the moon and stars it was hard to read the words on the page. When she found the spot where they were due to start she noticed that they seemed to be skipping most of the dialogue and were heading to the scene where Danny attempts to make out with Sandy, but she resists. She put the script down on the dashboard and waited for Jason to make his move. Sure enough, he slowly lifted his right arm and pretended to stretch. He reached across and slid his arm around her shoulder.

'Danny, what are you trying to do?' she said.

'I really like you, Sandy,' he replied. 'And now that you're wearing my ring.....'

Jason leant across and kissed her on the mouth. His breath stank of cigarettes. Baby pushed him away.

'Danny, what are you doing?'

'Come on Sandy,' he said, leaning in and attempting to kiss her again. She held him off successfully by pressing her hand into his chest, but then to her surprise, he took method acting to a whole new level when he reached out and grabbed a handful of tit.

'*Danny!*' she yelled, defiantly, pushing his hand away. 'Stop it, I've never seen you like this.'

Jason was much more forceful than Baby had expected. Considering it was only a rehearsal he was extremely rough. His hands kept finding their way onto her tits and she kept grabbing his wrists and pushing him off. Eventually he gave up on the tit lunge and shoved his face into hers, planting a sloppy kiss on her mouth. Baby turned her head away and his tongue slobbered all over her cheek.

'Come on *Baby*, you know you want it!' he said.

'Don't you mean, *Sandy?*'

Jason ignored her and slid his hand inside her blouse. She felt his sweaty palm on her breast as he tried to force his way into her bra. She slapped him across the face.

The slap was loud too. And it seemed to have the desired effect. Jason looked surprised by it and retreated back to his seat.

'Sorry, Baby, was that too rough?' he asked, looking a little embarrassed.

Baby adjusted her blouse to preserve her dignity. 'I just wasn't sure if we were still acting or not for a minute there,' she said.

Jason blinked a few times. 'Neither was I,' he said. 'We kind of got carried away in the moment, didn't we?'

'Well, *you* did.'

'I'm sorry, Baby. It's just that, well, you really turn me on, you know?'

'It's just rehearsal, Jason.'

Jason grabbed her by the wrist. He pulled her hand towards him and placed it on his crotch. Baby could tell straight away that he was turned on, *very turned on*. But he had a firm grip on her and she couldn't pull her hand away.

'See,' said Jason. 'That's how much you turn me on. I'm really hard for you, Baby.'

'Let go of my hand!'

He lurched forward again and kissed her neck, pressing her hand even harder onto the stiff bulge in his pants.

'Come on, Baby. It will be a lot easier to rehearse this scene if we could get rid of the sexual tension.'

With each passing moment Baby seemed to be sliding further down underneath him. If she didn't get him off soon, it was going to become impossible. She pulled her hand away from his crotch and pressed it into his chest in the hope of keeping him at bay.

'What are you doing?' she asked, panicking.

Jason was breathing heavily. 'I was just thinking it would be easier for me to do this scene if we could get rid of this boner I've got,' he said.

'Well why don't you think about something else, or go for a walk to clear your head?'

'I was thinking you could give me one of those blow-jobs that you're famous for. Then afterwards I'd be able to concentrate on doing the scene properly, you know?'

Before Baby could respond, Jason slid his arm around the back of her head and pulled her down towards his groin.

'Stop, I don't want to!' Baby yelled. She rolled her head to one side and pulled away, pressing her back up against the car door to get as far away from him as possible.

'Hand job then?' Jason ventured.

'NO!'

'What's wrong?' he asked. He looked confused.

'I'm not ready for all this,' said Baby. 'I hardly know you.'

It looked like she had finally gotten through to him. He sat back. His brow was furrowed. He seemed to realise he'd misjudged the situation.

'Okay, sorry. *I get it*,' he said reaching into a pocket on his jeans. He pulled out a twenty-dollar bill. 'I'm such an idiot. It's twenty bucks right? That's what you used to charge back in B Movie Hell, isn't it?'

'What? Who told you that?'

Jason held the twenty-dollar bill out. Baby made no attempt to take it, so suddenly without warning he lunged at her again. He slipped the twenty inside her blouse and into her bra, pressing his hand onto her chest again. Baby already had her back pressed up against the door and had nowhere further to go. Instead she tried to force him away with her feet, but all that achieved was that it put her into a more vertical position for him to continue with his assault. He clawed at her top and ripped it open. She felt a button come off her blouse and the next thing she knew her bra was half off, exposing her boobs. Jason's eyes lit up, and not in a good way.

'That's more like it!' he said, ogling her chest.

He pressed his mouth against hers and gave her another unwelcome waft of stale cigarettes. He began caressing her left breast, rubbing his thumb against her nipple while he persisted in trying to kiss her with an open mouth.

He had cleverly manoeuvred her into a position from which she couldn't fight him off and she'd backed herself into a corner up against the car door. She twisted her face away and tried to find something to grab hold of. Her hand settled on his car stereo. Her fingers pressed down on some of the buttons and it suddenly burst into life. Carly Simon was blaring out the chorus of *Nobody Does It Better*.

'Come on Baby, you know you want it,' said Jason, attempting to chew on her ear. 'I'm not like those seedy guys you used to fuck. I'll make you my number one girl, I promise.'

'Get off!'

Baby couldn't make it any clearer that she wasn't interested, but Jason just wasn't listening. Or if he was, he just didn't care.

And then she heard the car door open on his side. She prayed to God he hadn't invited a bunch of the other jocks along to join in the fun. And then she heard a voice. One she hadn't heard for a long time.

'Hey you, get your fucking hands off her!'

The look of lusting on Jason's face was replaced by a look of surprise. He had no chance to react before he was dragged feet first from the car with his hands still outstretched, trying for one last grab at Baby.

Baby covered herself up and peered out of the open car door. Dragging Jason out by his left ankle was a man wearing black jeans, a red leather jacket and a yellow mask with a red mohawk on the top. Baby felt her skin tingle. The feelings of terror and helplessness from moments earlier were rapidly replaced by a feeling of excitement. She hadn't seen Joey Conrad in a long time. In her lonelier moments she'd wondered if she would ever see him again. But there he was, outside the car, dragging Jason Moxy by his ankle towards the cliff edge.

The cliff edge. Oh fuck!

She scrambled across the seats and stumbled out of the car. She landed on her knees on the grass. 'Joey don't kill him!'

Too late.

She climbed to her feet just in time to see the Red Mohawk swing Jason by his ankle, tossing him over the edge of the cliff.

She heard Jason's voice yell out *'Shiiiiiiiit!'* but with each passing millisecond his voice became more distant until eventually it was silenced by an unpleasant thudding sound far below them.

Baby stood stunned, her mouth agape, silently screaming as she replayed in her mind what she'd just seen.

'Oh my God, you killed him!'

The Red Mohawk peered over the edge of the cliff and took a look down. Then he turned back to face her. 'No, I didn't,' he said.

'You mean he's okay? He's not dead?'

'No. He *is* dead.'

'So you *did* kill him?'

'No. He fell.'

'I *totally* saw you throw him over the cliff!'

For a moment the Mohawk considered what Baby was saying. 'No, *he fell*,' he repeated, before adding, *'when I let go of his leg.'*

Inconsequentially it suddenly occurred to Baby that she might look a mess. She rearranged her blouse and then ran her hand through her hair tucking some stray hairs behind her ear.

'Oh my God, we're in so much trouble,' she said as the realisation of what had happened began to sink in. 'What did you have to go and drop him for?'

'Because he was hurting you.'

Baby stared at him. It was so hard to read his face because it was hidden behind the scary mask and she could only see his eyes. But it was so good to see him again. And he'd just killed the lead actor in the stage production of *Grease* because the guy had been trying to date-rape her. Something inside her took over. She forgot about Jason Moxy and how awful it was that he was dead, his skull probably caved in on the rocks at the foot of the cliff. Instead she found herself gazing at the Halloween mask on the Red Mohawk, remembering all the dreams she'd had about him. Her heart fluttered at a million miles an hour and every cell in her body came alive like nothing she'd ever felt before. *To hell with inhibitions and self-control.* She ran up to him, threw her arms around his waist and buried her head in his chest.

'Oh God I've missed you,' she said.

Fourteen

Devon Pincent hadn't travelled on the underground for years. He'd had no need to. And he'd had no desire to, either. The underground was for *other* people. Unfortunately these days he was being followed everywhere he went by spooks from within his own agency, and the underground was the easiest way to lose someone in a crowd.

He loitered near a northbound platform, hiding within a large crowd of people, keeping one eye on an agent who had tailed him on foot from his home. When the tube train arrived, Devon hopped aboard and sat down next to a woman with two noisy kids. Out of the corner of his eye he saw the agent step onto the train two carriages further down. So right at the last second Devon jumped up from his seat and squeezed through the closing doors and back out onto the platform. Tempting though it was to wave goodbye to the agent as the train pulled away from the platform, Devon kept up the feeble façade that he had no idea he was being followed. A minute later he was on the southbound platform, boarding the train that would take him to a meeting with Blake Jackson.

The walk from the underground station to the Holy Chapel of St John the Evangelist took less than two minutes, which Devon was grateful for because a few spots of rain had begun to fall from the night sky. He'd wrapped up warm in a long brown coat, which was perfect for hiding a folder containing sensitive information.

When he arrived at the chapel, Blake Jackson was already there, sitting in the back row of pews that looked up at a statue of the Virgin Mary at the far end of the hall. Devon recognised Jackson by his tight curly black hair, which was protruding from underneath a brown tweed Trilby hat he was wearing. He'd also wrapped up warm in a long brown coat similar to Devon's, with the collar pulled up. There didn't appear to be anyone else in the chapel, not even a preacher.

Devon sat down on the pew and sidled along until he was next to Jackson. 'Good choice of meeting place,' he said.

Jackson nodded. 'Yeah. It's always quiet in here.' He pulled a cell phone from his pocket and held it up for Devon to see the display. On it was a text message from someone called Rupert. It read –

I've lost Pincent. Think he knew I was following him.

'Your man wasn't exactly hard to spot,' said Devon.

'Good. Now let's cut to the chase before he tracks your cell phone and works out where you are.'

Devon reached inside his jacket and pulled out the folder he had been carrying with him. He handed it over to Jackson.

'You need to show the contents of that folder to Alexis Calhoon,' he said.

Jackson opened the folder, which was full of photos Devon had printed off from Jack Munson's phone. 'Okay, talk me through it,' he said, pulling out the first photo.

'These pictures were taken last week in a secret military bunker in Romania. The one you're looking at there is of three men who are planning on hijacking Calhoon's big event with the Pope on Saturday.'

Jackson eyed him suspiciously. 'The Christmas Miracle event?'

'Yeah. The man in the photo with the eye patch, that's Solomon Bennett.'

'*The* Solomon Bennett?'

'Yes.'

'I thought he was dead?'

'Well he's not, and neither is Frank Grealish.'

'Frank Grealish?'

Devon pointed at a man in the background on the photo. 'The big dude with the bolts in his neck who looks like Frankenstein. *That's* Frank Grealish. He was an operative on Blackwash.'

'I know who he is. Calhoon told me all about him the other day. But she said he died.'

'That's what we all thought. But he's just landed in the USA with Solomon Bennett. I think they're going to hijack Calhoon's "Christmas Miracle" event because they intend to steal the remaining Mistralyte.'

Jackson looked confused. 'What Mistralyte?'

'You know the stuff Calhoon is using as her cure for skin cancer? It used to be called Mistralyte. Solomon Bennett tried to use it years ago to create bulletproof skin. There's not much of it left in existence these days, but Calhoon has all of it. Every drop of it is going to be at her event on Saturday. Now Bennett is back and I think he wants that Mistralyte. It's probably him who's planning to kill the Pope too.'

Jackson rubbed his chin and stared at the photo. 'Are you one hundred percent sure about this?'

'Absolutely.'

'Because if you're wrong, there'll be no way back for you. Calhoon has already got it in for you. She's just waiting for you to do something stupid like make contact with the Red Mohawk. Then that's it, you're history.'

'Well, she'll be waiting a long time. You can have your spooks follow me for the next ten years and you won't see me talking to Joey Conrad. I don't know *where* he is and I'll be honest, I don't *want* to know.' Devon wasn't being honest at all and he suspected that Jackson knew it, but secrets were secrets and they had to stay that way, and besides, Joey Conrad was a separate issue.

'Okay,' said Jackson, closing the folder and sizing it up to tuck inside his jacket. 'I'll show her this tomorrow. She'll be pissed that I agreed to meet up with you though. You know that don't you? I'll be in the shithouse!'

'There's one other thing.'

'There always is with you.'

'You know the guy Mozart, the man of many faces?'

'I've heard of him. What about him?'

'It's not been made public but he's escaped from prison. Bennett broke him out. And Mozart is a master at plotting high profile robberies, which just adds weight to my theory that they're going to hijack Calhoon's event.'

Jackson raised his eyebrows. 'How do you get all this information?'

'I have very reliable informants.'

'Got any photos of Mozart?'

'No, but I have it on good authority that he was in Romania with Bennett and the others.'

The doors at the back of the chapel creaked and both men looked around. An old man with a walking stick shuffled into the hall. They waited for him to make his way past them before they carried on their conversation.

Devon whispered in Jackson's ear. 'Just get Calhoon to cancel the event. I couldn't give two shits about the Mistralyte, but if the Pope gets assassinated, it could start a fucking religious war. And God knows we don't need that.'

Jackson seemed to be in agreement. 'Okay, okay,' he said. 'I'll convince her to cancel the event. She'll be livid though, so throw me a bone here. At least tell me how you got all this information? Have you got a mole in Bennett's organisation? Because if it was Joey Conrad that got you all this info I'm not sure I want to be involved.'

'I told you already, I've not had any contact with him. Besides, as you already know, he was butchering that kid and his family in the gas station the other day. He can't be in two places at once.'

'So who then? Who took these photos? And who saw Mozart?'

Devon took a deep breath. 'Alright, but you keep this to yourself.'

'Scouts honour,' said Jackson, looking to the heavens and crossing himself.

'It was Jack Munson. He infiltrated their hideout. He's still just about the best secret agent we have you know.'

'I *do* know that. But Calhoon hates him almost as much as she hates you!'

Devon snorted a laugh, but then checked his watch and realised time was in short supply. 'I'd better go before your spook works out where I am,' he said, getting up.

Jackson grabbed Devon by the sleeve of his coat to stop him from leaving. 'Devon, you really should give up Joey Conrad. With what you've given me here, if you were to give him up, Calhoon would forgive you and bring you back into the fold.'

'I can't do that,' said Devon. 'Like I said, I don't know where he is.'

'Alright, but think about it. I'll call you as soon as I've spoken to Calhoon.'

'Thanks, Blake.'

Devon got up and left the chapel, leaving Jackson behind to mull over the contents of the folder.

The first thing Blake Jackson did when Devon left was make a call on his cell phone. After two rings a man with a deep voice answered. It was Solomon Bennett.

'Hey, what's up?' he said.

'It's Blake. I just met with Pincent. He knows *everything*. He's even got photos of you from Romania.'

'How?'

'Jack Munson.'

'Alcoholic Jack? Are you sure?'

'Positive. Pincent says he infiltrated your hideout and took the photos. I've got them all here.'

Bennett sounded mighty pissed. 'Fucking hell!' he snapped. 'Fucking Devon Pincent and his fucking undercover people. How are you only telling me about this now? You were supposed to be keeping an eye on him.'

Jackson didn't take too kindly to Bennett's attitude. 'Don't have a go at me. You're the idiot who tried to be clever by sending that phoney death threat from the Red Mohawk to Alexis Calhoon.'

There was a pause on the other end of the line as Bennett took on board what Jackson had just said. 'What are you talking about?' he grumbled.

'That note you sent Calhoon. The one that said the Red Mohawk is going to kill the Pope.'

'I sent no such thing.'

Jackson was baffled. 'If you didn't send it, then who the hell did?'

Fifteen

A cool breeze brushed through Baby's hair and her lungs sucked in the fresh forest air. Every one of her senses was working overtime. She couldn't remember ever feeling more alive. If an owl had hooted a mile away she would have heard it. If a skunk up a tree half a mile away farted, she would have smelt it. Things she had only dreamt about for the last few months were suddenly happening. *It was all real.* The touch of Joey Conrad's hand, wrapped around hers had made the whole world come to life, particularly the woodland. Strolling hand in hand through the woods at night with a masked serial killer wasn't everyone's idea of a great night out, but Baby couldn't think of anything she would rather be doing.

'Where are we going?' she asked.

'I'm taking you home.'

'Right now?'

'Yeah. It's for the best.'

'Why?'

'Because when someone discovers your boyfriend's body at the bottom of that cliff, the cops are going to ask you where you were. If you're at home you've got an alibi, your dad.'

'He wasn't my boyfriend,' Baby replied, ignoring everything else Joey had said after the words *"your boyfriend"*.

'Who was he then?'

'He was Danny Zuco in the Grease stage play. We were rehearsing. I'm Sandy.'

'I killed Danny Zuco?'

'Yeah.'

'That's so cool.' He suddenly came to his senses. 'Even so, I have to take you home. Your dad can be your alibi.'

'I think he's gone out bowling,' Baby lied. 'I'll be better off staying here with you.'

Joey stopped walking. His eyes stared out through the holes in his mask, looking deep into her eyes, searching for the truth. Baby looked away.

'Can you take the mask off?' she asked.

'Why?'

'I want to see your face.'

He yanked the mask off his head and screwed it up into a ball. The mask was really lightweight and fitted easily into his jacket pocket. Baby stared at his face. He looked exactly how she remembered him when she thought of him every night before she fell asleep, in the hope that she would dream about him. His hair was a little messy from wearing the tight mask, but his face was so much more welcoming without it. His brown eyes looked softer, less black. His stubble and sunken cheekbones hinted at a man who could be anything he wanted to be without even trying. And his lips looked so inviting, so kissable.

'Your mask was bigger before,' she said, noting how flat his hair looked.

He nodded. 'The last one was too loose. Half the time when I turned my head, I couldn't see *shit*. So I got a bunch of new ones made. They're skin tight and lightweight, like Spiderman's mask.'

'It looks better.'

'Yeah.'

Baby loved chatting to Joey again. The conversation might not be intellectual or even flirtatious, but it was just great to be talking to him. After all, this was the guy who risked his life to rescue her from B Movie Hell. The man who murdered half a town to make sure she got home in one piece.

'I never asked you this before,' she said. 'But why do you wear the mask?'

Joey spun around as if he was distracted by something. He surveyed their surroundings, looking for any sign of movement within the trees. Eventually he answered her question, but he spoke in a softer voice as if he feared someone else nearby was listening.

'Why do you think I wear it?' he asked.

Baby had a theory lined up. 'Is it to protect the people you care about?'

'No.'

'Oh.' *That was a surprise*. She was almost certain that would be the reason. It was certainly her first choice, but there were other options. 'So it's to protect your identity from the cops then?' she said confidently.

'No.'

'So what is it then?'

Joey stopped looking around at the trees and bushes and turned his full attention on Baby. 'I wear the mask,' he said, ' because it looks cool.'

She smiled and waited for him to admit that he was kidding. It quickly became evident that he wasn't.

'Oh,' she said. 'Of course, I should have known. I mean, I *did* know that it looks cool, I just thought there might be another reason too.'

'Why do you still call yourself Baby?' he asked.

Baby glanced down at her feet for a split second, embarrassed that he had asked. She didn't like her real name, Marianne. It wasn't the name of a character from *Dirty Dancing*, therefore it wasn't..... *cool.*

She looked back up and stared him in right the eye. 'Because Baby's a cool name,' she grinned.

'Yes it is.'

She felt an overwhelming urge to reach out and touch him. She had never wanted to hug someone so much, but she needed an excuse. And she didn't really have one so she settled for reaching out and stroking the red leather on the sleeve of his jacket.

'Don't take me home yet,' she said. 'Can't you show me where you live?'

Once more he was distracted by something. He stared over her head at the woodland behind her.

'Did you hear that?' he asked, his voice lowering with every syllable.

'No. What?'

'I think someone's following us.'

Baby let go of his jacket and looked around. The woodland behind her was motionless, like a photo. There wasn't even so much as a slight breeze causing any of the leaves to flicker. 'I can't see anyone,' she said.

He took her by the hand again. 'Let's get out of here. Stay quiet.'

Baby hurried along behind him as he led her through the woods. Joey was light on his feet and seemed to know exactly where he was going, in stark contrast to her. She seemed to stumble over every outstretched tree root and tread on every snappable twig.

When they neared the roadside at the edge of the wood, Joey let go of her hand and headed for a thick bush that was close by. He pulled aside a wall of leaves, revealing a shiny metallic red motorcycle behind the bush. Baby loved motorbikes, even though she had never been on one. Her favourite scene in the movie *Purple Rain* was when Apollonia hitched a ride on the back of Prince's motorbike. Riding through a country lane listening to the song *Take Me With You* would be perfect.

Joey wheeled the bike out of the bushes. It looked brand new. The red paintwork was impeccable and there wasn't a spot of dirt on it. The seat was made of bright yellow leather and to Baby's inward delight it had room enough for two. Joey slung his leg over it and gestured for her to hop on behind him.

'Get on,' he said.

'Where's your car?'

'Couldn't bring it. It gets noticed.'

He started up the engine on the bike. It roared loudly as he revved it a few times. 'Come on. Get on.'

Baby's heart was pounding, almost to the point that it was embarrassingly loud. This was exciting, but also dangerous and scary at the same time.

'Is it safe for two of us?' she asked.

'Do you trust me?'

'Always.'

'Then jump on, put your arms around my waist and hold on tight.'

That was an offer Baby couldn't resist. She hoisted a leg over the back of the bike and sat down on it. The leather seat was firm but spongy too. She wiggled her backside around on it until she was comfortable. Eventually she settled in with her chest pressed up against his back. She slid her arms around his waist. Her hands were trembling and her mouth had gone dry. The bike vibrated just enough for her to get a feel for how powerful it was. She was barely able to contain her excitement. And they hadn't even moved yet.

She whispered into Joey's ear. 'Do I need a helmet?'

'Only if you fall off.'

Before she could respond, he squeezed the accelerator and steered the bike out of the woodland onto the road. To Baby's relief, when they hit the road the ride was much smoother. Joey flicked on the headlight and then hit the gas. The bike sped off down the middle of the road, getting faster all the time. Baby took a deep breath and pressed her head into his back, squeezing him even tighter than before. As they raced towards the first bend in the road, she glanced back to the opening where they had come out of the woods. Standing there watching them ride off was a man dressed from head to toe in black with a hood pulled up over his head, concealing his face. Baby only saw him for a fleeting moment before he vanished from sight as they sped around the bend. Within ten seconds she had forgotten all about him. Her dream date with the Red Mohawk had begun and it was all that she cared about.

Sixteen

Devon hadn't walked through the city at night in a long time. The flashing bright neon signs above the shops and nightclubs made the place look exciting. If you were to scratch beneath the surface though, most of the neon lights merely added a touch of glamour to what was really a seedy underbelly of the city, crawling with low-lifes and sex workers.

In spite of everything, Devon enjoyed strolling along the sidewalk looking up at all the lights and displays. His meeting with Blake Jackson had gone well and he was feeling optimistic that he'd be welcomed back into Phantom Ops and thanked for his work in uncovering Solomon Bennett's plot to hijack the Pope's visit to Calhoon's fundraiser.

He was roughly halfway home when it crossed his mind that Blake Jackson's spook might be tailing him again. He'd lost the spook earlier but if the guy was worth a damn he would be following him again by now.

Up ahead Devon spotted a Range Rover parked by the side of the road. He walked up alongside it and stooped down and pretended to tie his shoelaces. In reality he was looking into the Range Rover's wing mirror to see if he could spot anyone behind him. Approximately a hundred metres back he saw a man in a long coat, walking slowly. Rather predictably the man stopped and stared into a shop window when he suspected that Devon might be checking him out in the Range Rover's mirror.

Devon smiled to himself and stood back up. He didn't mind being followed through the streets by a government agent. It was actually very reassuring to know that if anyone tried to mug him there would be a trained agent nearby who could come to his aid. He carried on walking down the street, occasionally slowing up or stopping to look in a shop window, just to mess with the man tailing him.

He was on a quiet street just two blocks from home when a taxi-cab pulled up alongside him. The passenger side window was down and the driver leant across the seat to shout to Devon.

'Hey buddy could you tell me the way to Gordon Street?'

Devon stopped and pondered the whereabouts of Gordon Street. He'd never even heard of it. He stepped over to the kerb and poked his head through the window of the cab.

'Gordon Street?' he said, querying what the driver had said.

When he looked at the driver he recognised him straight away. The big giveaway was his bright orange curly hair. It was Henry Jekyll, *the mad doctor.*

'Henry?' said Devon, confused.

'Nice to see you again, Mr Pincent,' Jekyll replied.

Devon backed away from the cab. Before he had a chance to look down the street for a sign of the man tailing him, someone grabbed him from behind. A hand wrapped around his waist from one side and another slammed a handkerchief onto his mouth and nose. The handkerchief was laced with a powerful anaesthetic. If it had been chloroform Devon would have stood a fighting chance, because, in spite of what TV shows like *Dallas* and *Charlie's Angels* would have people believe, chloroform takes more than half a second to render someone unconscious. As he sucked in the fumes through his nostrils he knew he was being drugged by something far more powerful. He twisted his head to try and free himself from his attackers grip, but with each passing moment he drifted closer into a state of unconsciousness.

As he weakened he heard the sound of a car door opening. He was bundled into the back of the cab by his attacker, all the while with the handkerchief pressed over his face. Just before he passed out completely he caught sight of the man who had attacked him. It was Solomon Bennett.

'Devon,' said Bennett, shuffling into the backseat of the cab alongside him. 'We've got lots of catching up to do.'

Seventeen

Devon Pincent had spent most of the morning fretting about the fact he was about to lose his precious Blackwash project. He'd racked his brains to try and think of a decent argument to present to General Calhoon to convince her to reconsider her plan to scrap the operation. But his thoughts always returned to the events of the day before when Calhoon ruthlessly had Solomon Bennett and his crazy doctor friend escorted off the premises to be executed.

Word had spread that Bennett and Jekyll had vanished, along with the two MP's who had escorted them off the base. Devon was fairly confident that it meant Bennett and Jekyll were dead and the two Black Ops agents masquerading as MP's had been reassigned.

He arrived at Calhoon's office on time, virtually to the second. She'd shown her true colours the day before so Devon was in no doubt how important it was not to piss her off. And if that meant being punctual, then punctual he would be. At all times. He'd even brought two cups of coffee with him. One for himself and one for Calhoon, black with no sugar, just how she liked it.

Calhoon was sitting behind her desk when he walked in. She was dressed in a khaki military outfit. To Devon's surprise she greeted him with a warm smile.

'Take a seat, Devon,' she said, gesturing to the two chairs on the opposite side of her desk. A large window behind her was open but no one would hear their conversation because they were three floors up.

'I brought you a coffee,' said Devon.

'Thanks.'

He set the two coffees down on Calhoon's desk, which was completely bare except for a brown folder she had in front of her. He pulled out a chair and sat down, careful not to let his legs go too far under the desk for fear of any inappropriate "foot touching" antics with the General. Calhoon took the lid off the plastic coffee cup and inspected the contents.

'You got my coffee right,' she said. 'You'd be amazed how many people fuck it up. I mean, it's just black with no sugar. How hard can it be to get that right?'

Devon smiled politely, but changed the subject immediately. 'Jack said those two men that arrested Solomon were really Black Ops.'

Calhoon took a sip of the coffee. 'Uh huh. You think I overreacted yesterday don't you?'

'It seemed a little excessive to have Solomon killed. He fucked up, no doubt, but he deserved a fair trial, in my opinion.'

'Devon, *he escaped.*'

'Of course.'

Devon was working on the assumption that Calhoon was keeping up the façade that Solomon Bennett and Henry Jekyll were still alive, which was why she was going to stick with the whole *"They escaped and we'll never find them"* story. He was confident that the truth was somewhat different.

'Listen,' said Calhoon. 'Even though I don't need to justify myself to you *ever*, I'm going to on this occasion. There's a lot more to this situation than meets the eye. Now you and I have only been working together for a few months, but as I'm sure you've worked out by now, I'm here to clean up this department. My predecessor allowed you assholes way too much freedom to do as you pleased. And he never questioned anything. That's all going to change.'

'But my Blackwash Operation....'

'Your Blackwash Operation is finished.'

Devon sighed, a deep heavy sigh. He knew he wasn't going to win this argument but he felt the need to explain himself. 'We've made so much progress,' he said. 'I shouldn't be punished for Solomon's fuck up. I didn't want any of my soldiers taking part in that experiment and you know it.'

'I do, but Devon, there's a whole other story here that you don't know about. This goes back a long way to a case you were involved in fourteen years ago.'

'What?'

'Your old friend, Lionel Conrad and his wife Mary, remember them?'

'Yes.' Devon couldn't hide how confused he was. He'd run through how this conversation with Calhoon would go in his head many times since the day before, and at no point had he ever expected to hear the names of Joey Conrad's parents mentioned. 'What's this got to do with them?'

'You found their son in the closet when they were murdered, right.'

'I remember it like it was yesterday.'

'Well there's a lot more to those murders that you don't know about.'

'You know who did it?'

'I do *now*. For the last twenty-four hours we've been investigating Solomon Bennett, going through his emails and phone calls, digging up as much dirt on him as possible. Him and his buddy Dr Jekyll go way back. All the way back to the murder of the Conrads.'

'What?'

Calhoon opened her folder and pulled out a two-inch thick pile of papers and photos. 'As you know, Lionel Conrad and his wife both worked for a medical research company called Cybertech. Well, about twenty years ago, Cybertech got their hands on a meteorite that landed in the desert about five miles from their factory.'

'Yes I remember that. Lionel talked about it. He said it was like nothing he'd ever seen.'

'And he was right,' Calhoon continued. 'Lionel and his wife extracted a substance from within the meteors core. After two years of research they found that it might be a possible a cure for skin cancer. It seemed that at the right temperature the stuff in this meteorite was able to meld itself to human skin and destroy any cancerous cells. And it looked like the effects would be permanent. It was going to be one of the major breakthroughs in human history.'

'Lionel never said anything to me.'

'I should hope not. His work was of a highly sensitive nature. But one of his young apprentices, a doctor named Henry Percival saw an opportunity to make a name for himself.'

'Henry Percival. Is that Henry Jekyll?'

'Yes, and he wanted the meteor substance for himself. He hired someone to kidnap Mary Conrad and forced her to hand over all of the substance from the meteor. We're only talking about maybe fifty gallons of the stuff, so it wasn't hard for Jekyll's people to transport the stuff off the Cybertech factory. But they had one problem; Lionel Conrad kept his research with him at all times. Without his notes, the stuff was useless in anyone else's hands. That's when Lionel and Mary were murdered and you found Joey Conrad in the closet.'

'Are you saying Henry Jekyll murdered Lionel and Mary?'

Calhoon scoffed. 'No. Jekyll's way too much of a pussy to do that. He got someone else to do his dirty work for him.'

'Solomon Bennett!'

'Actually no.'

'Oh.'

'Solomon Bennett *was* involved though, of course. Jekyll went to him with his plans. I'm guessing he told Solomon how he could make him the richest man in the world and blah blah blah. Solomon hired someone who would happily do all the killing for them.'

'Who?'

'Take a guess.'

Devon had no idea, but Calhoon was giving him a look as if to say the answer was obvious. He scratched his head and tried to think who Bennett would have hired to kill someone fourteen years ago. Eventually one name popped into his head. 'Not his brother?'

Calhoon nodded. 'Terry Bennett.'

'I thought he was dead.'

'Everyone did. Solomon's been in contact with him the whole time. I've got emails, phone calls, the whole lot, all in these files. And this is just what we've found in the last twenty-four hours.'

'That sonofabitch. I worked that case for years and never got close to finding the killer.'

'Don't beat yourself up about it. I'll bet Solomon was keeping a close eye on you the whole time. If you'd gotten close he would have screwed things up for you.'

'But what did Solomon want with a cure for cancer?'

'Nothing. Him and Jekyll both felt that the cancer cure was a waste of time because there wasn't enough of it to make a difference. They preferred the idea of using it to make a bulletproof suit. They figured they could patent it, sell it to the military and become billionaires.'

'Fucking assholes.' Devon picked up his coffee and took a sip. It was cooling rapidly. 'So where are they keeping all this, what's it called, *Mistralyte?*'

'You know, the darndest thing,' said Calhoon. 'It's all *here*. The only place Jekyll and Bennett could formulate this stuff was in our very own labs. Every single barrel of that liquid is stored here.'

'Does anyone else know it's here?'

'Only Bennett and Jekyll.'

'But they're dead, right?'

'No they're not Devon. They escaped. I don't know how, but they killed my two Black Ops people and got away.'

'For real?'

'I'm not kidding. You can't tell anyone about this.'

'Do you think Bennett will come back here to get the stuff from the lab?'

'I'd like to see him try.'

'Me too.'

Calhoon leaned back in her chair and looked up at the ceiling. 'Devon, what do you plan to do with this information I've given you.'

It had been a lot to take in and Devon hadn't really had the time to process it all. 'What do you mean?' he asked.

'As I've already explained, your Operation Blackwash is finished. The remaining soldiers are being sent home. They'll be given a full military pension in exchange for their silence. If any of them ever speak about Operation Blackwash, I'll see to it that they disappear.' She slid a few sheets of paper across the desk to Devon. 'These are the terms of their release. I want you to give them their severance packages this afternoon. But I want to know what you plan to tell Joey Conrad when you give him his.'

Devon frowned. It took him a few seconds to realise what Calhoon was saying. 'You want me to tell him who killed his parents?'

Calhoon tapped her finger on the paper she had slid across to Devon. 'Terry Bennett, the man who killed Joey's parents is hiding out in Boston. He rarely goes out in public, but Solomon sends him money from time to time, envelopes of cash. When Terry makes appearances in public to pick up his money, he goes out dressed as a nun named Sister Claudia. You might want to mention that to Joey Conrad when you give him the news that Operation Blackwash is over.'

Devon allowed himself half a smile. 'Thank you General, I just might do that.'

Eighteen

Baby kept her arms wrapped tightly around Joey's waist while he took her on a ride around the quieter parts of town. His motorbike could accelerate from zero to warp speed in a split second, at least that's how it felt to Baby who had never experienced a bike ride before.

They sped through a long winding country road surrounded by trees for a couple of miles until Joey eventually steered the bike down a private lane that led up to a huge country estate known as Landingham Manor. The Landingham estate was well known as a home for protected wildlife. Foxes, deer and badgers were seen regularly within the grounds. But its focal point was a mansion with over 50 bedrooms. A ten feet high wall to keep out poachers and burglars surrounded the entire hundred acres of land.

Joey slowed down and they cruised up towards a set of large black iron gates at the front of the estate. Baby was surprised when, as they neared the estate the gates slowly opened inwards. As soon as the gap between the gates was big enough, Joey accelerated through them.

A stone fountain was positioned in the middle of the driveway. Joey's steered the bike around it and continued up to the main building. He stopped outside a set of large red doors at the front entrance.

'This is home,' he said.

'No way do you live here!' said Baby, gawping up at the marvellous old building in front of her. It was even bigger than the whorehouse she had grown up in. Only someone incredibly wealthy could possibly live there.

Joey killed the engine and gestured for Baby to hop off. She slid off the back of the bike and watched him wheel it over to the side of the entrance. He flicked down a kickstand and left the bike next to the wall.

Baby was more than a little confused at how they had come to stop in such a prestigious place. 'Seriously? How do you live here?' she asked.

'Your dad set me up here. He's got another job for me to do soon and he wanted me to stay here in the meantime.'

'So you *are* still in contact with my dad then?'

'Yeah. I'm due to meet him tomorrow to find out what he wants me to do next.'

'Do you speak with him a lot?'

'No. We meet once a month in a bar. Last time I saw him he gave me a job killing some folks at a gas station.'

'I heard about that on the news!'

'Yeah. That job got quite a bit of publicity, although mostly negative.' He nodded towards the doors at the front of the house. 'Come on, let's go inside. It's getting cold.'

'Okay, but seriously, how did my dad get you in here?'

'The landlady Mrs Landingham is a friend of his. She was married to a guy in your dad's department. And now she rents rooms in the house out to the agency if anyone ever needs a place to stay. Fortunately at the moment, I'm the only one staying here. And I think Mrs Landingham likes having me around.'

'Does she know who you are?'

Joey shrugged. 'I don't know, but your dad says she knows not to ask questions and she never talks about the guests who stay here.' He pushed open one of the doors and held it open for her. 'Try not to make too much noise. Mrs Landingham's probably in bed.'

The house was even more impressive inside. The reception hall had a shiny marble floor and a staircase in the centre that led up to a balcony, which branched off in two directions. Everything inside looked antique and therefore probably worth a small fortune.

'Follow me, you're gonna love this,' said Joey taking her by the hand.

He led her down a corridor and into a room that was straight out of a Cary Grant movie. The far wall was made up entirely of bookshelves from top to bottom. Hundreds of ancient hardback books filled the shelves. On a large antique wooden table in the centre of the room there was an old fashioned bright red telephone with just one button in the middle of it where the dial should have been. Next to it was a bronze bust of a man who Baby didn't recognise.

Joey ambled over to the bronze bust and placed his hand on its head. 'Cool, huh?' he said.

'Who's that supposed to be?' Baby asked, staring at the bust.

'Adam West.'

'Who's Adam West?'

'He was Bruce Wayne in the old Batman TV show.'

Baby screwed up her face to show how baffled she was. 'That's kind of random isn't it?' she said.

'Mrs Landingham's husband was a secret service agent when he was younger. That's how your dad knew him. He had this room kitted out like the study in Wayne Manor, except instead of a bust of Shakespeare he had a bust of Adam West made.' He pointed at the red telephone. 'That's a special phone. Mrs Landingham uses it to call me when dinner is ready.'

'She makes your dinner?'

'No, the kitchen staff do, but Mrs Landingham brings it in here for me.'

'This is your room?'

Joey shook his head. 'No, this is how I get to my room.'

Baby wondered exactly what that meant. 'Huh?'

'Watch this.' Joey pulled back the head on the bronze statue. It folded back, separating from the shoulders, revealing a small button in the middle of the neck. 'Press that button.'

Baby pressed the button and almost immediately she heard a gentle grating noise over by the wall of books. A portion of the wall slid to one side, revealing an elevator behind it with bright metallic walls.

'Oh wow,' she said. 'That's so cool.'

Joey closed the head on Adam West. 'Come on,' he said.

He took her by the hand again and led her into the elevator. There were two buttons on a display pad inside. One with an "UP" arrow on it and another with a "DOWN" arrow. Joey pressed the "DOWN" button. The bookshelf slid back across in front of them and the elevator moved downwards.

'I do remember seeing that Batman show once,' said Baby. 'Didn't they slide down to the basement on firemen poles?'

'Yeah. Mrs Landingham had the elevator put in here to replace the poles after her husband died.'

'How long has he been dead?'

Baby wasn't entirely sure why she asked how long Mr Landingham had been dead, but she was suddenly starting to feel nervous. She was alone with Joey just like she had dreamed about and all of a sudden she couldn't think of anything interesting to say.

'He died last year,' said Joey. 'He was eighty-six. Not a bad age really.'

'What happened to him?' Baby asked as the elevator came to a stop.

The doors slid open and Joey stepped out. He turned back to face her and answered her question. 'He broke his neck sliding down the fireman pole.'

Baby barely heard him. She was dumbstruck by the sight of the room behind him. The underground basement had been constructed to look like a giant cave, only it was full of high tech equipment like computers and some very modern gym equipment. The thing that really caught Baby's eye was situated at the back of the cave in front of a large metal shuttered door. Rotating around slowly on a giant silver

110

disc was Joey's yellow and red stock car, the one he had taken her home in after he rescued her from B Movie Hell.

'Cool isn't it?' said Joey. 'Mr Landingham had the walls built to make it look like a real cave.' He pointed at a desk in the middle of the room. It had a bank of television monitors neatly stacked on it and a control panel in front of them. 'Those monitors show everything that's happening in and around the grounds,' he said. 'That way if anyone breaks into the estate I can kill them before they get inside the building.'

'Kill them?'

'I'm kidding. I usually just cripple them.'

'What?'

'It's a joke Baby. No one has tried to break in since I've been here.'

Baby laughed politely. She looked across to the other side of the room. There was a large screen television, almost the size of a cinema screen, with a black leather sofa facing it.

'That TV is huge!' she said.

'Yeah. Wanna watch Karate Kid 3?'

'Uh, not just now, thanks.' Baby walked towards the car. That car had been in most of her dreams. The day that she and Joey had spent in it driving home was one of her favourite memories. She longed to go for another drive with him one day, in his Mohawk-mobile. She noticed a door in the wall not far from the car. 'What's through there?' she asked.

'Bathroom. You need a piss?'

'No, I'm good, thanks. What about your bed? Where do you sleep?'

Joey was standing by the security desk. He flicked a switch on the control panel. A portion of the wall behind Baby started moving. In Landingham Manor walls were often *not walls at all*. This one rolled out like a drawbridge being lowered, revealing a large double bed with a yellow duvet and a set of red pillows.

'Holy shit. That's awesome,' said Baby. 'This place is crazy.'

'I think Mr Landingham was a little eccentric,' said Joey. 'I mean he'd have to be crazy to still be sliding down a fireman's pole in his eighties.'

'Yeah.'

'You want a drink?'

Baby shook her head. She made her way over to the bed and sat down on it. The talk about Mr Landingham being crazy had reminded her of something that she was curious about. 'Joey, can I ask you something?' she said.

'Sure. What?'

'Are you really planning to kill the Pope?'

Joey laughed, loudly and boisterously for a moment. 'No, no, no. I don't know what that's about. I think the papers have just made that up.'

'But my dad said you killed a nun because you don't like church people, and that's why you got sent to a mental hospital. Is that true?'

Joey looked surprised that she had asked, but not offended, which was a relief. 'Did your father not tell you why I killed the nun?'

'No. So you *did* kill a nun then?'

Joey pulled out a cushioned office chair from under the security desk and sat down on it. 'Yeah, but your father arranged it.'

'What?'

'The nun was really a man. He'd murdered my parents. Your father told me where I could find him.'

Baby felt guilty about asking, but also extremely pleased that she now knew the truth. 'Oh. I'm sorry I didn't know about your parents.'

Joey wheeled his chair over to her. She looked up into his eyes. He had a look about him that convinced her she would believe anything he said. For all his faults Joey had honest eyes.

'The man who killed my parents was a paranoid sociopath, a real fuckin' weirdo. After he killed them, he moved to Boston and went into hiding. He rarely went out, but when he did he dressed as a nun so that no one would recognise him. I guess he had a lot of enemies, and he was wanted for a whole bunch of different things, not least of all the murder of my parents.'

'If he killed your parents then he deserved it,' she declared.

'So you'd have done the same thing?'

Baby smiled. 'Yep.' It was reassuring to know that he hadn't murdered a defenceless holy woman for no reason. 'How did you do it?' she asked. 'My dad said you stabbed the nun in a diner. Is that part true?'

Joey nodded. 'The man's name was Terry Bennett. I'd been told that when he needed money he would go to a diner in the city centre where an associate of his would deliver an envelope full of cash to him. So I found out who the associate was and I followed him everywhere, waiting for the day he went to the diner. And eventually after a couple of weeks he went. And that's when I saw Terry Bennett sitting there in a booth in his nun outfit. When he murdered my parents he was wearing a balaclava so I'd only ever seen his eyes before. Your father had shown me some photos of him, but it was the eyes that gave him away. Once I saw those I knew it was him.'

'So what did you do?'

Joey became more animated, using his hands to keep her attention as he delved deeper into the story. 'I'd prepared ahead for what I was going to do. I'd written a message on a piece of paper telling him that someone in the diner was going to kill him. I put it in an envelope with the name *Sister Claudia* on it. That's what he called himself. I wanted to see the fear in his eyes when he read the note. So when the waitress wasn't looking, I slipped it onto her tray. And I can tell you now, the best part of killing that sonofabitch was seeing his expression change when he read that note. He was fucking terrified.'

'Did he see you and realise it was you?'

'No. I was with a girlfriend.'

'You had a girlfriend?'

'Meghan was one of the other recruits from Operation Blackwash. When the project was scrapped she and I dated for a while. Neither of us really knew anyone in the outside world so it was easier to reintegrate into society together. I convinced her to take a vacation to Boston with me. But I didn't tell her what I was there for. I probably should have done, but she was the perfect cover. We were just sitting at a table in the diner looking like a love-struck young couple, so I think he ruled us out.'

'So what did he do?'

'He sat there crapping his pants for like, five minutes. He can't call the cops because let's face it, he's a dude dressed as a nun and he's wanted all across America. And then purely by chance a big fucker at another table gets up and walks over towards Terry Bennett's table. I can see Bennett thinks he's the person who sent the note. He's got a fork in his hand and he's ready to slam it into this guy's neck.'

'Oh God.'

'Yeah. Well the big fucker walks right past Bennett's table. See, he's just going to use the bathroom and the toilets are at the back of the diner. Bennett waits 'til he's gone past, then gets up from his seat. He's watching the guy walk into the washroom. So now he's got his back to me. And that's when I made my move.'

'What did you do?'

'Stand up. I'll show you.' Joey stood up and kicked his chair away. He grabbed her hand and hauled her up from the bed, without waiting to see if she was planning on standing up herself. 'Okay, turn around,' he said.

Baby turned her back on him. He pressed his body up against her. Even though he was about to demonstrate how he had murdered someone, having him up pressed up against her back made Baby's heart race. She felt weak at the knees and all of a sudden it became an issue just trying to breathe like a normal person. Joey slid one arm around her waist and yanked her in tight. His other hand came up higher, around her throat. He spoke softly in her ear.

'I grabbed him like this,' he said. 'I pressed a knife up underneath his chin and I told him, *"You killed Mary and Lionel Conrad. They were my parents."* I had just enough time to say that before he could really struggle. I slammed the knife in through the bottom of his chin, into his mouth.' He demonstrated on Baby by using his index finger. He traced the finger back down from beneath her chin, lightly stroking her neck until he reached her collarbone. 'I sliced him all the way down,' he said. 'Then I pushed him to the floor. I still remember the look on his face. When he looked up at me. Blood was spurting out of his throat. I sat on his chest and looked into his eyes. And I watched him choke on his own blood. I made sure that the last thing he saw before he died was *me*.'

'And what happened then? Did you get away?'

Joey shook his head. 'I hadn't planned an escape. I didn't care if I got caught or not. Someone flagged down a passing police car and they charged into the diner, guns drawn and arrested me.'

'What about your girlfriend Meghan?'

Joey lowered his hands so that they were both around her waist. 'They arrested her too. Even though I told them she had nothing to do with it she got a couple of years in prison for being an accomplice to murder. And me, I got sent to a mental institution. Your father fixed that up for me. I could easily have had the death sentence, but because of what had been done to me in the Blackwash project I was able to plead insanity and make it stick. Meghan wasn't so lucky though. She pleaded innocent and was found guilty.'

'Do you still see her?'

'No. She hates my guts now. I can understand that. I should never have involved her.'

Baby was pleased that throughout the story he had kept his body pressed up against her back, one hand around her waist and another just above her chest. He was staring off into space, lost in the details of his own story. She could feel the warmth of his breath on her neck. She wanted the moment to be romantic, but the talk of murders and prison sentences had dampened the mood, so she tried to lighten things up.

'Grabbing folks from behind, is that one of your big moves?' she asked, hoping he didn't let go any time soon.

'Yeah. You like that?'

Baby smiled. It felt like they were flirting in a weird kind of way. 'Okay, don't move,' she said. 'You wanna see *my* big move?'

'Okay.'

She took a deep breath. Having announced that she had a big move she now had to back that claim up, which only added to her nerves. Her heart was thumping harder than ever.

'When I worked at the Beaver Palace we had this one creepy customer who used to grab the girls from behind as soon as he was in the room. He was really forceful and even though he was paying for the sex and it was consensual, he liked to make it feel like it wasn't.'

'Nice guy,' Joey said sarcastically.

'Yeah. But I worked out a move that screwed up his plans. You ready for this?'

'Go on.'

Baby hoped to hell she could still pull off the move. 'This is called *the Penguin*,' she said.

'Okay, I'm waiting,' said Joey.

'Done.' Without him realising it, Baby had reached back with one hand and unbuckled his belt and the top button on his pants. She elbowed him in the ribs and spun away from him, yanking his pants down at the same time in one fluid movement. The combination of the elbow in the ribs, coupled with the realisation that his pants were falling down worked perfectly on every single guy she'd ever done it to. Baby had yet to come across a man that didn't panic when his pants dropped past his knees unexpectedly. She spun around to face him, a beaming smile on her face. She felt a great sense of pride in the knowledge that her trick had worked so perfectly on him. Joey looked completely bewildered. He was open-mouthed, staring down at his pants that were wrapped around his ankles. When Baby looked down to see what kind of underwear he had on, she got a surprise of her own.

'Oh God. You've gone Commando!'

'Yeah.'

Baby had seen a great many dicks in her time, but this was different. She felt her face burn red with embarrassment. 'I'm sorry I didn't realise.'

Joey got over the initial shock pretty quickly. He raised his eyebrows and looked at her with mock disapproval. 'I don't really know what to say.'

'You don't have to *say* anything.' Baby took a few steps back and sat back down on the bed. 'Come here,' she said coyly. Her previous feelings of embarrassment were fading rapidly.

Joey took two steps towards her, but because his trousers were round his ankles he ended up waddling awkwardly.

Baby giggled. 'And that's why it's called *the Penguin!*'

Joey closed his eyes and shook his head. 'I've killed people for less than this.'

Baby took a deep breath and let her eyes wander down to his exposed penis again. It was an impressive size and as she was looking at it, she could see it was getting bigger with every passing moment. She looked back up at his face and stared into his eyes, willing him to come closer. This was the moment she had been waiting for.

Within a matter of seconds they were both naked and writhing around on the bed. For all her sexual experience, Baby had never known what real passion was like. *This was it.*

For the next twenty minutes the two of them were so wrapped up in each other that they forgot about the existence of everything else in the whole world. Neither of them noticed the live footage on the security monitors. If they had they would have seen a brutal murder take place in the woodland outside the estate.

Nineteen

Alexis Calhoon had spent a lot of time reflecting on what had happened within Phantom Ops in recent times. The biggest concern, as usual was that she didn't know which of the men in her command she could trust. *One hundred percent trust.*

Devon Pincent was still the biggest problem. His intentions were always good and he believed in protecting the weak. His methods though, were completely immoral. She couldn't figure out what his involvement was in the threat to kill the Pope, if he even *was* involved. That was the problem with Devon, he was always one step ahead of the game. By the time people cottoned onto what he was up to, he'd always covered his tracks and created a diversion that wasted everyone's time and bought him the space he needed to erase his involvement in whatever the hell he'd been up to.

Calhoon arrived outside the penthouse suite of the Ritz Hotel, none the wiser about Devon's involvement in any of it, and she'd grown tired of even thinking about it. She had too many other things on her mind, not least of all her imminent meeting with the Pope. She had dressed in military whites for the meeting, even though she had spent an hour contemplating all manner of informal outfits. This was business after all. She arrived with a bunch of flowers of all colours too, seeing as how the Pope had just undergone a serious lifesaving operation.

Rufus, the Pope's personal secretary and head of the Papal household showed her into the Pope's private suite. Rufus was a man of average height, with a decent head of grey hair and a face that belonged on a man in his forties rather than a fifty-eight-year-old. He was wearing a long black cassock with red lining on the sleeves and collar. Calhoon had seen him before on television and on her one and only previous meeting with him had been pleased to find that he was as affable in person as he was on screen.

'Please take a seat,' said Rufus.

'These are for His Holiness,' said Calhoon, handing him the bouquet of flowers.

'Thank you.'

Rufus took the flowers and placed them on top of an antique grand piano in the corner of the room.

The Pope and his entourage sure knew how to pick a nice hotel. The penthouse suite they were renting was better than any place Calhoon had ever stayed in. She sat down on a gold coloured three-seater sofa and looked around, marvelling at the high ceilings and sheer expensiveness of everything in the room, from the grand piano in the corner, to the enormous television screen built into the wall. She would have liked to spend much more time showing herself around but with it being such an ungodly hour she was conscious that she needed to be brief.

'I have two reasons for coming at such a late hour,' she said. 'First of all and most importantly, I wanted to know how the Pope was recovering from the operation?'

Rufus sat down in an armchair opposite her. 'Good news,' he said with a generous smile that belied his tired eyes. 'The operation has been a complete success. The Mistralyte worked exactly as you said it would. The surgeons have confirmed that all of the cancerous cells have been destroyed.'

'Oh that's wonderful.' Calhoon inwardly breathed a sigh of relief even though she'd been certain that the operation would work based on all the tests they had done. 'Is he awake? I'd love to see him.'

'He's probably sleeping, but by all means come and take a look at him.'

Rufus stood up and beckoned her to follow him over to a bedroom door near the grand piano. He knocked gently on the door and then pushed it open. He stepped inside and Calhoon followed, careful not to make any noise. The sight inside the bedroom was quite unnerving. The Pope was lying in a single bed with tubes from machines attached to his arms. He looked pale but he had a contented smile on his face. There were candles all around his bed, offering a dim, eerie light that wouldn't look out of place in a morgue.

'Oh my goodness,' said Calhoon. 'What's with all the tubes?'

The Pope stirred and opened his eyes. He looked across at them both and smiled.

'Has she come to give me a bed bath?' he asked.

'No, Your Holiness,' said Rufus. 'This is General Calhoon. She's the lady who provided us with the cure for your skin cancer.'

'Good for her,' said the Pope. 'Has she brought any cake? I fuckin' love cake.'

He closed his eyes again and appeared to drift back off to sleep with an even bigger contented smile on his face, occasionally muttering the word "cake" to himself.

Rufus ushered Calhoon back out of the room and into the main lounge. 'I do apologise,' he said. 'It's the drugs. I've never heard him swear before, but he is dosed up on morphine for the pain, so he's probably not sure what he's saying.'

118

'That's all right,' said Calhoon. 'As I understand it, the stinging sensation from the skin graft can burn quite a bit, but it goes within a day.'

'That's what we've been told,' said Rufus, pouring himself a drink of scotch from a glass decanter on a drinks cabinet. 'And don't worry, we will still be attending your event on Saturday. You've saved the Pope's life, so I promise you, he will be there to endorse this wonderful cure you have developed. It's the least we can do. Would you like a drink?'

'No, I'm okay thank you.'

'Let's sit back down then.'

Calhoon handed him an A4 sized envelope she had brought with her and kept tucked under her arm since she'd arrived. Rufus accepted it and sat down in his armchair again. Calhoon sat back down on the sofa and watched him open the envelope. He pulled out the contents and the first thing he saw was the picture of the Pope with the death threat written on it. It didn't evoke any kind of reaction from him. He swiftly moved on to the Top Trump playing card with the picture of the Red Mohawk. Again, he showed no emotion.

'How concerned do we need to be about this?' he asked, looking up at her.

'I'm almost certain it's a hoax,' said Calhoon. 'But, I just can't be one hundred percent sure. So I believe out of courtesy I had to let you and *His Holiness* know about it.'

Rufus took on board what she had said and studied the playing card for a while, his face still giving nothing away. Eventually he put the card and the photo of the Pope back into the envelope and slid it across the coffee table back to Calhoon.

'I used to love Top Trumps when I was a kid,' he said with a smile. 'We get death threats all the time. This one is of little concern compared to some of the others I've seen. Have you beefed up security for the event on the back of it?'

Calhoon fidgeted on the sofa. For all its expense the darned thing wasn't all that comfortable.

'Security is ramped up to the max. You'll have more armed guards than the President gets. Only very distinguished guests have been invited, and everyone who enters the premises will be thoroughly checked for weapons. We have metal detectors on the entrances too.'

'Is that normal for an event of this kind?'

'It's *excessive* for an event of this kind. But as an added precaution I'm switching the event to our contingency site. It's just as secure, but the benefit of it is that no one will be informed of the new location. All of the guests, caterers and entertainment staff will be driven there on the morning of the event. Even my security team won't be informed of the location change until the night before.'

Rufus took a sip of his scotch and then swilled the glass around in his hand, staring into the contents, deliberating his options.

'I'm impressed,' he said eventually. 'I have the utmost faith in you, General. And I have a feeling that one day, not too far from now, you'll be recognised for all of your work, not just with saving the Pope's life with your cancer cure, but also for giving it to the Pharmaceutical companies so that they can give it to the world. You'll go down in history, ma'am.'

'Thank you, you're very kind.'

'So are you able to tell *me* the new location?'

'Of course. I'll have a military escort to accompany you there on the day anyway, but in case you wanted to look the place up and find out more about it before you attend, it's called Landingham Manor. It's on the outskirts of the East side of the city.'

'Landingham Manor,' said Rufus, sniffing his drink. 'It sounds like a lovely place. But I'll check it out all the same.'

'Great,' said Calhoon, standing up. 'I'll leave you in peace now. If you have any queries about Landingham Manor, feel free to call my office. If I'm not there ask for Blake Jackson, he's the only other person who knows about the change of venue.'

Twenty

Baby was perched on the edge of the bed frantically putting her clothes back on. It was past midnight and she'd promised her father she would be home by eleven.

'I'm so late. My dad is going to go mental!' she said, trying to express the urgency of the situation to Joey who was far more casual about it. He had slipped his jeans back on but was now sifting through a selection of vests in a closet that had previously been concealed within the cave walls.

'Don't worry,' he said. 'I'll have you home in next to no time.'

'Can we go in the car this time?' Baby asked, keen to avoid riding on the back of a bike again, particularly with no helmet in the dead of night.

'Yeah, okay.'

Joey slipped a black sleeveless vest over his head. It suited him and really showed off his bulging biceps. His upper body was totally ripped and as Baby had recently discovered it was as solid as granite. She had seen a fair few torsos in her time, but never anything quite as solid as Joey's.

As she put her shoes on she watched him running his hand through his hair, which was a tad messy from their sex session. Without his Mohawk mask and trademark red leather jacket he looked so normal. He had a pleasant way about him and good manners, none of which was in keeping with the persona he emitted when he was in his Red Mohawk attire.

'If my dad is waiting up for me, what am I going to tell him?' Baby fretted.

Joey picked his red jacket up from the floor by the bed. 'Tell him you walked home from *Dead Man's Drop*. You know, say about how you left that dickhead Jason on his own out there. Don't let on that you know anything about him being dead.'

'My dad's no fool. When he hears Jason Moxy is dead, he'll know you were involved.'

'He won't be able to prove it though, and neither will the cops. Stick to your story.'

Baby wished she had some clean clothes to put on. Hers felt sweaty and creased since they had been flung onto the floor. Although deep down she also wished that she hadn't had to put her clothes back on at all. She could happily have stayed in bed with Joey and fooled around all night, but she knew there would be more opportunities for them to get together in future, as long as she didn't screw up and get herself arrested for the murder of Jason Moxy.

'Here, catch,' said Joey, snapping her out of her maudlin thoughts. He tossed a cell phone to her. She caught it and looked at him, puzzled. 'Put my number into your phone, and put yours into mine.'

Swapping numbers wasn't the world's biggest commitment, particularly when you've already slept with that person but Baby felt a surge of excitement. This was a sign that they would be seeing more of each other.

She saw Joey head over to the car so she quickly followed him. She climbed into the car on the passenger side and buckled up her seat belt then got to work typing numbers into phones. Joey settled in behind the wheel. He twisted a key in the ignition and started up the engine. The roar from beneath the stock car's hood reminded her of the first time she'd driven with him, the first time she'd ever known what it was like to feel truly safe.

'Have you still got that Dirty Dancing CD?' she asked.

'Glove box.'

She handed him back his cell phone and opened the glove box. It was full of junk. The first things that caught her eye were a handgun and a big knife in a leather sheath. She pushed them aside and grabbed two CD's from the back of the compartment. One was the soundtrack for the movie Road House, but the other one was the one she wanted, the Dirty Dancing CD she had given to Joey when they last saw each other. It was pleasing to know he had kept it. The CD had been the soundtrack to her life. It reminded her of so many events from her days at the Beaver Palace, some good, some bad, but all part of what had made her into the person she was today.

She pulled out the disc and slid it into the car stereo. While they waited for the music to start they watched the metal shutter gate roll up into the ceiling. Behind it was a long dark tunnel with a sprinkling of spotlights in the walls to show the way.

'Wow,' said Baby. 'That's so cool.'

'It's an underground road. It comes out in the woods right on the edge of the estate.'

Joey released the handbrake and drove the car into the tunnel. The song Be My Baby by The Ronettes kicked in as Baby looked back and watched the shutter gate roll back down behind them. Everything about Joey's hideout was so cool. She gazed at him, a beaming smile across her face. She couldn't remember ever feeling so happy.

The tunnel carried on for about a quarter of a mile before it came to a dead end in a circular opening. Joey slowed up and stopped the car.

'What's happening?' Baby inquired.

'Watch and see.'

The car started moving sideways. It rotated ninety degrees and then when it stopped, the floor beneath them rose up like an elevator. After about ten seconds they stopped moving completely. They were in total darkness. And Joey hadn't turned on the car's headlights.

'Where are we?' she asked.

'An abandoned electricity outhouse on the outskirts of the estate.'

A sliver of light appeared on the ground in front of them and Baby realised she was staring at another metal shutter gate that was slowly rolling upwards. The sliver of light was coming from the moonlight outside. Once the gate had risen high enough Joey hit the gas and cruised out under it. They were back out in the woodland surrounded by trees.

'Shouldn't you put your headlights on?' Baby suggested, fearing they might plough into something in the darkness.

'Not yet,' Joey replied. 'We need to get out of the woods first. Otherwise people might wonder where we suddenly appeared from.'

The car bounced over a tree root and Baby almost smacked her head on the roof. She was thankful she had buckled up.

'This re-entry is a little bumpy,' said Joey. 'But I know the route to the main road. I could do this with my eyes shut.'

He did seem to know where he was going. Baby was grateful he kept his speed down though because visibility was extremely poor. He steered around some bushes and into an area dense with trees. He was navigating his way through them with great skill until –

BANG!

Baby looked around. 'Shit, what was that?'

Joey fought with the steering wheel but the car began leaning over to one side and heading towards a large tree. He hit the brakes in the nick of time and they stopped just short of the tree's trunk.

Joey banged his fist on the steering wheel, venting his frustration.

'What just happened?' Baby asked, lightly touching his arm in the hope of calming him down.

'People dump all kinds of shit out here. I think we went over something and got a flat tyre.'

He opened his door and climbed out of the car. He looked around for any sign of what he had driven over. He spotted something and started tutting and cussing about having a burst tyre. He made his way round to the front of the car to take a look at it.

'Can I help?' Baby called out, hoping secretly that the answer would be no. She unbuckled her seatbelt and scuttled across the car seats onto the driver side to see what he was doing. He was kneeling down inspecting the front tyre. It was obviously bad news because he shook his head and stood up. He walked back and poked his head around the door. 'Yeah it's a flat,' he confirmed. 'I'm just gonna have to change the....'

Before he could finish the sentence his head jolted forward and he grimaced in pain. Baby saw something sticking out of his neck. It looked like a small feather. Joey reached up to touch it. It was a dart of some kind. But before he could pull it out, his body snapped forwards again. A second dart hit him in the arm just below the shoulder.

'What's happening?' Baby gasped, looking around to see if she could see where the darts were coming from.

Joey didn't reply. He dropped to his knees and tried once more to grab hold of the dart in his neck. A flash of white raced past the car door and a third dart slammed into the back of Joey's thigh. This one seemed to do the trick, either that or the effect of the first two had finally kicked in because Joey slumped down onto his back, staring up at the sky, blinking slowly in an effort to stay conscious. He was in some serious trouble. He twisted his neck around to look at her.

Baby poked her head tentatively out of the car door, hoping not to get hit by any stray darts herself. 'Are you okay?' she asked.

Joey opened his mouth to speak but no words came out. His eyes stopped blinking and closed as if he'd fallen into a deep sleep. Baby heard footsteps approaching from the woods. She ducked back inside the car and crawled back into the passenger seat. It was hard to know what to do. She didn't want to desert Joey, but she also had nowhere to hide. She kneeled on the car seat and squinted her eyes to get a look through the back window. A man dressed from head to toe in woodland camouflage gear was stalking up to the car, heading towards Joey.

Baby remembered the gun she'd seen in the glove box. This might be a chance to prove to Joey that she could handle herself, but did she have the guts to use it? There was only one way to find out. She opened the glove box and tentatively pulled out the gun. For a brief moment she considered the knife, but dismissed the idea when she realised that she would look scarier with a gun. Besides, a knife had to be used at close quarters and could therefore be taken from her easily before she did any damage with it.

She held the gun in both hands but kept it out of sight in the gap between the car seats. The camouflaged man ignored her and walked past the car door. He stooped down to check on Joey. He was stocky and had a black ponytail, which was poking out through the back of a camouflaged cap. In the dark it was hard to make out any facial features on him, but it looked like he had black paint smeared across his cheeks and nose to help stay out of sight in the dark. Strapped across his back was a lightweight rifle and an ammo belt filled with darts. Who was he and what did he want?

When the man was convinced Joey wasn't a threat he stood up and walked back to the open door. He peered in to get a look at Baby. He had a horrible upturned piggy nose. His eyes glanced down at Baby's hands, which were concealed between the two seats.

'Don't even think about pointing that gun at me,' he said, reaching for a hunting knife on his belt.

Baby had a tough decision to make.

Twenty One

When Devon woke up he was tied to a chair. His eyes felt heavy and his brain was swirling around in his head. He was aware of some other people nearby moving around and talking. Eventually one of them said something that he was able to make sense of.

'He's waking up. See, I told you he would.'

Devon squeezed his eyes shut and reopened them hoping that his vision would clear. Everything was still blurry but he found that by squeezing his eyes shut a few more times his vision sharpened each time he reopened them.

'How are you feeling, Devon?' He recognised the voice. It was Solomon Bennett.

Devon had been focussing mostly on the feet of the other people in the room. Bennett's voice had come from the direction of a man in black boots and combat pants. Devon lifted his head. His eyes followed up the man's body. The black combat pants led up to a black T-shirt, bulging old veiny man muscles and then the chiselled, grizzly face of Solomon Bennett and his crap eye-patch and rubbish flat top haircut.

'What the hell are you doing?' Devon asked, the words falling out of his mouth without much rhythm to them. He felt pleased with himself that he'd managed to get the whole sentence out without any slip-ups because he felt like he'd drunk ten pints of lager and been awake for three days solid.

'Give him a minute. He's a bit groggy,' said another man's voice.

Dr Henry Jekyll was leaning against a desk, smirking at him. He was wearing a long white lab coat over a pair of grey trousers and a blue shirt. His curly ginger hair was totally out of control, making his head look huge. Devon hadn't quite got his wits back and consequently another sentence fell out of his mouth.

'You look like an orange on a pencil.'

'I've heard all the insults before,' Jekyll replied.

A hand slapped Devon across the face. It stung and it certainly helped wake him up a bit. The hand belonged to Solomon Bennett.

'Devon, I haven't got time to mess around with you. How many people have you talked to?'

Devon frowned. 'Talked to? About what?'

'Don't fuck with me!' Bennett said angrily. He raised his hand as if to hit Devon again.

'Wait up,' said Jekyll. 'I'll liven him up.'

126

Dr Jekyll hopped off the desk he was sitting on and sauntered over to Devon. He held his hand underneath Devon's nose and squeezed something. A puff of gas blew into Devon's nostrils. It gave off a strange ice cold burning sensation, albeit for just a second. But it made his head snap back, and suddenly he felt more awake than he had in years.

'What the hell was that?' he asked.

Jekyll didn't reply. He walked back to the desk in the middle of the room and resumed his position leaning against it.

Devon took a good look around him. He was in an office of some kind. There was a desk in the middle of the room and a cream sofa against the wall. His coat was draped across the sofa, with its pockets turned inside out.

Devon was tied to a wooden chair against a wall. His hands were wrapped tightly behind his back, which was arched in an uncomfortable position.

'Where the hell am I?' he asked.

'This is my new office,' said Bennett. 'It used to belong to a bunch of drug dealers but they're all dead now, thanks to my bulletproof friend Frankenstein. Remember him?'

Frank Grealish was standing in the corner of the office by the door. Devon wondered how he hadn't noticed him before, but there he was, all six feet six inches of him, complete with metal bolts in his neck, looking exactly like had the last time Devon had seen him, when he pronounced him dead.

'Frank? How are you alive?' he asked.

Bennett slapped him across the face again. 'Don't ask Frankenstein questions. It unsettles him.'

Devon's cheek was stinging. He pulled a few odd faces as he tried to shrug off the pain.

'Is it really necessary to keep bitch-slapping me?' he said.

'Where's Jack Munson?'

'Jack? How the hell would I know?'

SLAP!

Bennett crouched down in front of Devon to get right into his eye line.

'Devon, I know you sent Jack to spy on us in Romania. Don't play all these innocent games with me. We already know that you know everything we're planning. If you persist with playing dumb you know exactly how this is going to pan out. And let's face it, you and me are old friends so I really don't want to have to start cutting off your fingers.'

'You won't have to,' said Devon. 'I've nothing to hide. What do you want from me?'

'I want to know what your contingency plan is.'

'My contingency plan? For what?'

SLAP!

Devon grimaced. The slaps were getting harder.

'That was a perfectly reasonable question,' he groaned. 'I have lots of contingency plans on the go at all times. Which one are you referring to?'

Bennett stood up straight, as if all the crouching had started to make his old knees ache.

'You know perfectly well I'm talking about General Calhoon's big *"Christmas Miracle"* event.' He put the words *"Christmas Miracle"* in air quotes to demonstrate his contempt for the whole thing. 'You know the one, the event where the Pope is showing up, but no one is supposed to know about it.'

'Oh, that one,' said Devon. 'Even I don't know where that is. In case you haven't heard, I've been suspended.'

'Yes, I heard. You got suspended because of your links with Joey Conrad. Yeah, that's right, I know who the Red Mohawk is.'

'How did you know that?'

'I have my sources, Devon. Just like you do.'

Devon looked around the room. Dr Jekyll and Frankenstein weren't giving anything away. Neither of them could have discovered the Red Mohawk's true identity. Frankenstein was too dumb and Dr Jekyll was just too much of an oddball. So how the hell had Solomon Bennett found out? He hoped it was simply guesswork, but Bennett seemed far too sure of himself.

'Well then,' said Devon, 'you'll also know that the Red Mohawk has gone rogue. I'm not in contact with him at all. He's working for himself.'

Bennett smiled. 'Are you referring to that gas station massacre?'

'Yes, you read about that?'

'I know all about it, Devon. I know what the newspapers and the cops haven't worked out yet, that the family who owned that gas station were long suspected of drugging late night customers and then serving them up for dinner.' He sneered at Devon, his eyes filled with contempt. 'Joey Conrad showing up and murdering a bunch of redneck cannibals, that's got your fingerprints all over it!'

For a moment, Devon was speechless. How could Bennett know all of this information? Devon had been working on the gas station case for years but had never acquired enough proof to make an arrest, until a

128

few weeks ago. But then instead of obtaining a warrant for the arrest of the family of cannibals, he had sent the Red Mohawk in to administer his usual brutal form of justice.

'I don't know what you're talking about,' Devon bluffed.

Bennett laughed. 'No one was supposed to know the Red Mohawk had anything to do with it were they? But he showed up while the cannibals were drugging another woman with their poisoned coffee. So even though he saved her she became the witness who identified him to the cops. How many other assignments have you given the Red Mohawk where no one was left alive to identify him, eh? Loads, I'll bet!'

Devon did his best to look like he had no idea what Bennett was talking about. He tried shrugging, which was actually pretty difficult because he was tied to the chair.

'You have a vivid imagination, Solomon, you really do.'

'Yes I do,' Bennett agreed. 'Which is why I want you to tell me where Joey Conrad is, because I suspect you've forewarned him about my plans to hijack Calhoon's big charity event.'

'Like I said already, I don't know where he is. He's gone rogue. There's nothing I can tell you.'

Dr Jekyll stepped forward and whispered in Bennett's ear, loud enough for Devon to hear it. 'Let me torture him. I'll get him to talk.'

Bennett waved him away. 'We won't be torturing Devon,' he said with a smirk. 'He'll be coming with us to Calhoon's event. You see, Devon, when the dust settles and everyone, including the Pope, is dead, all that will remain of Calhoon's "Christmas Miracle" event is some video footage of you killing Calhoon in cold blood.'

'I'll do no such thing!'

'Oh you will, Devon. You're the perfect fall guy. Calhoon just suspended you indefinitely. And everyone knows you like to get even with people who cross you. *And so do I.* In fact, I even hope your friend the Red Mohawk shows up and tries to carry out his threat to kill the Pope, because we'll be there waiting for him. Then you and him can take the fall for the whole thing. Don't think I've forgotten that Joey Conrad killed my brother. I'll bet you gave him that mission too, didn't you?'

Twenty Two

Baby wasn't sure if she would pull the trigger or not, but she knew she had to convince the man with the "pig face" that she had the guts to shoot if it came to the crunch. A thousand thoughts were racing through her mind all at once. Like who was this ugly bastard? Who was he working for? And could he afford surgery to fix his horrible snout?

If Baby shot at him and missed, it would almost certainly lead to some serious unpleasantness. Understandably too, people generally didn't take too kindly to being shot at. And Pig Face had a knife and a dart rifle with him. But with Joey out cold on the ground, it was Baby's turn to step up to the plate. She pointed the gun at Pig Face and tried to think of something cool to say.

Pig Face beat her to it. 'Put the fucking gun down, honey,' he said calmly. 'You'll only hurt yourself. You're not even holding it right.'

'Who are you?' Baby said with a fake level of confidence. She felt like she should be trembling with fear, but she was holding it together, *just.*

'What's your name?' Pig Face asked, with an evil glare.

'Baby.'

'Your *real* name?'

A plan popped into Baby's head, a decisive plan. Not necessarily a good one, but she'd made up her mind about it and decided to give it a try.

'I'll give you the gun,' she said. 'If you tell me who you are.'

Pig Face deliberated her offer for a moment before responding. 'My name is....'

Baby picked her moment well. It was what she thought Joey would have done. *Shoot your enemy when they least expect it, right when they're in the middle of answering a question you asked them.* She'd lined up the shot and took aim at the end of his stubby nose. She closed her eyes and squeezed the trigger. Nothing happened. She opened her eyes.

Pig Face looked livid. 'You've got the safety on, you dumb bitch!'

Baby glanced down at the gun. She'd heard of this cliché in movies where an occasional dumbass tried firing a gun without flicking off the safety switch. Now *she* was that dumbass. But unlike the dumbasses in the movies, Baby didn't intend to dither. She spotted the safety catch and flicked it off with her thumb, impressing herself with her speed of thought in the circumstances. She looked back up at Pig Face, who still looked livid, but now also looked surprised at Baby's attempt to take another shot at him straight away. He started to move, ducking his head out of the way of the next shot. Baby squeezed the trigger again.

CLICK.

Pig Face poked his head back around the open door. '*No bullets!*' he sneered. 'That's too bad.'

Pig Face pulled the car door wide open and propped his knee on the driver's seat. He reached across and grabbed the gun from her. He slung it out into the woods behind him. Then he held up his knife. The end of the blade was jagged and very unpleasant looking, much like Pig Face.

He grabbed Baby by the arm and dragged her across the driver's seat. 'You're coming with me,' he snarled.

He backed out of the car and glanced down to check that Joey was still incapacitated. Baby was unable to take advantage of the situation because she was stuck spread-eagled across the front seats. Pig Face hauled her out of the car. Her hands and chin brushed against the coarse, dirty woodland ground. Pig Face grabbed her by her hair and pulled her to her feet. He slammed her up against the car, straightening her up so he could get close and personal. Baby could smell his breath. It reeked of garlic. Out of the corner of her eye she saw his knife moving slowly up towards her throat.

'Now then,' he said, his face less than six inches away. His eyes were staring hard into hers, bulging with anger. 'You're gonna tell me your real name, or I'm….'

What happened next was really strange. His right eye, which looked slightly bigger than his left anyway, started getting bigger. *And bigger.* Or as Baby came to realise quite quickly, it was actually getting closer. But his left eye stayed where it was.

In the space of half a second Pig Face's right eye had lurched forward, right out of its eye socket. It stopped an inch from Baby's face, staring at her.

What the fuck?

His eye was poking out, stuck on the end of a thin piece of metal. For a fleeting moment, Baby considered the possibility that he was some kind of half man half robot, but then he fell sideways and collapsed on the floor in a heap.

That's when she realised that his eyeball was impaled on the end of a sharp arrow. The back end of the arrow was sticking out of the back of his skull.

Baby looked around the woods to see where the arrow had come from. It was so dark that it was difficult to see anything. And there wasn't time to stare hard at every branch or bush in the woods.

She heard Joey mumble something that sounded like *"Get in the car"*. But she ignored him because she had caught sight of someone moving within the dark shadows of the woodland. A ghostly figured dressed all in black moved silently between the trees. As he neared her, Baby saw that he was wearing a long black coat with the hood pulled up over his head. And he had a crossbow strapped across his back. It was the man she had seen coming out of the woods at Dead Man's Drop when she was on the back of Joey's motorcycle.

'Did my dad send you?' she asked nervously, when he was less than two metres away.

He ignored her and headed over to Joey instead. He bent down and moved Joey's face around with his hand, checking to see how bad his condition was.

Baby called out to him. *'Who are you?'*

The man stood up and grabbed the end of the arrow that was impaled in Pig Face's head. He yanked it out, which caused a yucky squelching sound that made Baby want to gag. Then he rolled Pig Face onto his back and rifled through his pockets, where he found a cell phone and a wallet.

'Who was that guy?' Baby asked him.

Again she received no response. The hooded man tucked Pig Face's phone and wallet into a pocket inside his coat.

Baby made another attempt to ignite some conversation, because the fact that this guy hadn't even acknowledged her was really creeping her out. 'He fired some darts into my friend,' she said. 'I think they might be poisonous. Can you help us?'

The man lowered his hood. She could just about make out his face in the dark. He was unshaven, with shoulder length dark hair and, well, he was *just nasty looking*.

On the floor, Joey stirred some more. 'Leave Baby alone,' he mumbled.

Baby ran around the hooded man and crouched down next to Joey. She stroked his face. 'Are you okay?' she asked.

He looked up at her, his eyes glazed over. 'Who's that guy?' he asked.

'I don't know,' Baby whispered. She looked back at the hooded man again. 'Who are you?' she repeated.

The man ignored her *again*. But this time he pointed at Joey and asked a question of his own. 'Where's his mask?' he said, his voice evoking a deep gravelly tone.

'I don't know what you mean,' Baby spluttered, bluffing for all she was worth.

The man pushed her away from Joey and pulled his crossbow from its holster on his back. He pressed his foot onto Joey's chest and aimed the crossbow at his face. 'Where's the mask?' he asked again, his voice even more determined this time.

Baby reacted without thinking. She dived onto Joey, placing herself in between his face and the end of the other man's crossbow. 'Don't kill him!' she screeched. *'Please!'*

There was a prolonged tomblike silence as the hooded man considered his options. Baby was risking her life to protect Joey. After a macabre delay he stopped aiming the crossbow at them and lifted it up. He slung it back over his shoulder into its holster and took his foot off Joey's chest.

'Without the mask, you're nothing,' he said.

And with that remark floating in the air, the hooded man stepped away and vanished back into the woodland, effortlessly blending in with the other shadows.

Baby rolled off of Joey. She spotted a dart still sticking out of his thigh. Normally she wouldn't have considered pulling it out, but after all that had just happened she had a huge burst of adrenaline. She reached down and tugged it hard, yanking it out. Joey winced.

'Is that all of them?' he asked.

'I think so.'

Joey's strength was returning. His immune system was fighting back, thanks in no small part to all the experiments carried out on him years earlier in the Blackwash operation. The drugs that had been tested on him as a youth had improved his immunity so much that he was flushing out the poison from the darts much quicker than any normal person would. Baby helped him up into a seated position and checked his back. She brushed a bunch of leaves and twigs off his vest and arms.

'I think that's all of them,' she said, noticing a couple of other darts on the ground that Joey had pulled out himself.

Joey looked across at the dead body of Pig Face. 'We need to get that fucking body out of here.'

'I really should tell my dad about all of this,' said Baby.

'That might not be possible,' said Joey. 'I mean doesn't it seem odd to you that you're almost two hours late and your father hasn't phoned?'

Baby felt a chill, as if a ghost had passed through her. 'Do you think something's happened to him then?'

'It's possible.' Joey stopped to think for a moment and concocted a plan very quickly. 'You still need an alibi,' he said. 'Is there a friend you can trust who lives nearby?'

'Just Jasmine, but she's staying in a motel with Jack Munson.'

'That's perfect.'

'It is?'

'Yeah. Tell Jack everything and tell him to meet me at ten a.m. tomorrow morning at the Olé au Lait.'

'Aren't you coming with me?'

Joey shook his head. 'I'm going to dispose of this dead body, then I'm gonna swing by your dad's house and see if he is there or not.'

He picked up Pig Face by his armpits and started dragging him towards the back of the car. 'Grab his feet, Baby. We gotta throw this guy in the trunk and then change the flat tyre.'

Baby grabbed Pig Face's feet and helped toss his body into the trunk. Joey then set about replacing the flat while Baby watched, impressed by his speed of thought.

'Will I see you tomorrow?' she asked.

'Yep. I'll pick you up from your rehearsal in the afternoon.'

'I'm not sure I want to go to the rehearsal now.'

'Baby, you *have to go*. The leading man in the show is dead and everyone knows you went out with him tonight. If you don't show, you're gonna look guilty as hell when they find his dead body.'

Twenty Three

Solomon Bennett was sitting behind the desk in his newly acquired office, drinking a glass of whiskey and flicking through the movie channels on the television trying to work out which film to watch. It was a tough choice between Weekend At Bernie's and The Revenant. He opted for Weekend At Bernie's and was enjoying it, but then right at the best bit where the characters go water-skiing he had a knock at the door. He paused the television and was about to shout, *"Come in"* at the door when it opened and Mozart walked in. He seemed troubled and it was clear that something important had come up because he looked like he'd just got out of bed. He was wearing nothing but a pair of blue boxer shorts and a white vest.

'What's up?' Bennett asked.

Mozart held his cell phone up. 'Something's gone wrong,' he said.

'What are you talking about?'

Mozart was momentarily distracted by the paused image of a dead guy water-skiing on the television. He stared at it for a second before shaking his head and then perching himself on the edge of Bennett's desk.

'I sent two men to Landingham Manor to check out the security around the perimeter, just like you asked,' he said.

'And?'

'And they're both dead.'

'What?'

'Check my phone.' Mozart handed Bennett his cell phone. 'They both texted me ten minutes ago to say they were dead.'

Bennett tried to make sense of what Mozart had just said. Dead men sending text messages? Was this a fancy new phone app that he hadn't heard of? One that texted your friends for you if you died?

'What the fuck are you talking about?' he snapped.

'Take a look for yourself,' said Mozart, pointing at the phone in Bennett's hand.

Bennett saw a text message from someone called Martin. It said simply –

I'M DEAD

'Who the hell is Martin?' he asked.

'He's the one who looks like Miss Piggy.'

'And he sent you this text?'

'I don't think so. I think the person who killed him sent it. Look at the next message from Logan.'

Bennett flicked to the next message. It was from Logan and it had three words, although the message was as clear as the one from Martin.

I'M DEAD TOO

'Have you tried calling them?' Bennett asked.

'Yeah. Both the phones are dead, probably destroyed by the person who sent the messages.'

'So do we have any idea who killed them? Assuming that they are actually dead, that is.'

Mozart shrugged. 'I've haven't had time to think about it. I came straight to you.'

Bennett tried to piece together what could have happened. The first thing he had to do was switch the television off, because the water-skiing dead guy was making it difficult to concentrate.

He voiced his thoughts out loud. 'Blake Jackson assured me that there would be no security people around the perimeter of the site. That fucking clown, he doesn't know his ass from his elbow.'

Bennett used Mozart's phone to call up Blake Jackson. Jackson took an eternity to answer and sounded like he was half asleep.

'Do you know what time it is?' he groaned.

'Fuck what time it is,' Bennett replied. 'I've just lost two men.'

'What are you talking about?'

'I sent two men to Landingham Manor to check out the surroundings for escape routes and stuff. Now Mozart's just had text messages from both of them saying they're dead. Someone's fucking with us! You said no one knew that the venue had been switched to Landingham Manor.'

'No one does know. Well, apart from me and Calhoon and the Pope's secretary.'

'Well then who the fuck is killing my men?'

The line went quiet while Jackson took some time to think things over. Eventually he came up with an answer. '*Joey Conrad.*'

Bennett scratched his head. 'What?'

'It's that motherfucker Devon Pincent. He's been one step ahead of us the whole time!'

Bennett exchanged a look with Mozart who could hear everything Jackson was saying on the other end of the line. Mozart didn't appear to have a clue what Jackson was ranting about either.

'What do you mean?' Bennett asked. 'We've got Pincent here. He couldn't have contacted Joey Conrad. We're not letting him use the phones you know!'

'Of course you're not. But it's classic Pincent,' said Jackson. 'He would have done this weeks ago.'

'How?'

'He knew that if we received a legitimate death threat to the Pope we would switch the venue to a contingency site. And I'll bet he knew the only place we could have moved to at short notice was Landingham Manor. And his old friend Dorothy Landingham would have been more than happy to tell him her manor was the contingency site for the event.'

Bennett rubbed his forehead. 'So what are you saying exactly?'

'I'm saying it was Devon who sent the death threat from the Red Mohawk. He fucking knew we would switch the venue to Landingham Manor. And he's got Joey Conrad or someone else there already, waiting to fuck up our plans!'

'Pincent sent the death threat?'

'Yep. Sneaky fucker.'

'Blake, when I asked you to keep a close eye on Pincent did you actually do anything?'

'It's not my fault,' Jackson protested. 'Maybe you should be doing a better job of getting him to talk. He's obviously got something up his sleeve to try and fuck up our plans.'

'I'll deal with Pincent,' said Bennett. 'He'll start talking soon enough.'

'He won't,' said Jackson. 'He's old school. Torturing him won't get you anywhere. A better idea would be to head to the School of Performing Arts tomorrow morning.'

'What for?'

'His daughter Baby is rehearsing there for the show Grease. You grab her and Devon will tell you everything you need to know. His daughter is his whole world these days.'

'Done.'

Bennett hung up the phone and handed it back to Mozart. 'Did you hear that?' he asked.

'Loud and clear,' said Mozart, sliding off the desk. 'The School of Performing Arts, tomorrow morning.'

Mozart walked towards the door to head back to his sleeping quarters. Bennett switched the television back on and was greeted by the sight of the freeze-framed dead guy once again. Before resuming the film he had a thought and called out to Mozart.

'I'm going to come with you to get Pincent's daughter tomorrow. And we'll take Frankenstein too. I don't want any more mistakes.'

Twenty Four

Sharkey's was the seediest bar in town. It stayed open all day and all night and it attracted the worst kinds of people. At ten o'clock in the morning some of the customers were asleep, some were just arriving and some were drunk and looking for a fight.

In the darkest corner of Sharkey's, Rodeo Rex, Elvis and the Bourbon Kid were sitting at a round wooden table. They were making a lot of noise that was attracting the attention of a few of the big time drinkers. Actually it was Rex who was making most of the noise. He'd taken his Stetson off for a change and was wearing a dark blue headband to keep his hair out of his eyes.

'You had a chance to kill the Red Mohawk and you passed it up?' he ranted, loud enough for half the bar to hear.

Rex's fury was directed at the Bourbon Kid who was sitting with his back to the wall smoking a cigarette. He was wearing a long black coat but he had the hood down for a change. And he had a glass of bourbon in front of him.

Elvis was sitting in between them. He was kitted out in a black leather suit, a replica of the Elvis Presley outfit from the '69 Comeback special.

'Let the Kid speak,' said Elvis. 'He must have had a good reason, right?'

The Kid shook his head. 'This Mohawk guy is not going to kill the Pope.'

'How do you fucking know if he's gonna kill the Pope or not?' Rex grumbled.

The Kid ran his index finger around the top of his glass of bourbon. He looked like he'd been drinking for three days solid and he was visibly in need of a shave and a shower. His normal two-day-old stubble had stretched to something more like five-days-old.

He looked Rex in the eye. 'He's not some crazy demonic monster like the Mystic Lady said. He's just an ordinary dude who wears a mask, but when I found him he wasn't even wearing it. This guy couldn't be more average if he tried.'

Rex picked up a bottle of beer from the table. 'He still killed hundreds of people for no good reason. He'll kill *hundreds more*. You coulda finished him off, and saved a lot of lives.'

'Like I told you just now, there were other people trying to kill him.'

'Yeah, yeah, and you killed them both. Good for you.'

'They were ex-military.'

'So fuckin' what! Not only did you *not* kill the Red Mohawk, but you killed two ex-military folks who would have done it for you! I'm telling you, the boss is gonna be real fuckin' pissed when he finds out about this.'

'I don't care.'

'Well you fuckin' should.'

The Kid blew some cigarette smoke out through his nostrils. 'What have you two found out from following Jack Munson?'

'Not a lot,' said Rex. 'Him and his girlfriend Jasmine don't do anything interesting.'

Elvis had been listening intently to the conversation but there was one thing he hadn't quite understood. 'You said the two people you killed last night were ex-military.'

The Kid nodded. 'Uh huh.'

'Why ex-military? Surely the real military should be after this guy?'

'That's why I think this Red Mohawk is like us.'

'What do you mean, like us?' Rex asked, frowning.

'He's a vigilante. I found him by following the girl he rescued from B Movie Hell, and I'm telling you, that girl would die for him. The people trying to kill him, they were mercenaries not government soldiers or cops. They're the ones planning on killing the Pope.'

Rex scowled. 'I need to see this Red Mohawk fella for myself, and if I think there's anything not right about him, I'm taking him down.'

'Good for you,' said the Kid. 'I'm staying here. I've got some other shit to figure out.'

'Like what?'

'I want to find out who Mozart is.'

Elvis was in the middle of taking a sip from a bottle of *Shitting Monkey* beer. He spat half of it out and put the beer down on the table. 'I know who Mozart is,' he said.

Rex and the Kid both looked at him and waited for him to explain. Elvis used his jacket sleeve to wipe some stray beer spit from his face before continuing.

'Mozart was a German composer. Did some real good stuff, hundreds of years ago.'

'That's not who I meant.'

'Maybe you were thinking of Beethoven?' Elvis suggested.

The Kid ignored Elvis. 'The two guys I killed, I checked their cell phones. They both had just one contact, someone called Mozart. I think he works for a catering company, so I'm going to check that out.'

Rex downed the rest of his beer and put the bottle back down on the table. 'That sounds like a major waste of fucking time,' he said. 'I'm going after this Red Mohawk fella. You got any idea where he's gonna be today?'

The Kid picked up his glass of bourbon. 'Nope,' he said. 'But his girlfriend will be at the School of Performing Arts. She goes there every day for rehearsal.'

'Rehearsal for what?'

'She's Sandy in Grease.'

Rex slapped Elvis across the chest. 'Come on. Let's go find ourselves a Red Mohawk.'

As the two of them got up to leave, the Kid tapped Elvis on the wrist. 'Hey, Elvis, do me a favour,' he said.

'Sure. What?'

The Kid nodded towards the bar. 'There's a guy over there in a red shirt.'

Elvis looked around and saw a mean looking fucker in his late twenties leaning against the bar, staring over at them. He had the physique of a bodybuilder, and he was wearing a skimpy red vest to show off his muscles. His head was shaved almost down to the bone and he had a whole host of jailhouse tattoos on his arms.

'What about him?' said Elvis.

'He keeps staring at me.'

'So?'

'So on your way out, tell him I don't like him.'

The Kid downed his glass of bourbon in one and slammed the empty glass back down on the table.

Rex tugged at Elvis's sleeve. 'Come on let's go,' he said.

Elvis grabbed his half full bottle of *Shitting Monkey* and followed Rex over to the exit. As they passed the big guy in the red vest, Elvis stopped. He whispered in the man's ear. 'See my friend over there in the corner? He says you're a fag.'

The man in the red vest took a moment to digest what Elvis had said. As soon it sunk in he jumped up from his stool and stormed over to the corner table to confront the Bourbon Kid.

Elvis and Rex headed out of the bar and into the street. It was still mid morning. The light outside was dazzling after being inside the dark and dingy premises of Sharkey's. Rex's chopped Harley was parked out front on the sidewalk. Elvis's purple Cadillac was fifty yards down the street.

'I'm gonna head straight to the School of Performing Arts,' said Rex, climbing onto his bike. 'You wanna meet me there?'

Elvis shook his head. 'I'm hung over. I'm gonna finish this beer and get some sleep.'

Rex gave him a disapproving look. 'At least make yourself useful and stake out Jack Munson's motel room. See if he does anything interesting.'

Elvis reached into the breast pocket on his jacket. He pulled out his sunglasses and slipped them on. 'See ya around,' he said.

Rex started up his Harley, revved the engine a few times and then rode off down the middle of the street in heavy traffic. Elvis walked on down the sidewalk towards his car, pausing only momentarily to avoid being hit by the flying body of a big bald guy in a red vest who came crashing through a sheet glass window on the side of Sharkey's bar.

On his way to the motel to spy on Jack Munson's apartment, Elvis stopped off and bought a six-pack of *Shitting Monkey* beer. If he'd known what was going to happen at Munson's place later that day, he probably would have had a coffee instead.

Twenty Five

Jack Munson's plans for a quiet life and an early retirement spent with Jasmine had to be put on hold for a while. Just when it looked like his days working on dangerous life-threatening cases were over, he'd had a knock at the door in the middle of the night. He'd been sleeping alongside Jasmine in the local Bates Motel when Baby woke them up. She was deeply upset about something and it had taken about ten minutes just to calm her down so that she could tell them what she was so distressed about. And naturally, it involved some dead bodies and the return of the Red Mohawk. There was also the possibility that her father was missing too.

In the morning Jack kept a promise to Baby headed to the Olé au Lait to meet Joey Conrad. The traffic was a lot busier than he would have liked. So by the time he arrived at the Olé au Lait it was ten past ten. His back was aching and his neck was stiff. Sleeping on a sofa, no matter how comfortable, was no substitute for a good bed.

The Olé au Lait was a coffee shop that also doubled up as a café that served fried breakfasts. It was part of a chain that had sprung up in recent times and was rapidly spreading its way across America. When Jack walked through the door, he spotted Joey sitting at a table in the corner. Joey blended in well, considering he was a psychopath. He was wearing a pair of blue jeans and a black sleeveless vest. His dark hair was ruffled and his face unshaven. In general he had a rumpled look about him, but there was nothing at first glance that screamed "Serial killer" at you. Unless you happened to notice the red leather jacket on the back of his chair, which had a screwed up Red Mohawk mask concealed inside one of the pockets.

There were only about fifteen tables in the Olé au Lait and half of them were empty. Those that were occupied generally had one or two people sitting at them, tapping away on laptops, pretending they were writers, or gossiping about some local scandal. No one paid Jack any attention and no one seemed to have noticed Joey sitting in the corner either.

Jack made his way to Joey's table and pulled out the chair opposite him.

'You're ten minutes late,' said Joey.

Jack sat down. 'I didn't get a great night's sleep,' he grumbled.

'I thought maybe you'd had a power cut or something.'

Joey had always been like this. Awkward to talk to because you never knew when he was being serious, or joking, or hinting at something, or just plain being weird.

'Why would I have had a power cut?' Jack asked, knowing the answer might make no sense.

'I just figured you got dressed in the dark. Otherwise, what's the deal with that shirt?'

The shirt Joey was so rudely referring to, was a thick pink cotton short sleeved shirt that Jasmine had picked out for Jack on a shopping spree the day before. Now that they were back in the USA, Jack and Jasmine needed new clothes. Jasmine in particular required some "non hooker" outfits if she was going to fit in at social functions. So Jack had taken her out and spoilt her by buying her about a thousand dollars worth of new clothes on his credit card. In return she had insisted on treating him to an entirely new image by buying him a bunch of new outfits too, also paid for on his credit card. As such, Jack was now wearing a pink shirt and a pair of ripped blue jeans. Ideal for a man of his age, with a partner of *her* age.

'Jasmine bought me some new clothes,' he said, not feeling the need to over-explain the situation.

'You must like her a lot.'

'Did we come here to talk about my clothes, or was there something important you wanted to discuss with me?'

Joey had a mug of steaming hot coffee in front of him. He picked it up and took a sip. 'So, did Baby tell you about last night?'

'Yeah. When she turned up at the motel she was absolutely hysterical.'

'Yeah, she's pretty funny, isn't she?'

'No, I mean she was stressed out, not funny.'

'Oh. Is she okay now?'

A waitress appeared at Jack's shoulder. 'Can I get you anything, sir?' she asked, holding a pen and notepad at the ready.

'Coffee, black, no sugar, thanks.'

'Anything else?'

'No.'

Jack waited for the waitress to fuck off before responding to Joey's question about Baby's wellbeing.

'She seems fine. She's gone off to her Grease rehearsal this morning, just like you told her to. Jasmine's gone with her to make sure she gets there okay.'

Joey seemed to relax a little upon hearing that Baby was okay. 'Did you get in touch with Devon?' he asked. 'I thought he might know who these guys were that were after me.'

Jack shook his head. 'I can't get hold of him. I drove by his place on the way here and no one is home. I think something might have happened to him.'

'Like what?'

'I gave him some information when I got back from Romania. He was going to show it to someone in the Agency. Something big was going to go down. But I'm wondering if some people got to him first.'

'What people?'

'Solomon Bennett is back in town.'

Joey's face switched into a mode that Jack recognised as "psycho-mode" meaning he was liable to do something crazy. Fortunately, the moment passed and he seemed to regain his composure and self control very quickly, a sign that he had matured a little since the days of Operation Blackwash.

'Why didn't I know about this?' Joey asked.

The waitress arrived back at Jack's shoulder with an unsavoury looking white mug of coffee. She placed it down on the table, gave Jack a quick fake smile and then thankfully she fucked off again.

'I was wondering that myself,' said Jack. He picked up his coffee and sniffed it before placing it back down on the table. 'There had been some unofficial sightings of Bennett in Romania, which is why Devon sent me to see if I could confirm it. But that's not the half of it. Frank Grealish was there too, and that freaky idiot who calls himself Dr Jekyll.'

'I thought Frank Grealish was dead?'

'We all did.'

'So what happened with him then? Did he fake his death, or what?'

Jack shook his head. 'I really don't know. I mean, I saw him die, but he's definitely alive now. There's something weird about it too because he's still got the metal bolts in his neck that were fitted to him before they tried to make him bulletproof.'

'Bulletproof,' Joey snorted a laugh. 'Who seriously thought they could make him bulletproof? What a dumb fucking idea.'

'It wasn't me,' said Jack. He pulled out his cell phone. 'Look, there's the proof.' He showed Joey a photo of Frank Grealish. 'I gave Devon copies of these photos. He was going to show them to someone in Phantom Ops, but ever since I gave them to him, he's gone quiet. He's not returning my calls or texts.'

'Maybe he's gone dark. You know Devon, he's always a step ahead of the game.'

'True.' Jack picked up his coffee and took a sip. It tasted pretty good, even though it was probably strong enough to wake the dead. 'So, Baby said some weirdo showed up and killed a man who attacked you last night. Is that right?'

'Yeah. It was bizarre. I don't know what the fuck it was all about.'

'I think I might have an idea.'

'Well please enlighten me because I haven't got a fucking clue.'

'From the description Baby gave me, it sounds like you met the Bourbon Kid.'

'Who the fuck is the Bourbon Kid?'

'Serial killer, all round bad guy, basically someone you don't want on your ass. I think he was hired to kill you, and I'm not sure why he didn't. That part doesn't make sense.'

'None of it makes any fucking sense, Jack.'

'I met him and two other guys on the flight back from Romania. They were told that you were going to kill the Pope. They knew about it before it became front page news.' Mentioning the Pope assassination plot interrupted Jack's train of thought for a moment. 'You're not *really* trying to kill the Pope are you?' he asked.

'Why the fuck would I want to kill the Pope?'

'Keep your voice down.'

Jack scratched his head and looked around. None of the other customers or the waitress seemed to be listening in on their conversation.

'It's all over the newspapers,' he said, lowering his voice to just above a whisper. 'Everyone seems to think you're going to kill the Pope. Why is that?'

'I don't know. Honest.'

Jack took a sip of his coffee and pondered the Pope situation. The coffee, as always, kicked his brain into gear. The ideas started flowing like fine wine.

'Someone must be trying to frame you. I bet there's a plot to kill the Pope, and when it happens, you'll be blamed.'

'Did Devon know anything about it?'

Jack held his hands up, palms open. 'I don't know. He didn't tell me anything. I guess he didn't want to involve me. You know Devon. He keeps his secrets close to his chest. Last year he didn't even tell me he'd sent you to B Movie Hell to rescue Baby. I had to work that one out for myself while I was looking for you.'

Joey took a sip of his own coffee. He had a robotic, vacant stare about him that meant he could pick up his coffee mug and drink from it without even looking at it, almost as if he didn't know he was doing it.

'Devon hasn't been in touch with me for over a week either,' he said, placing the mug back down on the table, but then picking it back up and taking another swig straight away. 'He set me up in this weird imitation batcave under Landingham Manor and told me to wait for him to get in touch.'

'You're staying in the bunker under Landingham Manor?'

'Yeah. Didn't Baby tell you?'

'No, she's like her father, keeps quiet about the important stuff. She just said you'd gone out for a drive together.'

Joey reached up with both hands and tugged at his hair, arching his back and stretching at the same time. 'So then how did these people know where to find me last night? Who told them?'

'It wouldn't be Devon. He wouldn't give you up under any circumstances. Maybe someone was following you?'

'I would know if someone was following me.'

'Then maybe they were following Baby?' Ideas and theories were racing around in Jack's head. 'You should go and get her back from her Grease rehearsal. Talking of which,' he lowered his voice even further, 'did you *really* throw Danny Zuco off a cliff?'

'That's a whole other story, Jack.'

'Fair enough. But from now on, keep your wits about you.'

'Same goes for you, Jack.' Joey stood up and slipped his arms into the sleeves of his red leather jacket. 'I'll go and get Baby and maybe we'll swing by your place later.'

'Okay. I'm gonna grab some takeaway food and head back to the motel. Keep your head down. And if you suspect anyone is following you, give me a call.'

Twenty Six

A white van had been parked in the street opposite the School of Performing Arts for much of the morning. Inside it three men were watching and waiting for the arrival of Baby. Solomon Bennett was sitting behind the wheel with Mozart in the passenger seat next to him. Behind them, concealed from view in the back of the van was Frank Grealish, a man best consigned to the shadows out of view where his appearance wouldn't draw the attention of any cops.

'I told you,' Mozart complained. 'She knows we're after her. Whoever killed our people and sent me those texts last night could have warned her. I think it's dangerous for us to be hanging around here. It could be a trap.'

Bennett felt something crawling on his neck. He smacked it with an open hand and then inspected his fingers. He had killed a fly. He wiped its remains on the dashboard and returned his focus to staring at the front entrance of the school. Students were frequently making their way up and down the concrete steps at the front. Occasionally a passing bus would block the view from the van for a short time, but Bennett was quietly confident that they hadn't missed Baby going in.

'You're being paranoid,' he said to Mozart, in response to his fears about a trap.

'Am I?'

'Yes.'

'Does anyone else think I'm paranoid?'

'No.'

'You're just saying that, aren't you?'

'Shut up a second. I think I just saw a girl that looked like Pincent's daughter.'

'Where?'

'She just walked behind that bus.'

The two of them spent the next few seconds craning their necks trying to get a view over or around the bus. Eventually it pulled out into the street and they were able to get a good view of the entrance to the school. Standing on the top step was a girl wearing a red and white striped sleeveless top and a pair of three-quarter length jeans. She had wavy brown hair and looked like a perfect match for the girl they had only ever seen photos of before.

'See,' said Bennett, 'there she is. Dumb bitch.'

Baby didn't go straight into the school. She stopped and blew a kiss to someone at the bottom of the steps. Someone Bennett recognised even though she had her back to him. The skin-tight leopard print outfit was a dead giveaway.

Mozart grabbed Bennett by the arm. 'Fuck me,' he whispered. 'It's fucking Jasmine!'

Bennett could hardly believe it. 'What the fuck is she doing here with Pincent's daughter?'

'Because she's a fucking spy!' said Mozart. 'I knew it was fucking weird that there was an American hooker hanging around your base in Romania. How did no one ever suspect she was spying on you?'

Bennett was furious, with himself as much as anything. 'She must be the one who told Pincent everything. Goddamn it, I remember she used to ask a lot of questions about what we were doing.'

'And you never suspected she was a spy?'

Bennett rubbed his forehead in frustration. 'That girl was too damned stupid to be a spy. Pincent would never hire someone that dumb.'

'Well maybe she plays dumb. Spies can often be very good actors you know.'

'I'm aware of that,' said Bennett. 'But generally spies don't lick your asshole while they're jerking you off.'

Mozart stared at Bennett, unsure how to respond to the revelation that Jasmine had given him some trombone treatment. Bennett picked up on his disapproving look and backtracked pretty quickly.

'That was someone else that she did that to. I was just in the room at the time.'

'Even so,' said Mozart. 'Your guys shouldn't have been talking to her about business. I made a point of not telling her anything, even while she was tea-bagging me.'

Bennett ignored Mozart and turned his attention back to the front of the school. Baby had gone in but Jasmine was making her way back down the street without a care in the world. Bennett kept his one good eye focussed on her ass and slapped Mozart across the chest with his hand.

'I want you to follow her and see where she goes. She might not have been the only person spying on us in Romania,' he said. 'See where she takes you and give Denise a call before you do anything.'

'Why Denise?'

'She's good at interrogating women. I don't want you cutting Jasmine's face off until she's told us who she's working for and how many people she's talked to.'

'But I can kill her when we're done questioning her, yeah?'

'When Denise says so. Now go, before you lose her in the crowd.'

It would actually be pretty difficult to lose Jasmine, even in a crowd of thousands. Bennett watched her doing a weird dance as she walked along the sidewalk on the other side of the street and wondered just how she had duped him and his men in Romania. She'd played dumb, but she'd been so good at it. *Too good.* Being outwitted by someone so stupid was infuriating. And the thought that she had only licked his butt to get information from him made him feel cheap. He consoled himself in the knowledge that Denise and Mozart would make her pay for what she'd done.

Mozart jumped out of the van and started following Jasmine down the street, keeping a safe distance to avoid being spotted.

Bennett shouted to Frankenstein in the back of the van. 'It's time to go to work. Go and grab Pincent's daughter from the school. I'll meet you in the parking lot round the back.'

Twenty Seven

Baby arrived for her Grease rehearsal thirty minutes late. In truth she didn't want to be there at all. She had far too much on her mind, like what she would have to tell everyone about her ill-fated date with Jason Moxy, and more importantly she was concerned about her father's sudden radio silence.

In the main hall the rehearsal was already underway. The producer, Camberwick Bender was standing in the middle of the hall in a garish green sweater and a pair of cream coloured trousers, waving a cane around in the air, signalling to the actors like an orchestra conductor. All of the main cast members (apart from Jason Moxy) were there, standing in pairs in front of Camberwick and were doing their best to carry out the dance moves. A team of background dancers were supporting them in the scene, which was the important *High School dance sequence.*

As soon as Camberwick saw Baby walk into the hall he threw his cane down onto the floor and yelled, *"CUT!"*

Everyone stopped what they were doing and turned to look at Baby.

'Baby, you're late!' Camberwick yelled. 'And where's Jason?'

'I'm sorry,' said Baby. 'I was ill this morning. And I have no idea where Jason is.'

'No idea where Jason is!' Camberwick repeated in a poor impersonation of Baby. 'Pah, I'm trying to put on a Grease stage show but neither of my leads thinks it's important to show up on time. This isn't *Sunset Boulevard* you know!'

Camberwick put his hands on his hips in a double teapot pose and stamped his foot on the floor. Baby wasn't sure if she was supposed to say anything else and she was completely baffled by the *Sunset Boulevard* remark, which appeared to have no relevance to anything. Or did it?

'Well don't just stand there!' Camberwick yelled at her. 'Get into your position. We haven't got all day.' He turned to the others and clapped his hands together. 'Come on people, we go again. No time to waste.'

Baby hurried over to the front row of performers and took up her place in the line up. One of the male backing dancers was chosen to step up and fill in for Jason Moxy as Baby's dance partner. He was a strong, handsome guy but Baby could see in his eyes that he was nervous about filling in for the male lead. He seemed to be concentrating solely on remembering all the dance steps and wasn't in the least bit interested in working on any chemistry with her. She grabbed both his hands and entwined her fingers in his, ready for the music to start. As soon as everyone was in position, Camberwick switched on a shitty old silver ghetto blaster that he insisted on using during rehearsal. The song *Born To Hand Jive* by the *Na Na Na's* started blaring out.

Baby knew the moves pretty well. Concentrating on not screwing up was the perfect way to clear her mind of everything else that was going on in her life.

Unfortunately, half way through the scene, Camberwick yelled *"CUT!"* again at the top of his voice and turned off the music. He threw his cane down on the floor and put his hands on his hips again just so everyone would know he was in a huff. He was looking at someone behind Baby. She turned to see who had shown up late this time and was greeted by the sight of a giant man dressed in black and wearing goggles. He looked exactly like Frankenstein's monster. And rather alarmingly he had a holster hanging off his hip with a gun handle poking out of it.

'Who are you?' Camberwick yelled at him.

Frankenstein ignored him. He looked around the room, his head swivelling from side to side, slowly. Eventually he stopped and stared right at Baby. His goggled eyes locked in on her and he walked towards her with a real sense of purpose. Baby looked around to see if there was someone else nearby that he might have been looking at. But it became clear she was his target when he stopped in front of her and grabbed her by the arm.

'You're coming with me,' he said in a monotone voice.

His grip was unnecessarily firm. Baby slapped his hand in the hope he would release her, but he didn't.

Camberwick spoke up on her behalf. 'Will somebody tell this clown that the *Young Frankenstein* show isn't for another month!'

Frankenstein turned his head slowly and stared at Camberwick in a manner that suggested he didn't take too kindly to being called a clown. That was confirmed when with his free hand he reached down to his side and pulled the handgun from its holster on his hip. His movements were slow and robotic. He pointed the gun at Camberwick.

Camberwick raised his hands above his head. 'Don't shoot, I was just kidding when I called you a clown. I'm sure you're a very fine actor.'

Frankenstein either didn't hear the apology or wasn't impressed by it, because he squeezed the trigger on his gun. It made a low-key *bang* and a bullet flew out of the barrel and hit Camberwick in the chest. A patch of thick, crimson blood appeared in the middle of his green sweater. His jaw dropped open and he looked stunned as the realisation he had been shot struck him as hard as the bullet had done. He staggered back a step then toppled over, landing flat on his back staring up at the ceiling, gasping for breath as his life ebbed away.

That was the cue for everyone else in the room to shit their pants. One of the male dancers squealed like a dying pig, and then everyone started running for the exits, crying and screaming. *Everyone except Baby.* She couldn't move because Frankenstein had a vice like grip on her arm. He replaced his gun in its holster and pulled her closer to him.

'You're coming with me, or you die next,' he said in his dull voice.

Baby tried to struggle. 'What do you want from me?'

Frankenstein ignored her. He leant down and before she knew what was happening he had thrown her over his shoulder. She was staring down at the floor, disoriented and confused. He kept one of his giant arms wrapped around her thighs and carried her off towards the exit at the back of the hall. Baby clenched her fists and tried to punch him as hard as she could in the back. But punching someone when you're dangling upside down is surprisingly hard to do. She couldn't muster any strength, and even if she could it wouldn't have made any difference to Frankenstein.

'Put me down!' she screamed.

Frankenstein ignored her and carried on towards the exit. All Baby could see was the wooden floor and the back of his legs, which were like tree trunks. Suddenly all of the other actors and dancers were gone, their voices a distant echo as they vacated the school at high speed.

But then suddenly a man's voice bellowed out above everything else. Baby wasn't sure exactly where it came from, but it was loud and evoked a degree of authority.

'Put the girl down and drop the gun, *asshole.*'

Frankenstein stopped in his tracks and Baby braced herself for the possibility that she might be dropped onto the floor. From her upside down position she managed to crane her neck to look around for the owner of the voice.

She spotted him at the end of the hall, standing in front of a set of double doors. He was dressed from head to toe in blue denim, with brown cowboy boots and a head of wavy brown hair that was held in by a Harley Davidson headband. His left hand was teetering next to a gun that was holstered on his hip.

'Who are you?' Frankenstein inquired in his leaden tone.

'I'm Rodeo Rex,' the other man replied. 'Who the fuck are you?'

Frankenstein's response was emphatic. He'd obviously learned about gunfights at the school of *"Shoot first"*. Before Rex had a chance to reach for his six-shooter, Frankenstein whipped out his pistol, aimed it at Rex's heart and shot him three times.

Twenty Eight

Jasmine arrived back at her motel room and changed into some sexy underwear in readiness for spending the afternoon indoors with Jack. She wrapped herself up in her favourite pink dressing gown to cover up the silky black undergarments and settled down on the sofa in the front room. She had recently picked up a new DVD box set from a second hand store and was eager to catch up on her favourite TV show.

She was eating a tub of popcorn and watching the opening credits for the first episode when she got a call from Jack on her cell phone.

'Hi honey,' she said.

'Hey Jaz, what's that noise?'

She found the remote and muted the television. 'It was the TV. I was just catching up on the latest episode of *Săpun Gunoi.*'

'What the hell is that?'

'You know that Romanian soap that we watched while we were in Bucharest? I found it on DVD in a second hand store round the corner.'

There was a pause as Jack took the information on board. 'You don't even understand what they're saying on that show. And you're back in America now, remember? You can watch American TV!'

'Yeah, but I wanted to know who killed the blonde woman's husband.'

She heard Jack let out a deep sigh. 'When you work out who it is, let me know, but then we're not watching that show any more, okay?'

'Okay. It's getting good though.'

'Of course it is. Look I'm on my way home. I'm going to stop and get some Chinese food. Is there anything in particular you want?'

Jasmine thought hard. 'Umm, can you get me something with rice?'

'Something with rice? Like what?'

'I don't know. French fries?'

'French fries, right, of course. I'll grab a bunch of other things too, just in case. See you in a bit.'

'Okay sweetie. Love you!'

'Love you too. Bye.'

Jasmine hung up the phone and turned the volume back up on the television. She only watched another five minutes of *Săpun Gunoi* before there was a knock on the door of her motel room. A female voice called through the door.

'Room service!'

Jasmine jumped up from the sofa and dashed over to the door. She hadn't ordered any room service but if they'd brought some chocolate she figured she'd take it. When she pulled the door open she saw a face she recognised. It was Denise, a bisexual Jon Voigt lookalike from Romania. Denise was wearing blue jeans and a red sweater, not the sort of uniform Jasmine expected to see on an employee of the motel.

'Denise, hi!' she said, pretending to be pleased to see her. 'When did you start working here?'

Denise didn't reply, instead she barged her way into the apartment and shoved her hand into Jasmine's face, pushing her back as far out of sight of the open door as possible.

Jasmine staggered back unsteadily, but managed not to fall over. 'What do you want?' she asked.

Denise didn't need to reply. Jasmine already knew it was bad news and this was confirmed when a man wearing combat pants and a black vest appeared in the doorway. She recognised him straight away. It was Mozart, Solomon Bennett's deeply unpleasant sidekick.

'Hello Jasmine,' he said softly as he shut the door behind him.

'Hi.'

Mozart walked over to the television and switched it off. He pointed at the sofa. 'Sit down,' he said firmly.

Jasmine did as she was told and sat on the sofa before Mozart had to ask her a second time. She wrapped her dressing gown a little tighter around her chest to avoid showing off too much flesh.

'What do you want?' she asked.

Mozart reached behind his back and pulled out a pistol that was tucked inside his pants. He rubbed the barrel with his fingers as if he was polishing it. 'I want to know who you've been talking to.'

'I talk to lots of people. You know me, I'm a regular chatterbox. This one time, I was stuck in a place called Monkey World and there was this big orang-utan....'

Mozart nodded at Denise and she reacted swiftly. She grabbed Jasmine by the collar of her dressing gown and hauled her up off the sofa. She ripped the dressing gown open and took a look at what Jasmine had on underneath.

'Do you mind?' said Jasmine.

Denise slapped her across the face with the back of her hand. She had fat fingers and unusually large knuckles so the slap practically

156

doubled as a punch. It had enough force to knock Jasmine back down onto the sofa with her dressing gown wide open and looking more like a superhero's cape.

'OW!' Jasmine squealed and rubbed her cheek. She considered retaliating. The opportunity to punch Denise in the crotch had presented itself, but with Mozart in the room brandishing a gun, she wisely refrained from the cunt-punch.

Mozart cleared his throat and took a long lingering look at Jasmine's body. 'Now Jasmine,' he said. 'In case you didn't know, Denise here is a specialist in violence against women. She enjoys it almost as much as she enjoys beating up men, and she enjoys *that* a lot. I have bruised testicles to prove it. They're like great big blue plums. Maybe I'll show them to you later. But here's the thing Jasmine, I enjoy it when Denise tortures me. I'm kind of weird like that, I get a real kick out of it. But *you*, I don't think you'll like it so much. And Denise, she actually gets off on hearing her victims scream in pain. In fact, you know what? I'd like to hear you scream out in pain too.'

'So play some Barry Manilow tunes,' said Jasmine, tiring of his long-winded speech.

Mozart slapped her hard across the face. It knocked her sideways and her face thudded into a cushion. She wrapped her gown around herself again, fearing that Mozart might be getting a little worked up at the sight of her underwear, which was intended for Jack's benefit, no one else's.

'So,' Mozart continued, his composure regained after the unexpected slap. 'When you were dishing out blow jobs and God knows what else to the men in Bucharest, did any of them tell you what I'm renowned for?'

Jasmine stared at the floor. 'No,' she mumbled.

'Well, most people know me as the man of many faces, that's how the press liked to label me, and it seemed to stick. But my real talent, what my friends know me for....'

'You have friends?' said Jasmine, foolishly goading him.

'*Denise.*'

At the mention of her name, Denise smashed Jasmine across the face again with the back of her hand. This one hurt way more than the last and Jasmine decided not to make any more provocative remarks.

'As I was saying,' said Mozart, 'My friends know me for my ability to sniff out a lie. They call me *The Polygraph*, which in case you weren't aware is a type of lie detector machine. I'm sure you're thinking to yourself, that it's a shit name, and I would be inclined to agree with you, but it is a very appropriate nickname, because I have a gift. I can sniff out a lie before it's even spoken. There are a great many facial ticks that humans display when they are about to tell a lie and I know them all, from the simple ones like scratching your nose, to the more complex efforts of a seasoned liar. So next time I ask you a question and you decide to pretend you don't know what I'm talking about, just think about this, your body language will give you away. Pretending you don't know what I'm talking about when you do, is just another way of telling a lie, and lies disappoint me. Next time you disappoint me I will give Denise a little nod of the head, like this.' He nodded at Denise. 'And when I do that, Denise will drag you up from the sofa. She will remove your clothes, and then while you're standing there naked in front of me, she will begin to slice off parts of your body. Denise has a real talent for this too, because where I tend to go straight for the face and take the whole thing off, she will go for some of the more sensitive parts of the body, the parts that feel the most pain. She's a real *Michelangelo* when it comes to blood-work and scars, aren't you Denise?'

Denise sneered at Jasmine. 'I can keep you alive for days in unbearable pain, if I have to.'

Denise had a large hunting knife in a sheath strapped to her hip. Jasmine hadn't noticed it before, but the sight of it made her swallow hard. She felt a tear begin to well up in her eye, but she shook it off. There was no way she was going to let these two freaks know they had intimidated her.

Mozart crouched down and looked Jasmine in the eye. 'Do you understand what I'm saying here, Jasmine? Because I wouldn't want you to complain later on that you weren't clear on the rules of this game. Tell a lie, or even think about telling a lie and I nod at Denise, okay?'

Jasmine nodded.

'Good. Now let's begin.'

Twenty Nine

Rodeo Rex had encountered some big dudes in his time and Frankenstein was certainly the biggest he'd seen in a long while. When he spotted the metal bolts sticking out of Frankenstein's neck he figured either he was an actor in costume, or he was a psycho with a penchant for unusual body piercings. Either way, he was the cause of all the gunfire and the screaming hoards of people fleeing from the School of Performing Arts. And he had a girl slung over his shoulder. The girl Rex had come looking for.

'Who are you?' Frankenstein asked.

'I'm Rodeo Rex. Who the fuck are you?'

Frankenstein's response was rude to say the least. He whipped out a gun, aimed it at Rex's heart and fired three times.

BANG!

BANG!

BANG!

Any normal man would have been killed instantly. But Rex was no normal man. He had a magnetic right hand. He held it up in front of his chest and all three bullets diverted from their trajectory, landing perfectly in his gloved palm. He opened his fingers and dropped the bullets onto the wooden floor. They landed with a clatter and rolled away in different directions.

'Didn't see that one coming, did ya?' he said, pulling his own gun from its holster on his hip.

Frankenstein lowered Baby off his shoulder and dropped her onto the floor. She landed face first, her head smashing into the hard wood. The rest of her body rolled over the top of her and she ended up on her back, dazed and staring up at the ceiling.

Frankenstein took aim and fired unremittingly at Rex again until his clip was empty. This guy was a moron, every bit as dumb as he looked. Incapable it seemed, of learning from his mistakes.

Rex once again caught all of the bullets in his magnetic hand. Frankenstein's continued firing empties for a while, looking confused as if he was incapable of understanding why Rex was still on his feet. Rex dropped the latest batch of bullets onto the floor, one by one this time for dramatic effect. All in all, eight rounds hit the floor and rolled away.

'Thanks, dipshit,' said Rex. 'Now it's my turn!'

He took aim with his six-shooter, lining it up with Frankenstein's chest, which was a very substantial target. He fired off three shots in quick succession, just like Frankenstein had done when he chose to shoot first. Each bullet hit Frankenstein in the centre of his chest, but the impact of each shot only knocked him back a step. Not one of them pierced his skin. They went through his grey T-shirt just fine, creating tiny ripped holes so Rex knew he hadn't missed. But the bullets bounced right off their target.

Rex muttered to himself under his breath. *'What the fuck?'*

In all his years of shooting people, Rex had never come across anyone that could withstand a bullet. He'd met a few who could stay on their feet for a while, but they all had holes in them, and they all bled. This guy didn't even have a dent in him. *What the fuck, indeed.*

Frankenstein didn't like being shot at any more than Rex did. He shrugged off the attack and steadied himself. He tossed his empty gun to the floor, arched his shoulders back and started walking towards Rex.

Rex (blissfully unaware of the irony) fired his last three bullets at Frankenstein. The first two hit him in the chest again, and when they had no effect, he fired the last one at his head in the hope of finding a weak spot. And he quickly discovered that there wasn't one. Every single bullet that hit his adversary served only to knock him back a step.

Rex sighed and slid his gun back in its holster.

'Fair enough,' he said. 'Fist fight it is then.'

Now Rex was no slouch when it came to a fistfight. He'd been a bareknuckle fighter for many years, earning a perfectly good living that way when there was no other work available. One of his strengths was working out his opponent's weaknesses. He had a keen eye for any flaw in an enemy's technique, or a physical defect.

Frankenstein lurched towards him like an angry rhino. Rex knew immediately that he had the beating of the big lug because Frankenstein was rigid, heavy footed and attacked head on, a common mistake made by big guys. Something most of Rex's opponents over the years had failed to realise was that in spite of Rex being a big fellow, he was deceptively quick and had the flexibility of a ballerina, not that he would appreciate anyone suggesting he had anything in common with men who danced around in tights.

Rex raised his fists and waited for Frankenstein to get close. When they were just a metre apart Frankenstein reached out with both hands and lunged at Rex's neck. Rex ducked back and moved with ease to one side, looking like he was in fast-forward compared to his opponent. Before Frankenstein even realised he was clutching at thin air, Rex threw an almighty uppercut with his metal hand.

CLANK!

The punch registered perfectly on Frankenstein's jaw. It jarred the giant oaf's head right back. He took a couple of backward steps as he tried to balance himself. His heavy feet weren't helping his cause.

'How does that feel, bitch?' Rex goaded.

Frankenstein shook himself off like a wet dog, then launched into another clumsy attack. He marched towards Rex and swung a right hook that arrived only slightly quicker than a telegram from the North Pole. Rex ducked it easily, stepped inside and landed another huge uppercut.

CLANK!

This one was even harder than the first. It lifted Frankenstein off his feet and sent him flying through the air. He landed six feet away, flat on his back a few feet away from Baby, who was now on her knees watching the fight with a befuddled look on her face.

'Don't worry, honey,' said Rex. 'This'll all be over in a sec.'

Rex strode over to Frankenstein and kicked his hand away from under him as he tried to get up. He circled the fallen giant, kicking his limbs away from beneath him every time he tried to use them as leverage to get up.

'Who the fuck are you?' he asked. 'What do you want with the girl?'

He repeated the questions again and again as Frankenstein continued to ignore him, concerned only with climbing back to his feet.

Frankenstein for all his brute strength and his ability to withstand a bullet wasn't quick to learn from his missteps. There was no way he was going to answer Rex's questions while he was on his back. And there was no way Rex was letting him up until he explained *"Who the fuck he was? And what he wanted with the girl?"*

But then came the distraction neither of them was expecting.

Baby screamed out. *'Joey!'*

Rex stopped circling Frankenstein and looked to see what Baby was screaming at. A man had entered the hall through a fire exit in the corner.

Thirty

When Joey arrived in the rear car park at the School of Performing Arts it was obvious straight away that something was wrong. Hoards of screaming actors and actresses were flooding out through the fire exit at the back of the building.

He parked his motorcycle right outside the exit and barged through the onrushing swarm of fleeing thespians into the building. What the hell were they running from? Had they run out of mirrors to stare into lovingly? Were they re-enacting the cinema evacuation scene from the movie *The Blob?* Or had they been asked to read the entire works of Shakespeare? Or even just a page of it?

Joey grabbed a hold of one of the actors dressed as a T-bird and shoved him up against a wall of lockers, keeping a tight grip on the collar of his black leather jacket.

'What the fuck is going on?' he asked.

The man made a futile attempt to wriggle free from Joey's grasp but he soon realised it would be quicker to respond to the question.

'There's a freak dressed like Frankenstein shooting the place up!' he wailed.

'Where?'

'The main hall. Fucking let go of me for fucks sake!'

'Where's the main hall?'

The guy pointed down the corridor. 'That way! Take a left and it's on the right.'

Joey released him and the guy wasted no time in bolting for the exit out of the building. His race to the doors was easier now because only a few stragglers were still making their way out.

Joey hurried down the corridor and followed the directions he'd been given, turning left at the end. He found himself in an empty corridor. Empty, but not quiet. There was a lot of noise coming from a room up ahead. A fight was going on and it involved a lot of shouting. Joey sprinted down the corridor until he came to a fire door on the right. It had been forced open and through it he could hear a man's voice inside shouting, *"Who the fuck are you?"*

Joey poked his head around the door. The first thing he saw was Baby backing towards him. Further on, at the far end of the hall, two men were in the middle of a fight. One of them was on the floor being kicked around by the other, who was a big biker dude with muscles upon muscles.

'Baby!' Joey whispered loud enough for her to hear him, but not loud enough to attract the attention of the two scrapping men.

She turned around and her face lit up when she saw him.

'Joey!' she squealed.

The big biker dude, who was kicking the man on the floor, stopped for a moment and looked over at Joey, his eyes drawn to his red leather jacket.

Baby sprinted towards Joey. 'We've gotta get out of here!'

'Why? What's going on here?'

She grabbed a hold of his jacket with both hands. 'The Frankenstein guy tried to kidnap me,' she said. 'Then this Rodeo Rex fella turned up and they started shooting at each other.'

Rodeo Rex shouted across to them. 'Are you the Red Mohawk?'

Joey wasn't keen on announcing his secret identity to a stranger. And he'd just realised that the man on the floor, who Rex was kicking was Frank Grealish.

'I think Rex is on our side,' Baby whispered.

Rodeo Rex was staring at Joey and waiting for an answer. He had taken his eye off Frankenstein and as Joey knew from his years in the Blackwash operation, Frank Grealish could handle himself in a fight, even when he was on the ground. The big thug grabbed a hold of Rex's leg just below the knee and yanked it hard and fast. Rex lost his footing and toppled over onto the floor, banging his head hard on the wooden panelling.

Baby tugged at Joey's jacket, pulling him towards the corridor outside. 'We need to get out of here,' she said. 'That man shot Frankenstein a whole bunch of times but the bullets bounce off him!'

Joey ignored her and called out to Frank Grealish who was now sitting up with his back to them. 'Frank! What are you doing here?'

Frankenstein looked around. Through his black goggles he stared at Joey for a moment, then he reached over and grabbed Rodeo Rex by his hair and smashed his head down onto the floor again. Rex rolled away, looking dazed and just a little bit pissed.

Frankenstein climbed to his feet and stared at Joey. He said nothing though, so Joey called out to him again.

'Frank, it's me, Joey, remember?'

Rodeo Rex hauled himself up onto his knees. He still looked dazed and confused, but he had enough wits about him to shout a warning to Joey. 'He wants the girl!'

Baby tugged at Joey's arm, trying to pull him away from Frankenstein and into the corridor. 'Seriously we've got to go. That guy's invincible!'

'He can't be,' said Joey. 'Stay here!' He shrugged Baby off and walked towards the approaching figure of Frankenstein. It was evident straight away from Frankenstein's body language that he was spoiling for a fight.

'Frank, remember me? From Operation Blackwash?' Joey said, raising his hands to try to calm his former comrade.

As soon as he was close enough, Frankenstein swung a haymaker punch at the side of Joey's head. Joey ducked it with ease and adopted a crouched pose, ready to hit back. It seemed that Frank Grealish hadn't picked up any new moves since the days when they had sparred together. Joey threw a short jab hard and fast into Frankenstein's crotch. The old *"Punch in the nuts"* was a sure-fire way to incapacitate just about any man. But on this occasion it was Joey who came off worse. Instead of connecting with a soft target it felt like he'd punched a two-tonne iron bell. It hurt his fist far more than it should have. He swivelled to one side to avoid Frankenstein's follow-up punch, which was once more aimed at his head.

For his next attack, Joey ducked inside and threw a short sharp punch into Frankenstein's midriff. And this punch *hurt like hell*. Hurt Joey, that is. It felt like he'd smashed his fist into a wall of concrete. He jumped back out of swinging distance and wiggled his fingers to make sure none of them were broken. Frankenstein wasn't even winded by the blow to his stomach. Maybe he really was invincible and bulletproof?

At the other end of the hall Rodeo Rex had climbed to his feet. 'Get out of here!' he shouted. 'You can't beat him. He's a fucking robot or something!'

'Please!' Baby yelled. 'Listen to him. We've got to get out of here!'

Joey ducked another wild swing from Frankenstein and retreated a few steps. In doing so, he unintentionally coerced Frankenstein into a position from which Rex could attack him. Rex came charging across the hall like a wild bull. When he was close enough to Frankenstein he launched himself into the air and threw a flying punch that landed flush on the side of Frankenstein's head. Unlike Joey's punches this one made a loud CLANK that sounded like a baseball bat connecting with a football helmet. It turned Frankenstein's head sideways and he staggered away, badly off-balance. He planted his left foot down on the ground and then swung a punch at Rex. It caught the giant biker on the shoulder as he was coming in for another attack. The sound wasn't a loud clank this time, more of a dull thud, but it was powerful enough to knock Rex back down onto his ass. Rex looked up and shouted at Baby.

'Run for fuckssake! Your boyfriend will follow you!'

Baby looked at Joey with pleading eyes and then did as Rex suggested. She raced out into the corridor and started running for the exit. Joey had two choices, stay and help Rex fight Frankenstein or run after Baby. It was an easy choice. He sprinted out into the corridor and charged after her. He caught up with her quickly and grabbed her arm.

'Come on. My bike's outside. Let's get the fuck out of here.'

They sprinted to the end of the corridor. As they turned the corner Joey glanced back and saw Frankenstein had left Rodeo Rex behind and was plodding along the corridor behind them, pursuing them like something from a low grade horror movie.

Joey and Baby raced down the corridor to the fire exit at the back of the school and burst through it into the parking lot. Joey's bike was right by the exit where he'd left it. A crowd of people had congregated at the rear of the parking lot to get a view of what might be going on inside, but they all looked ready to run if any psychotic gunmen appeared. Joey jumped onto his motorbike and started it up. Baby hopped on behind him and slipped her arms around his waist. She buried her head into his back.

'Hold tight Baby, this could be a rough ride,' he said, turning the bike around. Baby squeezed him tight as he accelerated out of the parking lot through the crowd of onlookers and into the street at warp speed.

As they raced off, they heard more screams of panic from the crowd. Frankenstein had reappeared, barging through the fire doors into the parking lot.

■■■

Frankenstein marched over to Solomon Bennett's van, which was parked in a disabled bay. He opened the door on the passenger side and climbed in. Bennett started the engine.

'He got away. I'm sorry boss,' said Frankenstein.

'It's not a problem,' Bennett replied. 'I saw Joey Conrad show up, so I took the liberty of planting a tracking device on his bike while he was inside. We'll catch up with him and the girl later.'

'What about the other guy?' Frankenstein asked.

'What other guy?'

'Rodeo Rex.'

Bennett frowned. *'Rodeo Rex?'* he scoffed. The name sounded like something from a low budget Seventies Western. 'I don't know who that is. What does he want?'

The sound of approaching police sirens rang out nearby. It was time to make a hasty exit. Bennett steered the van out into the street.

'We'll worry about Rodeo Rex another time,' he said. 'For now, let's see where Joey Conrad takes us.'

Thirty One

Jack Munson parked his car in the designated parking spot outside apartment 17 at the Bates Motel. He'd bought enough Chinese food to feed four people even though it was only for him and Jasmine. She had been kind of vague about what she wanted to eat so he'd ordered a whole bunch of different appetizers and chicken dishes.

He grabbed the big brown paper bag containing all the food and hopped out of the car. He slammed the door shut but before he could move, a powerful motorcycle roared into the motel parking lot. He turned around and saw Joey Conrad cruising towards him on his yellow and red motorbike with Baby on the back clinging onto him for dear life.

They parked up in the vacant spot next to Munson's car and Joey killed the engine. Baby hopped off the bike.

'Oh God Jack, *thank God* you're here!' she cried. It was clear she was in a state of distress, much like she had been the night before when she showed up at Munson's door with tales of Danny Zuco being thrown off a cliff. Munson wasn't sure if it was Joey's reckless bike riding that had upset her this time, or something else.

It was something else.

'You guys okay?' Munson asked.

Joey climbed off the bike. 'Not really,' he said. 'I just got into a fight with Frank Grealish.'

'Frankenstein's here? You saw him? Where?'

'He was at Baby's drama school.'

Baby butted in. 'He threw me over his shoulder and tried to kidnap me. But then this other man called Rodeo Rex showed up and they got into a fight.'

'Rodeo Rex?'

Joey confirmed it. 'I saw him. He and I took turns trying to kick Frankenstein's ass. I'm telling you, Frank Grealish is fucking invincible. You can kick him, punch him, *Hell* you can shoot him, he doesn't feel pain, he doesn't bruise and he doesn't bleed. Once I figured that out, we got the hell out of there and came straight here.'

Munson was listening to what Joey and Baby were saying and just about taking it in even though it was a rather scattergun story, but he'd seen something else that warranted his attention.

'Joey, you can't be here,' he said.

'What? Why not?'

He pointed at Joey's bike. 'You've got a tracking device on your bike.'

Joey looked at where Munson was pointing. There was a small plastic device attached to the underside of the seat.

'Where the fuck did that come from?' he said, reaching for it.

'Leave it,' Munson snapped.

'Huh?'

'It's a hasty job. Someone's done that in a hurry. Whoever it is could be following you right now. You should keep moving, head across town, then take that device off and stick it in the back of a pickup truck or something, anything that's likely to keep moving.'

Joey put his hands on his head. 'Shit.'

'Get going,' said Munson. 'Baby can come with me. We'll nip inside and grab Jasmine then we'll head off somewhere safe. Call me later, but when we speak if I use the word *delightful* it means something's wrong, okay, got that?'

Joey nodded. '*Delightful*, yeah, got it.' He grabbed Baby and planted a kiss on her lips. 'Everything will be fine. I'll see you in a bit.'

'Okay, *hurry. Go!*' she said, recognising the urgency of the situation.

Joey jumped back on his bike and started it up. 'Jack, save me some of that Chinese food I can smell,' he said.

'Don't worry, there's enough here to feed the five thousand.'

Joey swung his bike around and raced out of the motel parking lot and into the street amid a chorus of screeching tyres, beeping horns and drivers shouting *"Dickhead!"* at him.

'Come on, Baby,' said Munson. 'Let's grab Jasmine and get out of here.'

He walked over to apartment 17, slid his key into the lock and pushed the door open.

'After you, Baby,' he said, with a reassuring smile.

Baby walked into the motel room. Munson followed her in and closed the door behind them.

And Baby screamed. *'Oh my God!'*

Thirty Two

Stakeouts were one of Elvis's least favourite things. Sitting in a car watching an apartment and waiting for someone to show up was tedious beyond belief.

He'd arrived at the Bates Motel at just before nine o'clock in the morning and parked his purple Cadillac near the motel entrance. The entrance was a good distance away from apartment 17, so it didn't look like he was staking the place out, even though he was.

He took a look at himself in his rear view mirror and was disappointed to see that he looked as shit as he felt. His eyes were red and puffy, his hair was a mess and he had a feeling he didn't exactly smell too great either. That was often the case when he went out drinking in his black leather suit. He slipped his sunglasses on and cracked open a bottle of *Shitting Monkey* from the six-pack he'd brought with him.

Shitting Monkey was a great cure for a hangover. It was also what had *caused* Elvis's hangover, but there was something about the stuff that helped clear his head first thing in the morning. Elvis wasn't an alcoholic or anything, but when he went on a booze bender, he liked to make it last at least forty-eight hours. The current binge was about thirty hours old and would most likely end at midnight; leaving him enough time to catch up on sleep so he'd be in good shape to help prevent the Pope from being assassinated on Christmas Eve, or as it was also known *tomorrow*.

He stared at the label on the beer bottle. It had never occurred to him before, but *Shitting Monkey* was an odd name for a beer. And the logo, a picture of a defecating primate holding a bottle of the beer, what was that supposed to signify? Drink this beer and you'll end up shitting like a baboon in the morning? Elvis pondered it for a moment. Maybe it was some kind of subtle health warning, like the SMOKING KILLS captions on the cigarettes he smoked. The more he thought about it, the more he considered the likelihood of it being true. There had certainly been some occasions when after a night on the *Shitting Monkey* beer he had spent a lot of time on the toilet crapping like a baboon.

The big problem for Elvis though, was lack of sleep. As soon as he started trivialising over the deep suggestions of the beer logo, his mind started to switch off. And his eyes were burning, so he closed them and slowly drifted off into a gentle sleep, one that lasted for less than half an hour. It ended when he was woken by the sound of a motorbike roaring past his car.

It took him a few seconds to remember where he was, by which time the motorbike was long gone. Elvis's mouth was dry and his leather suit had glued itself to his skin thanks to a profuse amount of sweat that had poured out of him while he slept. He fidgeted around in his seat and spotted the time on the dashboard. It was 10:38. He needed a soda. And when he thought about it, he decided he needed a cheeseburger too. He looked across at apartment 17 and saw that Jack Munson's car was back. *Typical, you nod off on a stakeout and miss all the action. This really was the dullest stakeout ever.*

He stretched his arms and thought about what to do. Should he take a stroll past apartment 17 and see if he could see through the window? Or should he stay in his car and watch from a safe distance?

The answer was simple. He wound down the window on the driver's side and tossed his half empty bottle of lukewarm *Shitting Monkey* out into parking lot. Then he started up the engine and reversed the car back.

It was time to go get a cheeseburger from McDowell's on the corner of 4th and Main.

Thirty Three

Baby screamed. *'Oh my God!'*

Munson spun around to see what had upset her. When he saw it, it upset him too. Jasmine was lying on the floor by the sofa. The side of her face was bruised and bloodied, and her normally immaculate long dark hair was matted with streaks of blood. *Her blood.* Her dressing gown was on the floor on the other side of the room. Her bra was nowhere to be seen and her black panties were halfway down her ass. She had bruises across her back, and the stockings she was wearing were ragged and down by her knees.

Baby rushed over to her. 'Jaz! Are you okay?' She leant down and stroked the hair away from Jasmine's face.

Munson went temporarily numb at the sight of his beautiful partner lying in a bloodied mess on the floor. The bag of Chinese food slipped from his grip and dropped to the floor. His first thought was to join Baby in rushing to Jasmine's aid, but then his years of training kicked in. What if the person who had done this was still in the apartment? His eyes settled on the door to the bedroom. His mind was overcrowded with thoughts, the most disconcerting of which was that he didn't have his gun with him, it was on the bedside table in the bedroom.

He took one tentative step towards the bedroom door. But that was as far as he went. The bedroom door burst open and a man with a gun stormed out. Munson recognised him straight away. It was Mozart, *the man of many faces.*

Mozart grinned at him and then pointed the gun downwards. Munson knew what was coming. There was a silencer on the end of the gun. He heard the muffled gunshot, but he couldn't tell if he heard it before or after the bullet burst into his kneecap. The pain was agonising. He collapsed to the floor as if someone had snapped his leg in two. His head banged on the wall behind him and he yelled out in pain.

'Nice of you to show up, Jack,' said Mozart.

A butch woman in a red sweater who looked like a young Jon Voigt followed Mozart out of the bedroom. She barged past him and grabbed Baby, hauling her away from Jasmine. She thrust a handkerchief over Baby's face. The hanky was laced with a powerful anaesthetic that caused Baby's to lose consciousness almost immediately. Her legs gave way and she fell back into the woman's arms.

'Good work, Denise,' said Mozart. 'Call the boss and tell him we've got Pincent's daughter.'

Denise pulled a cell phone out of her pocket and moved away to make the call to Solomon Bennett.

Mozart turned his attention back to Munson. 'So Jack, it's really good of you to show up and even kinder of you to bring Devon's little girl with you.'

Munson grabbed his shattered knee with both hands and tried to stem the flow of blood. There was a hole in his jeans that wasn't meant to be there and blood was gushing out through it. He'd been in some painful situations in his time, but a shot in the kneecap was by far the most agonising.

'What do you want?' he asked, grimacing in pain.

It wasn't Mozart's voice that he heard next. It was Jasmine's. She was still alive, in spite of the fact she looked half dead on the floor a few feet away from him.

'Jack, I'm so sorry,' she spluttered. She sounded like a drunk. A *punch-drunk* to be more exact.

He looked into her eyes. She looked in so much pain that for just a brief moment he forgot about the agony of his own injury. Even with a bloodied and bruised face, Jasmine was still the most beautiful woman he had ever seen. It hurt him more to see her brutalised than any suffering Mozart could inflict on him. He had to stay strong for her.

'Don't worry, Jaz,' he said. 'It'll be okay.'

Mozart loomed over Munson. He tucked his gun away in the back of his pants.

'Look at you, Jack,' he said, a hateful look upon his face. 'You think you're so clever don't you, huh? Just because you've got the law on your side, you think that somehow what you do has more honour than the rest of us don't you? But without the law on your side, you're just as bad as the people you spy on, if not worse.'

'What are you talking about?'

Munson's vision was beginning to swim in and out of focus. He was losing a lot of blood and feeling faint. But he had to stay conscious for the sake of Jasmine and Baby.

Through his blurred vision he saw Mozart was wielding a large jagged edged knife in front of his face.

'What am I talking about?' Mozart sneered, repeating Munson's question back to him. 'I'm talking about you being a two faced hypocrite.'

'Just let the girls go and I'll tell you everything.'

'You don't give *me* orders Jack. You hear me?'

'Okay, fine,' said Munson, his mind swirling, making it difficult to converse. 'What do you want?'

Mozart grabbed Munson's face with his free hand. He squeezed his jaw and cheeks hard. 'You wanna know what I want?' he hissed, pressing his face in close to Munson's. 'I want to take your face.....
off!'

Thirty Four

A quarter-pound cheeseburger from McDowell's was a marvellous cure for a hangover. Elvis washed it down with a large diet coke and then drove back to the motel with the intention of finishing off the bag of fries that came with it. And maybe washing them down with another bottle of *Shitting Monkey*.

He parked in the same spot as before. Jack Munson's car was still parked outside apartment 17, but there was now a white transit van next to it in the spot designated for apartment 18. Nothing seemed to be happening though so Elvis closed his eyes and started chomping away on his bag of French fries. He was so hungry he could eat in his sleep. The fries were greasy and slightly overcooked, just how he liked them.

His sleep-eating was interrupted by the sound of a car door opening. He opened his eyes and saw that an ugly woman in a red sweater had opened the double doors at the back of the white van. The door to apartment 17 was open too. A big dude who looked like Frankenstein walked out of the apartment carrying a young woman over his shoulder. Elvis took a closer look, without looking like he was taking a closer look, something that he was only able to do because he had his sunglasses on. The girl on Frankenstein's shoulder wasn't Jasmine. It crossed Elvis's mind that he might have been staking out the wrong apartment the whole time. That would be embarrassing.

Frankenstein tossed the young woman into the back of the van and climbed in after her. The other woman, the one that resembled a young Jon Voigt, closed the van doors and headed round to the passenger side.

And then another man walked out of apartment 17. A man with an eye-patch over his left eye. He was in his late forties and looked like a cross between Charlton Heston and a pirate. He jumped into the driver side of the van. Elvis had a decision to make. Go over and politely ask them who the fuck they were? Or finish his fries? It was a tough one.

He ended up doing neither because his cell phone vibrated in his pocket. Rex was calling. Elvis swallowed a mouthful of fries and answered it.

'Hey man, what's up?'

'I have had a fucking morning!' Rex moaned.

'What's happened? You sound pissed.'

'I found the Red Mohawk's girlfriend.'

'Cool.'

'Not really. Some big motherfucking Frankenstein cunt got to her first. I shot the sonofabitch six times and the bullets bounced right off him.'

'What?'

'Yeah, then the Red Mohawk shows up and we end up fighting this Frankenstein fucker together without much luck. So I let the Mohawk and his girlfriend get away, then Frankenstein fucked off, and I'm left with a fucking headache. I really don't know what to think.'

Elvis was listening to the story and watching the white van reversing out of its parking space, ready to leave the motel.

'Did you say Frankenstein?' he said, interrupting Rex who was still rambling on, complaining about the police blocking off all the roads or something.

'Yeah, Frankenstein. This dude looked just like him.'

'What about the girl? What did she look like?'

'Why do you care?'

'I think I just saw Frankenstein dump a girl into the back of a white van.'

'What?'

'A guy with bolts in his neck just came out of Jack Munson's apartment. He was with a lesbian and a pirate.'

'What about the Red Mohawk? He was wearing a red jacket. Is he there?'

Elvis could feel his hangover coming back. The conversation was confusing, especially while he was watching the white van heading out of the parking lot. 'They're all in a white van,' he said. 'Shall I go have a word with them?'

'NO!' Rex shouted. 'Don't do that whatever you do!'

'Why not?'

'Were you not listening when I said I shot that Frankenstein asshole six times?'

'Not particularly no. Look, they're leaving with the girl in the back of the van. What do you want me to do?'

'Follow them. But don't get too close. Call me when they get where they're going.'

Elvis checked his reflection in the rear view mirror and was reminded that he looked like shit. His hair was all over the place. And more importantly, his fries were getting cold.

'What about Jack and Jasmine?' he said. 'Shouldn't I check on them? I mean all these people just came out of their apartment.'

'Fuck them,' said Rex. 'Follow the van. I'll head to the motel and check on Jack and Jasmine. I'll be there in five minutes.'

'Okay.'

Elvis hung up the phone and stuck it back in his pocket. The white van had driven up to the exit and was waiting for an opening to pull out into traffic. Elvis reached over to grab another handful of French fries from the bag on the passenger seat, but because he was watching the van he accidentally knocked them onto the floor instead.

'Fuck!'

He reached down and picked up the bag of fries. Half of them had fallen out and were stuck to the floor, probably covered in hair and stale beer. He put the bag with the last few edible fries in it back on the passenger seat and checked the rear view mirror again. The white van had gone.

'Shit!'

To hell with it, he decided. The right thing to do now was check on Jack and Jasmine, and hopefully use their bathroom to sort out his hair and find some mouthwash. He clambered out of his car and stood up. He had no idea what he was going to find in apartment 17, or even what his excuse would be for knocking on the door, but hey, he didn't have time to come up with one either.

He rolled his shoulders and neck around a few times to loosen up and then swaggered across the parking lot with all the confidence of a man who had no plan whatsoever and didn't give a fuck. He rocked up to the apartment and raised his fist to knock on the door. His knuckles were an inch away from it when he heard a scream from inside. Every hair on his body prickled. It was Jasmine screaming.

And that's the great thing about Elvis. When he hears a woman in distress, he doesn't stop and think about what to do. He just gets on with it.

He took a step back and then barged into the door with his right shoulder. Over the years he'd knocked plenty of doors off their hinges. A shitty motel door was a piece of cake to the King. The lock shattered and the door swung open. Elvis's momentum threw him into the motel room. The first thing he saw was a dead body slumped on a sofa on the far wall. It was Jack Munson. Well, *it was probably Jack.* It was hard to know for sure because much to Elvis's disgust and horror, the corpse had no face. Right where the face should have been, there was just a skull covered in chunks of bloodied gristle.

Elvis looked away. Most people would have puked at the sight of a dead guy with no face. *Shit*, Elvis had puked at the sight of far less in his time, but no dead body, no matter how badly mutilated was going to stop him from rushing to the aid of Jasmine, a woman he'd taken a genuine liking too when he'd allowed her into his cockpit on the flight

176

back from Romania. So from being a hung-over mess just moments earlier, Elvis was suddenly right on his game.

He heard Jasmine scream again. Whatever was occurring in the apartment was coming from the bedroom. He charged at the bedroom door and smashed it open. Inside was a sight that made his blood boil. Jasmine was lying face down on the double bed in the middle of the room. Sitting astride her, pushing her head down into the pillow was a stocky man with dark hair. With his free hand he was unbuckling his belt, ready to carry out a rape. The sight of Elvis barging in took him by surprise. But Elvis was taken aback too, for a different reason. This man on the bed, this brutal rapist who was attacking Jasmine was doing it while wearing Jack Munson's face as a mask. It was secured around his head by a pair of elastic bands. It stopped Elvis in his tracks as he processed the sick image in his head and tried to make sense of it.

The other man reacted quickly. He let go of Jasmine and pulled a bloodied knife out of a sheath on his right thigh. And *this* was one *big fucking knife*. He moved away from Jasmine and took up a kneeling position on the bed. He lunged at Elvis with the knife, more in hope of getting him to back away than anything else. Elvis did backtrack a step, the sick image in front of him, confusing him momentarily. The man in the Munson mask rolled off the bed, landing on his feet with the knife primed and ready to attack.

Elvis put the horrifying scene to the back of his mind and raised his fists, ready to fight. 'Who the fuck are you?' he snarled.

'What do you care?' said the face behind the Jack Munson mask.

'I don't, I just like to know whose ass I'm kicking.'

The man jabbed his knife towards Elvis, feeling him out. 'Name's Mozart,' he said. 'You might have heard of me, I've got quite a reputation.'

'Not for much longer.'

Mozart lunged forward, thrusting the knife up towards Elvis's throat. Elvis (in spite of all the alcohol and junk food he'd consumed) shifted to one side effortlessly. The knife whooshed past his face and he retaliated by grabbing Mozart's wrist, preventing him from swinging the knife again. He followed that up with a hard stamp from his right boot, straight down onto Mozart's left knee. A sickening crunch followed as the knee crumbled. His leg gave way and he toppled forward right into Elvis's second kick, which smashed him in the face. Three of Mozart's teeth flew out of his mouth, accompanied by a spray of blood that splashed against the side of the bed.

From there, disarming Mozart was a piece of cake. Elvis relieved him of his knife and pressed his foot down onto his chest. He leant down and yanked off the elastic band around Mozart's head and pulled the human facemask off. He tossed it onto the floor and grimaced at the sight of the blood it left on his fingertips. Mozart was at his feet, groaning in pain. Elvis loomed over him and pointed the sick bastard's own knife up against his eyeball.

'Don't kill him!' Jasmine cried out from the bed. She had crawled up onto the pillows and was curled up in a ball against the headboard.

'Why not?' said Elvis, keeping his eyes firmly fixed on his enemy.

'His friends took Baby. He knows where she is! He can take us to her.'

Elvis pulled the knife away from Mozart's eye, but pressed his boot into his chest to keep him pinned to the floor. Mozart's face was fucked up and covered in blood, some of it his and some probably Jack Munson's. He sneered and spat some blood onto Elvis's boot.

Elvis glanced over at Jasmine and saw what a distraught, traumatised state she was in. She had bruises and swelling around her eyes and her nose was bloodied. She was naked from the waist up and her upper body was streaked in blood. And on top of that she'd obviously been crying, *a lot*. He looked back down at Mozart and removed his foot from the other man's chest. Elvis wanted to kill him, but knowing that he couldn't, he did the next best thing instead.

He stamped on Mozart's face a bunch of times until he was unconscious.

Thirty Five

Joey rode his motorcycle through the city streets for fifteen minutes, checking regularly to see if anyone was following him. He saw nothing suspicious, but nevertheless, the knowledge that he had a tracking device on his bike had made him paranoid. He eventually pulled into a multi-storey parking garage and rode up to the third floor where everything seemed relatively quiet. He pulled into a space and jumped off the bike.

The tracking device planted underneath his seat had been stuck on with double-sided tape. A real hurried, amateurish way to install such a device. He looked around the garage. The third floor was only half full. More importantly though, there weren't any people wandering around on foot. He ripped the tracker off his bike and sidled over to a pickup truck nearby. He tossed the device into the rear cargo area and took a look around. No one had seen him do it. And no one seemed to have followed him there. He ran back to his bike and called Baby on his cell phone. To his dismay, her phone was switched off, so he tried calling Jack Munson instead. The phone rang six or seven times, and he was about to hang up when finally someone answered. Someone who wasn't Jack.

'Hello,' said a man's voice.

'Who's this?' Joey asked.

'Rodeo Rex. Who's this?'

Joey frowned. 'What are you doing with Jack's phone?'

'Is this Joey?'

'I asked what you were doing with Jack's phone.'

'Look buddy, if you are who I think you are, you need to get your ass back to the place you dropped your girlfriend off.'

Joey considered the possibility that Rodeo Rex had planted the tracking device on his bike. Rex had been at the School of Performing Arts, so he was a prime candidate, and now he was being vague. But how did he know Joey had dropped Baby off somewhere?

'What have you done with Baby?'

'Me? Nothing,' said Rex.

'Then how have you got Jack's phone?'

'Jack's dead.'

'What?'

'Frankenstein got here before I did. He's taken Baby with him, so why don't you get back here and we can talk about how I can help you get her back?'

Joey was shaken by the claim that Jack was dead. He'd known Jack since he was a kid and he'd always believed the guy was indestructible. And he was a good friend too. And Baby, had she really been taken? He hoped to God that Rex was lying about all of it.

'What happened to Jack?' he said sharply.

'Just get back here and you can see for yourself. I'll give you five minutes but after that I'm leaving. Cops are gonna be all over this place soon.'

Rodeo Rex hung up the phone. Joey took a few deep breaths. Was this a trap? Had Baby really been taken? He considered the facts for a second. Baby hadn't answered her phone and Jack's phone was in the hands of Rodeo Rex. If Joey wanted to know *what was real* and *what wasn't* then heading back to the Bates Motel was his only option.

Rex had said he'd wait for five minutes, which meant that Joey was going to have to seriously hit the gas if he wanted to get there in time. He hopped back on his bike and flew through the crosstown traffic at dangerously high speed. Every other driver suddenly seemed to want to switch lanes without indicating, or pull out in front of him at busy junctions, and every single streetlight changed to red as he approached it. But none of these things was going to stop him. He swerved around cars and zipped through red lights at every turn until he reached the motel.

When he arrived in the parking lot he saw a big Harley Davidson parked up outside apartment 17. Sitting astride it in a pair of jeans and a sleeveless blue denim jacket was Rodeo Rex. Rex was one of those guys, once seen, never forgotten.

As Joey rode towards him, Rex held up his gloved hand, offering half a wave. Joey slowed up and scoped his surroundings. Both of Rex's hands were visible and there was no one else in sight. So, unless there was a sniper in a building across the street, Joey had to assume Rex had come in peace.

He parked up alongside Rex's Harley and dismounted. Straight away he noticed that the door to apartment 17 had been damaged. Someone had smashed the lock. Rex reached out and grabbed Joey's arm with his gloved hand. His grip was fierce.

'I wouldn't go in there if I was you,' he said.

'Well you're not me,' Joey replied. 'So get your fuckin' hand off.'

'They cut Jack's face off.'

'What?'

'If you really need to see it for yourself, he's on the floor in the front room. But be quick because we need to get out of here. My buddy

180

Elvis got here in time to save Jasmine and he caught one of the guys that did it. Come with me and we can question this asshole and find out where they took your girlfriend.'

Rex let go of Joey's arm. Joey rushed into the apartment. As soon as he stepped through the door he saw the mess inside. The corpse on the floor by the sofa was horrifically mutilated. He recognised Jack's pink shirt from when they'd met earlier in the day at The Ole au Lait. It was covered in blood, thick chunks of it. Rex had warned him that Jack's face had been cut off. He'd hoped that it was some kind of exaggeration or metaphor, but the sight of it was very real and a hundred times worse than he could have imagined. Jack had been mutilated, butchered in a way that was completely unbefitting of a man of his stature. He had been a good, decent man who had dedicated his whole life to protecting those who couldn't fight for themselves. It was an inglorious ending for someone who deserved so much more, who had endured so much more.

Joey shuddered for a moment, and put the horrific sight out of his mind. He hurried over to the backroom. There was yet more blood on the floor and the bed was a mess. A lot of violence had taken place in that motel apartment. He opened the bathroom door and saw that it was empty. There was some blood in the sink and on the mirror. He had secretly hoped to find Baby safe and well somewhere inside the apartment. He should have known better. The only way to find out what had happened to Baby was to go with Rex.

He walked back outside, avoiding looking at Munson this time. Rex was waiting on his Harley. He offered Joey a sympathetic look.

'I'm sorry, man.'

'Who killed him? Was it Frankenstein?'

Rex shook his head. 'A guy called Mozart. He wore Jack's face like a mask while he tried to rape the girl, Jasmine. Elvis has taken them both to a secret hideout of ours. Jasmine knows exactly what went down in there but she's distraught and barely able to communicate at the moment. This asshole Mozart, he's our ticket to finding out where Frankenstein is and what they're planning to do with your girl.'

'He's not really Frankenstein you know.'

'Yeah, I worked that out by myself, thanks.'

'I knew him years ago. His name was Frank Grealish. We were part of the same government operation, designed to make us into invincible assassins.'

'It worked well,' said Rex.

'No it didn't. Frank died.'

'He what?'

'He died. At least, that's what everyone thought. A fucked up weird scientist who calls himself Dr Jekyll tried to make him bulletproof. It went wrong, but as you and I have recently seen, the bulletproof skin seems to work pretty damn good.'

Rex took on board what Joey was saying remarkably well. 'Frankenstein and Dr Jekyll,' he said with a nod of the head. 'This is what God put me on earth for.'

Joey didn't know what to make of Rex. He seemed okay, kinda cool, but who the hell was he?

'How do you fit into all this?' Joey asked him. 'Jack told me you were looking for me. Are we gonna have a problem?'

'No, I just heard you were trying to kill the Pope. Are you?'

Joey shook his head. 'No. But everybody seems to think that.'

'It was in the news.'

'I know, but I can only assume someone is trying to frame me for it. I couldn't give two shits about the Pope. He's certainly done nothing to make me want to kill him.'

'Good,' said Rex. 'I wouldn't be surprised if Frankenstein is involved in it all somehow. So let's go ask his friend Mozart about it. Maybe we can get your girl back and save the Pope too.' He tapped his wristwatch. 'We've got twenty-two hours and sixteen minutes.'

'Until what?'

'Until someone kills the Pope.'

Thirty Six

Joey tailed Rex's chopped Harley across town. After cruising through the streets at a pace Joey considered far too leisurely, Rex eventually took a turn down a side alley next to a Hell's Angels clubhouse. The place looked as broken-down and dilapidated as the rest of the neighbourhood. Rex parked up underneath a sheltered area and strode towards a rusty metal door at the back. Joey parked up next to him and joined him just as Rex typed a number into a very sleek, high-tech keypad next to the door. There was a soft click followed by the door releasing itself ever so slightly from the lock. Rex pushed it open and walked through. Joey followed.

'This is your hideout?' Joey asked.

'This place is owned by a gang of Hell's Angels called *The Outsiders*. And I'm welcome anywhere in the world where there's a Hell's Angel.'

They walked into the backroom that looked like it was used for storing junk. There were boxes stacked high around the perimeter of the room and a few benches with motorcycle parts scattered around on them. Joey paid little attention to any of it though. What he'd come for was the man at the far end of the room, the man who killed Jack Munson and knew where to find Baby. Mozart was slumped in a chair, only semi-conscious. The ropes around his chest, legs and arms were the only things keeping him upright. His face and shoulders were covered in blood, as were his hands and feet. And his hair was a mess. The two people who had worked him over were in the far corner of the room. Jasmine was sitting on a workbench with her slim brown legs dangling down just above the floor. She was wearing a pair of red hotpants and a black bra. Her face was bruised and she had some pretty severe swelling around her eyes and cheeks, but Joey still recognised her from the time he'd seen her in the Beaver Palace while he was cutting her former employer's head off. Elvis was tending to Jasmine's face wounds with a damp cotton pad and some warm water from a china bowl. Joey didn't know if Elvis was his real name or not, but he sure did look like Elvis Presley. From the black leather outfit Elvis wore in the '69 Comeback Special, through to the quaffed black hair and gold-rimmed sunglasses, this guy was a dead ringer for The King.

Joey called out to Jasmine. 'Hi Jasmine, remember me?'

'You're Joey?' she said, forcing a brave smile. Her teeth were stained with blood, making the smile less appealing than usual.

'Yeah.'

'You look pretty normal without the mask.'

Elvis stopped wiping Jasmine's face and took a look at Joey. 'This is the Red Mohawk?' he asked Rex.

Rex patted Joey on the shoulder. 'Yeah, Joey meet Elvis.'

Elvis pointed at Mozart. 'Help yourself to fuckhead over here.'

'Thanks, I will,' said Joey, walking up to the prisoner in the chair.

'He's kind of a dick,' said Elvis, tossing a bloodied cotton pad onto the floor and reaching for another one from a pack next to Jasmine. 'But he's the only lead we have.'

Jasmine jumped down from the bench and picked up the bloodied cotton pad Elvis had thrown on the floor. She walked up to Mozart and put her hand over his nostrils. He jerked back to reality and his mouth flopped open involuntarily so that he could breathe. As soon as he opened it she shoved the bloodied cotton ball into his mouth.

'You can torture him as much as you like,' she said to Joey. 'Just don't kill him until he tells you where Baby is.'

Mozart spat the bulk of the cotton pad out onto the floor and tried to scrape the rest off his tongue using the few teeth he had left.

'This guy is a stubborn asshole,' said Elvis. 'I've ripped all his toenails off and Jasmine's stubbed out two cigarettes on his dick.'

'Nice,' said Joey. 'Has he told you anything yet?'

'Nope. He's got a very limited vocabulary.'

Joey stood in front of Mozart and grabbed his jaw. 'Is Mozart your real name?' he asked.

'*Fuck you.*'

'Where's Baby?'

'*Fuck. You.*'

'See,' said Elvis.

Joey let go of Mozart's face. 'What are we gonna do with him then?'

Elvis reached into his back pocket and pulled out a brown leather wallet. He tossed it to Joey. 'That's got all his ID's in it. He's got about ten different names.'

Joey opened the wallet and flicked through the different forms of identification. Elvis was right. Mozart had a bunch of aliases and different disguises on a series of security passes and drivers licenses. And none of them were providing any clues.

'How do you know Frank Grealish?' Joey asked him.

'*Fuck. You.*'

184

Joey was already exasperated. '*Jesus,* I was in a mental hospital for five years and most of the patients there had better conversational skills than this dickless bastard.'

Rex pushed Joey aside. 'Let me try.'

He marched up to Mozart, his colossal figure looming over the prisoner. He grabbed Mozart's balls with his metal hand. And he squeezed hard. *Really hard.*

Mozart screamed out in agony. The screaming went on and on. But at no point did he offer to give up any information. Eventually Rex relinquished his grip and stepped back.

'Why don't you cut his dick off?' Jasmine suggested.

Rex visibly winced. 'That's not something we generally do.'

'Why not?' said Jasmine. 'I'll do it.'

Elvis placed his hand on Jasmine's shoulder. 'We don't do that. It's kind of a last resort.'

'So what? Fuck him. He deserves it,' said Jasmine defiantly. 'Where's the knife?'

Rex intervened. 'Jasmine, I think what Elvis is trying to say is that once you cut a guy's dick off he's got no reason to live. You've got nowhere to go once you've done that. A guy with no dick won't tell you shit.'

Joey crouched down in front of Mozart and got right in his eyeline. He grabbed a clump of his hair and pulled hard. 'Look buddy, why don't you tell us where Baby is before we let this young lady get her hands on a rusty knife. Seems to me she's just itching to slice your cock off.'

'*Fuck you.*'

Joey punched Mozart hard in the face. Mozart's nose made a horrendous crunching sound as it broke beneath his fist. Blood spurted out over Joey's hand. He stepped back and wriggled his fingers, which were hurting from the punch. A few specks of Mozart's blood dribbled off his knuckles and onto the floor.

'Okay,' said Rex, calling for calm. 'Maybe we're asking the wrong questions. This fucker obviously isn't going to give his people up, so let's try something different.'

'Like what?' said Joey.

Rex ushered him away and took on a softer approach, crouching down in front of Mozart in a non-aggressive pose. 'Mister Mozart, I just need to know who's going to kill the Pope. Is it your friend Frankenstein?'

'*Fuck you.*'

'Fine. Just tell me how to kill Frankenstein, and I'll make sure you die quickly. Say *fuck you* again and I'll let Jasmine loose on your dick.'

Mozart looked up at Rex. Blood was spilling from his nose and he was visibly struggling to breathe. 'Frankenstein can't be killed, dickhead,' he spluttered. 'Once they find out where I am, he'll show up here and kill all of you.'

Joey had heard enough. 'Look fucknuts, if you think your friends are going to find you by following the tracking device they put on my bike then you're gonna be sorely disappointed. That thing's long gone.'

'See,' said Rex. 'No one is coming for you. So why don't you tell us where we can find Frankenstein? If you're so sure he can't be killed then you won't mind us finding him, will you?'

Mozart spat some blood out onto Rex's boot. 'I don't care what you do to me. My friends will be doing all this same stuff to your precious little girl, Baby. She's probably given you all up already.'

Joey gently pushed Rex aside so he could get to Mozart again. He hit Mozart in the face with another jab. It knocked Mozart's head back and caused him to yell in pain, his cries accompanied by a delightful spray of blood.

'This is no use!' Joey complained, shaking some more blood off his fingers. 'This motherfucker's not going to tell us anything. We're wasting our time!'

'*Fuck you,*' Mozart said for what felt like the hundredth time.

'God this guy's annoying,' said Joey, contemplating hitting him again but realising the futility of it.

'Why not shove a knife up his butt?' Jasmine suggested.

Rex looked over at Elvis. 'What do you think?' he said.

'I think you should head to the bar around the corner.'

Rex nodded.

Joey didn't know if they were talking in code or what, but heading out for a drink wasn't on his list of priorities. 'What the hell is in the bar around the corner?' he snapped.

'You know that friend of ours you met the other night?'

'The Bourbon Kid?'

'Yeah,' said Rex with a wry smile. 'He's in the bar around the corner.'

'And?'

'And we should go get him, because he'll make this guy talk.'

Thirty Seven

When Baby woke up she felt a searing pain in her head. Her clothes were stuck to her as if she'd been wearing them for days. And there were a few stray sweaty hairs stuck to her forehead too. She was lying comfortably on her side on something soft. She rolled over and opened her eyes. She wasn't in her own bed, but she was in *a* bed. But where the hell was it?

She heard her father's voice call out. 'Baby, are you awake?'

She turned her head. She was in a dark room. At first she thought it was a kitchen because there was a sink and a draining board on the opposite wall, but as she took in the bigger picture she saw that she was actually in a caravan. Her father was sitting in a chair by her bedside. He was wearing a smart pair of pants and a white shirt she had bought for him a few weeks earlier.

'Daddy, where are we?' she said, sitting up and rubbing her eyes.

Devon got up from the chair and sat down on the bed next to her. He rubbed the small of her back. 'You're safe now, Baby.'

Baby grabbed him and hugged him tightly. 'I'm so sorry I got caught,' she said. 'I messed up.'

'You didn't mess up, Baby. I messed up, I should have seen this coming.'

A few unpleasant images flashed through Baby's head. She remembered seeing Jasmine spread-eagled on the floor of the motel room. And Jack was there too. She pulled away from her father.

'Dad, what happened to Jack and Jasmine?'

Devon stroked some stray hairs away from her forehead. 'I don't know, but you should prepare yourself for the worst.'

Baby tried to put the thoughts of what might have happened to Jack and Jasmine out of her head. 'What do these people want with us?' she asked.

Devon kissed her on the cheek. 'We'll be okay,' he said. 'Just leave it to me to do all the talking.'

The sound of someone unlocking the caravan door interrupted them. The door opened and Solomon Bennett walked in. He was accompanied by the hulking figure of Frankenstein, who had to duck down to avoid hitting his head on the ceiling. They left the door open behind them, allowing in a sliver of light. Bennett was wearing a black T-shirt and a pair of matching combat pants. He looked annoyed about something.

'Okay Devon,' he said. 'Who the fuck is Rodeo Rex?'

'What?'

'Rodeo Rex, who is he? Frankenstein says he showed up at Baby's drama school with Joey Conrad. So who is he?'

'Rodeo Rex?' Devon repeated the name, pretending to try and make sense of it. He actually knew who Rex was. And he knew Rex was back in the country because Jack Munson had shared a plane ride from Romania with him.

'Yeah, Rodeo *fucking* Rex,' Bennett sneered. 'What kind of a fucking name is that anyway?'

'It's the name of a dead guy.'

'Don't play smart with me Devon, not unless you want to watch your daughter die.'

'I'm telling you the truth,' said Devon. 'He was on my radar some years back. We had numerous reports from all around the world about him and his sidekick, some fella who thought he was Elvis. They killed a lot of people, although nothing was ever officially pinned on them.'

'So you do know him then?'

'I know *of* him, but like I said, he's dead, at least that's what I heard. Do you remember Miles Jensen?'

Bennett nodded. 'The black dude who thought he was Fox Mulder. What about him?'

'Years ago he vanished without trace in a place called Santa Mondega. Just before he went missing he reported the deaths of both Elvis and Rodeo Rex. We never got confirmation of it, but there haven't been any Rodeo Rex sightings since then. So whoever you saw can't have been him.'

Bennett marched over to Baby and grabbed her by the arm. He hauled her to her feet. The sudden jarring movements made her headache feel ten times worse. 'You were there,' he said, shaking her. 'Tell your dad what you saw.'

Baby nodded apologetically at her father. 'A big guy showed up and tried to stop Frankenstein from taking me. He said his name was Rodeo Rex.'

'See!' said Bennett.

Frankenstein, who wasn't generally one for saying much, chipped in. 'He had a metal hand,' he mumbled. 'It catches bullets.'

'So come on,' said Bennett, sliding his arm around Baby's waist in a creepy, predatory way to unsettle Devon. 'Who's he working for?'

Devon looked twitchy. 'It certainly sounds like Rodeo Rex. I mean, the one thing above all else that made that guy easy to identify was that he had a metal hand. But like I said, word on the street is he's been dead for years. Him and his buddy Elvis, *both dead*.'

'Devon, you do know why we brought your daughter here don't you?'

'Because you're an asshole.'

'Quite. But if you value your daughter's life and don't want to watch anything unpleasant happen to her, you'll tell me where Joey Conrad is. And while you're at it you can tell me where Rodeo Rex and Elvis are too. If you've hired these guys to fuck up my big day tomorrow, then you'd better give them up right now.'

'Let Baby go now and I'll tell you everything I know.'

Bennett held out his hand and Frankenstein slapped a pistol into it. He pointed the pistol at Baby's head and scowled at Devon. 'Don't act all naïve Devon, you know it doesn't work like that. What's waiting for us at Landingham Manor tomorrow?'

There was no way Devon was going to do anything other than cooperate at this point. 'Look, I have no idea about Rodeo Rex or Elvis,' he said, 'but I can give you Joey Conrad.'

Baby's heart sank. She knew her father had no choice, but the knowledge that Joey would be hunted down by Frankenstein and co was devastating.

Bennett pushed his gun under Baby's chin. 'That's a start,' he said. 'Go on.'

'On the ground floor in Landingham Manor, there's a study room. It has a bronze bust of Adam West. Lift the head up and press the button inside. It opens a secret passage with an elevator behind it. The elevator takes you down to an underground bunker. That's where Joey Conrad is hiding out.'

'That wasn't so hard, was it?' said Bennett. 'Now tell me more about Rodeo Rex.'

Devon held up his hands. 'I swear Solomon, on my daughters life I don't know. Kill me if you want, but just know that I would *never* risk her life to protect anyone else's.'

Bennett lowered his gun and nodded. 'I believe you,' he said. 'But you and your daughter are coming with us tomorrow. And if Rodeo Rex, Elvis, Michael Jackson or even the fucking ghost of Prince shows up, you're gonna have to watch her die.'

Thirty Eight

Joey and Rex had found the Bourbon Kid in a sleazy bar around the corner within minutes of leaving the Hell's Angels clubhouse. He looked the same as always, *drunk and wearing a long black hooded trench coat*. At first, while they brought him up to speed on everything that had happened, he seemed disinterested in what they had to say. But when they mentioned that his skills were required to torture Mozart, well, he sobered up pretty darned quick.

By the time the three of them returned to the Hell's Angels clubhouse, Mozart looked even worse than when Joey and Rex had left him. He was still tied to the chair in the centre of the room but his face was more bloodied and swollen than before, and he had a fine selection of bright red sores on his chest and stomach that looked like they were causing him a lot of discomfort.

Elvis and Jasmine were sitting on one of the workbenches a few feet away from Mozart. Elvis had successfully calmed Jasmine down after her traumatic ordeal and had somehow managed to get her to join him in a drink. The two of them were drinking bottles of *Shitting Monkey*. Jasmine was now wearing a pair of jeans that she had acquired from somewhere, and Elvis's leather jacket was wrapped around her shoulders. Elvis had slipped a white T-shirt on, which was tighter than it needed to be. Most curious of all though, for some reason Jasmine was wearing a black mask on the top half of her face, the kind one would normally associate with The Lone Ranger or one of Batman's sidekicks. She had a lit cigarette in her hand too.

Rex shouted over to Elvis. 'Did you get any information out of him while we were gone?'

Elvis burped up some fizz from his beer before replying. 'Nah, we haven't even bothered asking him anything.'

'Well he looks worse than he did when we left.'

'Jasmine's been hiding cigarettes up his butt hole.'

Jasmine held up a pack of cigarettes. 'You want one?' she asked, offering them up to everyone.

'No thanks,' said Rex. If she'd had cigars he would have considered it, but cigarettes, no way. He clicked his fingers and gestured to the Bourbon Kid. 'Go on, do your stuff.'

The Kid lowered the hood on his coat and walked up to Mozart. He stopped a yard short of him to get a good look at what had been done to him, so far.

'Are you positive that this cunt is Mozart?' he asked.

Elvis grabbed Mozart's leather wallet from the worktop and tossed it over to the Kid. 'There's a bunch of ID's in there,' he said.

The Kid opened the wallet and started flicking through all the different ID badges inside it. One of them grabbed his interest. He took it out and slipped it into a pocket inside his coat, then he folded up the wallet and tossed it back to Elvis.

'I'll take one of those cigarettes,' he said to Jasmine.

Jasmine chucked the pack of cigarettes to him. The Kid caught it and put it up to his mouth so he could pull one out with his teeth. The cigarette duly lit up when he sucked on it, and he threw the pack back to Jasmine. Instead of reaching out to catch it with her hands she entertained everyone with one of her party tricks and caught it perfectly in her cleavage.

Elvis clearly approved. 'Nice catch,' he said, staring at the cigarette packet.

The Kid looked at Jasmine too, studying her closely. Even though he was probably impressed by her catching skills, he was much more interested in something else. 'Why is she wearing a mask?' he asked.

Elvis replied. 'I gave it to her. It covers up her bruises.'

'What bruises?'

Elvis pointed at Mozart. 'That asshole punched her in the face a bunch of times this morning.'

The Kid took a drag on his cigarette and blew the smoke back out through his nostrils, leaving the cigarette hanging out of the corner of his mouth. For a moment he was deep in thought, evidently unimpressed by the notion of Mozart beating on Jasmine. He soon made up his mind on how to best deal with the news though. He took a step back and reached into his coat. He pulled out a handgun that he kept holstered out of sight. *And this was a big fucking gun.* He straightened his arm and pointed the gun at Mozart's crotch.

Rex and Joey both tried in vain to stop him, by shouting out, *'NOOOOO!'*

It was a wasted shout. Even if the Kid had heard it, it wouldn't have stopped him. It was noticeable to everyone present when he squeezed the trigger that the gun didn't make the obligatory "BANG!" that they had all come to expect from such a weapon. The noise it made was much more of a deep and thunderous "BOOM!" more in keeping with a cannon.

Whatever it was that the Kid fired out of that gun, it sure as hell packed a punch. It didn't just blow Mozart's dick and balls off, it blew the ass out of the seat he was on too. The chair collapsed onto the floor in a pool of smoke, with Mozart falling through it. What was left of his ass splattered against the floor with a loud squelch.

Before anyone (including Mozart) could react, the Kid fired another shot, this time into the stunned, gawping face of the dickless prisoner.

The second bullet didn't just hit Mozart in the face and leave a hole, or even make his head explode, it was much more unusual. His head flew right off his shoulders, as if an invisible train had hit it. And as it parted company with his neck it transformed into bright red goo and flew back towards the wall behind him. As the sound of the BOOM faded, it was overlain with a loud *SPLAT* as what was once Mozart's head splashed across the wall ten feet behind him. It looked like someone had thrown a can of lumpy red gravy at the wall.

There was a momentary silence while everyone took in the sight of the big red splodge on the wall and the headless upper body of Mozart, which had separated from his legs. As the remains of his torso fell backwards, a fountain of blood spurted up out of his neck, gushing onto the floor. And boy, oh boy did it stink.

The Kid blew some smoke away from the barrel of his gun and then replaced it inside his coat. Joey and Rex were standing behind him, open-mouthed.

Rex put his head in his hands, grasping at his own hair, seriously considering pulling some clumps of it out. He of all people should have known that this was the most likely outcome. The Bourbon Kid almost always did the opposite of what was required.

Joey said out loud what Rex was too angry to verbalise. 'You weren't supposed to kill him, you fucking dick! Did you not listen to anything we said? We said *don't kill him!*'

'He was our only lead,' Rex added, disconsolately, closing his eyes and hoping that when he reopened them it would all have been a bad dream, which it obviously wasn't.

The Kid blew some more smoke out of his nostrils, before justifying his actions. 'I didn't like him.'

'None of us fucking liked him!' Joey ranted, squaring up to the Kid. 'We *all* wanted to fucking kill him, but we *needed* him. He was our only fucking lead!'

Jasmine piped up with a question. She was staring at the remnants of Mozart's head, which were sliding down the wall. 'Why did his head turn into ketchup?' she asked.

'It's a special gun,' said the Kid. 'I made it myself.'

Joey pushed the Kid in the chest. 'Are you listening to me?' he snarled.

'Gold Star Catering,' the Kid replied.

Joey waited for him to explain the random remark. It quickly became evident that he wasn't going to. 'Is there more to that, or am I supposed to guess?' he said angrily.

The Kid reached inside his coat again. This time he pulled out the ID card he had taken from Mozart's wallet. He handed it to Joey. It was a black plastic card with a picture of Mozart's face and the name *Vincent McLane* next to it in gold lettering. Across the top of the card in capital letters were the words GOLD STAR CATERING.

'What the fuck is this?' Joey asked, hoping for a decent explanation.

The Kid produced two more cards, this time from the back pocket on his jeans. He handed them to Joey. They were both similar to the other one. They were photo ID's of two more Gold Star employees. Joey recognised the face on one of the cards. It was Pig Face, the asshole who had attacked him and Baby with the dart gun in the woods, right before the Bourbon Kid had shown up and shot him in the back of the head with an arrow.

Joey looked back up at the Kid. 'I don't get it?' he said.

'Gold Star Catering,' the Kid repeated. 'I killed two people last night and they both had these ID cards.'

Rex grabbed the cards from Joey and flicked through them. 'These guys aren't caterers,' he scoffed.

The Kid took a drag on his cigarette and blew out a smoke ring while the others waited, hoping for some kind of explanation. When he was ready he eventually spoke. 'Gold Star is an exclusive company that does catering for very important clients, namely Government, Royalty, Celebrities, that kind of shit. Tomorrow they're catering at the charity event that the Pope is attending.'

'For fuckssake!' Rex yelled. 'Why didn't you tell us this before?'

'You didn't ask.'

'Goddammit! So do you know where the event is taking place?'

'Yeah. But before I tell you,' he paused and pointed at Joey. 'I wanna know who *he* is working for?'

'What?' said Joey, surprised by the question.

'Who are you working for?'

'No one. What are you talking about?'

'It's a simple question,' the Kid said calmly.

'What the fuck do you care who I work for?

'It matters. Answer the question.'

Joey sighed, irritated by the seeming lack of relevance to the Kid's questioning. 'A man called Devon Pincent, my girlfriend's dad, he points me in the direction of bad people and I deal with them, okay?'

'Where is he now?'

'Who? Devon? I don't know. I can't get hold of him. I think Mozart's people have got him. We might have found that out if you hadn't painted the wall with his face!'

The Kid took one really deep drag on his cigarette and looked into Joey's eyes. 'Did he set you up in Landingham Manor?'

Joey frowned. 'Yeah, why?'

'You ever wonder why that guy fired darts into you the other night when he could have just killed you?'

Joey's mind flashed back to the incident when he'd been peppered with poisoned darts. 'No, I haven't had time to think about it. Why, have you got a theory?'

'Yes I have, thanks for asking.' The Kid dropped his cigarette on the floor and stubbed it out with his boot. 'There were two guys in the woods outside Landingham Manor last night. They were checking the place out for escape routes, hidden security cameras and stuff. They probably thought you were a security guard who they could interrogate.'

'Interrogate?' Joey repeated. 'About what?'

'The Pope's charity event is being held at Landingham Manor tomorrow.'

Rex shouted out. *'Hallelujah!'*

The Kid was still eyeballing Joey. 'So why did your boss set you up in a room at Landingham Manor?'

Joey felt a cold shiver run down his spine. 'He said he had a big job for me. He told me to stay in the underground bunker at Landingham and he was going to come and meet me to tell me what the job was, but he never came.'

Rex made a suggestion. 'Maybe he wanted you to protect the Pope?'

'Or kill the Pope,' said the Kid.

Joey breathed a sigh of frustration. 'I'm *not* going to kill the Pope, okay? I think Rex is right. Devon probably wanted me to *protect* the Pope. It's these assholes working for Gold Star Catering. They'll be the ones trying to kill the Pope. But I don't get how they got jobs at Gold Star. They must have someone on the inside working for them, or something.' He paused. 'Fuck it, I don't know.'

The Kid had an answer. 'They don't work for Gold Star. At least, not yet.'

'Huh?'

'Gold Star employees are never told the location of the events they're catering for. They get picked up in the morning and driven directly to the event, which in this case is at Landingham Manor. But a bunch of *these* assholes,' he pointed at the fake ID's Rex was still holding, 'are going to hijack the Gold Star bus tomorrow, execute all the employees and take their place catering for the event. Then they're going to steal something called Mistralyte.'

Rex crushed the ID cards in his hand. 'And they're going to kill the Pope!' he said, raging at the Kid. 'You should have told us all this stuff as soon as you found out about it!'

The Kid reached inside his coat and pulled out a small Kinder Surprise Egg wrapped in orange and white foil. He offered it to Rex. 'Here, have a chocolate egg. It'll calm you down.'

'I don't want a fucking chocolate egg!" Rex scowled. 'Stop offering me fucking chocolate eggs. What's wrong with you?'

'It's got a toy in it.'

'I don't fucking care.'

Elvis had been listening intently throughout, knowing from experience that it was best not to get involved when Rex and the Kid were bickering. He jumped off the workbench he'd been sitting on.

'Are Frankenstein and Dr Jekyll gonna be there?' he asked.

The Kid slipped his chocolate egg back inside his coat and shrugged. 'I guess so. Jekyll is going to poison all the guests with some fucked up champagne. Frankenstein is the muscle.'

'How the hell did you find all this out?' Joey asked.

'I asked one of the guys in the woods before I killed him. He told me all sorts. I think he thought I might let him live if he cooperated.'

Rex laughed out loud to everyone's surprise. 'Boy, did that guy misjudge the situation!'

Joey was more concerned with other, more personal matters. 'Do you know where they've taken Baby?' he asked the Kid.

'No, you can ask them yourself tomorrow when they show up at Landingham.'

Elvis kicked Mozart's headless upper body across the floor. It smacked into the wall and a little more blood splashed out.

'So, Joey?' Elvis said, 'can you get us into Landingham Manor tonight?'

'You bet.'

Rex checked his watch. 'Well at least we know Mozart wasn't the assassin,' he said. 'The time is still counting down. According to my watch the Pope is still due to die in just under twenty hours. So let's get moving.'

Joey couldn't hide his confusion. 'You have a watch counting down the hours 'til the Pope dies?'

Rex rolled his eyes. 'I'll tell you about it on the way.'

Thirty Nine

Blake Jackson had always excelled at hiding his true feelings. Right now he was feeling extremely nervous. Solomon Bennett had phoned to warn him that Joey Conrad was staying in a bunker beneath Landingham Manor. The one person who could fuck up their plan to kill the Pope was living beneath the building where the assassination was to take place. So when Jackson arrived at Landingham Manor accompanied by two of Bennett's mercenaries who were pretending to be marines, his ass was twitching a lot more than usual. The three of them were dressed in woodland camouflage gear, which had been chosen as the standard uniform for all on-patrol officers at Landingham. And they were armed with MP7 submachine guns.

They pulled up outside the main building in an M38 Military jeep. A supplies lorry, driven by another phoney marine parked up behind them.

The lorry was carrying enough crates of *Dr Jekyll's special champagne* to knock out all the guests who had been invited to Calhoon's Christmas Miracle event, and still have enough left over to knock them all out again if necessary.

Mrs Landingham greeted them at the front entrance to the building. She was a seventy-year-old widow, but her vast wealth had enabled her to retain a youthful look. She had auburn hair that was cut short into a bob style that took twenty years off her. She was wearing a smart yellow cardigan over a white blouse with a matching yellow skirt.

Jackson greeted her with a warm smile. 'Lovely to see you again Mrs Landingham.'

'You too, Blake,' she replied, courteously. 'Are you the first of many arriving tonight?'

'No it's just us for now. No one else will be along until 5 a.m. tomorrow. May we come inside?'

'Of course. Can I get you and your men a drink?'

'No, we'll be fine, thank you.'

They entered the main house and Jackson marvelled at the wondrousness of the reception hall. It was huge, with a high ceiling and balconies that ran around the wall on the next level up.

'We just have a few last minute things to attend to,' he said, hoping that Mrs Landingham would take the hint and leave them alone. 'My two colleagues are from the bomb disposal unit. They're just going to take a look around and check there are no explosives hidden anywhere.'

Mrs Landingham looked shocked. 'Is there a bomb on the premises?'

'I very much doubt it, Mrs Landingham. But it would be foolish not to check everywhere just in case, especially with such an important day ahead tomorrow, we can't be too cautious.'

'Please call me Dorothy,' said Mrs Landingham casually. 'Now Blake, I was told that all this security stuff had already been done.'

'It has,' said Jackson. 'Like I said, I'm just being over-cautious. But anyway, more importantly, we've brought you a truck full of champagne for tomorrow night's event.'

'We already have plenty of champagne,' Mrs Landingham said, sounding more than a little offended at the intimation that her own champagne might not be considered up to scratch. 'The cellar here is full of the finest wines and champagnes from around the world. And the Government supplies them all so I don't mind you drinking them. It's what they're there for.'

'Oh, I'm aware of the wonderful cellar you keep here, Dorothy. But we've managed to acquire several crates of a very exclusive Diamant Bleu. This stuff is to be poured out for the guests when the Pope gives his speech tomorrow. It seems only appropriate that such a big occasion be toasted with the finest champagne in the world.'

'Oh I see.'

The lorry driver appeared at the entrance behind them, wheeling in a trolley containing two crates of champagne.

'Where am I taking this?' he asked.

Blake Jackson put his arm around Mrs Landingham's shoulder and smiled at her. His big brown eyes and film star looks worked like a charm on her.

'Could you take my colleague to the kitchen area and show him where to store the champagne, please?' he asked, politely. 'It needs to be kept chilled, but in a place that it can be reached quickly.'

Mrs Landingham seemed to melt within in his arms. Her vulnerability since her husband's death was easily played upon.

'Certainly, Blake,' she said, fluttering her eyelashes.

'Good,' said Jackson, ushering her away. 'While you're doing that, we'll take a look around if you don't mind.'

'Of course.'

Mrs Landingham led the lorry driver off down a corridor towards the kitchen. Jackson gestured for his two colleagues to follow him in the opposite direction, towards the study.

Jackson had never been into the study before but he knew what he was looking for. On a table in the middle of the room was a bronze bust of Adam West. Solomon Bennett had told him all about it. He headed straight for it and pulled the head back. It was heavier than it looked, but the head came loose, just like Bennett said it would. In the centre of the neck was a small white button. Jackson pressed it and almost immediately, one of the bookshelves on the opposite wall slid to one side, revealing an elevator behind it.

'Perfect,' he said, turning to the others. 'I want you two to head down there. If you see Joey Conrad, or anyone else for that matter, shoot on sight, understood?'

'Yes sir,' the two men said in unison.

'And disable the elevator. I don't want anyone coming back up.'

One of the men frowned. 'What about us? How are we supposed to get back up here when we're done?'

'I'll send someone to get you when Joey Conrad is dead.'

'What if he's not there though?'

'You'll wait there for him until he does show up.'

'But what if he doesn't?"

Jackson took a slow breath and resisted the urge to shout. 'If he doesn't show up, you'll have to wait down there all night. Someone will come and get you tomorrow.'

'When?'

'When the Pope is dead.'

Forty

Back at the Hell's Angels Clubhouse, Joey and Rex spent the evening cleaning up the messy remains of Mozart that were splattered all over the floor and walls. Elvis hung out with Jasmine, doing his best to keep her calm after the horrible day she'd had. She stayed fairly quiet and kept her thoughts to herself, possibly not wanting to open up to a bunch of guys she barely knew. The Bourbon Kid headed out on his own, claiming he had better things to do with his time.

After a break for a spot of food, Elvis changed into a light blue suit with gold cufflinks that he kept in a wardrobe in one of the rooms in the clubhouse. Jasmine was still wearing his black leather jacket and he didn't have the heart to ask for it back. Besides, it looked better on her than him.

At around midnight they set off for Landingham Manor, with the intention of arriving at the time when the fewest security people would be on the lookout for them. Elvis drove the four of them there in his purple Cadillac. The car was his pride and joy and he drove it like he was on a Sunday morning cruise through the countryside. Joey was in the back seat with Jasmine who seemed to be enjoying the Bugs Bunny Christmas hits CD that was playing on the car stereo. She was wiggling from side to side and singing along to every track even though it was quite clear that she had no idea what the lyrics were. In her defence she tended to have the chorus sussed by the third time it came up in each song. Considering what a traumatic day she'd had she was surprisingly unaffected by it all. She'd been a quivering mess only a few hours before, but half an hour of Bugs Bunny and the Looney Tunes gang and she was a new woman. Joey did consider the possibility that underneath the mask she was wearing on the top half of her face she might actually look deeply troubled. But that's the thing about people in masks, you just can't tell what the fuck they're thinking.

Rodeo Rex was sitting up front with Elvis. The Bugs Bunny music wasn't really doing it for him, but every time he reached out to eject the CD or switch to the radio, Elvis would slap his hand away.

As they approached the area of woodland that led to the underground tunnel beneath Landingham Manor, Joey reached forward and tapped Elvis on the shoulder and shouted over the music.

'Turn off the road up ahead, between the two trees with the overhanging branches.'

Elvis eased up on the accelerator and steered the car off the road into the bumpy woodland. Joey continued to give him directions through the woods until they saw the abandoned electricity outhouse up ahead. Elvis pulled up outside it, facing the large metal garage door that prevented intruders from breaking in.

'What now?' he asked.

Joey pressed a key fob on a key ring in his pocket. It activated the garage door, which rolled upwards into the roof.

'Drive on in,' he said.

Rex peered through the windscreen to get a better look at what was inside. 'This place looks real shitty,' he commented.

It was pitch black inside the outhouse so Elvis drove in slowly, fearing the worst for his beloved Cadillac. Once they were inside, the metal entrance gate rolled back down behind them. To the untrained eye it looked like they had parked inside an old barn, but as soon as the gate touched down behind them, the floor beneath the car began to move. Jasmine stopped singing along to the *Looney Tunes* for a moment.

'This is weird,' she said. 'We're going down.'

'Don't panic,' said Joey. 'This is perfectly normal.'

Rex disagreed. 'It fuckin' ain't.'

The car dropped down into pitch darkness until it eventually stopped moving. Before anyone could say *"What the fuck is going on?"* a bunch of streetlights came on up ahead. They were in a tunnel, fifty feet below the surface and wide enough for two cars.

'Just drive straight on until you come to another gate,' said Joey.

'Wow!' said Jasmine, clapping her hands together. 'This is so cool. An underground road!'

'It's called a tunnel, honey,' said Rex.

Elvis drove the Cadillac through the tunnel until they reached another reinforced steel garage door at the end. He turned down the volume on the stereo right in the middle of Bugs Bunny (and Jasmine) singing *"Deck the halls with boughs of holly"*.

Elvis looked at Joey through the rear view mirror. 'What now?' he asked.

'Hold on a sec,' said Joey. He pressed the key fob in his pocket again and the sheet gate slid up slowly into the ceiling.

As soon as the gate started moving upwards it became clear that they had a situation. *A fucking serious situation.* Two pairs of army boots came into view, and as the gate rose higher, two pairs of camouflage pants worn by the owners of the boots became visible too.

'You expecting anyone?' Elvis asked.

'Shit no!' said Joey.

There was no way of stopping the metal gate once it was on its way up. As it slid up further, they first saw the black leather belts on the two soldiers, and then their hands and arms. And the submachine guns they were pointing at the car.

The two men, the marines despatched by Blake Jackson, were standing in front of Joey's yellow and red stock car that was always parked just inside the entrance. As soon as they made eye contact with the passengers in the car, the two marines opened fire. The front windscreen of Elvis's Cadillac was peppered with bullets from the two MP7 submachine guns.

Joey grabbed hold of Jasmine and pulled her down behind the front seats out of sight of the gunmen. She hadn't spotted the danger because she was so busy singing. But surprisingly, neither Elvis or Rex bothered to duck down either, not even when the two gunmen opened fire. The sound of bullets from the submachine guns drowned out Bugs Bunny too. Rex poked his head over the back of the seat and looked down at Joey and Jasmine.

'It's okay,' he said. 'We've got a bulletproof windscreen.'

Joey sat up tentatively, pulling Jasmine up with him. She had stopped singing, which was a blessing of sorts. The gunfire didn't let up though. The two marines continued unloading bullets at the car and advanced towards it when they realised they weren't hitting their targets. It didn't seem to dawn on them that they weren't going to penetrate the glass on the car, so their efforts continued to achieve very little, other than occasionally damaging the Cadillac's paintwork.

Elvis held his hand out to Rex and said something that Joey couldn't hear over the gunfire. Rex nodded and opened the glove box. He reached in and pulled out a golden Desert Eagle handgun, which he handed over to Elvis. Elvis took it and checked to see if it was loaded. Then he turned the volume back up on the stereo.

See the blazing Yule before us,
Fa la la la la, la la la la.
Strike the harp and join the chorus,
Fa la la la la, la la la la.

By the end of the second *Fa la la la la* part, which had coincided nicely with the *"rat-a-tat-a-tat"* sound from the guns, both of the marines were out of ammo.

Elvis wound down the electric window on his side, leaned out and fired two shots from the golden gun, one at each of the gunmen. The first man took a bullet to the face and staggered back. His friend hit the ground before him though, courtesy of Elvis's second bullet, which hit him in the throat and carried on up into his brain. A nice spray of blood flew out of the back of his head as he toppled over. The other gunman landed alongside him a moment or two later. *Two bullets, two dead men. Nice shooting.*

Elvis retreated back into his seat, swivelled the gun around in his hand and then passed it back to Rex, handle first. Rex put it back in the glove box next to a few half empty packs of cigarettes.

Elvis wound his window back up, and then looked back over his shoulder at Joey.

'Where should I park?' he asked.

Forty One

Rex and Elvis were extremely impressed with Joey's underground hideout. The two of them spent a good few minutes marvelling at all the gadgets, weapons, computer technology and cool furniture. Jasmine had taken an immediate interest in the private bathroom and after getting permission from Joey, she disappeared inside to take a shower.

'We need to get a place like this,' said Rex, admiring the computer monitors that showed the activity around the estate.

'It's the nicest place I've ever stayed in,' Joey admitted. 'I'm gonna miss it.'

'I bet,' said Rex with genuine sympathy. 'But after tomorrow, regardless of how things pan out, this building is going to be crawling with cops and FBI agents.'

Elvis took some time to admire the double bed that came out of the wall at the press of a button. Truly a work of art, he thought. Unfortunately, after staring at it for a while it reminded him of the awful moment he'd seen Mozart attacking Jasmine in her motel room. He wondered just how badly she had been affected by it. Judging by the sound coming from the bathroom he guessed she was coping pretty well. He could still hear her singing *Deck the Halls* in a Bugs Bunny voice over the sound of water bursting from the showerhead as she freshened up.

Rex walked passed Elvis and over to the elevator. He pressed the button in the wall next to it. The doors opened and he stepped inside and took a look around.

'They fucked with your elevator,' he yelled out.

'What did they do?' Joey yelled back.

'They fucked with your elevator.'

'You already said that. What did they do to it?'

Rex stepped back out of the lift. 'They ripped all the wires out and destroyed the cables in the lift shaft. That thing's going nowhere.'

Elvis stopped admiring the bed for a moment and headed over to Joey to see what he was looking at on his computer screen.

'Whatcha doin' man?' he asked.

'Looking at tomorrow's guest list for the Cancer event.'

'You have access to the guest list?'

'Devon set me up with a computer ID and password that gives me access to everything that Mrs Landingham has.'

On the screen, Joey was looking at photos of all the ID cards for the people on the Christmas Miracle guest list. There were some very ugly people, Elvis noted.

'Is that the Pope?' he asked pointing at one of the pictures on screen.

'Yeah.'

'I like his hat.'

Joey ignored him and carried on scrolling through the identities of each of the guests. Rex came over and joined them, looking over Joey's other shoulder.

'What are you looking for exactly?' he asked.

'Well, seeing as how the elevator is fucked, I'm looking for four people whose identities we can steal so we can get in through the front gates tomorrow.'

'Four?'

'Yeah, the Bourbon Kid is still coming, right?'

Rex laughed and patted his chest as if he'd nearly had a heart attack. 'You know, for a dumb moment there I thought you were talking about bringing Jasmine in on this.'

Joey shook his head. 'No, this is way too dangerous for her, especially after what she's been through today.'

'You're right there,' said Rex. 'That girl is a walking disaster zone at the best of times. And as for the Bourbon Kid, forget about him. If he bothers to show up, he won't want a fake ID. He'll walk in through the front doors, like an asshole.'

'Well that'll make things easier,' said Joey. 'I just need to look for a party of three then. Problem is it's got to be three guests who none of the other guests know, otherwise we'll be rumbled as impostors straight away.'

'How long is this gonna take?' Elvis asked.

'It could take a while so make yourself comfortable.'

Elvis was already bored. Staring at computer screens wasn't his idea of fun. He walked back over to his car to grab a pack of smokes. He'd left the windows down on the Cadillac to let some fresh air in, so he was able to reach through the passenger side window to the glove box. He flicked it open and a couple of packs of cigarettes fell out onto the seat. He reached down to pick one up, inwardly cursing Rex for moving everything around when he'd put the gun back.

As he stood up, ready to pull a cigarette from the pack, it occurred to him that Jasmine had stopped singing. The shower was still running, but for the first time in hours she had gone quiet. He tucked the cigarettes inside his jacket and walked over to the bathroom door.

Neither Rex nor Joey was paying him any attention so he opened the door and let himself in.

The bathroom was steamed up from all the hot water in the shower. But Elvis wasn't there to look at the steam. He wasn't even there to peek at Jasmine's naked body. He was there for a far more noble reason. To stop her from blowing her brains out with the gun that had vanished from his glove box.

Her clothes were strewn across the floor. Elvis followed the trail, which started with the leather jacket he had given her, followed by her bra, shiny hotpants, a thong and finally, next to her feet he saw the facemask she had been wearing to cover up the bruises around her eyes. She was sitting on the floor in the shower with hot water washing down over her naked body.

Her hands were wrapped around the handle of the shiny Gold Desert Eagle and the barrel of it was in her mouth. The thumb on her right hand was pressed lightly against the trigger. If she applied a tiny bit more pressure to it she could ruin her good looks forever.

'I'll really miss you if you pull that trigger,' said Elvis.

Jasmine looked up, startled. She hadn't seen him come in. In spite of all the water from the shower washing over her, he could see in her eyes that she was crying. And she was shivering too, even though the water was hot. He approached her slowly and crouched down beside her. He put his hand on her head and wiped her hair back, tucking a few strands carefully behind her ear.

'Can I tell you something?' he said softly.

Jasmine's head flickered up and down just enough to be classed as nodding her head and she whimpered something inaudible. Elvis took it as a *yes*.

'You're the most fun person I met this week,' he whispered tenderly in her ear.

She sobbed harder and coughed a little, her teeth chattering against the barrel of the gun. Her grip on the handle loosened a little and for just a brief moment, Elvis thought he saw the tiniest of smiles in her eyes. He reached out and gently unwrapped her hands from the handle of the gun, slowly pulling it from her mouth.

She lowered her head, pressing it down between her knees, sobbing uncontrollably. Elvis tucked the gun away down the back of his pants and rubbed her back and shoulders.

'I know it's been rough today,' he said. 'But you've got friends here.'

'I heard what you were all saying about me.'

Elvis cast his mind back to Rex shouting off about how Jasmine was a disaster zone who wouldn't be joining them in tomorrow's big mission. 'Take no notice of Rex,' he said, rubbing her back some more. 'He hasn't sussed you out yet, that's all. He just sees what you show on the surface. I can see through all that. You're as smart as you are sexy.'

She reached up and touched the swelling around her eyes. 'I don't feel sexy right now.'

Elvis gave her a comforting smile. 'If you weren't sexy then why the hell did I sneak in here to watch you in the shower?'

Success! Jasmine smiled. She had such a beautiful smile. Elvis had noticed it before, but now more than ever it really lit up her face.

'You snuck in here to watch me in the shower?' she said, feigning shock.

'Yeah. Why else would I be in here?'

The smile on her face broadened ever so slightly. She reached up and flicked the quiff on his hair. 'You'd better pass me a towel so I can cover myself up.'

Elvis stood up and grabbed a blue towel from a nearby towel rack. Jasmine stood up and allowed him to wrap it around her, giving him an eyeful of her naked body at the same time. Whether or not that was intentional he couldn't tell. Perhaps it was her way of rewarding him for showing up when he did. Either way, with or without the bruises and swollen face, she was unbelievably cute.

'You won't tell the others about this, will you,' she said, wiping the tears from under her eyes.

'There's nothing to tell.'

She smiled again, her natural warmth and glow returning. 'I wasn't going to pull the trigger,' she said.

'I know. You were just using the gun to work on your blowjob technique, right?'

'How did you guess?'

The two of them shared a knowing look. No more needed to be said. A bond of trust and friendship had been formed between them and it would never be broken. And Elvis would never mention to her that he knew there were no bullets left in the gun anyway. And she in turn would never tell him that she knew that too because she'd squeezed the trigger twice before he found her.

Elvis left the bathroom and closed the door quietly behind him. He pulled a cigarette out and lit it with a zippo lighter before re-joining Rex and Joey at the computer desk.

'You sneaky bastard,' Rex said, without even looking at him, keeping his gaze fixed on the photo ID's on the computer screen.

'What do you mean?' said Elvis, puffing on his cigarette.

'She's just seen her man killed this morning and you're hitting on her in the shower. That's low.'

'I just needed a piss. I didn't see anything.'

Rex shook his head, disapprovingly. 'Yeah, right,' he said.

'We should bring her in on this with us tomorrow,' said Elvis. 'Having a woman with us will make us look much less suspicious.'

Rex lowered his voice. 'No way. She should stay out of this. These guys aren't playing around. They've got machine guns. It ain't safe for a woman.'

Jasmine walked out of the bathroom. She was wearing nothing but the blue towel Elvis had given her and it didn't cover very much at all.

'I can hear you, you know!' she hissed at Rex. 'These people are responsible for what happened to Jack and they kidnapped Baby. So I'm coming too, whether you like it or not. Where you guys go, *I go*.'

Rex raised his hands defensively. 'Listen, sugar, I'm just looking out for you. We're your friends here and we just don't wanna see you get hurt. It'll take some serious skills to survive up there tomorrow.'

'I've got moves,' said Jasmine. 'I've been a hooker for most of my life. You don't last in that business if you don't have a few tricks up your sleeve.'

'You have moves?' Rex said, mocking her. 'Like what? Kung Fu?'

'Wanna see?' said Jasmine.

'*I do*,' said Elvis. He leant down and whispered in Joey's ear. 'Five bucks says she kicks him in the balls.'

'You're on.'

Jasmine walked up to Rex and stood in front of him with her hands on her hips. 'You ready?' she asked, defiantly.

'Go on,' said Rex, wearily.

Jasmine pulled her towel open, giving him an eyeful of her naked body. Rex's eyes bulged wide open and he swallowed hard. His face burned bright with embarrassment and he seemed unsure where to look.

'What do you think of my tattoos?' Jasmine asked, fiercely.

The strange thing was, Jasmine didn't have any tattoos. Rex was confused and unsure what he was supposed to be looking at. The temporary confusion was all Jasmine needed. She swung her right leg hard and fast at his crotch. Her foot caught him flush in the balls, hard enough to have nailed a fifty-yard field goal.

Rex grabbed his balls and dropped to his knees, groaning in pain. Jasmine wrapped her towel back around her, ending the peep show rather abruptly. Rex head-butted the floor and retched like he was about to be sick.

Elvis dropped his cigarette and started clapping. 'Good fucking show!'

'See,' said Jasmine. 'I've got moves, right?' She looked over at Elvis and Joey, smiling broadly.

Elvis carried on applauding. 'Best fuckin' move I ever saw, Jaz.'

'I'll second that,' Joey agreed, handing Elvis a five-dollar bill.

'So I'm in?' Jasmine asked. 'Can I be a Dead Hunter?'

Rex sat up in a kneeling position, rubbing his balls and trying to coax them back out of his stomach. 'You can come with us tomorrow,' he croaked. 'But you can't be a Dead Hunter.'

'Why not?'

'You gotta kill someone if you wanna become one of us. Me, Elvis and the Bourbon Kid, we're all outlaws wanted for murder.'

Joey wheeled his chair back round to get back to work, checking the photo ID's on the computer. Four faces were already staring back at him. Four ID cards featuring three men and a woman.

'I think I found what we're looking for,' he said.

'What you got?' said Elvis hurrying over to his side.

Joey looked round at the others. 'I need a photo of each of you.'

Jasmine's face lit up. 'I've got some great photos of me on my phone.'

'I only need one of your face.'

'Good, 'cause that's all your getting.'

Rex stood up and walked gingerly over to Joey. 'What have you found?'

Joey pointed at the four ID cards pictured on the computer screen. 'I'll put our faces on these ID's and create new cards. We can replace these four people at the event tomorrow.'

'Who are they?' said Rex, taking a closer look at the screen.

Elvis leaned in too and saw immediately why Joey had picked the four people on screen. 'I like it,' he said. 'This is a fucking great plan.'

Forty Two

Dante and Kacy had been working for Gold Star Catering for three weeks. They had never intended for it to be a long-term job. Kacy had befriended one of the women who worked there and found out the truth about what Gold Star really did. It was so much more than just a catering company. It was a gateway to the rich and famous. If a Hollywood movie star or a mega rich oil baron was hosting a private party and they wanted to guarantee discretion, Gold Star was the "go-to" company. And that's what attracted Dante and Kacy to the job, the opportunity to steal some shit from a bunch of rich folk.

Their first two assignments had been rather seedy affairs. The first had involved catering a sex party for the rich and famous. Every person at the party had been wearing a facemask, and virtually nothing else. It was like walking onto the set of the movie *Eyes Wide Shut*. That's not to suggest that Tom Cruise was there, but he might have been because plenty of other actors and actresses were. The big problem with that event of course, was that with all the dinner guests in the nude, there was nothing to steal from them. All of the wallets and purses had been locked away securely, which meant the only thing available to steal was the jewellery the guests were wearing. They had tried it, but when Kacy suggested Dante pinched a blonde lady's ring, he'd misunderstood and pinched her ass instead, which nearly cost him his job.

The second event had been far less glamorous. An old lady with more money than sense had thrown a secret million-dollar birthday party for her pet poodle. The poodle had invited all its friends and, well, poodles and spaniels don't have much in the way of cash on them, so there was little to be gained from that night apart from a tin of dog treats that Dante stole as a matter of principle.

But this third job, rumour had it, was going to be the big one they had been waiting for. Kacy's friend Suzy had heard rumours that they were being taken to a country mansion for a billionaires' charity event. And it was possible that the Pope would be there. And maybe, Bono from the band U2. Dante hated Bono, so the opportunity to steal something from him or even just to punch him in the face held great appeal.

At seven o'clock in the morning Dante and Kacy both received the same text message. It informed them to be at a vacant parking lot on the edge of town. Usual rules apply. Leave your phones at home and don't bring any cameras or recording devices.

Dante drove them there in a Volkswagen Beetle he had stolen the night before. He hadn't realised when he stole it that it was a piece of shit. It spluttered and bounced for fifteen miles before it finally broke down on a deserted highway with nothing in sight but rocks. And more rocks.

Kacy looked across at her husband with a disapproving look, something she seemed to do a lot. 'You've got a real knack for stealing shit cars haven't you?' she moaned.

He picked up on her judgmental look and responded accordingly, with a grin. They'd been together as a couple for so long now that he knew he only had to grin at her when he'd fucked something up. They had both recently turned thirty and should have grown up by now. But he still loved stealing things and she loved going along for the ride.

He leaned across the front seat and kissed her on the mouth, his floppy dark hair, tickling her face. And she kissed him right back. Just like she always did.

'We're gonna have to run from here,' he said.

Kacy sighed and pulled down the sun visor so she could take a look at her reflection in the mirror on the other side of it. She tied her long black hair back into a ponytail and checked her make-up.

'You look gorgeous, babe,' said Dante.

'I might not after I've run two miles.'

'You look sexy when you've been running.'

She threw him another evil stare, which melted away as soon as she made eye contact with him. Him and his stupid, heart-melting grin.

'Come on then, let's go,' she said. 'We're already late.'

They got out of the car and started walking down the highway. There were no clouds in the sky so the early morning sun was glaring in their eyes.

'They really do choose some shitty places to pick us up from,' Dante complained.

'It's so journalists can't track where we're going.'

'All a journalist would have to do is follow us, or your friend Suzy with the bright red hair.'

'I suppose,' said Kacy. 'But let's face it, if they'd been following us for the last week they'd have wasted a lot of time.'

The sound of a bus's horn screeched through the air. Dante grabbed Kacy and pulled her to the side of the road. A silver bus sped past them down the highway.

'Shit,' said Kacy. 'I bet that's our bus!'

Gold Star Catering had a fleet of buses. One thing you could guarantee is that the bus wouldn't be gold coloured or have the words

Gold Star Catering on it anywhere. The only way it could be identified was by its registration number. Only the people hosting the party would be made aware of the number. Even the Gold Star employees would not be told. They only ever knew it was a Gold Star bus because the driver was always the same, a fat guy called Bubba who sweated a lot.

Dante grabbed Kacy by the hand and dragged her down the road after the bus. Fortunately they only had to run about a hundred metres before a station wagon pulled up alongside them and stopped. Kacy looked in through the window and saw Chantelle, a middle aged blonde lady who as luck would have it, was one of the Gold Star supervisors. Chantelle had two other Gold Star employees riding in the back of the car already. She reached across and opened the passenger side door.

'You two need a ride?' she asked.

'Fuck yeah,' said Dante.

'One of you can squeeze in the back. The other can ride up front with me.'

Kacy wasted no time and jumped in the front seat. Dante hopped in the back with the two other passengers. As soon as the doors were slammed shut, Chantelle pulled away again, with the tyres screeching on the road.

Dante looked across at the two other passengers in the back. He didn't recognise either of them. The one next to him was a butch lady who looked a bit like a young Jon Voigt. On the other side of her was a thin fellow in his mid-thirties with a big ginger perm.

'You guys new?' Dante asked them.

'Yeah,' said the woman.

'Nice to meet you. I'm Dante and that pretty lady up front is my wife, Kacy.'

The woman smiled. 'I'm Denise,' she said. 'And this is Henry. We're good friends of Chantelle. We're filling in for a couple of others who rang in sick this morning.'

'Oh cool, who's sick?'

Denise didn't reply. She tapped the back of Chantelle's chair instead and instructed her to turn up the music on the car stereo. Chantelle turned it up to EXTREMELY LOUD, so for the rest of the journey, it was impossible to have any further conversation.

The pick up point was a parking lot outside a giant superstore. When they arrived, the bus was already there and all of the other Gold Star employees were already on board. Chantelle parked her car in a space between two BMWs and killed the engine, and thankfully the loud music too.

'Looks like we made it in the nick of time,' she said.

Dante jumped out of the station wagon and opened the passenger door, hauling Kacy out before she was ready.

'What's the big rush?' she grumbled.

Dante whispered in her ear. 'Hurry up, the bus is almost full. I don't want to have to sit next to anyone else.'

Kacy understood his haste immediately. They'd been separated once before and she'd had to sit up front in a shitty little seat next to Bubba. Bubba was a nice guy, but he had terrible flatulence and after half an hour of inhaling his sweaty farts, Kacy had felt ill for the rest of the day. So with that in mind the two of them raced across the parking lot to the bus.

They showed their ID badges to Bubba through the glass door at the front of the bus. He granted them permission to board and opened the door. To their dismay, the only two-person seat still available was at the front, directly behind Bubba. Dante, ever the courteous husband, allowed Kacy to have the window seat, just in case Bubba had eaten anything spicy for breakfast.

The next person to board the bus was Henry. He insisted on sitting on the small seat at the front with Bubba. Dante and Kacy nudged each other and sniggered, amused by the thought of watching Henry sniffing Bubba's farts for the entire journey.

A further minute passed by before Denise boarded the bus on her own. She spotted a free seat halfway down the aisle and headed towards it.

'Where's Chantelle?' Kacy asked her as she walked past.

'She's not feeling well,' said Denise. 'She'll catch up with us later.'

The bus pulled away and drove out of the parking lot. On the way out they passed Chantelle's station wagon. Chantelle was still sitting in the driver's seat. To the untrained eye she looked like she was asleep. But much later that day, a passer-by would notice that she had cheese wire wrapped around her neck. Denise had used it to strangle her from the back seat.

Chantelle's death would be the first of many that day.

Forty Three

When Rex, Elvis and Joey got started on working out their plan for the next day, Jasmine felt like she was watching one of those musical montages in an episode of *The A Team* where the guys build a tank out of whatever crap they can find lying around. Rex and Elvis had filled a sports bag up with guns and ammunition. Joey created some cool Gold Star ID badges and Jasmine entertained them all by singing along to some more of the *Bugs Bunny Christmas album.*

At about 4 a.m. they all took a break and caught up on some sleep. Jasmine snuggled up to Elvis in the double bed. Rex slept in the back of Elvis's Cadillac and Joey slept in his red and yellow stock car.

Three hours sleep was all they managed. But it was enough.

At seven a.m. they got back to business. The sports bag with all the guns and ammo was left behind in the bunker, to be collected later. The plan was to lower someone back down on a rope or ladder via the elevator shaft once they were inside the main building. There was no other way to get the guns past security. It wasn't the best plan in the world. As a matter of fact everyone was in agreement that it was a "shit plan", but it was the *best* "shit plan" they could come up with.

By seven-thirty, the four of them were hiding out in the woods, and according to Rex's stopwatch they had less than five hours until the Pope's assassination. They watched a number of limousines and other very expensive vehicles drive past on their way to Landingham Manor for the *Christmas Miracle* event. Over an hour passed before the vehicle they were waiting for showed up. A huge brown bus with blacked out windows cruised down the country lane headed for the Landingham mansion. On the side of the bus in big red letters were the words "DOUBLE FANTASY".

Elvis nudged Jasmine. 'Go do your stuff, honey.'

Double Fantasy was the name of a well-known quartet of Rock star impersonators. Four performers who travelled the world dazzling people everywhere with their impersonations of Jon Bon Jovi, David Bowie, Britney Spears and Elvis Presley.

Jasmine was rather excited about the fact she was going to take the place of the Britney Spears impersonator even though she had argued for some time that she did a good Jon Bon Jovi impression. But as it was explained to her, that would mean Rodeo Rex had to impersonate Britney Spears and he didn't quite look the part.

The first part of the plan involved Jasmine utilising her amazing skills at "pretending" to be stupid. She ran out into the middle of the road as the bus approached and began waving her arms around begging them to stop. Because she was only wearing a pair of hotpants and a black bra and her face was covered in bruises, she genuinely looked like a damsel in distress. So it was no great shock when the bus stopped and a Jon Bon Jovi impersonator stepped off. He was wearing a yellow sleeveless T-shirt and black leather pants. And he had a magnificent eighties mullet haircut.

'Are you okay, honey?' he asked, approaching her.

Another man stepped off the bus behind him. Jasmine figured he was supposed to be David Bowie from his Ziggy Stardust phase. He had a ghostly white face and bright orange hair. He was wearing a creepy skin-tight onesie with green and red vertical stripes on it and a pair of bright orange boots.

'What the fuck are we stopping for?' he shouted to Jon Bon Jovi.

Jasmine did as Rex had instructed her earlier. She stood still and played dumb. Rex, Joey and Elvis crept out of the bushes at the roadside behind Bon Jovi and Bowie. Elvis sneaked aboard the bus, while Rex and Joey tiptoed up behind the two guys.

David Bowie obviously heard them coming because he spun around to see what was going on. And he walked right into a face-smash from Rex. There was a loud CLANK as Rex's metal fist connected with his forehead. His bright orange wig flew off and he fell backwards. He was unconscious before he even hit the ground.

Joey walked past Rex and up to Jon Bon Jovi. Bon Jovi raised his fists, prepared to fight back.

'Put your hands down or you're gonna get hurt,' Joey warned.

Bon Jovi ignored him and foolishly swung a punch. Joey ducked under it, moved inside like a boxer and retaliated with a short sharp jab to Bon Jovi's stomach. The wannabe rock star doubled over and staggered back a few steps as he struggled for breath, clutching his stomach.

Rex walked up alongside Joey. 'Why didn't you knock him out?' he asked, his voice rife with disapproval.

'I gave him a *shit-punch* instead,' said Joey.

Jasmine wasn't sure she'd heard him correctly. 'What's a *shit-punch?*' she inquired.

Joey didn't need to answer. Jon Bon Jovi demonstrated the effects of a *shit-punch* as soon as she asked. He suddenly farted really loudly. He stopped holding his stomach and instead grabbed his ass with both hands. His eyes were filled with panic. A loud squelching sound came from the backside of his leather pants, he dropped to his knees and then toppled backwards, landing at Jasmine's feet, writhing in agony, accompanied by an awful stench of shit.

Jasmine covered her mouth and nose. 'Ooh, what have you been eating?' she asked him.

Rex wandered over and peered down at the Jon Bon Jovi impersonator. The guy was in considerable distress and looked very embarrassed. Rex looked back at Joey.

'You made him shit himself? Why?'

'It's something I learnt when I was in Operation Blackwash,' said Joey. 'Hit a guy in the sweet spot just below his abdomen, with the perfect level of force and you can cause his bowels to open, and it makes him shit himself.'

Rex tutted. He didn't seem impressed at all. He raised his right boot above the head of the shitting Bon Jovi impersonator and stamped on his head, rendering him unconscious and giving him a nosebleed.

'Far easier just to knock him out,' Rex said, overstating his point.

Joey nodded. 'I know that, but I figured this dude wanted to go down in a *blaze of glory!*'

Rex sighed. 'That's the only reason you did that isn't it? You wanted to shoe-horn in the name of a Bon Jovi song. You're worse than my friend Sanchez.'

Jasmine tapped Rex on the shoulder and made a suggestion. 'Maybe he had some *bad medicine?*'

'Don't you start' Rex grumbled. 'This is no time for shit jokes.' He pointed at Joey. 'You can be the one to carry this stinky bastard into the woods. I ain't touching him.'

'Fair enough.'

Joey grabbed the foul-smelling Bon Jovi by his armpits and dragged him off the road into the bushes. Rex picked up the David Bowie impersonator and followed him in.

Jasmine looked around. There was nothing left for her to do. She ran up to the bus to see how Elvis was getting on inside, dealing with the two other singers. As she approached, Elvis poked his head around the door and gestured for her to hurry up.

'Jaz, come here, I need you to do something.'

She jumped aboard the bus behind Elvis. It was immediately obvious that things had gotten messy on board the Double Fantasy tour bus. It looked like the place had been smashed up. A table lamp was on the floor, the bulb of it smashed into tiny pieces. Next to it, bleeding from a cut to his head was another Elvis impersonator, a fat guy in a white jumpsuit. His wig had come off, and without it he looked less like Elvis and more like Jasmine's favourite actor, Elias Koteas.

'Don't worry about him,' said Elvis. 'He's asleep.'

Jasmine soon became aware of the real problem. Elvis stepped aside so she could get a look at the attractive young Britney Spears impersonator cowering at the back of the bus. She was wearing the red catsuit from the *Oops I did It Again* video and she looked terrified. She saw Jasmine and pleaded with her.

'Please don't hurt me.'

'I'm not going to hurt you,' said Jasmine, offering her some reassurance.

Elvis cleared his throat. 'Yeah, Jaz, I can't knock her out. I don't hit ladies, so I kind of need you to do it.'

Jasmine pushed Elvis aside and backed away from him towards Britney Spears. 'It's okay honey,' she said, looking over her shoulder at Britney. 'I won't hurt you.'

She positioned herself in a way that made it appear as if she was shielding the Britney Spears impersonator from Elvis.

Elvis frowned. 'What the fuck are you doing?'

'I told you, we're not hurting her!' Jasmine retorted. Then she winked at Elvis so he would know she was lying.

When she was close enough to Britney, she demonstrated another one of her amazing fighting moves. It was even better than the *"Look at my tits and I'll kick you in the nuts"* routine she had performed on Rex the night before. Jasmine was a very flexible young woman. And one of her best party tricks was the ability to swing one of her legs over her head from a standing position. She flung her right leg up in a kicking motion that kept on going until her foot flashed past her ear. The toe end of her high-heeled shoe hit Britney hard in the face. Her head jolted back and smashed into the bottom of a cupboard on the wall behind her. She turned cross-eyed and crumpled to the floor in a heap, completely unconscious, just like Elvis had asked.

'How's that?' Jasmine asked with a beaming smile.

Elvis's peered over his sunglasses at her. 'That was fuckin' awesome,' he said. 'You've given yourself a nasty case of camel toe though.'

'I can soon get rid of that.'

The overhead kick had caused Jasmine's red hotpants to ride up into what looked like an uncomfortable position. Instead of rearranging them, she pulled them right down to her ankles and flicked them off the end of her leg. Elvis caught them in his right hand. Jasmine undid her bra and threw that at him too.

'Don't just stand there staring!' she said. 'Help me get this catsuit off Britney Spears.'

Jasmine was now wearing nothing but her high-heeled shoes. And although Elvis was a gentleman, he still reacted the same way every other guy did when Jasmine was naked. He stopped listening to what she was saying and looked her up and down.

She clicked her fingers at him. 'Hello, *Earth to Elvis*, help me get the catsuit off Britney Spears!'

Elvis snapped out of his gawping, although not before Jasmine noticed the bulge appearing in the pants on his blue suit.

'Uh yeah, right,' he said. 'Catsuit. Off.'

'I'm gonna need you to zip me up too. Hurry up before the others show up. This ain't a peep show you know!'

For the next two minutes, Elvis helped Jasmine remove the catsuit from the unconscious Britney Spears and then zipped her up in it. It turned out to be a perfect fit.

'How do I look?' Jasmine asked, twirling around.

'Not bad at all,' said Elvis.

Jasmine kissed him on the cheek. 'Thanks for everything.'

Rex and Joey boarded the bus. Rex took one look at the unconscious fat dude in the white jumpsuit and then at the Britney Spears lookalike who was on the floor wearing just her underwear.

'What the fuck have you two been doing?' he grumbled. 'We've already tied the other two up in the woods!'

Elvis sat down on a pull-out sofa by the windows. 'I've been helping Jasmine get changed,' he said, breathing heavily.

'Yeah, I'll bet you have,' said Rex. 'Well you can carry this fat dude off the bus. I ain't doing it for you.'

'Just gimme a minute,' said Elvis. 'I need to sit down for a while.'

'He's got a boner,' Jasmine added.

Rex sighed. 'He's always got a fuckin' boner.'

The sound of a car approaching reminded them all of the urgency of their situation. Joey pressed his face up against one of the windows, safe in the knowledge that it was heavily tinted so no one would see in.

'Holy shit!' he said.

'What is it?' said Rex.

'That's the Pope!'

Everyone, apart from Elvis got up and stared out of the windows. Four Black Bentleys drove past one after the other with just a few feet in between them, like a funeral procession. The Pope was sitting in the back seat of the third car.

Rex looked at his watch. According to the timer, the Pope would be dead in three hours time.

Forty Four

The Gold Star Catering bus had travelled barely a mile towards its destination when Bubba the driver suddenly started choking and collapsed, sliding off his chair onto the floor. For a few shaky moments it looked like the bus might crash but Henry, the new guy with the big ginger perm, slid over to the driver's seat and stopped the bus.

Kacy was about to offer Bubba some assistance, but before she could get out of her seat, Henry's friend Denise barged past and shoved her back down. Denise insisted she was a qualified nurse and could handle the situation on her own. She hauled Bubba up from the floor and performed the Heimlich manoeuvre on him. It didn't seem to achieve much. If anything it looked like she was trying to perform some kind of wrestling move. The incident eventually ended with her hauling him up and slamming him down on the floor in the middle of the aisle.

Henry carried on driving and Denise stood in the aisle assuring everyone that the drama was over.

'Nothing to see here!' she shouted several times.

Kacy looked down at Bubba's head, which was right by her feet. His eyes were bloodshot red and his mouth was open, gasping for air.

'I think he's had an allergic reaction to something,' she suggested.

'And I think you should keep your mouth shut,' said Denise, aggressively. 'I'm a fucking nurse, all right? What he needs is to be left alone.' She addressed the rest of the bus again, raising her voice in order to be heard at the back. 'Everyone remain in your seats. We're carrying on to our destination. Bubba's going to be just fine.'

Denise stayed in the aisle, on her knees, occasionally thumping Bubba in the chest for no obvious reason, while Henry drove the bus much faster than Bubba had done, as if he was in a desperate hurry to get to their destination.

After about half a mile, Dante leaned forward and tapped him on the shoulder. 'So do you actually know where we're going?' he asked.

Henry glanced over his shoulder. 'It's a secret. I can't say.'

Kacy tapped him on his other shoulder. 'Do you know if there's going to be any famous people there?'

Henry's big ginger perm brushed in Dante's face as he turned to look over his other shoulder at Kacy. His hair didn't smell good. Dante grimaced as he took a full waft of it up his nose. *"This guy must wash his hair in dog shit!"*

220

'We're almost there,' Henry said. 'You're gonna love it, I promise.'

Kacy grabbed a hold of Dante's hand and whispered in his ear. 'Won't it be great if there really are some movie stars or pop stars at this event?'

'I heard a rumour that Dirk Benedict was in town.'

'Who's he?'

Dante didn't reply. He'd spotted a sign post up ahead. 'This doesn't look too promising,' he said.

'What's that?'

'We're heading to the old industrial estate. The one where all the drug dealers hang out.'

'What drug dealers?'

'Remember LeBron and Tina?'

'The tracksuit millionaires?'

'Yeah. They ran their operation out here.'

Kacy squeezed Dante's hand. 'Please tell me you didn't steal from them.'

Dante kissed her on the forehead. 'You worry too much.'

A few minutes later they arrived at the industrial site where LeBron and Tina ran their operation. Henry drove the bus into a large warehouse and parked up. Dante had been inside the warehouse once before. It had been full of boxes and bags filled with drugs back then. Times had obviously changed. It no longer looked like the headquarters of LeBron's drug empire. The place was empty.

'What the fuck are we doing here?' he said, tapping Henry on the shoulder.

Henry ignored him and pulled a handle to open the doors at the front of the bus. A burly man with a military flattop haircut jumped aboard. He was wearing the same black and white uniform as everyone on the bus, but he definitely didn't work for Gold Star. *And he was carrying a machine gun.*

'Everybody off the fucking bus!' he shouted. 'You've got ten seconds. Anyone still on the bus after that is getting shot in the face!'

His warning worked remarkably well. Within ten seconds everyone had exited the bus, whether it was by the front exits or the emergency exit at the back. Everyone that is, apart from Henry and Denise (and Bubba, who was trampled underfoot by many of the fleeing caterers).

Two more gunmen, also dressed like Gold Star employees ushered everyone away from the bus and over to the wall furthest away from the entrance. Sixty caterers in all were shepherded over there.

Anyone who dared to question what was going on was either kicked in the back or had a gun pointed at him or her in a threatening manner.

One of the gunmen, a bearded fellow with a shaved head, shouted out an order. 'Everybody get down on your knees and face the wall. Anyone who looks around will be shot! Don't test me on this. Do as you're told and no one will get hurt!'

Having been the first two off the bus, Dante and Kacy were lined up furthest away from the gunmen in the far corner of the warehouse. So Dante, in spite of being down on his knees facing the wall, was able to see what was going on out of the corner of his eye.

A second group of caterers, all dressed exactly like the Gold Star team, were boarding the bus. Even Dante, who was not a particularly smart man, could see that they were being replaced by a group of robbers or terrorists.

But there was one man who stood out from the others. He wasn't boarding the bus and he wasn't dressed like a Gold Star employee. This guy looked like Frankenstein because he had a pair of metal bolts protruding from his neck. He was dressed in black and he had a gun holstered on his hip. And he was standing next to a really cool silver motorbike. Dante considered the possibility that it might be worth stealing the bike if they could get out of this alive.

With a nod of his head, Frankenstein gave a silent order to the two gunmen who had lined everyone up against the wall. They immediately dashed off to board the bus with the others.

A man with an eye patch over his right eye poked his head out of the bus and shouted across to Frankenstein. 'Lock up when you're finished here. I'll see you at the estate!'

Frankenstein nodded but said nothing.

Kacy nudged Dante and whispered in his ear. 'What the fuck is going on?'

'I don't know. Just stay close to me.'

The man with the eye patch ducked back inside the bus and it drove out of the warehouse with the new Gold Star crew on board.

Kacy was beginning to panic. 'That Frankenstein guy is going to kill us all.'

'Don't worry,' Dante whispered back. 'I'll think of something.'

Further down the line of imprisoned caterers, one of the men burst out crying. Dante recognised him. It was Ramjam, a young Asian gentleman who was renowned for his panic attacks when under pressure. 'Please do not kill us!' he shouted, foolishly.

A few of the other Gold Star employees shushed him, but his sobbing grew louder and more hysterical. He kept repeating the phrase,

"I do not wish to die today". If Dante had had a gun he would have shot him just to shut him up. Ramjam was doing no one any favours, least of all himself. Predictably his whining began to irritate Frankenstein. The giant brute unholstered his gun.

'Be quiet, bitch,' he said in a monotone voice. 'No one has to die. You all wait here.'

Unfortunately Ramjam didn't believe him. In a moment of panic he made a run for it. He sprinted past Frankenstein and off towards the opening where the bus had exited. Frankenstein turned slowly, watching him run. Then in an almost mechanical fashion, he pointed his gun at Ramjam's back and took aim.

BANG!

The bullet burst through Ramjam's back and a spray of blood burst out through his chest as it passed right through him. His legs gave way beneath him and he collapsed to the ground, dead.

The death of Ramjam should have served as a warning to everyone else. Unfortunately it had the opposite effect. It sparked a major panic. A midget who Dante knew only as Little Bo, made a run for it too and was gunned down in similar style without covering half as much distance as Ramjam. Suddenly like a pack of lemmings, half of the catering staff decided to make a run for it, as if it was a good idea, which it obviously wasn't. Frankenstein started gunning them down one by one, making sure no one got close to the exit.

Dante grabbed Kacy and shouted above the gunfire. 'Wait until he runs out of bullets and has to reload! Then run like hell for the exit. I'll distract him.'

'Come with me!' Kacy yelled back, her voice barely audible over the noise.

'Trust me I've got a plan.'

'I'm not leaving you!'

Frankenstein gunned down at least ten people before he had to stop and reload. Dante pushed Kacy towards the exit. 'Go!' he shouted. 'I'll catch up with you. I gotta plan, *honest*. Go!'

Kacy kissed him and then sprinted for the exit along with everyone else. Dante took a deep breath and bolted over to Frankenstein's blindside. The big oaf never saw him coming because he was too busy reloading his gun, ready to open fire on the rest of the fleeing caterers. Dante remembered what he'd learned when playing high-school football. Always tackle the big guys low around the knees. He charged full pelt at Frankenstein and ploughed into the back of his legs. They were without doubt the sturdiest legs Dante had ever encountered and for a moment, he wasn't sure if his plan was going to work. But just as he'd been taught to always aim for the knees, he'd also been told to always see a tackle through to the end. It took a while but eventually Frankenstein's knees bent and he toppled forward into a kneeling position. Dante climbed onto his back and wrapped his arm around his neck. He squeezed as hard as he could. Frankenstein's neck was as solid as his legs though. It was like trying to strangle a lamppost. It had no effect on the bastard whatsoever. Frankenstein climbed back to his feet with Dante clinging onto him from behind.

Any normal man would have been preoccupied with ridding himself of the person hanging on his back trying to strangle him. *Not Frankenstein.* He ignored Dante and focussed on gunning down the escaping prisoners. Kacy was at the front of the pack, close to the exit. Dante kept his eyes on her the whole time, and to give her a fighting chance he placed one of his hands over Frankenstein's goggles to try and blind him. It worked. Dante breathed a huge sigh of relief when Frankenstein missed Kacy but gunned down five or six other Gold Star employees instead.

Eventually when all of the fleeing caterers were either dead or outside and still running for their lives, Frankenstein decided to rid himself of the irritant hanging around his neck. He reached up with his free hand and grabbed Dante by the collar on his shirt. He lifted him up and threw him over his shoulder. Dante landed flat on his back on the concrete floor, with the fight knocked right out of him.

Frankenstein straightened up and loomed over Dante. He took aim with his gun, pointing it at Dante's forehead. Dante stared down the barrel, waiting for a bullet to fly out and hit him in the face. Frankenstein was a millisecond away from pulling the trigger when, out of nowhere, he was distracted by the sound of screeching tyres. He took his eye off Dante and looked over at the exit.

Dante lifted his head too, to see what was coming. A black Pontiac Firebird had raced into the warehouse and was speeding towards them. Dante mustered enough energy to roll out of the way before it reached them. The Firebird roared past him and ploughed into Frankenstein. The giant thug tried to jump out of the way at the last moment, but his feet barely left the ground before the car hit him. He bounced onto the hood, into the windscreen and then over the roof. He landed with an almighty thud on the concrete floor. The driver of the Firebird pulled a handbrake turn and the car skidded to a halt. The door on the passenger side opened and to Dante's surprise, Kacy jumped out.

'I got some help!' she shouted.

Considering she'd only been gone for a matter of seconds, Dante had to applaud her ability to find help so quickly. Before he could congratulate her though, Frankenstein lumbered to his feet. The impact of being pummelled by a car at high speed had done nothing to hurt him. This guy was like a fucking Terminator, or one of those ants that just refuses to die, no matter what you spray it with.

But when Kacy says she's going to get help, she sure does come up with the goods. The door on the driver's side of the Firebird opened and the Bourbon Kid stepped out.

Forty Five

Joey and Rex tied the Britney Spears and Elvis lookalikes to a tree next to Jon Bon Jovi and David Bowie. All four captives had their mouths taped over so that they couldn't yell out for help. And there was a distinctly shitty smell around, courtesy of Jon Bon Jovi's soiled leather pants.

As soon as Rex was sure that there was no way the prisoners could free themselves, he and Joey headed back to the tour bus. Rex settled in behind the steering wheel, assigning himself the role of driver without consulting the others. While he was working out what all the controls on the dashboard did, Joey grabbed the David Bowie impersonator's orange wig, which was blowing around in the middle of the road.

It had long been decided that Joey would take on the David Bowie role, but that was before he'd seen the outfit. A Ziggy Stardust costume did not look scary or even *masculine*. So, in spite of the others all looking like the singers they were impersonating, Joey decided he wasn't changing out of his black jeans and T-shirt, or even his red leather jacket. Elvis and Rex hadn't had to change because they already looked like Elvis and Jon Bon Jovi. Joey was willing to concede that he'd wear the wig if he had to, but the tight fitting onesie suit, *no fucking way*.

He headed to the back of the tour bus where Elvis and Jasmine were sitting together on a comfy padded bench, leaving him to sit on a plastic chair by the kitchen sink.

Jasmine had slipped her facemask on again, which didn't really go well with the red catsuit, but she didn't have a lot of choice. Her bruises would draw too much attention, whereas the mask could be passed off as part of her outfit.

'Try the wig on,' she said, eyeing up the orange ball of hair in Joey's hands.

'I'm not sure this is going to make me look like David Bowie,' Joey replied.

Elvis peered over his sunglasses. 'Maybe not,' he said. 'But it'll stop you looking like *you*.'

'What's that supposed to mean?'

'Well,' Elvis said diplomatically. 'Everyone thinks you're planning to kill the Pope. It might not hurt to change your appearance a little bit.'

Jasmine's face lit up. 'I'll put some makeup on you,' she said, beaming. 'I'll paint your face white and draw a red line across it like Ziggy Stardust used to do.'

Up front, Rex had finally sussed out how to get the bus moving and they began cruising along the road at a speed normally associated with curb crawling. Several fancy cars bombed past them, but they soon arrived at the gates to Landingham Manor and joined the back of a queue of cars and limousines waiting to get in.

It took a further twenty minutes to move forward thirty metres because a group of marines guarding the gates were taking a long time checking the credentials of all the guests. But that gave Jasmine plenty of time to paint Joey's face a bright white colour with the makeup that belonged to the Double Fantasy singers. She used a red lipstick to paint a diagonal line from his chin to his hairline.

When his transformation into a poor David Bowie lookalike was complete, he joined Rex up front, just in time to see a stocky blond-haired marine in a woodland camouflage uniform approaching the bus.

Rex whispered to Joey out of the side of his mouth. 'This had better work, otherwise we're fucked.'

'That's not our biggest problem,' said Joey.

'It's not?'

'No, my big worry is that we don't know if these soldiers are real, or part of Solomon Bennett's gang.'

'What difference does it make?'

'Solomon's people are probably expecting us to try something as lame as this. The real soldiers aren't.'

Rex grimaced. 'I'd feel better if we had some guns.'

'So would I, but we don't, so *quit bitching.*'

'*You quit bitching!*'

The marine tapped on Rex's window. Rex wound the window down and gave a fake smile. 'Morning, officer,' he said.

The marine peered in and looked around. 'Good day to you,' he said. 'I'm Private Downey. How are you today?'

'All good, thanks,' said Rex.

'You're the band, Double Fantasy, correct?'

'That's right,' said Rex. 'I'm Jon Bon Jovi.' He nodded over his shoulder. 'That's David Bowie. Elvis and Britney Spears are in the back.'

Private Downey checked his clipboard. 'Okay.' he said. 'Can I see your ID passes please?'

Joey had all the ID cards in his hand. He leaned across Rex and held them out of the window for Private Downey. 'I've got all our ID's here,' he said.

Downey looked at him, studying his face for a moment. It looked like he was going to comment on the amount of makeup Joey was wearing, but after a long pause he chose not to. He took the ID cards from Joey and pulled a small device the size of a cell phone from his pocket. He scanned the cards onto it, checking each one against the photo that came up on his device. Joey had changed the photos on the main database so they all matched. The only problem would be if Private Downey recognised their faces from any criminal databases he'd seen, *or newspapers*. When Downey was done he handed the cards back to Rex, who passed them along to Joey.

'Open up, please,' said Downey. 'I still have to come aboard.'

He walked around the front of the bus to the electric door on the other side. Rex pressed a button on the dashboard to open the door. The windscreen wipers came on. He pressed it again and turned them off. Then he pressed another button and water squirted onto the windscreen.

'What are you doing?' Joey asked.

Rex whispered out of the side of his mouth. 'Which button opens the fucking door?'

Joey got up and opened the door by hand. Private Downey stepped aboard and gave Rex a funny look.

'Worried it was going to rain?' he asked.

'You can never be too careful,' said Rex.

'True,' said Downey. 'I don't suppose you've seen another bus full of caterers have you?'

'No. Why?' said Rex.

'We're only expecting two buses today. I saw you guys coming round the bend and I hoped you were the catering bus. Those assholes are late again.'

'Caterers, eh?' said Joey. 'Bunch of bastards.'

'Yeah. Anyway, this will only take a minute.'

Private Downey had a see through plastic bin liner with him. He spent the next few minutes checking every single area of the bus for hidden explosive devices or weapons. He obviously knew his way around a tour bus because he found every single hidden cupboard or storage space. Everything he found that he didn't like the look of he threw into his plastic bin bag. The original *Double Fantasy* band had concealed a number of items that were unsuitable for the event. By the time Private Downey had finished his search, his bin bag contained

228

three different types of recreational drugs, two dildos, a bong, a butt plug and a string of anal beads.

'You singers sure know how to have a good time, huh?' he said to Elvis and Jasmine as he took one last look around the back of the bus.

'None of that stuff is ours,' said Jasmine.

'Whose is it then?' Downey asked.

'Oh, it all belongs to the....'

Elvis elbowed Jasmine and cleared his throat, hoping she wouldn't give away that they'd stolen the tour bus from the real singers.

Downey eyed them both suspiciously. 'Belongs to the *what?*'

Jasmine had to think quickly. 'Belongs to the *driver*,' she said. 'He's a real pervert.'

Private Downey looked over at Rex and then back down at the bag full of sex toys and drugs. He was obviously visualising Rex using the items in the bag because he visibly winced.

'Fair enough,' he said. 'Does he use all this stuff on himself?'

Jasmine nodded. 'I think he's got another set of anal beads too.'

'Where?'

'Where do you think?'

Private Downey pulled a face like someone who'd just drunk a mouthful of sour milk. 'Eeew, he can keep those.'

Private Downey made his way off the bus, keeping a safe distance from Rex. He closed the door behind him and waved them on, then signalled to his colleagues on the gate that they were okay. Rex turned the windscreen wipers on again a couple of times before sorting himself out and releasing the handbrake so they could proceed. The tour bus cruised through the gates and into the grounds of the estate. Joey checked the wing mirror to see if Private Downey was still watching them. Downey had moved onto another bus that was queuing further back, behind a string of limousines. This was the one he had been waiting for. The Gold Star catering bus.

Forty Six

Baby and Devon had been marched onto the Gold Star Catering bus along with all of Solomon Bennett's mercenaries. Like everyone else on the bus they were dressed to look like caterers. Baby was wearing a black skirt with a white blouse and black waistcoat. Devon had black trousers to go with a shirt and waistcoat and a bow tie. They were sitting on the backseat of the coach, cloaked by two of Bennett's mercenaries who were under orders to make sure they behaved.

Bennett was standing in the aisle at the front of the bus, leaning over the driver, Dr Henry Jekyll. He was constantly pointing at stuff on the road, and generally getting on Jekyll's nerves, kind of like the way Keanu Reeves stressed out Sandra Bullock in the movie *Speed*.

Baby whispered in Devon's ear. 'Are they going to kill us?'

Devon didn't want to panic Baby, but she needed to know the truth, or part of it at least. 'They won't kill you,' he said with a calm level of reassurance. 'Solomon promised me that. And in spite of the fact he's a total asshole, he's also a man of his word. But on the other hand, I'm pretty sure if his plan comes off, the only loose end he's going to have is you. So if you see any window of opportunity to escape, I suggest you take it.'

He knew Baby didn't particularly want to hear that news. She would much rather be told that everything was going to be all right. But everything *wasn't* going to be all right. Devon was certain of it.

'What about you?' Baby inquired, her voice creaking with anxiety as they got nearer to their destination. 'Are they going to kill you?'

Devon grabbed her and kissed her on the forehead. 'They're setting me up to take the rap for this whole thing,' he said. 'I can't see a way for them to do that without killing me.'

Baby was still clinging to the hope that things would work out fine. 'Joey will save us. I know it,' she whispered.

'Well if he doesn't, his body will end up alongside mine. He's an even better fall guy than I am.'

The man on Baby's left who had been assigned to keep her in line, pinched her arm.

'Will you two shut up?' he scowled. 'You're getting on my fucking nerves.'

Solomon Bennett must have heard it because he spun around and marched down the aisle to the back seats. Watching him storm towards them, it occurred to Devon that of all the people on the bus pretending to be caterers, Bennett was the one who looked least convincing. He was wearing an unsightly black eye patch, which wasn't something you would expect to see on a caterer at an event attended by the Pope. But then again, in these times of equal opportunities, maybe it was perfectly normal? Who knew?

'I don't want to hear another peep out of you and your daughter, Devon, is that clear?' Bennett said, getting his face in close to Devon's.

Devon ignored him and asked a question that had been bothering him. 'What happened to the original caterers? Are they dead now?'

'Probably,' said Bennett, with a shrug of his shoulders. 'Frankenstein tends to get a bit trigger happy when he's left on his own.'

Devon shook his head. 'I can understand your reason for wanting to steal the Mistralyte, and even for wanting to kill the Pope, but murdering innocent people? I'm disappointed in you.'

'Oh fuck off.'

Just as Devon had suspected, Bennett was starting to feel the pressure. It was now easier than ever to wind him up. Unfortunately the window of opportunity for goading Bennett closed quickly when Dr Jekyll shouted to him from the front of the bus.

'Solomon, we're here!'

Bennett regained his cool and smirked at Devon. 'Watch how easily we get into Landingham Manor,' he gloated.

He quickstepped back to the front of the bus and took up his position at Dr Jekyll's shoulder. The bus was queued behind a bunch of other vehicles, mostly limousines. A team of marines were checking all of the passengers and vehicles for anything suspicious.

After a ten-minute wait, the bus arrived just short of the front gates and a young blond-haired marine boarded the bus. Devon recognised him straight away. It was Private Downey, a young man he had known for years. He was a good, decent officer.

Downey took Dr Jekyll and Solomon Bennett's ID badges. He scanned them with a small device in his hand. They must have checked out okay, because after a brief conversation with Bennett, Private Downey addressed the rest of the bus.

'Could everyone please have their ID passes ready?,' he said.

Devon whispered in Baby's ear. 'I know this man. He'll know something's wrong when he sees me. Hopefully he won't say anything to anyone until he's off the bus.'

Private Downey walked down the aisle, checking everyone's ID cards. Solomon Bennett followed behind him, spending most of the time looking over his shoulder and smirking at Devon. When Downey reached the back of the bus, he stopped and stared at Devon and Baby and the two men sitting either side of them.

'ID cards please,' he said.

Devon and Baby both held up the ID cards they had been given. Downey scanned them on his handheld device, then handed them back. He then scanned the ID badges of the two other men on the back seat. At no point did he acknowledge Devon. When he was done, he turned around and bumped heads with Solomon Bennett who was uncomfortably close behind him.

'Anything I need to know about?' Bennett asked.

'Everything seems to be in order,' said Downey. 'You can carry on up to the house. There's a second security checkpoint at the front doors to the main building. Everyone will have to pass through a metal detector there too, so don't try sneaking any bombs in, okay!'

Bennett laughed politely. 'Of course not.'

'Good,' said Downey. He sidled past Bennett and was about to head back down the aisle to get off the bus when he hesitated. 'There's one other thing,' he said.

'What's that?' said Bennett.

'Joey Conrad showed up on a bus with three other people, pretending to be singers. I let them through. I take it that was the correct thing to do.'

Devon overheard what Downey said and for a moment he couldn't make sense of it. But then he saw a huge grin break out on Bennett's face.

'Perfect,' said Bennett. 'You did the right thing. If word got out that Joey Conrad was here this whole event would be cancelled immediately. Good job soldier.'

'I don't know who the other people were that were with him,' said Downey, 'but they didn't look like they'd be much trouble. I searched their bus and they had no weapons, just a bunch of creepy sex toys.'

'That's good to know. Thanks.'

Private Downey headed back down to the front of the bus, leaving Solomon Bennett behind to gloat at Devon.

'Every soldier has his price,' he sneered. 'You'd be amazed how many of your people are working for me.'

232

Forty Seven

Frankenstein stood up straight and dusted himself off. Being hit by the Bourbon Kid's car had torn his black vest just below the neck, but there wasn't a drop of blood to be seen, or even a scratch to show that he'd been in an accident that would have killed any normal person.

The Bourbon Kid was dressed all in black, but instead of his trademark trench coat he was wearing a sleeveless black jacket. He reached inside it and pulled out a gun. He aimed it at Frankenstein's heart and fired three times in quick succession. All three bullets hit Frankenstein in the chest and knocked him back s step. But he stayed on his feet and the bullets bounced off him.

The Kid realigned his gun, aiming this time at his opponents face.

BANG!

Again, Frankenstein staggered back half a step, but the bullet bounced off his nose. He shook himself off again and took another stride towards the Kid.

BANG!

Another, more carefully aimed shot smashed into Frankenstein's black goggles. And it too bounced off. Not only was Frankenstein bulletproof, but his eyeglasses were too. What a bastard.

There was nothing else for it. The Kid tucked his gun back inside his jacket. It was time for a fistfight.

Frankenstein trudged forward again. This time instead of walking into a bullet he got close enough to walk straight into a punch. The Bourbon Kid connected with a sharp right hook onto his chin. It would have been powerful enough to put any other man down, and keep him down for a week. But with Frankenstein all it did was twist his head to the side. He shrugged it off with ease and tried to grab the Kid.

Dante and Kacy stayed back out of the way as Frankenstein repeatedly lunged at the Bourbon Kid. He missed each time and picked up a punch to the face or a Kung Fu kick to the stomach in return. It was turning into one of those fights that went nowhere. The Kid was way too quick and agile to get hit, but Frankenstein was impervious to pain. He couldn't be injured, not by a bullet and certainly not by a punch or a kick.

Eventually the Bourbon Kid backed away from Frankenstein and pulled his gun out again. He aimed it at Frankenstein's head again. As the bigger opponent lurched towards him once more, the Kid shouted out to him.

'What's your name?'

Dante decided to help out. 'His name's Frankenstein!'

The Kid ignored him and carried on circling Frankenstein, whose main weakness seemed to be an inability to turn quickly. The Kid shouted at him again.

'What are you doing here?'

Dante yelled back on Frankenstein's behalf again. 'He's part of a group who hijacked our bus!'

The Kid glanced across at Dante and gave him an evil look.

'What's the matter with him?' Dante said to Kacy.

'I think I know.'

'What?'

'He's trying to get Frankenstein to speak so he can shoot him in the mouth.'

Dante frowned. It usually took him a little while to cotton on when Kacy explained stuff to him. He watched the Kid and Frankenstein dance around a little more. The Kid repeatedly goaded Frankenstein, sometimes with questions, other times with insults, but not once did his enemy respond. It was entirely possible that in spite of his meathead appearance, Frankenstein knew exactly what the Kid was trying to do because he kept his mouth shut at all times.

Dante tapped Kacy on the arm. 'Do you think I should help?' he said.

She smacked him back on his arm, only much harder. 'No, *stay here!* The Kid always wins these fights, doesn't he?'

Kacy had a point. They had met the Bourbon Kid a few times in the past and even though they hadn't seen him for a few years, on every other occasion they'd encountered him, he had beaten the shit out of someone, and the "someone" was usually bigger than him.

This fight was different though. It had already outlasted every other bout by a few minutes, and was starting to look like a pay-per-view boxing match between two fighters who were under orders to drag the fight out. Things soon changed though, when the Bourbon Kid gave up on his plan of trying to get Frankenstein to speak. He replaced his gun back inside his jacket again and charged head first at his bigger foe.

Frankenstein welcomed the move and opened his arms invitingly. If he could get the Kid in a bear hug, he would gain the upper hand significantly. But just as he swung his arms in a grabbing motion, the Kid slid down onto the floor and swiped Frankenstein's feet out from under him. The giant thug toppled over and landed flat on his back.

As quick as a flash the Kid pounced upon his stricken opponent. He sat astride his chest and pulled his gun out again. He pressed it against Frankenstein's mouth, trying to force his lips open. When that didn't work he used his free hand to press Frankenstein's nostrils shut. Blocking off his nasal passage seemed like the only way to force him to open his mouth.

Frankenstein retaliated by reaching up and grabbing the Bourbon Kid around the throat with both hands. He squeezed hard, his intention to close off the Kid's windpipe and choke him to death. What ensued was a Mexican standoff revolving around who would run out of breath first.

Unfortunately the Bourbon Kid was unaware that Frankenstein had a huge advantage in the *"suffocation stand off"*. The metal bolts sticking out of his neck were actually air valves. He was breathing just fine.

Forty Eight

After Rex parked the tour bus in an allotted spot behind the main house, the Double Fantasy impostors headed to the front entrance for the second security check.

The private security team who were in charge of the front doors were a little more relaxed and informal. They were well aware that anyone who had made it past the marines on the front gate was probably going to be okay. And they weren't bothered about checking for weapons because they had a metal detector inside to do that for them. They scanned the foursome's ID cards again and chatted about what songs the four of them were intending to sing.

Two things did slow the group up though. First of all, the guards insisted that Jasmine remove her mask so that they could check her face against the one on her card. When they saw her bruises she had to make up a story about how she had been attacked by a gang of angry sheep when she was out running. The guards were fascinated by the story and asked her numerous questions about it, which served only to slow up the process.

The other thing that slowed them up was the rather inevitable moment when Rex's metal hand set the alarm off when he passed through the detectors that were installed just inside the front doors. What followed was a delay of several more minutes, first while the security guards raised their doubts and suspicions about it, and then a further delay when they accepted it but marvelled at how cool it was. Once they'd gotten over it and realised that there was a queue of guests building up outside they allowed the phoney *Double Fantasy* singers into the building.

A young lady named Lucy who was in charge of entertainment was waiting for them in the reception hall. Lucy was a petite thirty-year-old blonde lady. She wore a pink uniform that made her look like an airline hostess. Her hair was scraped back into a ponytail and she had a headset strapped on with its microphone pointed at her mouth.

She escorted them to their dressing room while giving them the lowdown on the history of the building and its ornaments and furnishings. Jasmine was the only person taking any interest in the guided tour and she frequently asked questions about the statues of celebrities that were dotted randomly around the corridors. It worked out well for everyone though. Lucy seemed to enjoy explaining stuff to Jasmine, and the guys got a chance to check out which areas weren't heavily guarded.

Their dressing room was on the second floor at the rear of the building. Lucy showed them inside and informed them that they were to stay there until three o'clock when they would be summoned to perform for the guests. She wished them luck then left to attend to something else that sounded urgent, judging by the tutting and cussing she was making into her microphone.

On one side of the dressing room was a long desk with a mirror above it that stretched the length of the wall. Jasmine bounded over there and took a seat in front of the mirror to check her make-up and hair and also to make sure her mask was on okay.

Rex headed for the window at the back of the room and peered out of it. He could see the parking lot at the back of the building. Even though they were only on the second floor, it looked a long way down.

Elvis walked up alongside him. 'So what do we do now?' he asked.

Rex checked his stopwatch. 'Well, the good news is, we won't have to sing anything. We're not due on stage for five hours, but according to my stopwatch this will all be over in ninety minutes.'

'Do you really think that stopwatch is correct about the time of the assassination?' Elvis asked. He was still having reservations about the accuracy if it, although he was no more sceptical than Rex.

'I called Scratch last night,' said Rex, 'and he's adamant about it, so I guess we just have to go with it.'

'Let's not hang around here then. Let's get going.'

Rex stopped staring out of the window and looked round. 'Where's Joey gone?' he said, scouring the room.

Elvis looked around too. Joey was nowhere to be seen.

'Jasmine, did you see Joey leave?' Elvis asked.

Jasmine shook her head. 'I didn't even see him come in.'

Rex hustled over to the door and looked out into the corridor. There was no one in sight. He shut the door and looked back at Elvis.

'He's gone.'

Elvis looked troubled. 'Imagine if Joey really did want to kill the Pope,' he said. 'We just helped him get into the building.'

'I don't think Joey wants to kill the Pope,' said Rex. 'He doesn't seem to have a reason to.'

'I agree,' said Elvis. 'I like Joey, but you know, we haven't met the Red Mohawk yet. Joey told me that when he puts on that mask he loses control and something takes over. Maybe the Red Mohawk wants the Pope dead. I mean, Joey might *seem* normal but he was in a mental asylum wasn't he?'

Rex had to admit, Elvis had a point. Joey was okay, but what about the Red Mohawk? Unfortunately time was in short supply. They couldn't afford to waste any of it searching for Joey who might just have gone to the toilet for all they knew.

'Okay, this is the plan,' said Rex. 'Jasmine, you wait here in case Joey comes back. If he does, tell him Elvis and me have gone to find the study.'

'The study?' said Jasmine, looking confused.

'Yeah. That's where the opening to the lift shaft is. I'm going to lower Elvis down the elevator shaft so he can grab the weapons we need, to do whatever the hell it is we need to do.'

Elvis baulked. 'You're not lowering me down,' he said. 'I'll lower *you* down!'

Rex headed for the door. 'Let's argue about it on the way.'

Forty Nine

Frankenstein was choking the life out the Bourbon Kid. His giant hands wrapped around the Kid's throat so tightly it looked as if the Kid's head would pop off at any moment. Dante and Kacy had to make a decision quickly because the Kid's face was turning blue.

Dante grabbed Kacy by the hand. 'I think we'd better split,' he said, dragging her towards the warehouse entrance.

'What about the Kid? Shouldn't we try and help?'

'There's nothing we can do. I mean, what *could* we do?'

Dante had a point. Kacy couldn't think of a single thing either of them could do that would hurt Frankenstein. And the way things were going, Frankenstein would be after them any second now.

She looked into Dante's eyes. She knew that if there was anything they could do to help the Kid, Dante would try. He was the bravest man she knew. It was part of what she loved about him. He'd risked his life to protect her many times and she supposed that's what he was trying to do now. The pair of them started running as fast as they could towards the daylight outside the entrance. Kacy gave an apologetic smile to the Bourbon Kid on the way out, but whether he noticed it or not, she couldn't tell.

As soon as they were out of the warehouse and into the open air they saw a group of the other Gold Star employees in the distance, running down the desert highway back towards town. Kacy cursed the stupid rule Gold Star had about no employees taking cell phones with them to jobs. They were stuck in the middle of nowhere without any way of contacting anyone for help.

'Let's follow the others!' she suggested, already struggling for breath.

Dante pulled her in the opposite direction, towards another derelict warehouse across the way.

'No way,' he said. 'If Frankenstein comes out, he'll head straight for them. We're better off on our own.'

The second warehouse had a huge metal entrance gate fifty feet wide. It was secured shut by heavy-duty padlocks on the bottom corners.

'There must be another way in here?' said Dante, looking around for an easier way to break in.

Three gunshots rang out loud from inside the warehouse they had fled from. Dante and Kacy looked at each other, both thinking the same thing. Who had fired the shots? The Bourbon Kid, or Frankenstein?

Kacy spotted a green dumpster. She pulled Dante towards it.

'Let's hide in there!' she said, desperately hoping he would see the merits of her plan.

They raced over to it. Dante threw the lid back and Kacy started climbing in. She managed to get her upper body up onto the edge and Dante did the rest for her, pressing his hands against her ass and shoving her into the dumpster. Luckily there was nothing but flattened cardboard boxes inside so the impact was minimal. Dante climbed in after her and pulled the lid back down, leaving a small enough gap for them to see out of.

They heard an engine start up across the yard in the other warehouse. A few seconds later, Frankenstein rode out of the warehouse on his silver motorbike, revving its engine loudly. He had a gun in his right hand, ready to shoot down all the fleeing Gold Star employees who had foolishly headed for the highway.

Kacy kissed Dante on the cheek. 'Sometimes you surprise me,' she said.

Dante smiled but didn't answer. He watched Frankenstein zoom off down the highway. The other Gold Star folks were out of sight around a bend in the road, but their fate was easy to predict. Their screams filled the air for a while before they were snuffed out one by one by Frankenstein's gunfire.

Kacy's joy at having escaped Frankenstein was immediately quashed by the knowledge that more of her friends and colleagues were being slaughtered. On top of that there was the small matter of what had become of the Bourbon Kid? There was no sign of him coming back out of the warehouse.

'Do you think he killed the Bourbon Kid?' she whispered.

Dante took a moment to consider his answer, which was unusual for him. He stared at the warehouse, almost willing the Bourbon Kid to walk out, or drive out in his car at high speed. But he didn't.

'I don't believe he's dead,' he decided eventually. 'I don't see the Kid getting killed like that.'

'Then why isn't he coming out?'

'I don't know. But let's wait in here for a while, just in case Frankenstein comes back looking for us. If the Bourbon Kid doesn't come out of the warehouse in the next ten minutes we'll go in and see what's happened.'

'And what do we do if he's dead?'

'We take his car and get the hell out of here. I'm pretty sure he would want me to have his car.'

Kacy did like the idea of Dante driving her around town in a cool black Pontiac Firebird. The pair of them stared in silence at the warehouse entrance for a while, waiting for a sighting of the Kid. It was starting to turn cold and Kacy took a look at her situation. She was on her knees, peering out of a dumpster. This was not how she'd imagined life as a married woman would be.

'If we do get out of this alive, I'm quitting this job,' she declared.

'Me too,' said Dante. 'I bet we don't even get paid for today.'

He let go of the lid of the dumpster and it dropped shut, leaving the pair of them in darkness. He ran his hand through Kacy's hair, in a way he often did when he was making a move on her.

'What are you doing?' she asked, suspiciously.

'I figure the safest thing to do is hide in here until it gets dark. Then we can sneak out.'

He leaned forward and kissed her softly on the mouth.

'It's cold in here though,' she said, pulling away.

'All this danger is a real turn on though, don't you think?'

Kacy closed her eyes and felt his lips press against hers again.

'Honey, this isn't the time,' she said, pressing her hand against his crotch. He was already fully aroused. One of the things she loved most about Dante was knowing that he wanted to fuck her all the time, especially at the most inconvenient times. He kissed her again, more passionately this time.

'We've never done it in a dumpster before,' he said, his hands frantically unbuttoning her blouse.

Kacy started kissing him back and unbuckling his belt. 'Okay, let's make it quick then.'

Fifty

Jasmine had been on her own in the dressing room for ten minutes when she started to feel restless. It was the first time she'd been unaccompanied since Jack had been murdered, and she didn't like it. Images of what had happened to him kept flashing into her mind. She needed something to occupy her thoughts. But there wasn't even a television in the dressing room. She wished she had her cell phone with her so she could call someone, but cell phones weren't allowed on the premises.

She thought about whom she would call. In a lonely moment it's nice to know that there's someone you can call just to say hi. It struck Jasmine that she no longer had a person like that. Phoning Jack to ask him what he was doing had been one of her favourite pastimes. But even if she had her phone with her now, she wouldn't have anyone to call. When she'd worked at The Beaver Palace none of the girls had been allowed a phone, so she had lost contact with all the other hookers apart from Baby.

She promised herself that in times of loneliness she would still call Jack and leave messages on his voicemail. Maybe in some crazy afterlife he would be able to hear them and send her an invisible hug. If he were alive now, as her lover he would tell her everything was going to be all right. But as an undercover spy he would tell her to stop dwelling on the death of a colleague. *Stay focussed on the mission or you'll get yourself killed*. He'd told her that many times.

Her current mission was to try and become a member of Rodeo Rex's team. Becoming a Dead Hunter would guarantee her some new lifelong friends. Their lifestyle seemed exciting and dangerous. And it would give her some new acquaintances to call when she was lonely. She had a feeling she'd be able to get Elvis's number. He'd be a good guy to have around in a crisis, and rather like Jack he seemed to understand her better than most people. Plus, he was the kind of guy who would take her somewhere nice to eat too, like KFC or Burger King.

Her daydreaming was interrupted by a knock on the door. She spun her chair around. The door opened and Lucy the entertainment organiser poked her head into the room again.

'Hi,' said Lucy, scouring the room. 'Where are the others?'

'Uh, they went to get some gear from the tour bus.'

'What sort of gear?'

'Different outfits, you know, for costume changes and stuff.'

242

'Are they going to be long?'

'They might be.'

Lucy looked agitated. 'Okay, well *you'll* have to do then. You're Britney Spears, correct?'

'No,' said Jasmine, shaking her head. 'I'm Jasmine. Britney Spears is probably halfway across the world.'

'That's not what I meant.'

'Are you getting her mixed up with Christina Aguilera? I do that sometimes.'

Lucy looked baffled, like she couldn't work out if Jasmine was being serious or not. 'No,' she said. 'What I mean is, you're the Britney Spears impersonator in your group *Double Fantasy*, yes?'

'Oh. Yeah. *Yeah,* I'm a Britney Spears impersonator. That's right.'

'The red catsuit is the giveaway,' said Lucy. 'Apart from that you don't really look much like Britney. Have you ever considered becoming a Janet Jackson impersonator? You look much more like her.'

The Janet Jackson compliment was quite flattering and for a moment Jasmine imagined herself earning a living singing *"What Have You Done for Me Lately?"* But she quickly snapped out of it and reminded herself to stay focussed on the mission.

'It's not my looks that got me the part,' she said. 'I actually sound *exactly like* Britney Spears when I sing. If you shut your eyes and listen, you'd think I was the real thing.'

'Good, because we need you on stage right now.'

'I beg your pardon?'

'We've had a problem. The catering staff showed up almost an hour late. The guests are getting agitated, so we need you on stage to sing a couple of songs now.'

'Eh?'

'Come on, hurry up. You've got to come now.'

Jasmine wasn't keen on leaving the safety of the dressing room. 'I should wait 'til the guys get back,' she said.

'There's no time. The boss wants you right now. We're paying you people a lot of money. Either get your ass on stage now, or get off the premises!'

It was obvious from the tone of Lucy's voice that she wasn't kidding. And the frown on her face suggested she wasn't someone to be fucked with. Jasmine tried to think of a clever excuse.

'I think all the instruments are still in the bus,' she said, pleased with herself for coming up with something that seemed believable.

'What instruments?' said Lucy, suspicion creeping into her voice.

'Guitars, drums, sax, you know. I play the triangle.'

'But your manager sent us a CD containing all your backing tracks. You *don't need instruments*. You just have to sing along to the backing tracks.'

'Oh,' said Jasmine. 'It's one of *those* gigs is it? *Riiiii-ight.*'

'Yeah. I'll just rejig the set list to bring two of your sings forward. You can get up and sing *Oops I did it Again* and *Toxic*. That okay with you?'

There didn't seem to be a way out of this situation. Jasmine was going to have to play along until she came up with a good reason to get out of it. Although, the more she thought about it, the more she figured it could be good fun. She'd always wanted a crack at being a pop star and this was likely to be as close as she ever got to that dream becoming a reality.

'*Oops I did it Again* and *Toxic*,' she said, repeating what Lucy had said. 'Yes, that's fine. Do you have one of those TV screens with the lyrics on, in case I forget the words?'

Lucy tilted her head to one side and gave a sarcastic smile. 'Very funny,' she said. 'Come on, get moving. We need you on stage and singing within five minutes.'

Fifty One

Private Downey's defection to Solomon Bennett's cause had given him sleepless nights. He'd always considered himself to be a patriot not a traitor, but Bennett had convinced him that stealing the Mistralyte to use it for the noble cause of defending the country was a patriotic thing to do. Selling it off to a bunch of millionaires and pharmaceutical companies (as General Calhoon was planning to do) wasn't in the interests of the masses. But now that the day had arrived and Downey had played his part in helping Bennett and his men onto the premises of Landingham Manor, he was having serious doubts. It was too late to back out of any of it now, and the money Bennett was paying him was too much to walk away from. But people were going to die. In the long run, Bennett's plan might well save thousands of lives, maybe millions, but in the short term, innocent people were going to die. *Today.*

Anxiety had been a problem for Tim Downey for as long as he could remember. And poor sleep was only one of the symptoms. Chronic stomach pain was usually how the anxiety really bit him.

By 11.30 a.m. his stomach was in knots, gripped by the invisible fist of anxiety. And the reason for that was the knowledge that as soon as Frankenstein showed up at the Manor, Downey was under orders to do something he dreaded more than anything in his whole life. He was going to have to shoot his friend Private Dane O'Kane. Downey and O'Kane were the two marines designated to stay and watch the front gates after all the guests passed through. As soon as Frankenstein arrived, Downey was supposed to put a gun to O'Kane's head and blow his brains out. Every time he thought about it, his stomach churned. So with the unpleasant event less than thirty minutes away, he decided to take advantage of his last chance to take a dump. He reminded himself of his father's dying words of wisdom. *"It's better to kill your best buddy after you've had a good shit."* Okay, so maybe they weren't his father's exact last words, but he'd said something along those lines.

He left O'Kane behind manning the front gates and headed for the main house. Even jogging down the driveway was uncomfortable. As he dashed through the metal detectors at the front of the building his pistol set off the alarm.

One of the security guards, a young chap named Liam made him hand his gun over and walk through the metal detector again as a precaution. When he'd successfully made it through, Liam handed him his gun back.

'Where's the nearest shitter?' Downey asked, trying his best not to do a "poo dance" like a child does when he or she is desperate to go.

Liam pointed at the staircase in the middle of the reception hall. 'Up there,' he said. 'People carrying firearms aren't allowed to use the same toilets as the guests. You've got to go up the stairs and round to the right.'

'Thanks.'

As Downey sprinted for the stairs, Liam shouted out to him.

'Go careful. They've had an accident up there. Someone was sick in the urinal trough. It's all blocked up and overflowing. There's piss everywhere!'

Downey didn't care how much piss or vomit was on the floor. As far as he was concerned he was going to be sitting in a nice clean stall with quilted toilet paper. That was the dream.

He hurried along a corridor on the upper floor until he found the Gents washroom that Liam had told him about. He burst through the door and started unbuckling his belt to save time. The stench of piss and puke inside the washroom was far worse than he had expected. Train station facilities smelled better than this place. There was background music coming from a set of speakers on the walls, perhaps designed to drown out the kind of noises Downey was about to make. He recognised the current song. It was *Little Drummer Boy* by David Bowie and Bing Crosby. Yet another Christmas tune, as if he hadn't heard enough of them over the last month.

On his left he saw the long old-fashioned urinal trough that Liam had warned him was overflowing. This was one of the problems with Landingham Manor. Some of the stuff was so old fashioned. The urinal was like a pig trough stuck on the wall, wide enough for six men to stand alongside each other, pissing into it, whilst talking about football (and staring straight ahead at all times). It was made of metal and its trough, which was at knee height (and no doubt caused a lot of awkward "splash-back" incidents) was six inches deep. It was filled to the brim by a sea of dark yellow urine with chunks of vomit floating in it. Some of it had spilled over onto the floor and was seeping across towards a set of three stalls on the opposite side of the room.

And this place was supposed to be posh!

Downey tiptoed through the sick on the floor and made his way over to the first stall. It had a piece of paper sellotaped onto the door with three words written on it black lettering.

OUT OF ORDER

For fuckssake!

The imaginary timer in Downey's guts had already started counting down to the moment of release, and he knew that when it got to zero, whether he was sitting on a toilet seat or not, his ass was going to be unloading last nights curry. Big Time.

Five.

Four.

Thankfully the second stall along had no OUT OF ORDER sign on the door. He barged through it and was about to pull down his pants when he saw that the toilet had no seat on it. And it had a spray of piss all around the basin. There was no way he was sitting on that, or even squatting over it.

Three.

Two.

There was nothing left for it. He would have to use stall three, *or shit on the floor!*

He backtracked from stall two and barged through the door on the third and final stall. He didn't get a look at the state of the toilet in this one though, because standing in his way was a big dude in a red jacket, wearing a yellow skull mask with a red crest on the top.

The Red Mohawk.

One.

The Red Mohawk reached out and grabbed Downey by the jaw, hauling him off his feet. Downey's ass cheeks clenched even harder than before. He stared into the holes in the skull mask at the eyes peering back at him. They were dead eyes, devoid of any emotion.

And suddenly, without warning he was thrown backwards towards the horrendous stinky, overflowing urinal trough behind him. His butt cheeks could no longer stay clenched either. He landed on the floor by the trough, right at the exact moment his asshole burst open and his underpants filled up with a mountain of excrement, which did little to soften the blow. The shit in his pants squirmed out everywhere, all down his legs and up his back.

The Red Mohawk walked out of the stall. He leant down and grabbed a handful of Downey's blond hair. He hauled him up and smashed his head back against the metal urinal trough. The impact was accompanied by a *clanging* sound and a tremor that caused a tidal wave of piss and puke to splash over the trough and onto the back of his head, down his neck and inside his shirt.

He tried to scramble to his feet so that he could fight back but his boots kept slipping and sliding in the piss on the floor. He reached back in a futile attempt to get a firm hold on something. His hand grabbed onto the urinal trough and his fingers sank deep into the pool of warm piss and puke. The Red Mohawk yanked him up by his hair again, twisted his head around and then thrust him face down into the trough.

Urine, chunks of vomit and sweetcorn flooded into Downey's mouth and nostrils. It caught him off guard and a mouthful of it slid down his throat and the back of his nasal passage. He struggled, unable to breathe as he tried desperately to lift his head back out of the trough, but the Mohawk's grip was too strong.

Downey thrashed around in the urinal, using his hands to grip onto the edge of it in the hope of applying some pressure to elevate himself upwards and pull his head out from the six-inch-deep lake of piss. His fight lasted for less than a minute before he finally succumbed and drowned in the trough of unspeakable vileness, with his underpants full of his own shit.

The Red Mohawk dragged Downey's body away from the urinal trough and across the floor to the stall with the OUT OF ORDER sign on it. He kicked it open and hauled his victim inside. He propped Downey's corpse up on the toilet seat and took a moment to look down upon his lifeless, gawping face. The first of the day's murders was complete. It felt good to be wearing the mask again. And it felt even better to be killing people.

He relieved Downey of his gun and washed it clean in a nearby sink, cleaning his own hands with the complimentary soap at the same time. A glance up into the mirror reminded him just how good he looked when he was wearing the mask. He felt invincible again. A voice in his head spoke to him.

Find Baby and Devon. Kill everyone else.

Fifty Two

It took Rex and Elvis a little longer to find the study than it should have done. Several wrong turns triggered by the pair of them arguing over such things *as "My left? Or your left?"* had taken them on a rather unnecessary tour of the ground floor of Landingham Manor.

Eventually Rex opened one of the doors and peered into the correct room.

'This is the one,' he said triumphantly.

Elvis followed him in and looked around.

'This looks the same as all the other rooms,' he groaned. 'What makes this one so special?'

'The bust of Adam West is on the table.'

There was a large antique wooden desk in the middle of the room. On top of it was the bust he had referred to. Rex headed over to it and yanked its head back, just like Joey had instructed. In the middle of the neck was a small button. Rex pressed it and looked around, waiting for something cool to happen. After a short pause, the bookshelf on the opposite wall slid to one side, revealing an elevator shaft, but no carriage.

Elvis took a quick look out into the corridor to make sure no one had seen them enter the study, then gently closed the study door to prevent any passers-by from spotting what was going on.

'Okay, what now?' he asked.

Rex walked over to the elevator shaft and stared down. 'Fuck,' he said. 'That's deep.'

Elvis sashayed across the room clicking his fingers and humming along to the invisible jukebox that played rock 'n' roll music constantly in his head. He removed his sunglasses and took a look at what Rex was seeing. At the bottom of the elevator shaft, thirty feet down was the carriage they had seen in Joey's basement hideout.

'That's a heck of a fall,' he said, stating the obvious.

'No shit,' said Rex. 'Reckon you can get down there?'

'No fucking way, man! *You* should go down.'

'Why the fuck should *I* have to be the one to go down?'

'You've got a magnetic hand. You'll be able to grab on to something metal on the way down.'

Rex screwed his face up into a contorted scowl. 'I swear to God this hand is a fucking curse sometimes,' he grumbled.

'I'll keep watch.'

'Well you'd better do *something.*'

Rex sat down and let his legs dangle into the lift shaft. He twisted around and then lowered himself down, gripping onto the edge with his normal hand. There were metal girders running down the sides of the shaft. He reached across and grabbed a hold of one with his metal hand. The magnetic grip was strong enough to stop him from falling while he flailed around to find something else to latch on to with his other hand. Slowly, little by little he began to descend down the lift shaft.

'This ain't as fuckin' easy as I'm making it look,' he called up to Elvis.

'It looks easier than that shit Tom Cruise did in Mission Impossible 4.'

'What?'

'You know, when he climbed around that building using a magnetic glove. At least you've only got a thirty foot drop.'

'Elvis.'

'Yeah.'

'Shut the fuck up.'

It took Rex just over a minute to get down far enough to be able to drop onto the top of the elevator carriage. The sound he made as he landed echoed all the way up the lift shaft.

'Easy, man,' Elvis called down. 'Try not to wake the dead while you're down there.'

Rex ignored him and opened the hatch on the top of the carriage. It was a tight squeeze for a man of his size but he managed to wriggle himself through it. He dropped to the floor inside the elevator.

'Okay, I'm in!' he yelled up to Elvis.

'Cool. Fuckin' hurry up then.'

Rex stepped out of the lift and looked around Joey's cave. It looked the same as when they'd left it earlier in the morning and it was a relief not to be confronted by any armed soldiers lurking around like last time.

He headed straight for the desk in the centre of the cave to get a look at the monitors that showed what was happening in and around the building. He took a minute to watch each monitor, to see if he could spot Joey anywhere and even more importantly, see where the Pope was and what he was doing. There was plenty of footage of security guards walking the corridors around the main building, but no sign of Joey anywhere.

Most of the monitors changed their viewpoint every few seconds, flicking from one camera angle to another. One of the central monitors was relaying a live feed from the dining hall which was

250

packed full of dinner guests. The dining hall was huge. There were approximately forty round tables spaced around the hall and a raised stage area at one end. It reminded Rex of the MTV awards. He'd been a member of security at the awards once and had been assigned to stop the other guests from spitting at a young Canadian singer while he performed. It had been one of the worst assignments he'd ever had. Half the night was spent listening to halfwit singers waffling on about politics and preaching to the masses to give money to various charities. He shuddered when he thought about it.

Fortunately Bono was nowhere to be seen amongst the two hundred guests in the dining hall at Landingham Manor. The Pope was easy to spot though because he was sitting at a table near the stage and he was wearing a big white cassock, or "dress" as Rex preferred to call it. All of the other men were wearing black dinner suits and white shirts. The women were mostly in black or silver cocktail dresses. At this point there was no sign of any trouble, or more importantly, of Frankenstein. Everyone was seated and everything seemed calm.

Rex turned away from the monitors and headed over to the sports bag they had filled with weapons the night before. There was a thick rope next to it that he was going to have to toss up to Elvis so that he could haul the bag up through the elevator shaft. Rex remembered thinking it was shit plan when they came up with it the night before. But so far it was going quite well.

He had taken barely two steps towards the sports bag when his mind flashed back to something he had just seen on one of the monitors. Was his mind playing tricks on him? Had he really just seen the image that was now ingrained in his mind? He spun back round and stared at the monitor relaying the live feed from the dining hall again. The Pope was gesticulating to the other guests who were sitting with him at the head table. It looked like he was pointing at something and laughing. Perhaps he was telling a joke? Rex feared that was not the case. The view on the monitor switched away from the Pope to another area of the room. It took three more camera switches before the view flashed back to the one that Rex was fretting about. His worst fears were confirmed. Jasmine was up on the stage singing and dancing in front of the audience.

Fifty Three

After some initial trepidation about singing in front of a large audience, Jasmine decided that the best thing to do was go with the flow and try to enjoy it. If people thought she sucked, so what? How many chances in life do you get to pretend you're Britney Spears and sing for a bunch of rich people? Having a mask that covered half of her face made it a little easier too because no one could really see how nervous she was.

Her biggest problem was that she didn't know the lyrics to the songs she was supposed to sing. She could just about bluff her way through the choruses but the verses were a nightmare, particularly the bit in *Oops I did it Again* when she had to try and remember some fucking nonsense about dropping something in the ocean and then diving down to get it again. What the fuck was that all about? *"Someone was on drugs when they wrote this garbage!"* she thought.

Fortunately Jasmine could dance. She didn't have any specific routines to go with the songs, but she definitely knew how to shake her ass. So whenever the lyrics escaped her (which was most of the time) she started grinding, twerking and writhing against imaginary backing dancers.

The audience seemed to get into it anyway, including quite a few of the older gentlemen. There was an old guy at the front table wearing a white dress, a long necklace, and a little white cap. Jasmine wondered who this rich transvestite was. Was he Elton John going through a Bjork phase? No matter, he was an appreciative transvestite and Jasmine liked that in a man. He was frequently elbowing the other gentlemen at his table and pointing at her as if he thought the others hadn't noticed her. When she performed her own unique version of the splits she feared he was going to have a heart attack.

Halfway through her second song, the huge double doors at the back of the dining hall opened and a team of waiters and waitresses entered. They wheeled in a set of trolleys loaded with bottles of champagne and nibbles. While all of the guests were distracted by Jasmine's performance the caterers delivered a bucket of champagne to each table and began pouring it into glasses for each of the guests.

Jasmine was in the middle of a particularly impressive Moonwalk when her eyes met with one of the waitresses pouring champagne at one of the tables near the front. She recognised the waitress straight away. It was Denise, the ugly bitch who had showed up at the motel with Mozart. Denise was as much to blame for Jack's murder as Mozart. Jasmine's blood ran cold at the sight of her. She looked away and hoped that her facemask was enough to prevent Denise from identifying her. Only time would tell.

When the song came to an end the audience clapped politely, with the exception of the old guy in the white dress. He stood up and applauded boisterously. Whoever he was, he seemed to carry a bit of sway because the whole room soon followed suit and gave her a standing ovation. Jasmine smiled and waved at her new fans. She looked around the room at all the faces smiling back at her and wondered which one was the Pope. She couldn't tell because all the men looked the same, apart from the guy in the dress at the front.

Lucy the entertainment manager strolled onto the stage and stood next to Jasmine, beaming a fake smile and applauding along with everyone else. She shouted into Jasmine's ear over all the noise.

'Okay, thanks. You can go now.'

'Are you sure?' said Jasmine, in between blowing kisses at the men in the audience. 'I don't mind doing another...'

'Get off the stage, please.'

Lucy nudged her to one side and took control of the microphone. 'Ladies and gentlemen,' she said, quietening the crowd. 'It's time for the highlight of today's event. I would like to ask you all to put your hands together for the organiser of this wonderful occasion, General Alexis Calhoon!'

Jasmine stood next to Lucy and clapped loudly along with everyone else as General Calhoon walked onto the stage from the wings. The General was a handsome lady, dark skinned and although probably in her fifties she had a very athletic figure. And she was wearing a black dinner dress that made Jasmine quite envious.

As Calhoon approached, Lucy whispered in Jasmine's ear. 'Seriously, fuck off. Get off the fucking stage!'

Jasmine reluctantly made her way off stage. She passed Alexis Calhoon on the way and whispered into the General's ear.

'There's no need to be nervous, I've warmed them up for you.'

Calhoon smiled politely, but didn't respond. She walked up to the microphone and graciously accepted the warm applause the audience gave her.

Jasmine waited in the wings to hear what Calhoon had to say, hoping she might also catch a glimpse of the Pope. She'd heard that it was a big deal to meet him. She supposed it was the equivalent of meeting someone like Nelson Mandela or Christian Slater. It would be a good story to impress people with. The Pope was very famous and well connected, so Jasmine was hoping he might come up on stage and tell some great stories about other celebrities.

Unfortunately she never got a chance to hear the Pope tell any jokes because she was attacked from behind before General Calhoon had even managed to quieten the audience. Denise had left the dining hall and snuck up on her. She wrapped one arm around Jasmine's waist and pressed a silver dinner fork up against her eye.

'Listen you dumb bitch,' she hissed. 'Make one sound and I'll ram this fork into your eye.'

She pulled Jasmine away from the stage area and marched her down a short flight of steps to an empty corridor below. The silver fork stayed dangerously close to Jasmine's eye the whole time. But it was just a fork. Not a gun. If Jasmine was going to escape, she would have to do it soon, before they bumped into any of Denise's comrades.

'Where are we going?' Jasmine asked.

'I'll ask the fucking questions,' Denise hissed, her voice dripping with anger. 'You can start by telling me what happened to Mozart!'

Denise was attempting to make Jasmine walk along the corridor, but she was struggling to maintain a grip on her because the red catsuit was so slippery.

'Mozart's head fell off,' said Jasmine.

Denise slammed her up against the wall and pressed the fork up against her eye again. 'Don't fucking test me you dumb bitch!' she snarled. 'Is he alive or not?'

Jasmine thought about all the things Jack had taught her about how to react when threatened. It was definitely now or never if she was going to stand a chance against Denise. So she took a chance.

She pretended she was about to answer Denise's question, but then head butted her instead, pushing the fork out of the way to avoid getting it in her eye. Denise staggered back, her eyes wide with shock. Like most bullies she didn't like getting a taste of her own medicine. She instinctively reached up to rub her head where Jasmine had butted her.

Jasmine knew she wasn't a match for someone with Denise's military training so she made a run for it. She raced down the corridor and up a set of stairs on the right. Denise chased after her cursing and yelling at her to stop.

Jasmine's high-heeled shoes made it difficult to run up stairs at high speed so she tried taking the steps two at a time. It worked well until she mistimed the last step and tripped over. She landed on her front on the landing at the top of the stairs. She rolled over onto her back ready to kick out at Denise.

But that's when she realised she had nothing to worry about. Concealed from Denise's view behind the wall at the top of the stairs was the Red Mohawk, waiting for her. Jasmine crawled backwards to entice Denise to keep running, Denise played into her hands by bounding up the stairs, fork in hand, ready to dive onto her.

The look of spite and anger on Denise's face vanished in an instant when the Red Mohawk's arm swung across her neck, giving her a kung-fu chop to the throat. From the neck down she carried on surging towards Jasmine, but her head snapped back and a moment later her feet left the ground. She tumbled back down onto the stairs and bounced down four or five steps before coming to a stop, struggling for breath and holding her neck.

The Red Mohawk walked menacingly down the stairs and grabbed one of Denise's legs. He pulled on it and dragged her back up the stairs. Her body twisted back and forth and her head bounced hard on each step on the way back up, making it hard for her to catch her breath. He let go of her when her legs were on the landing but her upper body was still hanging down the stairs. He reached over and grabbed a clump of hair on the top of her head and yanked her up a few inches. In his other hand he was holding the silver fork she had threatened Jasmine with. He held it above his head and then plunged it down, stabbing it into Denise's left eye. It made a disgusting squelchy, popping sound, which was followed by Denise screaming. He pressed his hand over her mouth to snuff out the cry for help before it got too loud. What followed ranked fairly high on the list of nasty things Jasmine had seen in recent times. She had to look away as the Red Mohawk squeezed Denise's eyeball out of its socket, still impaled on the end of the dinner fork. He forced it into her mouth and slammed her jaw shut, then he yanked the fork back out so that the eyeball came off against the back of her teeth.

Jasmine stood at the top of the stairs and watched with her hand over her mouth as Denise choked and spluttered, and struggled in vain to fight back. It was a wasted effort. The Red Mohawk rolled her over onto her front.

"What's he doing now?" Jasmine wondered.

Denise spat out her severed eye and it bobbled down the stairs. And that's when Jasmine realised what the Red Mohawk had planned. Normally she would have closed her eyes, but after what Denise and Mozart had put her through the day before, she wanted to see the ugly bitch bite the dust. Or in this case, *bite the stairs*. While her mouth was open, the Red Mohawk stamped his right boot down hard on the back of her head. Her face split in half on the step. To the sound of a loud *CRUNCH*, her jaw separated from the rest of her skull. The blood and brains that had once been tucked neatly inside Denise's head slid down the stairs, chasing after her severed eye.

Jasmine offered the Mohawk her approval. '*Nice!* That *bitch* had it coming.'

The Red Mohawk stepped away from the corpse and yanked his mask off. He pulled an earpiece out of his left ear and a tiny MP3 player from his inside pocket. The earpiece was lightly buzzing. He switched off the MP3 player and killed the buzz.

'What were you listening to?' Jasmine asked.

'Halloween soundtrack.'

'Is it good?'

'Perfect for my purposes, but wearing an earpiece is distracting.' He pointed along the corridor. 'There's a sound booth down that way. It overlooks the auditorium. Get the deejay to play some John Carpenter music, and make sure it plays through every speaker in the building. I want to hear it wherever I go.'

Jasmine frowned. 'What for?'

'Because I'm about to go on a killing spree.'

'But why do you need music for that?'

'It reminds me of the moment my parents were murdered.'

Jasmine couldn't think of a suitable response to that particular remark so she changed the subject quickly.

'What if the deejay refuses to play any Carpenter stuff?' she inquired.

'*Be persuasive.*'

Before Jasmine could ask what sort of persuasion he was talking about, they were interrupted by the sound of gunfire somewhere outside the building. Joey slid his Mohawk mask back over his head and stared at her through the eyeholes, his pupils suddenly dark and deadened unlike before.

'When you're done sorting out the music, I suggest you find somewhere to hide,' he said. 'It sounds like Frankenstein has just arrived.'

Fifty Four

'Rex! What the fuck are you doing down there?'

Elvis had been waiting for Rex to reappear down below in the elevator carriage at the bottom of the lift shaft for what felt like an eternity. When his buddy finally did rematerialize he was carrying the sports bag and a length of rope. He shoved the bag through the hatch at the top of the elevator and then climbed up through it with the rope wrapped around his shoulder.

He shouted up to Elvis. 'We'd better hurry up. Jasmine's just finished singing.'

'*Singing?* What are you talking about?'

'I'll explain in a minute. Catch this rope!'

Rex hurled the rope up the elevator shaft. Elvis reached out and caught it, then ducked back inside the study. He tied one end of the rope around a table leg and pulled at it a few times to make sure it was secure, then he tossed the other end of the rope back down to Rex.

The plan was for Elvis to haul the bag of guns and ammo up into the study. Then Rex would climb up the rope and join him. But as usual, something had to go wrong.

There was a sudden burst of gunfire somewhere outside the main building. Elvis heard it loud and clear from where he was. Rex must have heard it too because he shouted up to Elvis.

'What the fuck was that?'

'We might be too late,' Elvis shouted back. 'I think shit just got started!'

Rex shouted something back but his voice was drowned out by the gunfire, which was getting louder. What had initially sounded like one gunman now sounded like five, or six. There was a gunfight going on somewhere.

Elvis ran over to the door in the corner of the room. He twisted the doorknob and pulled it open a few inches so that he could see out into the corridor. There was no one in sight, but from the direction that the gunfire was coming from, a lot of male voices were shouting out some inaudible nonsense.

Elvis stepped tentatively into the corridor and edged along it towards the sound of the gunfire. On the corner of the corridor he noticed a pair of life size waxwork statues of Keanu Reeves and Alex Winter's characters from the *Bill and Ted* movies. Normally Elvis would have taken the time to question why on earth someone would have such a random pair of waxworks, but then again this house was owned by someone who had built a replica Batcave beneath it, so a couple of odd movie statues was nothing in the grand scheme of things. And besides, Elvis had more important things on his mind, like who the hell is doing all the shooting?

As he reached the corner, the gunfire stopped. He pressed his back up against the wall and poked his head around the wall's edge to take a look. The team of security guards who had been checking everyone at the front entrance had been massacred. The reception hall was littered with the bodies of dead men.

He tiptoed around the corner to see if he could get a look at the gunman. Judging by the position of the dead men, it was evident that their killer had shot them from outside. Elvis hesitated when he saw a long shadow on the reception hall floor, looming over the fallen security guards. It was the shadow of a man walking down the driveway towards the front entrance. Just when it looked like the shadow couldn't get any bigger, the killer walked through the front doors.

Frankenstein.

He was a six-feet-six-inch tall, muscle-bound meathead in a torn black T-shirt and loose fitting combat pants, wearing a pair of black goggles over his eyes. Both his shirt and pants were riddled with bullet holes, but there was not one drop of blood on him. He had an Uzi pistol slung over one shoulder and his pockets were crammed full of ammo clips. He walked through the metal detector and it started beeping manically.

Elvis backtracked and ducked back behind the corner so he could watch from a safe distance.

Frankenstein walked through the strewn bodies of the men he had just killed. He pulled out an ammo clip and reloaded his Uzi as he surveyed his handiwork. When his gun was reloaded he turned away from Elvis, towards the corridor that led to the dining hall.

"EXCELLENT!"

Elvis had no idea why someone would want waxwork figures of Bill and Ted, but to have them shout out lines of dialogue too, was *beyond stupid*. The fuckhead who had installed the waxwork figures had fixed them so that every hour a recording device would go off and recite a line from the film.

Frankenstein heard it loud and clear. He spun around and unloaded his Uzi at Bill and Ted, peppering their statues with bullets. Within seconds they looked holier than the Pope. Frankenstein then caught sight of Elvis and aimed in his direction.

Elvis ducked back out of sight just in time. A volley of bullets flew past his nose and blasted into the wall behind him. He turned and sprinted back to the study. Frankenstein forgot all about the dining hall for a minute and headed after him.

Elvis charged through the door to the study and slammed it shut behind him. He rushed across the room to the open elevator shaft. Rex was crawling out of it, holding on tightly to the rope Elvis had tied around the table leg. He had the sports bag full of guns over his shoulder.

'Where the fuck have you been?' Rex grumbled. 'This bag weighs a fucking tonne!'

A barrage of bullets peppered the study door behind Elvis. Frankenstein was closing in on them and making his presence known.

'What the fuck is that?' asked Rex.

Elvis booted Rex in the face with the heel of his shoe. Rex lost his grip on the rope and vanished back down the elevator shaft he had just climbed up.

Elvis dived feet first into the elevator shaft and grabbed hold of the rope. He started rappelling down it just as Frankenstein kicked the study door off its hinges.

Fuck!

This badass was in so much of a hurry he couldn't even be bothered to open a door like a normal person. *What a shithead.*

Frankenstein opened fire again immediately. Elvis felt a spray of bullets bouncing off the wall above his head. Evasive action was required. He let go of the rope and dropped down towards the elevator carriage. Luckily for him, Rex was laid out on his back on the top of it, wondering why he'd been kicked in the face. Elvis landed on top of him and then quickly slid his legs through the open hatch. He dropped through it onto the floor of the carriage and rolled out of the way of any potential gunfire that might be coming their way.

Another salvo of bullets from Frankenstein rattled into the top of the elevator carriage. Then everything went quiet. Elvis heard Frankenstein pull the bookshelf back across the opening to the shaft. But he heard nothing from Rex. Not a sound.

He stood up. 'Rex? You still up there?' he inquired, staring up at the hatch, hoping to see Rex poke his head through it.

Rex didn't reply, but a bucket-load of bullets fell through the hatch and landed on the floor by Elvis's feet.

Eventually Rex poked his head through the hatch and scowled at Elvis. *'You asswipe!'*

'I just saved your life by kicking you back down the lift shaft,' Elvis protested.

Rex climbed back down through the hatch and dropped to his feet. He held up his gloved hand. The glove was ripped to shreds.

'I think that's a record,' said Rex. 'Reckon I caught about twenty of the bloody things.'

Having a magnetic hand, although creepy and off-putting to the opposite sex, did have its benefits in Rex's line of work.

'So anyway,' said Elvis. 'I was trying to tell you, Frankenstein just showed up.'

'No shit!' Rex took off his glove and threw it on the floor. 'Why did he come after you?'

Elvis brushed some debris off his shoulders as he answered. 'He killed the guards on the door and then he came after me like he had a real *hard on* for me.'

'Well it's probably a good thing he did,' said Rex. 'It might give Jasmine time to get the hell out of the dining hall before he shows up there.'

Elvis peered over his sunglasses. 'What exactly was she doing in the dining hall?'

'Take a look at this.' Rex strode over to the bank of monitors that were showing the live feed from around the estate. He pointed at the one he'd seen Jasmine on earlier. 'Check it out,' he said. 'She was on the stage singing just now.'

Elvis stared at the monitor. It seemed that the dinner guests hadn't yet heard all the gunfire. They were all happily watching someone giving a talk on the stage. When the monitor switched to the stage view, it was a relief to see that Jasmine was no longer there. Unfortunately, *the Pope was there*, giving a speech to the watching audience.

On another monitor they saw Frankenstein heading straight for the dining hall, reloading his Uzi again.

Rex looked at his stopwatch. 'Shit, we've got twelve minutes until he kills the Pope.'

Elvis shook his head. '*Twelve minutes?*' he said in disbelief. 'I'd say more like *twelve seconds!*'

Fifty Five

Alexis Calhoon had been unusually nervous all day, so it was a relief to finally be up on the stage for her big moment. A young male stagehand wheeled a trolley containing twenty canisters of Mistralyte onto the stage, which signalled that it was time for her to give a brief speech. Everyone present knew what the Mistralyte was all about. After all, it was the reason they were all there. They were investors, donators, buyers, or just plain rich and nosey. No one was really interested in Calhoon. She felt a bit like a magician's assistant, which wasn't too far off the mark, given the miracle cure.

After introducing herself and showing off the trolley containing the miracle skin cancer cure, she beckoned the Pope up onto the stage so that he could explain to the audience how it had saved his life. What better endorsement could she possibly have than a recommendation from a Pope who had been weeks away from death the last time he'd made a public appearance?

However, it was evident to Calhoon straight away that the Pope wasn't entirely fit and ready to be speaking at a public engagement. His secretary Rufus helped him teeter to the stage. The drugs he had been prescribed to soothe the pain from his life saving operation were obviously still making him very drowsy and unsteady.

Before handing the microphone over to the Pope, Calhoon made one last request of the audience.

'Ladies and gentlemen,' she said. 'We have some of the finest champagne in the world on your tables. So now is the perfect time to raise a toast to the first beneficiary of the miracle cure for skin cancer.' She took hold of the Pope's hand and helped him towards the microphone. 'I give you, the Pope!'

There were many boisterous cries of "Cheers!" as the members of the audience toasted the Pope by drinking champagne.

Calhoon stepped out of the way to allow the Pope to address the audience. If his unsteady walk had hinted that he was heavily under the influence of drugs, his slurred speech confirmed it without a doubt. Rather embarrassingly he seemed drunk, or even worse, *high*.

'Hey everybody,' he said, giving a peace sign with his fingers. 'I've been on a lot of meds, so forgive me if I sound a bit goofy. My secretary Rufus says I sound drunk all the time. I'm not drunk, but hey, *vodka rocks!*'

Calhoon felt the urge to "facepalm" herself. The Pope was attempting to be funny, which wasn't really his strongpoint. It was made worse by his thick European accent uttering faux-hipster words. Luckily, the people in the audience were finding his routine highly amusing because it was so unexpected. Calhoon was incapable of enjoying it though because she was worried that the Pope was going to fall over.

While the audience applauded his lame "vodka rocks" gag, the Pope steadied himself by pressing one of his hands down on the trolley containing the Mistralyte. The way he was leaning on it, Calhoon feared he'd push it off the stage. She imagined the fictional newspaper headline - "Wasted Pope Smashes Canisters Containing Miracle Cure For Cancer."

The Pope cleared his throat and began to regale the audience with an anecdote. As the audience quietened down, Calhoon picked up on some noise outside. The dining hall was supposed to be sound proof, but something was making an awful lot of noise. And to Calhoon's well-trained ears it sounded like gunfire. The Pope obviously didn't hear it, because he carried on telling the audience a tale about a time he'd been on an aeroplane with Bill Clinton.

Calhoon wasn't the only one to notice the gunfire. Some of the guests started murmuring amongst themselves and staring at the doors at the back of the hall.

But then came an even bigger problem. An elderly gentleman sitting at one of the tables near the front began having some kind of seizure. He clasped his hands around his throat and his face turned bright red. Before any of the other guests could get to him he let out a loud gasp and then collapsed forwards. His face smashed onto his dinner plate and knocked his champagne glass over. The woman sitting next to him started screaming. Several other guests jumped up from their seats and rushed to the man's aid.

Another loud crash at one of the tables in the back corner of the room signalled the demise of a second guest. This time it was a young lady. She fell from her chair and dragged the tablecloth with her, pulling glasses and cutlery to the floor, creating an almighty mess.

A third person went down. Then a fourth.

In the middle of all the panic, the Pope finished telling his aeroplane story and staggered back away from the microphone, mumbling the punchline to himself and laughing. He seemed to think that all the screaming and shouting from the audience had been in response to his amusing Bill Clinton parachute anecdote. If there was one person in the room who was oblivious to the danger they were all in, it was the Pope. Calhoon knew she had to get him to safety.

262

More of the guests were collapsing every second, either face first into the table, or off their chairs and onto the floor. The guests who were still conscious were screaming and shouting in a mad panic, fearing for the lives of their fallen loved ones and panicking that they might be next. The mystery virus had affected none of the caterers. Most of them were standing by, idly watching the guests drop like flies.

Calhoon rushed over to the Pope. He was still laughing at his joke and slapping his thigh. He was in quite a boisterous mood.

'That joke gets 'em every time,' he said, smiling at Calhoon.

'No, it's the champagne,' she said, hoping he would pick up on the distress in her voice. 'The *champagne* is doing this!'

'Eh?'

'These people are dying. They've been poisoned by the champagne!'

The Pope seemed to sober up. He stared down at the rapidly increasing number of unconscious guests at the tables below.

'Holy Christ!'

Calhoon's mind was working at a hundred miles an hour, processing what was going on. The most obvious possibility was a terrorist attack. She grabbed the Pope's sleeve and shouted in his ear.

'I need to get you out of here!'

The Pope pulled a hanky from a pocket within his robes and started blowing his nose. By now ninety percent of the guests were either unconscious or having a seizure. A handful remained conscious but looked utterly terrified and bewildered.

Calhoon was frustrated at the Pope's lack of urgency. He was too busy inspecting the contents of his hanky to realise he was in danger. He'd obviously been pumped full of far too many drugs because he wasn't fazed by what was happening. But could she shout at him? Or slap him across the face and tell him to get a hold of himself? How do you berate the Pope?

She attempted to drag him away to the back of the stage. But then a new problem materialised at the other end of the hall. A distinguished gentleman in his forties who hadn't been poisoned by the champagne opened the doors at the back of the hall and ran out into the corridor in an attempt to flee the chaos and perhaps run for help.

BANG!

The gunshot stopped everything. The gentleman who had run out into the corridor fell to the floor. Blood was gushing out of a bullet wound in his forehead. All the screaming and shouting ended the moment it became clear that there was a gunman on the loose in the building.

Calhoon dragged the Pope away from the chaos towards the stairs at the side of the stage. 'Come on, I've got to get you out of here!' she yelled.

He looked baffled. 'Why?'

'Because men are coming to kill you!'

'Kill me? Why?'

A voice at the bottom of the stairs shouted up to them. 'There's no use trying to escape!'

Calhoon recognised that voice. She hadn't heard it in years. It was the voice of Solomon Bennett. He was walking up the stairs, pointing a pistol at her. And he wasn't alone. Behind him, Devon Pincent and his daughter Baby were being shepherded along by none other than Bennett's idiotic scientist friend, Dr Henry Jekyll.

Calhoon's jaw dropped. 'Solomon?'

He smiled at her and jogged up the last few steps until he was on stage with her. 'Do you remember the last time you saw me?' he said, his voice getting louder with every syllable. 'You tried to *have me killed!*'

Calhoon backed away, sensing that Bennett might shoot her at any moment. His gun was pointed at her stomach. She stepped backwards and accidentally knocked into the Pope. He was unsteady enough on his feet without her knocking into him, and it seemed that the nudge from her was the final straw. He lost his balance and staggered backwards. Before Calhoon could grab him he tumbled over the edge of the stage and fell into the dining area. His head bashed against the edge of one of the dining tables and he collapsed unconscious on the floor next to some of the fallen dinner guests. His cassock ended up covering his head and revealing a pair of big white Y-fronts he had on underneath. Calhoon noticed inconsequentially that there was a big brown skid mark in the back of them.

Bennett grabbed Calhoon by the throat and pressed his gun into her ribs. 'Forget about the Pope,' he growled. 'You're the only person I'm interested in killing right now.'

'You came here just to kill me?'

'*No!*' Bennett seemed offended. 'You have such a high opinion of yourself, don't you? We've come for the Mistralyte you stole from us.'

Dr Jekyll shoved Devon and Baby onto the stage. They both had their hands cuffed behind their backs. Jekyll was supposed to be guarding them but as soon as he saw the trolley full of Mistralyte he dashed over to it and started stroking it as if it were a cat.

'Solomon,' he shouted. 'I'll take this trolley and load it onto the bus!'

'Good thinking,' said Bennett. 'Get a couple of guys to help you with it. It looks heavy.'

Calhoon raised her hands in surrender as Bennett pressed his gun harder into her ribs. 'You did all this for twenty canisters of Mistralyte?' she said incredulously.

'Damn right,' said Bennett. 'We can't let you waste it all on curing skin cancer for rich people. It's far too valuable for that. It should be used for what it was designed for, to make more invincible soldiers, like *Frank Grealish.*'

'Frank Grealish?' Calhoon remembered the name. *Hell* she remembered the whole incident that caused the death of Frank Grealish. 'What are you talking about? *He died.* Your stupid experiment killed him!'

'I have to disagree with you on that.' Bennett pointed at the entrance to the dining hall. 'Let me reintroduce you to Frank Grealish,' he said. 'Or as we prefer to call him these days, *Frankenstein.*'

Frankenstein was standing in the corridor outside the dining hall, staring in. Calhoon could hardly believe her eyes. She had pronounced him dead five years earlier. But there he was, and he looked exactly the same as the day he died, except that he now had short dark hair whereas he had been bald during the ill-fated experiment. He was holding an Uzi pistol, looking for someone to fire it at.

Bennett let go of Calhoon's throat and she staggered back, rubbing her neck, which was red and sore.

'What the hell have you done?' she said, staring at Frankenstein.

'Watch this,' said Bennett. He shouted out to all of the catering staff who were hanging around the perimeter of the room. 'People, all of the security guards are dead. Go forth and help yourself to some guns!'

The waiters and waitresses all rushed out of the room to go and loot the dead bodies of the many security guards and marines that Frankenstein had slaughtered since he'd arrived in the building. Frankenstein passed by them and entered the dining hall, looking for anyone else he could kill.

There were maybe twenty dinner guests still conscious because they hadn't drunk any of the champagne. When Frankenstein walked into the room, one of them, a young brunette lady who was cradling her husband's head in her arms, screamed out in terror.

A fatal mistake.

Frankenstein pointed his Uzi at her and gunned her down in cold blood. A brief, deathly silence followed and then the surviving guests in the hall started running for their lives in all directions. Frankenstein shot them down one by one without a flicker of emotion.

Fifty Six

Devon & Baby

Devon surveyed the carnage all around the dining hall. There were upturned tables and chairs everywhere he looked. Unconscious guests were piled up on top of each other and under tables. And then there were the *dead* dinner guests. Frankenstein had murdered every single one of the people who thought they'd had a lucky escape by not drinking the poisoned champagne. The one and only survivor on the lower level of the room was the Pope who was lying unconscious, out of Frankenstein's view, behind an upturned table with his cassock over his head.

Up on the stage Devon and Baby feared for their lives, as did Alexis Calhoon. The man who would decide their fate was Solomon Bennett. He was looking down at the mayhem he had created and marvelling at Frankenstein's contribution to his perfectly executed plan.

Dr Jekyll on the other hand, was only interested in the trolley full of Mistralyte. Two of the henchmen dressed as waiters were helping him to wheel it down the stairs at the side of the stage. Many more henchmen were returning to the dining hall armed with weapons they had lifted from the dead security guards that were lying all around the Landingham estate.

Solomon Bennett walked up behind Devon and used a small silver key to free him from his handcuffs. It felt good to be free of the cuffs and to be able to move his arms again. Having them clasped behind his back for such a long time had been extremely uncomfortable. He rubbed his wrists to try and improve the circulation, which had been stymied by the handcuffs.

'Is that better?' Bennett asked.

'How the hell do you expect to get away with this?' said Devon.

'Easily,' said Bennett, smugly. 'Because I'm amazing.'

'You've killed hundreds of innocent people here!'

'No I haven't. The people who drank the champagne are merely unconscious and will be up and about again in half an hour or so, by which time, we'll be long gone.'

'What about the people who didn't drink the champagne? You killed all of them. What was the point in that?'

Bennett smiled. 'I'm so glad you asked. I'm afraid we had to kill them so that they wouldn't witness what happens next.'

Devon asked a question he knew he wouldn't like the answer to. 'So what happens next?'

Bennett put his arm around Devon's shoulder and pointed at Alexis Calhoon. She was nearby with a henchman pressing a gun into her back.

'Devon, it's time for you to shoot Alexis in the face.'

'What?'

'You heard me.'

Devon pleaded with him. 'But you've got the Mistralyte. That was what you came for. You've already won, you don't need to do this.'

'That's right,' said Bennett. 'I don't. But *you do*.' He held up a cell phone he'd sneaked into the building and waved it at Devon. 'You see, I'm going to film you killing Calhoon. Before you shoot her in the face, you will announce to the world that you are responsible for all of today's murders because you're angry at Calhoon for suspending you.'

'I'll do no such thing.'

Bennett sighed. 'We've already been through this Devon.' He removed his hand from Devon's shoulder and grabbed Baby by her arm. He yanked her away from Devon's side and violently pushed her off the stage. She landed in a heap on the floor next to a bunch of unconscious dinner guests and cried out in pain. Having her hands cuffed behind her back had made it impossible for her to break her fall.

'You asshole!' Devon growled at him.

'You made me do it,' said Bennett. He shouted across the hall to Frankenstein. 'Frankenstein, show Devon's daughter what a great dinner date you are!'

Frankenstein marched across the hall, using the bodies of the dead and unconscious guests as stepping-stones. He grabbed Baby and hauled her up from the floor. He turned her around to face the stage and pressed his Uzi pistol against the side of her head.

Devon glared at Bennett. 'You promised me Baby wouldn't be harmed!'

'And I'm a man of my word,' said Bennett. 'But if you don't step up and kill General Calhoon, Frankenstein will have to blow your little girl's brains out all over the floor.'

'This is sick!' said Devon, shaking his head.

Bennett pressed a few buttons on his phone, preparing it to record. 'When the other guests wake up they will have no recollection of seeing me, or any of my men. The only evidence of what has happened here today will be recorded on this phone.'

'You can't be serious?'

'Oh I'm *very* serious.'

'The police will find this phone and see that you were responsible for all of this.'

'They'll never believe it.'

'Maybe, but you won't be alive to give your side of the story though, so they *just might*.'

Bennett pulled a gun from the back of his pants and handed it over to Devon. 'This gun has one bullet in it,' he said. 'Point it at Alexis, give a little speech about how you're doing all this to teach her a lesson for firing you, then shoot her in the face. It's a simple plan. Deviate from it in any way, mess anything up and Frankenstein will kill your daughter. Do everything like I just said and we'll let her go free before we kill you.'

Baby screamed out. 'NO!'

Deep down, Devon had known all along it would come to something like this. He'd spent most of the last few hours mulling over all the options available to him and come up with one solution. *Do as Bennett said.* There was no other way to leave Baby with any chance of survival.

'I have to do this, Baby,' he said. 'I have no choice.'

Baby was sobbing, staring up at him helplessly, hoping that he would find a way to save them both. Praying that he had a secret plan ready to make everything okay. But he didn't.

'Daddy, don't do it!' she screamed.

Devon stared at the gun in his hand. He had just one bullet. *One bullet.* What could he do with it? His options weren't good. If he fired that shot at anyone other than Alexis Calhoon, Frankenstein would kill Baby. He looked Bennett square in the eye. 'You promise you'll let her go?'

'I promise. But if you do anything stupid, you'll watch her die. And you'll know it was *your* fault.'

Devon looked at Baby one last time and tried to comfort her with a warm smile. 'You've made me proud. I love you,' he said.

Baby sobbed. 'Please don't do it!'

Devon took a deep breath. He began trembling all over as the reality of what he was about to do suddenly hit him. For the first time since he'd been handed the gun he made eye contact with Alexis Calhoon. She had been pushed down to her knees by a henchman, who had stepped away to make sure he was out of the view of Bennett's recording device. To her credit she hadn't shed a single tear. The woman was made of strong stuff, but it was obvious she was terrified because she was quivering. She looked into Devon's eyes and nodded.

'Do what you've got to Devon,' she said, her voice shaking.

Solomon Bennett stepped back and held up his cell phone. 'Devon, move up close. Stand right over her.'

Devon walked tentatively up to Calhoon. He stood over her and pointed the gun at her head.

'That's perfect!' Bennett shouted, joyously. 'Okay, murder of Alexis Calhoon, take one. *Action!*'

Fifty Seven

Jasmine

Jasmine found the sound booth quickly enough. Unfortunately there was only one way in and that was through a door at the back of the booth. The door was locked, but it had a small square window in it at head height that she could see through. A deejay was inside, sitting behind a mixing desk with a computer monitor on it. Behind the desk was a big glass window that looked down on the dining hall and the stage where Jasmine had recently performed her Britney Spears songs.

She rapped her knuckles hard on the door to grab the deejay's attention. He turned around to see who it was. As soon as Jasmine saw his face she knew she could get him to play any song she wanted, to any room in the building. He had rosy red cheeks and messy brown hair that looked like he'd been cutting it himself. And his chin was *massive. Fucking huge!* Or as Jasmine might call it *"Mahoosive!"* It had a huge dimple in the middle of it too. On top of that, his eyebrows were thick and joined in the middle like one giant hairy caterpillar above his eyes. This young man was a freak. Not that Jasmine was judging in any way. She happened to like freaky guys. The uglier and nerdier they were, the better. Nerds knew how to treat a woman. Well, actually they didn't have a clue how to treat a woman, but they tried hard. Every nerd Jasmine had ever met was like putty in her hands. Experience had taught her that if she could be bothered to just brush her hand against a nerd's crotch, he would probably be willing to give her his favourite *Silver Surfer comic.*

So yeah, Jasmine liked nerds, freaks, ugly blokes and harmless weirdoes every bit as much as she liked alpha males like Jack Munson. She beamed a flirtatious smile at the deejay. It took him less than two seconds to jump up from his seat, unlock the door and let her into the sound booth.

'Wow,' she said looking around at the very untidy and stale smelling booth. 'Are you in charge of all this?'

He nodded like an excited dog. 'Yeah.'

'What's your name?'

'Roland Chang.'

'Roland? *Cool,* that's my favourite name.' She brushed away some crisps that were stuck to Roland's dark blue sweater. 'Can you play a song for me?'

'You were Britney Spears just now, weren't you?' he mumbled, his cheeks burning red like he'd never spoken to a woman before. *'You were amazing!'*

'Cool, thanks! So you'll play a song for me?'

Roland looked around nervously. 'Umm, I can't right now, but definitely later. What song do you want?'

'Something by, umm,' her mind went blank for a moment as she tried to recall what music Joey had requested. 'Carpenter? Do you know who I mean? Scary music apparently.'

'I think so,' said Roland. 'But I can't play it right now. There's something going on in the dining hall. A lot of the people are passing out. If I start playing music, I'll get fired.'

'But I need you to play it right now,' said Jasmine, flicking some more crisps away from the front of his tracksuit bottoms and accidentally on purpose brushing her hand against his dick.

Roland visibly stiffened (*his shoulders*). He swallowed hard. 'I really shouldn't,' he said. 'Is there something else I can do?'

Jasmine took a close look at his mixing desk. It had a whole bunch of switches on it and it all seemed to be connected up to his computer screen. This was nothing like the CD player she had owned during her time in B Movie Hell, or the cassette player she'd used in Romania. She had no idea how to work this thing. She would need him to operate it.

Tough times call for drastic action, so Jasmine got down on her knees and crept under the desk. She swivelled round and looked up at Roland who had a confused look on his face, and some chocolate sprinkles.

'What are you doing?' he asked. 'You can't be down there.'

'If you play that Carpenter music into every single room of the building right now, I'll suck your dick all through the song.'

Roland's mouth dropped open. He didn't manage to say anything. And even though no more encouragement was needed, time was of the essence so Jasmine made one final offer.

'Play the whole album if you want,' she said.

Roland came to his senses. He rushed over to the mixing desk and started flicking switches and typing stuff on his keyboard. Jasmine tugged down his tracksuit bottoms until they were wrapped around his ankles, then reached up and yanked down his colourful *Captain Caveman* underpants.

His dick was already erect, and with her vast experience Jasmine could tell there was no chance of him lasting the whole song. On the plus side, there was a pretty good chance she could make him "shoot his load" without even touching his dick. A quick five seconds of ball tickling would probably suffice.

As Jasmine was *"umming"* and *"aahing"* over which technique to use, she heard a gentle chinking sound up above her head. And then just as she was reaching out to cup Roland's balls, he fell backwards. He landed flat on his back with his dick pointing upwards. She considered the possibility that he had fainted, overcome by the excitement of what was about to happen. But then she spotted blood seeping out of his head onto the hardwood floor.

She crawled out from under the desk and took a closer look. Roland had a hole in his forehead. His mouth was open, but it had been for a while anyway, so he still looked the same from that point of view. Jasmine nudged him in the chest.

'Roland,' she whispered. 'Are you okay?'

He didn't answer.

She prodded him again and even tried tickling his balls but he didn't stir. She was considering sticking two fingers up his butt when she heard another chinking sound. The glass window on the booth was breaking.

She listened carefully and suddenly heard a burst of gunfire from the dining hall beneath them. Whoever had shot Roland in the head was now shooting at a bunch of screaming people in the dining hall.

She pulled Roland's underpants and tracksuit bottoms back up to save him from the embarrassment of being found dead with a sweaty boner. Then she climbed to her feet and took a peek over the mixing desk to see what was going on below. There wasn't much to see without sticking her face up close to the glass, which she figured would be dangerous. Fortunately she was able to hear what was going on through the hole in the soundproof glass window. When the gunfire stopped she heard some people talking. Most of the chatter was coming from the stage area. But then she heard Baby scream out just below her.

"Daddy, don't do it!"

Jasmine took a chance and leaned over the desk a little more. She saw Frankenstein had hold of Baby in a tight grip, and he was pressing a gun against her head.

Even worse was what was occurring on the stage. Alexis Calhoon was on her knees with Devon standing over her, pointing a gun at her face. A dude with an eye patch on his right eye was filming it on his cell phone.

It was time for Jasmine to spring into action. She had to create a diversion. The only option available to her was the music desk. It was why she was in the sound booth anyway, so now was definitely the time to stick on the music Joey had requested.

She crouched down out of sight and stared at the computer screen. Roland had been in the process of setting up the scary music for her. On the screen she saw a green button with the word PLAY on it. She hit the ENTER key on the keyboard beneath the computer and hoped for the best.

To her relief, a song started playing almost immediately. Roland had done as she requested and set it up to play through every speaker in every room of the building. *And boy was it loud!*

Joey had requested some scary John Carpenter music. His instructions had gotten a little muddled on their way from Jasmine to Roland and from Roland to the computer.

"We've only just begun...."

Jasmine was no expert when it came to *John Carpenter*, but she knew *Karen Carpenter* when she heard her. So it wasn't exactly Halloween music, but it had the desired effect. It distracted everyone in the dining room and bought Devon some time.

Frankenstein looked up and saw Jasmine just before she ducked out of sight again. He pulled his Uzi pistol away from Baby's head, pointed at the sound booth and began shooting.

Jasmine crawled back under the mixing desk and put her hands over her ears to drown out the gunfire, and *The Carpenters*. Glass shattered all around her as the impact of the bullets started destroying the booth. She'd done her job. She'd bought some time. Now it was up to the guys to show up and do their stuff.

But where the hell were they?

274

Fifty Eight

The Red Mohawk

Joey crept along a corridor on the upper floor of Landingham Manor until he made it to the balcony above the reception hall. That's where all the gunfire had been coming from. He saw the main culprit, Frankenstein, marching off towards the dining hall, leaving a trail of dead bodies behind in the reception area.

Joey took cover behind a pillar on the balcony above the reception. He scoured the floor to see if Elvis or Rex were among the corpses. There was no sign of them, which meant they might still be alive.

He was about to head down the stairs, with the intention of following Frankenstein when a group of six Gold Star waiters ran into the reception hall and started lifting guns and ammo from the dead security guards.

Joey hid behind a huge marble pillar and kept quiet. He heard one of the men down below give a short speech to the others.

'Search the building and kill anyone you see walking around unless it's the Red Mohawk. Devon wants him alive. Got that?'

There were some grunts from the others to indicate they understood, and then they all rushed off in different directions, looking for people to kill. A group of them headed up the main staircase to the balcony Joey was hiding on.

He had no choice but to back away and try to find another way into the dining hall. Even though he had a gun, the chances of him winning a gunfight against a team of Solomon Bennett's mercenaries from his current position weren't good.

'FREEZE ASSHOLE!'

Shit. One of Bennett's henchmen had gotten lucky and walked around a corner in the corridor behind Joey. He was a big shaven headed thug, who looked like he knew how to hold a gun. He was crouched down on one knee with a pistol pointed right at Joey's chest.

'PUT THE FUCKING GUN DOWN NOW!'

The big skinhead's shouting had alerted the other nearby phoney Gold Star caterers to what was going on. Joey's training on Operation Blackwash meant that he could work out the odds of survival in a millisecond. His survival odds here were roughly one in a thousand. The only thing in his favour was that he'd heard one of the henchmen say that they were under orders to take him alive if possible....

"Play the percentages," he told himself. "An opportunity to kill all these guys will present itself eventually."

As the henchmen closed in on him from all sides he made the decision to surrender.

'Okay, I'm putting my gun down,' he called out.

He raised one hand in the air and bent down to put his gun on the ground, careful not to make any sudden movements. The skinhead moved closer. He had a two handed grip on his gun and was keeping it pointed at Joey as he edged towards him.

'On your head,' the skinhead said. 'Hands on your head!'

Joey stood up slowly and placed his hands behind his head. The skinhead hurried up behind him and shoved him in the back towards the staircase that led down to the reception area. Six other henchmen were on the landing with their pistols at the ready. The skinhead shouted out to them.

'Mikey, I've got him here. And I've got his gun.'

The leader of the group, Mikey was a ponytailed henchman straight out of *the 80's*. He was standing at the front of the group on the landing, trying to look tough, with a machine gun hanging from his shoulder on a leather strap.

'So you're the Red Mohawk?' he sneered as Joey approached.

The skinhead gave Joey an extra hard shove in the back that caused him to stagger forward into Mikey. Mikey pushed him back and yanked the Mohawk mask off his head. He held it in his hands and studied it with a conceited grin on his face.

'Not so tough without your little mask, are you?' he said, gloating.

While the henchmen were busy congratulating themselves on catching him, Joey was weighing up his options. There were four henchmen on the landing with him and another two just a couple of steps down the staircase. And then there was the bulky skinhead behind him pressing the gun into his back.

The easiest person to take out first was the skinhead behind him. A step back and a quick stamp on his knee joint would incapacitate him, making it easy to take his gun from him. Next would be Mikey. He would have to be used as a human shield. That part would be easy too because Mikey had a mask in one hand and a machine gun in the other that he couldn't fire one handed. That would leave five others on the landing and the stairs.

His planning was interrupted by the sound of music, which should have been his cue to start killing.

But it wasn't John Carpenter's *Halloween theme.*

276

It was Karen Carpenter singing, *"We've Only Just Begun."*

Well, it wasn't the kind of music he was hoping for, but it would have to do. He had already decided in his head the order in which he was going to kill all of the henchmen.

He grinned at Mikey. 'You're all going to die.'

Mikey responded with a sarcastic smile and a quick jibe. 'I'm going to enjoy watching you....'

SQUELCH!

To Joey's surprise, Mikey's head vanished before he could finish the sentence. The squelching sound morphed into a *SPLAT* as his head turned into a milkshake-style red goo and splashed against a window at the back of the landing. His body remained upright with blood gushing out of a hole at the top of his neck where his head had once been.

Joey knew of only one person owned a gun that could do that to a man's head. *The Bourbon Kid.*

Fifty Nine

Mikey's headless body eventually gave way at the knees and collapsed onto the floor. Blood continued gushing out of his neck and trickled down the stairs. His remaining comrades were all stunned. Unlike Joey they had never seen a man's head fly off his shoulders, turn to mush and splat against a wall. So Joey had a slight edge, in that he knew exactly what was going on.

The distraction enabled him to execute the plan of attack he had been working out in his head. He backed into the skinhead behind him, spun round and smashed the butt of his open hand into his enemy's jaw. The skinhead's teeth splintered and blood spurted from his mouth in all directions. The blow knocked him out before he hit the floor. Joey snatched his gun away from him and turned on the remaining henchmen.

SPLAT!

Another henchman's head flew past Joey's face like a gust of red wind and squelched into the wall not far from the window where Mikey's head had ended up.

BANG!

Joey used the skinhead's gun to blast the next closest henchman in the back of the head from close range.

BANG!

He took down another with a bullet to the face.

Two henchmen remained. They had nowhere to go and it was clear that both were petrified. One of them dropped his gun on the floor and raised his hands in surrender. His comrade obviously saw merit in the idea and did likewise.

That was the cue for the Bourbon Kid to show himself. He had been concealed behind the doorway at the front entrance on the ground level. He stepped into the building and walked through the metal detectors, causing them to go into meltdown due to the vast amount of metal he had concealed beneath his long black coat. He had a big fucking gun in his hand and it was pointed at one of the henchmen on the stairs.

The henchman shouted out. 'It's okay, we surrender!'

SPLAT!

Surrender wasn't an option when the Bourbon Kid was on a killing spree. The fool who shouted out lost his head just like the others. His mulched brains, skull, face and hair splatted into the chest and face of the final surviving henchman.

The final survivor, a lanky guy with cropped blond hair, which was now caked in blood and brains, dropped to his knees and spat out some of the blood that had flown into his mouth when his friend's head blew up.

The Bourbon Kid called up to Joey. 'You wanna kill this last one?'

Beneath all the sludge on the last guy's face it was clear he was terrified. Joey lowered his gun and tucked it down the back of his pants. He stooped down and picked up his Red Mohawk mask from the floor by his feet. He slid it over his head. It felt good to have the mask on again. Once it was comfortably secured he started walking down the stairs towards the final henchman.

He stopped three steps above the terrified prisoner and swung a karate-style kick. His foot connected sweetly with the man's chin. The man's head snapped back and the power of the kick lifted him off his feet. He toppled head over heels like a gymnast as he hurtled down the stairs. His shoulder bounced off the edge of a step halfway down which made his legs somersault over his head until he landed unsteadily on his feet at the bottom of the stairs. He toppled forwards again, straight into an *express train of a punch* from the Bourbon Kid. The impact snapped his head back with enough power that it almost came clean off his shoulders. He landed on his back on the stairs *and that was the end of that.*

The staircase was littered with corpses, some headless, some not, but all fucked up pretty bad. Joey jumped onto the shiny wooden banister and slid down it until he dropped off the end next to the Bourbon Kid.

'Good to see you wearing the mask at last,' said the Kid. 'But what's with this fucking music?'

'I asked Jasmine to put on some John Carpenter tunes.'

'That figures.'

Joey hadn't had a chance to get a good look at the Kid's gun before. It was an impressive, heavyweight piece of artillery.

'What's the deal this?' he asked. 'Could it kill Frankenstein?'

The Kid shook his head. 'Already tried.'

'Well I've been thinking, if we can get him to open his mouth, that's where he's most vulnerable. I'm a pretty good shot and....'

'Already tried.'

Joey was frowning beneath his mask. 'When did you try all these things?'

'This morning.'

'And what happened?'

'It took a while but I eventually found a way to kill him.'

'Then how come *he's still alive?*'

'He got on his bike and rode off, like a bitch.'

'Well he's here now and he's in the dining hall, so let's go and get him!'

Joey picked up a pair of Browning 9mm semi-automatic pistols that were lying on the stairs. He checked they were loaded while the Kid lit up a cigarette.

'You ready?' Joey asked.

'Do I look ready?'

'Yeah. Let's go kill everyone.'

The Red Mohawk and the Bourbon Kid walked side by side along the corridor towards the dining hall. Even though the dining hall doors were closed, they could hear a lot of noise coming from inside.

'So how do we kill Frankenstein?' Joey asked. 'You should probably tell me now, in case something happens to you.'

The Kid reached inside his jacket and pulled out a small object. 'This will do it,' he said.

'How?'

The Kid blew some smoke out of his nostrils. 'You'll work it out,' he said.

They stopped short of the double doors to the dining hall. The doors looked like Swiss cheese due to the infinite number of bullet holes in them, so they were no use as cover.

'I'm ready when you are,' said Joey.

'Hold on a second.' The Kid dropped his cigarette on the floor and stared back at the reception area as if he'd seen something.'

'What is it?' Joey asked.

'Can you hear that?'

Joey stopped and listened. The gunfire in the dining hall had ceased. *Karen Carpenter* was still singing, *unfortunately.* But there was also something else. At first it wasn't loud enough to drown out the singing, but that would soon change.

Sixty

Devon Pincent made a promise to himself that if he managed to make it out of Landingham Manor in one piece he would find a way to thank Jasmine. He'd been seconds away from shooting Alexis Calhoon in the face when she came to his aid, creating a distraction by playing *We've Only Just Begun* on the sound system. He'd seen her duck down in the sound booth just after the music started.

About thirty of Solomon Bennett's hired mercenaries had re-entered the hall, armed with guns they had taken from the dead security team. On Bennett's order they all started shooting up at the sound booth. Frankenstein kept a firm grip on Baby and started firing his Uzi too.

The noise was deafening as the glass on the booth shattered into a thousand pieces and much of it dropped to the ground. The walls and the double doors beneath the sound booth were also peppered with bullets. It was a bizarre sight, reminiscent of the scene in the movie *Predator* where Arnold Schwarzenegger and his buddies unload a few thousand rounds of ammunition at a bunch of trees and hit nothing.

The distraction gave Devon an opportunity to buy himself some more time. While no one was looking his way, he fired his gun at the ceiling. The bullet was supposed to be for Alexis Calhoon, but now it was embedded in the ceiling and no one noticed because they were all too busy shooting at Jasmine in the sound booth.

Alexis Calhoon took advantage of the diversion too. She rolled away across the stage and vanished beneath the hem of a large pair of red curtains at the back.

From the moment Solomon Bennett had ordered his people to shoot at Jasmine, he'd been shouting at them to stop again. Eventually when the shooting died down a little he managed to make himself heard.

'STOP SHOOTING FOR FUCKSSAKE!'

The gunfire ceased almost immediately. The dining hall should have been silent as a tomb as a result, except that there was still the *music*.

Although Devon had never been a fan of *The Carpenters*, it was so much better than listening to thirty testosterone fuelled idiots firing guns at one helpless young woman in a sound booth.

Solomon Bennett shook his head and rubbed his ears. '*Christ almighty!*' he said. 'I think that's enough. My fucking ears are ringing!' He turned back to Devon. 'Now where were we?'

For a brief second, Bennett looked smug again, but his face soon dropped when he realised that Calhoon was gone.

'*Shit!* Where is she?' he bawled at Devon.

Devon shrugged. 'Maybe your buddy Dr Jekyll took her with him?'

Bennett started looking around frantically, which was quite an odd sight, because having just the one eye, he had to move his head around a lot, giving the impression he was doing some serious neck exercises.

Bennett's plans were beginning to collapse. A loud roaring sound came from the corridor at the opposite end of the hall. Everyone in the room stopped what they were doing and stared at the double doors in the wall beneath the sound booth. Something was coming their way.

'What the fuck is happening *now?*' Bennett moaned.

Devon put his hands over his ears as every single one of Bennett's henchmen (including Frankenstein who still had a firm grip on Baby) pointed their guns at the double doors at the end of the hall, ready to open fire again.

CRASH!

A purple Cadillac burst through the doors, knocking them off their hinges. Wood shattered and splintered off in all directions. The car bounced over a few bodies on the floor, some of which were dead and some of which were merely unconscious guests who had drunk the champagne.

The driver of the Cadillac was an Elvis impersonator in a blue suit. He pulled a handbrake turn and the car stopped at a ninety-degree angle to the doors it had crashed through. It had already been a strange day, so Devon shouldn't have been surprised by the sight of an Elvis impersonator driving a purple Cadillac into a dining hall filled with gun-toting waiters and a bulletproof Frankenstein.

Right on cue, the gunfire started again. This time it was even worse than before. Frankenstein and all the henchmen aimed their guns at the Cadillac and unloaded on it. The car was peppered with bullets, most of which were intended for Elvis. But he had bulletproof windows on his car, so he was in the safest place in the room. His paintwork was being absolutely ruined though. To keep the gunfire focused on him, Elvis raised his middle finger and made obscene gestures with it, which was guaranteed to keep the idiots firing.

Three other men bundled out of the other side of the car and took cover behind it. Their firearms began intermittently popping up over the car and firing back at Bennett's men. Devon spotted Joey. The red stripe of hair on top of his mask made him instantly recognisable. He was kneeling down behind the hood of the car. The two other men alongside him were Rodeo Rex and the Bourbon Kid. *The cavalry had arrived.*

Devon followed Calhoon's lead and dived behind the big red curtain at the rear of the stage. He hoped to God that these guys could get the job done and kill Frankenstein and Solomon Bennett without hurting Baby.

But as things go, Devon had never seen this particular type of shootout before. He scurried over to the side of the stage and took cover, peering out through the edge of the curtain to see what was going on. Alexis Calhoon crept up behind him and tapped him on the shoulder.

'What's happening?' she shouted in his ear.

'You're still here?' said Devon. 'I thought you'd be halfway to Belize by now!'

'I would but there's no way out from back here.' She pointed at the purple Cadillac that was being destroyed by gunfire in the hall. 'Are those *your* people?'

'They're nothing to do with me, apart from Joey Conrad.'

The Red Mohawk, Rodeo Rex and the Bourbon Kid were outnumbered and it looked like they'd underestimated the firepower Bennett's men had. Elvis was stuck in the front seat giving the finger to everyone. The other three were under attack from so much heavy fire that they couldn't even poke their heads up in order to shoot back.

To Devon's annoyance, Frankenstein wasn't letting go of Baby. He was shooting at the Cadillac like everyone else but he was also walking towards it, dragging her with him.

'Oh God, Baby's going to get hurt, I can tell,' he groaned.

Calhoon pulled at his shoulder to restrain him in case he was thinking of trying to help. 'There's nothing we can do,' she said. 'Let's just hope they've got a plan.'

Devon patted her hand on his shoulder. 'You should go,' he said. 'Make a run for it.'

'I can't,' she replied, staring out at the chaos in the hall. 'The Pope is still out there. I can't let him die at an event I organised!'

Sixty One

The plan to take cover behind Elvis's Cadillac had seemed like a good idea at first. But that was before thirty henchmen armed with automatic weapons joined Frankenstein in shooting at them. Joey, Rex and the Bourbon Kid watched a storm of bullets fly over their heads.

'Tell me again, whose idea was this?' Joey shouted over the ear-piercing sound of gunfire.

'Mine!' Rex yelled back.

'Well it's a shit idea!' Joey hollered in reply. 'I just wanted you to know that.'

'You got a better one?'

Rex was sitting with his back against the car, in between Joey and the Bourbon Kid. He'd dragged the black sports bag full of guns and ammo out of the car and had it by his side. The Bourbon Kid elbowed Rex in the ribs and shouted into his ear.

'I've got a plan! Give me those two Glocks.'

Rex grabbed a pair of 9mm Glock pistols from the bag and handed them to the Kid.

'What are you gonna do?' he yelled.

'I need you to stand up and draw Frankenstein's fire until he runs out of ammo!'

'*You what?*'

'Just do it.'

Rex wasn't entirely convinced that his magnetic hand would be able to catch the vast number of bullets that would come his way if he stuck his head up over the roof of the car again. He'd poked his head up a few seconds earlier, *they all had*, but it hadn't worked out too well for them. They'd had to duck back down almost immediately and Rex now had a bullet hole in the top of his favourite Stetson hat to prove what a shitty idea it had been.

'Why does it always have to be me?' Rex complained.

Joey slapped him on the arm. 'Because it was your shitty idea in the first place!'

'And what were you going to do before me and Elvis showed up with the car?'

It was a valid point. Joey and the Bourbon Kid had been on the verge of walking into the dining hall without a car as cover before Elvis and Rex showed up, driving the Cadillac down the corridor of the stately mansion.

The Bourbon Kid hollered at Rex. 'Just fucking do it!'

Rex had to accept that it had been his idea to hide behind the car and he was the only one with a magnetic, bullet-catching hand, so in the unwritten rules of gunfights in dining halls, he had to stand up and face the gunfire. He reached back into the sports bag and grabbed a Winchester "Mare's Leg" short barrelled shotgun. It wouldn't fire off the volume of bullets of the Glocks or wield the power and accuracy of the Desert Eagle in Elvis's glove box, but it looked fuckin' cool. He had wanted one ever since seeing Woody Harrelson with a similar one in *Zombieland.*

Rex waved his metal hand above the roof of the car to test the waters. He caught two bullets in it within half a second. *This was not going to be fun.* He took a deep breath and stood up. He pointed his shotgun over the car's roof and fired off a shot at the first gunman he saw. A suicidal maniac had foolishly decided to charge towards the car with a machine gun. The shot from Rex's gun made an excellent mess of his face.

All of the other henchmen had taken cover behind upturned tables and chairs and were firing intermittently at the car. Frankenstein was at the far end of the hall. He was walking towards the Cadillac, holding Baby close to him with one hand and firing an Uzi blindly with the other.

Rex managed to catch about thirty bullets in his hand. Four or five more blasted through the top of his hat again, missing his head by mere millimetres. Inevitably though, two bullets hit him. One grazed past his left shoulder and another blasted straight into his right bicep. *And they stung like hell.* He dived back down to the floor, wincing in pain. He'd been shot a few times before in his life and he knew how to ignore the hurt. He put it out of his mind and shouted at the Bourbon Kid.

'Frankenstein is out. He's reloading now!'

Frankenstein had indeed run out of ammo and was reaching for one of the clips he had tucked away in the pouches on his combat pants. But it wasn't easy because he had one arm wrapped around Baby.

The Bourbon Kid was just about to stand up and start shooting when Joey shouted a last minute request at him.

'Don't shoot the asshole with the eye patch! He's mine!'

The Kid stood up and pointed his Glocks over the roof of the car. For the next ten seconds he fired off shots at anything and everything that moved, with the exception of Frankenstein and "the asshole with the eye patch".

When he was out of bullets he ducked back down next to Rex.

'I killed 'em all,' he said.

'All of them?' queried Rex.

'Yeah. Well I wasn't shooting at the chairs, was I?'

Joey echoed Rex's doubts. 'That's impossible. There's about thirty of them!'

'Thirty-two actually,' said the Kid. 'And I saved the asshole with the eye patch for you. So why don't you quit bitching and shoot the fucker?'

Joey didn't need a second invitation. He stood up and leaned over the roof of the car. Solomon Bennett was at the end of the hall, hiding behind an upturned dinner table. There was enough of his head in sight for Joey to take a shot. Bennett's good eye lit up when he saw the Red Mohawk mask appear above the car. He moved to take a shot at the mask with a gun he was holding in his right hand. But he never got a chance to squeeze the trigger. Joey's years of training in Operation Blackwash had made him a crack shot. He fired one round from his Browning semi-automatic pistol. One round was enough. The bullet went right through Bennett's good eye and blood sprayed out through the back of his head. It straightened him up and he staggered backwards like a boxer who'd been knocked out but hadn't realised it yet. A moment later when the rest of his body worked out what his brain already knew, he toppled over, landing on top of the unconscious body of the Pope.

The only person still moving in the dining hall was Frankenstein. He still had one arm wrapped around Baby and he had finally reloaded his Uzi. Joey ducked back down just before Frankenstein started firing blindly at the Cadillac again.

'Did you get the eye patch guy?' Rex asked.

'Right in the fucking eye!'

'Good for you! Now how do we kill Frankenstein?'

Elvis leaned across the front seat of the car and poked his head out of the passenger side window.

'Guys, whatever you do, you'd better do it quick,' he warned, 'because I don't think Frankenstein's gonna protect the girl from those zombies.'

There was a momentary pause as everyone reflected upon what Elvis had just said. Even *The Carpenters* stopped singing.

'Zombies?' said Joey, querying the information on behalf of everyone else. *'What zombies?'*

Elvis poked his gold Desert Eagle out of the window and aimed it at something over Joey's shoulder.

BANG!

The bullet whistled past Joey's ear. Rex, Joey and the Kid took a moment to see what he was shooting at. One of the dinner guests who had been lying unconscious by the side of the smashed doors had climbed to his feet. His appearance had completely changed. His skin had become thin and grey like tracing paper. Violent blue veins had sprouted up on his neck, face and hands, and his eyes had turned blood red.

Elvis's bullet hit him straight in the chest. His white dinner shirt turned crimson with blood and he collapsed against the wall, coughing up blood from his lungs. Unfortunately, he was not the only dinner guest who had transformed into a thick-skinned, blue veined, red eyed, mutant. They were springing up all around the hall. Some of them had started biting chunks of flesh out of the dead henchmen. But many of the others had their eyes set on the living, moving survivors.

Frankenstein wasn't in the least bit bothered about the rising dead. There was nothing they could do to hurt him. He started shooting at the car again and continued advancing towards it.

Rodeo Rex checked his watch. It was still counting down. He held it up and showed it to Elvis.

'The Mystic Lady's vision hasn't changed!' he yelled. 'We've got less than four minutes to stop someone in this room from killing the Pope!'

Elvis crawled head first out of the open window of the car. He landed on the floor on his front and then backed up alongside Rex.

'Let's start shooting some fucking zombies then!' he roared.

'Kind of difficult with Frankenstein shooting at us,' Rex grumbled.

Joey intervened. 'Don't worry about Frankenstein. Me and the Kid will take care of him.'

'Well you'd better fucking hurry up!' Rex said, expressing the urgency of their predicament. 'Because the Pope is on the floor at the other end of the hall and if one of these zombie motherfuckers spots him, he's *dead meat!*'

Sixty Two

Jasmine had been cowering under the mixing desk in the sound booth throughout the shootout. The floor all around her was covered in shattered glass and there were shitloads of bullet indentations in the back of the desk just inches behind her. During a brief break in all the gunfire, she heard a few familiar voices down below. Rex, Elvis, Joey and the Bourbon Kid were bickering amongst themselves.

She crawled out from under the desk, carefully avoiding the broken glass, and took a peek over the desk to see what was going on below. The first thing she saw was the dead body of Solomon Bennett. He was lying on top of the old transvestite in the white dress. He had a gaping hole in the back of his head. Blood was oozing out of it.

The next person she spotted was Frankenstein. He was dragging Baby towards Elvis's purple Cadillac, which was parked sideways near the entrance to the hall.

But then she saw a bunch of the dinner guests climbing to their feet. At first she thought they had recovered from the effects of the drugged champagne. But then she noticed that all of them were staggering awkwardly and not because they were still a little woozy from the champagne. They had bloodshot eyes and blue veiny faces. There was something seriously wrong with them. This was confirmed when a few of them started biting chunks out of the dead bodies that were lying around.

Jasmine smacked the ENTER key on the mixing desk keyboard to turn off *The Carpenters*, which she figured had become an unhelpful distraction. Then she leaned over the desk to get a better look at what the guys were up to below her.

Elvis crawled out of the passenger side window on the safe side of the car. He had his gold Desert Eagle in his hand. Rodeo Rex was sitting on the floor next to him brandishing a shotgun and using it to shoot down any zombies that came close. The Red Mohawk and the Bourbon Kid were crouched on either side of the car, looking like they were about to make a run at Frankenstein.

In between Elvis and Rex, there was a sports bag full of guns and ammo. It crossed Jasmine's mind that if she could get her hands on a gun she could shoot dead one of the mutant dinner guests. Now that they were no longer human it would be okay to kill one without feeling bad about it. And if she succeeded, then Rex would have to honour his promise and make her a member of *The Dead Hunters* gang. *Jasmine really wanted to be part of the gang.* She leaned over the desk a little further and shouted down to Elvis.

'Elvis, honey, throw me a gun!'

Elvis looked up and, in spite of the fact he had a couple of mutant dinner guests climbing to their feet near him he was good enough to reach into the sports bag and pull out a small pistol. He hurled it up towards the sound booth. It was an accurate throw. The only problem was, Jasmine's catching skills weren't quite so good. She grasped at it and caught the handle in her right hand, only to then knock it away again with her left. The gun fell back down and bounced off Rodeo Rex's head onto the floor.

Jasmine squirmed back into the booth, hoping to avoid a dirty look from Rex. She pressed her hand down on the keyboard as she steadied herself and inadvertently booted up the music system again. The song *Yakety Sax*, started blaring out of all the speakers.

Before she had a chance to turn it off, Frankenstein looked up. Something about the music seemed to really get under his skin. He pointed his Uzi gun up at the sound booth and opened fire again. Jasmine dived out of the way and crawled towards the door that led out into the corridor. If she was going to kill a zombie and become a *Dead Hunter* she was going to have to do it from downstairs.

As she pulled the door open and crawled into the corridor, Frankenstein ran out of bullets again. He'd used up his last ammo clip. So without realising it Jasmine had given the guys downstairs a window of opportunity in which to confront him.

Sixty Three

Baby had been fighting hard to try and break free from Frankenstein's grip ever since all the shooting had started. Her efforts were futile because her hands were still cuffed behind her back and Frankenstein was so strong that he'd barely even noticed her struggling with him. He was too darn busy shooting at everything. He'd emptied the clip on his gun several times and replaced it with a new one from his pockets. But after his most recent attempt to hit Jasmine up in the sound booth, he finally ran out of ammo. He tossed his gun away and started looking for another one amongst the scores of dead bodies lying around on the dining hall floor.

There was another Uzi pistol sticking out underneath a dead waitress's leg at one of the many overturned tables nearby. He dragged Baby over to it and stooped down to pick up it up. Baby knew this would be her best and possibly last chance to try and wriggle free from him. She writhed and squirmed but it made no difference. Even when Frankenstein was bent over and off balance she couldn't shake him off. In one last moment of desperation she thought about trying out her "big move". Joey was obviously thinking the same thing because from his hiding place behind the Cadillac, he shouted out to her.

'Baby. Give him the penguin!'

To anyone else that might seem like a very odd request in the current predicament, but Baby knew exactly what it meant. And it was reassuring to know that Joey had the same idea as her.

She reached back and grabbed the buckle on Frankenstein's belt. With one deft flick of her thumb and forefinger she unclasped it. The first part of the move was done. Frankenstein didn't even notice because he was busy unhooking the Uzi from the waitress's shoulder. Baby grabbed a fistful of his pants and yanked them down.

Like any man who has his pants unexpectedly pulled down and isn't wearing any underwear, Frankenstein's first instinct was to forget everything else and pull them back up. He released his grip on Baby, which finally enabled her to twist away from him, yanking his pants with her. Frankenstein lost his balance as his pants got tangled up around his ankles. The move had worked for Baby on numerous occasions in the past. And the golden rule was, *the bigger they are, the easier they fall.* She rolled away and dived for cover behind a table.

Frankenstein's right foot got crossed over his left and he had to press his hand down on the floor to prevent himself from toppling over. Realising that Baby had escaped from his grasp he foolishly tried to reach out and grab her at the same time. He took a couple of awkward "toddler" steps before he toppled over and landed on his chin with his big smooth naked ass pointing up at the ceiling.

The Bourbon Kid came storming out from behind the Cadillac and raced towards him. He leapt up in the air with his fist clenched. It looked like he was intending to ram his arm right up Frankenstein's ass, but then right at the last moment he grabbed a butt cheek with his hand and pulled on it, making Frankenstein's asshole gape open. With his other hand he plunged a *Kinder Surprise Egg* between the big brute's butt cheeks and punched it deep in to his colon. And that thing went all the way in. The smooth oval shape of the egg was perfect for infiltrating Frankenstein's yawning rectum.

Joey had also raced out from behind the Cadillac. He screamed at Baby.

'Get away from the zombies!'

Baby had seen a couple of mutated dinner guests rising up around the hall, but they hadn't been a priority for her while she was in Frankenstein's grasp. Now that she was free she started to notice just how many of them there were lying around. She scurried to her feet and rushed towards the raised stage area, dodging the outstretched arms of a few veiny-faced, red-eyed mutants, which wasn't easy to do because her hands were cuffed behind her.

Fortunately Rodeo Rex and Elvis had her covered. Any time a mutant got close, one of them would shoot it in the head or blow one of its limbs off with the high-powered guns they were wielding.

Baby ran up the steps at the side of the stage and looked back to see what had become of Frankenstein.

The giant *brain-dead-monster-man* had stopped trying to pull his pants up. He was focussing his anger on the Bourbon Kid, which was understandable because the Kid had just stuffed a decent sized chocolate novelty egg up his bum. The Kid was on his feet goading Frankenstein, beckoning him to stand up and fight.

Frankenstein duly obliged. He straightened up, seemingly no longer bothered by the fact that his pants were hanging around his ankles. But as soon as he was upright, the Bourbon Kid launched into phase two of his attack plan. He leapt up into the air and landed a punch on Frankenstein's jaw. It spun him around straight into the path of the Red Mohawk.

Joey had discreetly circled round behind Frankenstein while the Kid distracted him with the *"egg up the anus"* assault. When Frankenstein stopped spinning from the Kid's punch, Joey hit him with a short, sharp but very powerful jab to the stomach.

Baby expected to see Joey and the Bourbon Kid take it in turns continuing their assault on Frankenstein, but both of them backed away.

Frankenstein shook off the gut punch and looked around for another gun to pick up. He spotted an Uzi he had been close to retrieving before Baby had pulled his pants down. He took one step towards it, *but that was as far as he went.*

A noise like thunder suddenly drowned out everything else. It felt like the room was about to start shaking. But the burst of thunder had come from within Frankenstein's stomach. The repercussions of Joey's trademark *"shit punch"* to the gut had begun to take effect.

Frankenstein's whole body expanded rapidly. His arms stretched out into a crucifix pose and his chest heaved. His stomach growled louder and began to stretch. *His body was exploding from within.* The first thing to go was the set of black goggles that covered his eyes. They snapped and flew off his head, chased out by his eyes, which popped from their sockets and jetted off in opposing directions.

And then came the blood.

So much blood.

It didn't just gush out of his eye-sockets either. It erupted from his ears and his mouth and his nostrils. A fountain of red gunge burst out of his asshole too, like the worst case of diarrhoea in the history of diarrhoea.

Frankenstein's demise was swift. The life drained out of him as fast as the blood and bodily fluids did. His knees didn't even bend as he fell forwards and crashed onto the floor, smashing in what was left of his face. Frankenstein was no more. Killed to the sound of the *Benny Hill theme tune.*

With the big monster down and out of the equation, Elvis and Rex bounded out from behind the Cadillac. They started patrolling the dining hall, blowing away any mutant dinner guests they could find. Anyone whose face looked remotely blue, or whose eyes were slightly bloodshot got his or her head blown off. And if a mutant got too close to them while they were reloading, the butt of a gun was a handy way to cave in its skull.

Baby found the dead body of the henchman who had put the cuffs on her. He was on the floor just below the raised stage area and he had the keys to her cuffs on his belt. She grabbed them and got to work trying to free herself.

The Bourbon Kid was sitting on the hood of Elvis's purple Cadillac, smoking a cigarette and occasionally shooting at any dinner guests that looked like they might be moving.

Joey was in the middle of the hall, just absorbing the scenery. His jeans were covered in the spray of blood that had erupted out of Frankenstein. He pulled his mask off and smiled at Baby. She finished unlocking her handcuffs, dropped them to the floor and then bounded over to him. She jumped on him, wrapping her arms and legs around him. He wrapped his arms around her and they shared a kiss more passionate than anything she had ever experienced before. Her psychotic, mask wearing serial killer boyfriend had risen to the challenge again, killing the seemingly invincible menace that was Frankenstein.

She looked into his eyes. 'How did you do that?' she asked. 'How did you make Frankenstein explode like that?'

'I gave him a "shit punch".'

'But why did he blow up?'

'He had a bomb in his stomach.'

'A bomb?'

'Yeah, concealed inside a chocolate egg.'

'Why would you put a bomb inside a chocolate egg?'

Joey shrugged. 'I have no idea. But as soon I hit him in the gut and his stomach tightened around the egg, he was a dead man walking.'

Baby kind of understood that Frankenstein's insides weren't going to be bulletproof like his skin, but she still couldn't fathom why someone would hide a bomb in a chocolate egg.

'Seriously though,' she said, voicing her thoughts aloud. 'Why would you put a bomb inside a Kinder egg?'

'That's what I wanna know!' Rodeo Rex boomed from across the room. He had stopped searching for mutants to kill and was staring at the Bourbon Kid and wagging his finger angrily.

The Kid exhaled a lungful of smoke. 'It's a good place to hide a bomb,' he said, shrugging.

'Was it the fucking egg you tried to give me the other day?' Rex bellowed.

'It might be.'

'You rotten sonofabitch!'

Baby wasn't entirely sure how she felt about Joey's new friends. They were strange to say the least.

'I'd better go and stop them from killing each other,' Joey said, pulling away from her. 'You should go hug your dad. Tell him what a star he is.'

Baby looked around and saw her father and Alexis Calhoon. They had been hiding down at the side of the stage, keeping clear of the gunfire. Now that it was over they had ventured out. Devon looked tired, but mighty relieved to see his daughter in one piece.

'Baby! You're safe!' he cried, tears welling up in his eyes.

Baby left Joey and bounded over towards him. There was so much love in his eyes. No one looked at her the same way her father did. A cheery smile broke out on her face. Her father was beaming back at her. But then suddenly he wasn't. His face dropped.

'BABY!' he yelled, staring at something over her shoulder. 'LOOK OUT!'

Sixty Four

Alexis Calhoon had seen some unusual things during her time as head of Phantom Ops, but what she witnessed in the dining hall at Landingham manor would be impossible to describe to anyone without sounding like she had lost her mind. At some point though, she was going to have to explain to some important people how the Pope had come close to being assassinated by Frankenstein. Then there was the small matter of the missing Mistralyte, stolen by Dr Jekyll. And of course, the zombiefied dinner guests! *Fuck it,* she needed a good cover story. *And quick.*

She stood on the stage and surveyed the wreckage below. Hundreds upon hundreds of smoking corpses were littered around the dining hall. The smell of death and gun smoke was nauseating. There were only a handful of survivors and Calhoon was grateful to be one of them. She owed her life to the four men who had showed up in a purple Cadillac. Elvis, Rodeo Rex, the Bourbon Kid and the Red Mohawk were four of the most wanted killers in the civilised world. She had never imagined she might one day be pleased to see them. They had a fifth member in their gang though, one Calhoon had momentarily forgotten about. The Britney Spears impersonator in the red catsuit and black facemask, skipped into the dining hall through the smashed doors at the back.

The only other survivors were Devon and Baby, and more importantly, the Pope. Calhoon could see him still lying unconscious on the floor underneath Solomon Bennett's dead body.

But just when Calhoon thought the chaos and carnage was over, she saw one last dinner guest rise from the dead. It was a man she recognised. Tyrone Malone was a wealthy benefactor whom she had hoped would make a large bid for some Mistralyte. He had transformed into one of the mutated, bloodthirsty zombie creatures. He was quick on his feet too. He came from nowhere and lunged at Baby from behind. Before Calhoon could shout a warning, Devon Pincent beat her to it.

'BABY LOOK OUT!'

The mutant reached out and grabbed a hold of Baby's shoulder. His rancid teeth were bared and ready to take a bite out of her neck.

Devon Pincent hadn't moved so fast in years. He sprinted at Baby and just before the mutant's jaws closed around her shoulder, he thrust his hand into its mouth. The mutant bit down hard on Devon's hand, crunching into his finger bones. Devon howled in pain and fought to get his hand back while dragging the monster away from his daughter. He might not be as young and agile as he once was, but when his daughter's life was in danger there was nothing this man wouldn't do. A tussle ensued between him and the mutant. Devon successfully dragged the fight away from Baby, but the mutant lunged at his face, sinking its teeth into his neck. He managed to drag the creature to the floor with him, where they writhed around like amateur wrestlers.

Baby screamed and backed away, tripping over one of the many corpses strewn around the floor. Joey, Rex and Elvis rushed to Devon's assistance. Joey grabbed the mutant around the neck from behind and threw it to one side, away from Devon. It slid across the floor until it crashed into a pile of dead bodies. Red blood was pasted around its mouth. *Devon's blood.*

Elvis followed up on Joey's assault by grabbing the mutant and lifting it up off the floor. Like a wrestler, he threw it over his shoulder and slammed it down onto an upturned table leg. The back of the mutant's skull crunched loudly as the metal table leg bust through it and came out through the front of its face. Its body twitched for a few seconds before expiring in a bloodied heap.

Calhoon rushed down the stairs on the stage so she could check on Devon. He was in a bad way. There was blood leaking out of his neck and his eyes had lost their sparkle. Baby got to him first and cradled his head in her arms.

'Somebody help him!' she screamed.

Joey crouched down alongside Baby. He took one look at Devon and then looked up at Calhoon. He'd seen what she'd seen. Devon Pincent's time was up. In saving his daughter from the last zombie, he had sacrificed his own life.

A few moments later Baby realised it too. She burst into tears as it dawned on her that her father was about to die. Devon was coughing up blood and trying desperately to choke out a few final words to his daughter. But the words never came. Baby stroked his head and did her best to fight back the tears, to stay strong for him. But eventually he took one last sharp intake of breath before his body turned heavy and flaccid, and he died in his daughter's arms.

Sixty Five

The sound of Baby howling in agony at her father's death was more painful than anything Alexis Calhoon had endured that day. She had known Devon for a long time and in spite of their differences she had always admired his desire to do the right thing, even when it meant doing the wrong thing. Calhoon had lost her own father when she was young, but not in such a horrible manner. A part of her wanted to throw her arms around Baby and reassure her that everything would turn out okay, but sometimes the right words just aren't available to empathise with someone's pain. Joey Conrad (who was no doubt suffering himself at the loss of his mentor) put his arms around Baby and did his best to comfort her.

Calhoon stepped away to give them some private space. She made a beeline for Rodeo Rex who was standing on his own, wielding a shotgun and looking around the dining hall for any other surviving mutants.

'I'm Alexis Calhoon,' she said, offering a handshake. 'Head of Phantom Ops.'

Rex stopped checking for signs of life amongst the dead and took off his Stetson. He held it across his chest before he shook her hand.

'Rodeo Rex, at your service,' he said.

'I know who you are,' said Calhoon, before adding. '*All of you.*'

'I don't know what you've heard about us,' said Rex. 'But we came here to stop the Pope from being assassinated.'

'And you succeeded.'

Rex checked the stopwatch on his wrist for what felt like the thousandth time that day. 'Looks like we did it with a minute to spare, too,' he said.

'You knew the exact time this was all going to happen?'

'Kind of. A crazy fortune teller had a vision that the Pope was going to be killed about a minute from now.'

Calhoon wasn't sure if he was being serious or not, but he didn't look like the kind of person who made jokes. 'A fortune teller?' she repeated.

Rex rolled his eyes. 'I know, I didn't entirely believe it either. But I was told that this watch would stop counting down as soon as the Pope's killer was neutralised.'

'Well on behalf of myself and the Pope, I'd like to thank you,' said Calhoon. 'In fact, I'd like to *hire* you guys.'

Elvis rocked up alongside Rex. 'Hire us?' he said. 'What for?'

'My department could use some men like you.'

'We're all wanted murderers,' said Rex. 'I don't think you *could* hire us!'

Calhoon lowered her voice and spoke softly to Rex. 'I can make all your criminal records disappear.'

Rex raised an eyebrow. 'Really? How?'

'I have that kind of power. As long as you haven't murdered a President or a King or any kind of world leader, I can get you cleared of anything.'

Rex pondered the offer for a moment. 'So you can make *all* our criminal records disappear?' he said warily.

'Even his,' said Calhoon, pointing at the Bourbon Kid who was stubbing his cigarette out on Elvis's car. Luckily Elvis wasn't looking. His eyes were elsewhere.

Before Rex could respond to Calhoon's very generous offer, Elvis elbowed him in the arm. 'I thought your watch was supposed to stop counting down when the Pope was safe?' he said, pointing at Rex's stopwatch.

The watch had carried on ticking down, even though Frankenstein was dead. When Rex looked at the display there were *seven seconds* left on the countdown.

He was about to comment on it, when suddenly *out of nowhere*, Jasmine shouted out.

'THERE'S ANOTHER ZOMBIE!'

Rex and Elvis both reached for their guns and sprung into action. They spun around and scoured the room to see where the mutant was that Jasmine was screaming about. Jasmine had grabbed a gun from one of the nearby dead henchmen and was pointing it towards the stage, hoping to finish the mutant off herself.

Rex and Elvis shouted at the same time. *"JASMINE NOOOOOO!"*

Their warning shout fell on deaf ears. Jasmine fired her gun six times in quick succession. And who would have guessed that she'd be a crack shot? All six bullets hit the target she was aiming at.

The deafening gunshots were followed by the sound of Rex, Elvis and Calhoon all face-palming themselves as they realised what she had done.

She'd shot the Pope. Six times.

He'd crawled out from underneath Solomon Bennett's corpse and was in the process of climbing to his feet when Jasmine spotted him. She mistook him for a mutant dinner guest because one side of his face was covered in blood and brains from Solomon Bennett. Six bullets later, *the Pope was dead.*

If it was any consolation at all *(and let's face it, it wasn't)*, he died almost immediately. His suffering was extremely brief and probably dulled immensely by the vast amount of painkilling drugs he had consumed.

Calhoon felt her knees go weak. She reached out and steadied herself against Rodeo Rex's shoulder and for the first time she noticed that he had been shot too. He had a hole in his bicep where a bullet had hit him. To his credit, the bullet hadn't phased him in the slightest, but he shared Calhoon's look of utter despair at what had just happened.

Jasmine lowered her gun. A broad smile beamed across her face. 'Did you see that?' she cried, excitedly. 'I got one!'

Calhoon couldn't believe it. After all the trouble they had gone through to save the Pope, he had been executed at the last minute by a gun-toting, mask wearing, brown skinned Britney Spears impersonator.

Rex offered an excuse on Jasmine's behalf. 'She didn't mean it.'

'Yeah.' Calhoon sighed. 'Like I was saying earlier, I can clear all your criminal records, as long as you haven't killed a President, a King or any kind of world leader. But your friend Jasmine over there, she's just killed the Pope, so there's really nothing I can do for her.'

Rex checked his watch again. It had stopped at 0.00. He closed his eyes and hit himself in the forehead with his metal hand. He looked exasperated. Jasmine on the other hand, was looking extremely pleased with herself. She came bounding over with a cheery smile on her face. She tugged at Elvis's sleeve.

'Did you see that?' she asked.

'Yeah that was real good,' Elvis replied, politely.

'Do I get to be a member of *the Dead Hunters* now?'

Elvis stroked Jasmine's hair. He looked across at Rex who was putting his Stetson hat back on. It was Calhoon who gave Jasmine her answer.

'Honey, you just killed *the Pope!* That means that for the rest of your life you're gonna have government agents, bounty hunters, assassins and all kinds of fame hungry lunatics on your tail trying to kill you.'

Rodeo Rex took a deep breath and responded on Jasmine's behalf. 'Well you'd better get word out to all of those people and let them know this, anyone who tries to kill Jasmine is gonna have to get past me, Elvis and the Bourbon Kid. 'Cause she just became the newest member of *The Dead Hunters.*'

Jasmine clapped her hands with glee. 'This is so cool!' she cheered. 'And all I had to do was kill a Pope!'

Elvis put his arm around Jasmine and gave her a kiss on the forehead. 'Yeah, you did good, honey. Not quite what I was hoping you'd do, but well done anyway.'

Calhoon slapped Rex gently across his stomach. 'You guys had better get going because I called for backup five minutes ago while you were murdering all these dinner guests.'

'What are you gonna tell people?' Rex asked.

The Bourbon Kid jumped off the hood of the Cadillac and walked into the middle of the dining hall. He had a bottle of champagne in his hand. He'd stuck a burning piece of cloth into the neck of it.

'Her story is simple,' he said. 'The place burned down.'

Calhoon hadn't considered burning the place down and wasn't sure she liked the idea, but the Bourbon Kid threw the flaming bottle at the curtains on the stage. The curtains caught fire quickly. In the grand scheme of things, it was probably the right thing to do. Burning the place down might just save Calhoon from having to explain to the FBI that a man known as Frankenstein (who was created in an experiment she authorised) had showed up and murdered half the guests. Dr Jekyll (a former employee of hers) poisoned the rest of the guests and escaped with all the precious Mistralyte. And well, then there was all the stuff about *The Dead Hunters* and the accidental assassination of the Pope by someone who mistook him for a zombie. If she told anyone that story she'd end up in Grimwald's Asylum for the rest of her life.

Rex shouted over to Joey. 'Yo, Mohawk, we gotta go!'

Joey was trying his best to comfort Baby who was in pieces, distraught at the sudden horrific and brutal death of her father.

'I should stay with Baby,' he yelled back.

Calhoon approached Joey tentatively. She placed a hand on his shoulder. 'Honey,' she said, 'you've got to go. If you're still here in two minutes time, I won't be able to help you. Now that the Pope is dead, you guys need to get out of here.'

Joey took hold of Baby's hand and wiped some tears from her cheeks. 'You should come with us,' he said.

'No she shouldn't,' said Calhoon. 'Her father has just died. If she leaves with you now she won't be able to go to his funeral.'

Jasmine intervened with a generous but useless offer. 'She can stay at my place,' she said.

Calhoon grimaced and shook her head in disbelief, before addressing the whole room. 'Can someone please explain to Jasmine what it means when you kill the Pope?' she said. 'Baby can stay with me until things have calmed down. The rest of you seriously need to get out of here, *now!*'

Joey knelt down beside Baby and held her hand. 'I'll come back and get you when things have calmed down, I promise.'

A loud whoosh from the burning curtains served as a reminder that regardless of whether Calhoon's backup arrived in the next five minutes or not, they needed to be gone, and soon.

Rex picked up the dead body of Devon Pincent and slung him over his shoulder.

'What are you doing?' Baby asked.

'We can't let him burn in here. I'll carry his body outside for you, but then we've really got to go.'

Calhoon called after him. 'Thanks again for everything you've done here.'

'No problem,' Rex called back. 'And do *yourself* a favour. When this place is burnt to the ground, blame everything on us. We can handle it.'

At that moment Alexis Calhoon could have hugged Rex. Blaming everything on a gang of mass murderers who most people scarcely believe exist was so much better than trying to explain the truth.

Sixty Six

The night sky had drawn in but the gardens in front of Landingham Manor were lit up by flashing blue and red lights from a succession of ambulances, police cars and fire engines that had rushed to the scene. On top of that there were hundreds of flashing cameras from the many members of the press and media who had gathered to report on what just might be the biggest story of the year.

Within two hours of their arrival the fire department had managed to get the blaze under control to prevent it from spreading. But much of the inside of Landingham Manor was already beyond repair.

Alexis Calhoon and Marianne "Baby" Pincent were the only two survivors who had walked out of the building. They were both perched on the back of an ambulance with warm towels wrapped around their shoulders while they looked out at the mayhem outside. Calhoon was drinking coffee and trying to come to terms with everything she had seen.

A vast number of deep-fried corpses had been carried out on stretchers but so far none of them looked remotely like zombies. Most of them were bagged up in readiness for a trip to the coroners. Very few of them had any skin left on their bodies so it would be a monumental task just to identify them, let alone work out if anything other than the fire had killed them.

Calhoon felt fortunate compared to Baby, because even though she had seen many acquaintances and colleagues murdered, she still had her husband to go home to. But Baby had no one. Her mother and sister had burned to death in a mysterious fire many years earlier and now she had lost her father too. Quite what was going through her mind as Landingham Manor burned to the ground, God only knew.

Calhoon kept promising Baby that everything would be okay and that she could come and live with her for as long as she needed a home. She had also drummed into Baby the importance of sticking to the same story if any cops or FBI agents questioned them. It was a simple tale that involved telling the truth, with the exception of three things. Don't mention Frankenstein, Dr Jekyll or the zombies. All of the murders were to be blamed on *The Dead Hunters*.

It was a relief when the familiar and friendly face of Blake Jackson showed up. He'd arrived on the crime scene wearing a thick blue coat that stretched down to his knees and a trilby hat. Wearing a hat was a trick of the trade when at a chaotic crime scene. It hinted at authority and generally meant that even if you weren't important, you could bark orders at people and they would respond. People respect headgear at crime scenes (but no one has a fucking clue why). Anyway, it just so happened that Blake Jackson was a senior figure on site, but the hat speeded things up for him. He swiftly assumed command of the whole crime scene and began ordering people around. When he spotted Calhoon and Baby perched on the back of the ambulance he hurried over. He managed to look anxious and relieved at the same time.

'Alexis, *thank God you're alive*,' he said. 'How are you?'

'I've been better.'

'Of course, that's a dumb question,' he said apologetically. 'Can I get you anything?'

'It's okay. We'll be leaving shortly.'

Jackson grimaced and shook his head. 'I'm afraid to say, Baby won't be able to leave just yet. I need to ask her a few questions.'

'Like what?'

'Like how she came to be at Landingham Manor today when she was never on the guest list?'

Baby looked up at him and wiped a tear from her cheek. 'My father and me were kidnapped and brought here as hostages.'

Jackson looked surprised. 'Kidnapped?' he baulked. 'By whom?'

Calhoon interrupted on Baby's behalf. *'By Solomon Bennett!'*

She stood up and spoke softly into Jackson's ear. 'Blake, why don't you give your career a rest for a minute? She's been through quite enough today as it is.'

'I realise that,' said Jackson, 'and I don't want to seem like an asshole, but I'm doing everything by the book so we don't have any more fuckups.'

Calhoon sighed. 'We don't do things by the book in Phantom Ops. Not any more.'

'It's not that simple,' said Jackson. 'Unfortunately this one is out of our hands. We've had two eyewitnesses come forward to say they saw the Red Mohawk throw a kid called Jason Moxy off a cliff at *Dead Man's Drop*. And they both say Baby was with him.'

'When is this supposed to have happened?'

'Two nights ago. The cops found a body this morning too.'

'Shit.'

'I know,' said Jackson, sympathetically. 'But let me handle it. You see the problem is, I've heard that you told the Feds the Red Mohawk was here today and that he was part of the gang that killed the Pope. So with Baby here too, I've got no choice but to take her into custody.'

This new information took Calhoon by surprise. 'Oh come on, Blake, you've got to be kidding!' she said, pleading to his compassionate side.

Jackson levelled with her. 'I promise you I'll make sure she's taken care of. This is probably just routine stuff. I'll get her a lawyer and make sure she doesn't implicate herself, but for now we've got to take her into custody.'

There were a lot of cops and FBI agents milling around behind Jackson. If it wasn't him that took Baby into custody then there was a good chance one of them would eventually wander over with an arrest warrant.

Calhoon made one final plea to Jackson. 'Just let her come home with me tonight. We'll go now.'

Jackson took on a more authoritative tone. 'Alexis, you need to step aside. I'll make sure she's treated well and given all the counselling she needs, but I can't let her leave this crime scene without a set of cuffs on.'

'All right, just give me a minute with her.'

'You've got *one minute*, but then I'm coming back with a couple of officers.'

Jackson stepped away and started barking orders at some nearby policemen. Calhoon sat back down next to Baby in the back of the ambulance. She brushed some stray hairs out of Baby's face.

'I promise you I'll fix this,' she said reassuringly. 'Don't answer any of their questions until I get you fixed up with my lawyer. His name is Bob Sugar. Tell the cops and the Feds that you won't speak with anyone until Bob Sugar shows up. He'll know exactly what to do. He's a real weasel.'

Baby looked deflated. The last thing she needed was an interrogation from Jackson or the Feds. 'Okay,' she said, lowering her head like a broken doll.

'Your father was a good man, Baby, and I owe him a few favours. As long as I'm still breathing, you won't end up in prison, I give you my word.'

A minute later, Blake Jackson returned with two military police officers. One of them cuffed Baby's hands in front of her while the other read her the Miranda rights. They were as pleasant and apologetic as they could possibly be, but the whole thing left Alexis Calhoon with a heavy heart as she watched them lead Baby away to one of the nearby police cars.

Blake Jackson sat down next to Calhoon. 'I'm real sorry about all of this,' he said. 'If there was any other way, you know.'

'I know.'

Jackson looked up at the remains of the main building. 'So what exactly happened here?' he asked.

'The Red Mohawk and some other crazy assholes calling themselves *The Dead Hunters* shot everyone, including the Pope. Then they burnt the place down. At least, I think that's what happened. I missed most of the action because I was smuggling Baby out of there.'

'What about the Mistralyte?'

'They stole it, I think. Or maybe it burned in the fire. To be honest Blake, I'm too tired for all this right now.'

Jackson patted her on the shoulder. 'Of course, I'm sorry, I didn't mean to push. Can I get someone to give you a ride home?'

She shook her head. 'No it's okay. My husband will be here in a minute. He's taking me home.'

'I bet you'll be pleased to see him after all this.'

'Yeah. It's been a long day.'

Jackson gave her a sympathetic smile. 'Take some time off,' he said. 'I'll handle everything for a few days. Try and get a good night's sleep.'

'Thanks Blake.'

Sixty Seven

"It's been two weeks since the Pope was assassinated and the Government's anti-terrorist department are no closer to catching the men responsible. This morning the President of the United States gave this message...."

Alexis Calhoon switched the TV off. The regular news updates on the Pope's murder were visibly getting her down. It was hard to tell who was feeling the pressure most, Calhoon or Blake Jackson who was sitting on the other side of her desk. She had summoned him to her office for a private meeting. Jackson had turned up dressed smart in a grey suit with a white shirt and red tie. Beneath the impeccable appearance though, he was a bag of nervous energy. In the two weeks since the Landingham Manor catastrophe he'd barely slept, worrying that Calhoon might discover his involvement in the theft of the Mistralyte and his links to Solomon Bennett. One thing in his favour was that Calhoon had the weight of the world on her shoulders. Like him she was doing a great job of keeping up appearances. She'd been wearing the full green and khaki service uniforms for the last two weeks because she was constantly attending meetings with senior officials. If she survived with her job intact, it would be nothing short of miraculous. And if she did get fired, that's when Blake Jackson would get what he'd been after all along, *her job*.

Calhoon took a sip of coffee from her favourite mug, which had a picture of Robert Redford on it from the movie Spy Game. 'I wish someone would blow up the White House or something,' she said.

'I beg your pardon?'

It's about the only thing that would stop the news from going on about the Pope all the time.'

Jackson laughed politely even though he didn't find jokes about blowing up the White House particularly amusing. 'It'll die down soon, I'm sure,' he said. 'Have you heard anything more from the Secretary of Defence?'

'No, but people from his department still question me every day about something or other, and I tell them the same thing, I didn't see *anything.'*

Jackson tried to sound sympathetic. 'If they spent as much time searching for the Red Mohawk as they do harassing you, this whole thing would have been sorted out by now. I mean how hard can it be to catch a man who walks around in a Halloween mask the whole time?'

'Very difficult it would seem,' said Calhoon sarcastically. She leant back in her chair and stretched her legs. 'But if they do find him and discover his real identity I suspect they'll be bothering me a lot more.'

'Crazy isn't it?' said Jackson. 'Now we're protecting him just like Devon was.'

'We're not *protecting him*. We just have to find him before anyone else does. And that's what I called you here for. I've come up with a plan.'

'Is it a good plan?'

'No, it's an *excellent* plan, just like all my plans.'

'Go on, I'm all ears.'

'If Joey Conrad has gone into hiding, no one is going to find him, ever.'

'How is that a plan?'

'It's not, smartass. We won't find him, but he'll come and find us if we play our cards right.'

'Why on earth would we want him to come looking for us?'

'Not *us, Baby*.'

'You think he'll come back for her?'

Calhoon shook her head. 'He's insane but he's not stupid. Baby's locked up in just about the most secure holding cell in the world. He won't attempt to rescue her until an opportunity presents itself.'

'What kind of opportunity?'

'Remember how Baby was supposed to be playing the part of Sandy in the stage production of Grease?'

'Yeah. What of it?'

'The show opens in two weeks time and I've arranged it so that she will perform on the opening night.'

For a second, Jackson thought she was kidding. Her determined stare suggested that she wasn't. He scratched his head to see if he could find any logic in her plan. And also, he wondered if it would provide him with an opportunity to make Baby disappear. She was one of the only loose ends from the Landingham massacre.

'You've lost me,' he said eventually. 'What are you planning?'

'Exactly what I just said. Baby's going to be in *Grease*,' said Calhoon.

Jackson had only known about the plan for a couple of seconds and he'd already spotted a huge flaw.

'Wait a minute,' he said, holding up his hands as if he were trying to calm her down. 'Even if you *could* do this, Baby is an accomplice to the murder of Jason Moxy. *Remember him, the leading man in that show?* The rest of the cast will *hate her!* You'll never be able to make this work.'

'It's already done.'

'*What?* How the hell have you managed that?'

Calhoon picked up her mug of coffee and took a sip. 'One day Blake, when you're in my seat, and you're the one drinking from this lovely *Robert Redford* mug, you'll have the same power and influence that I have, and you won't be able to talk about it to your second-in-command either. That's how these things work. I called in some favours and pulled a few strings, let's just leave it at that.'

'But your neck is already on the line. If this goes wrong you'll be hung, drawn and quartered in the Oval office!'

'I realise that. But this is our only chance. I've pretty much been told that if the Pope's murderer isn't found soon, our whole department is going down. So we entice Joey Conrad out of his hiding place to watch Baby in Grease, or we all start looking for new jobs.'

'And if he's dumb enough to show up at the Grease premiere?'

'We take him down.'

'How?'

'Well first up, tomorrow it's going to be announced to the press that all charges against Baby have been dropped, but she's being kept in custody for her own protection. On the night of the Grease premiere you and I will escort Baby to the show. We'll sit in the audience and watch with everyone else. Meanwhile, we'll have a bunch of our guys dressed like civilians patrolling the entrances and exits in case Conrad shows up. If he's dumb enough, *and I think he is,* then our people will discreetly make him disappear, if you know what I mean.'

One thing was still bugging Jackson. 'This all seems a little too elaborate. Why does she have to be in the show? Can't she just sit in the audience with us?'

Calhoon stroked Robert Redford's face, wiping a dribble of coffee out of his hair. 'That's a good question Blake,' she said. 'You see, the thing is, call me an old sentimental fool, but Devon Pincent was so proud of his daughter for getting the part in that show, that I feel like I owe it to him to let her perform in it, just once.'

'You're a sentimental old fool.'

'Yes I am.'

'And what happens to Baby after the show?'

'She'll be given a new identity and move to New Zealand.'

'*New Zealand?* Why New Zealand?'

'Because when I watched those Lord of the Rings films, I thought it looked like a nice place.'

'Yeah, a nice place full of *orcs!*' Jackson sneered.

'There's no need to be snippy. This is the plan and we're rolling with it.'

Blake Jackson mulled over Calhoon's plan. As far as he could tell it fitted in perfectly with what he wanted. Although the thought of sitting through a three hour performance of Grease filled him with dread.

Sixty Eight

Blake Jackson was pleasantly surprised by how much he enjoyed the *Grease* stage show. Baby's singing was much better than he had expected, particularly her rendition of *Hopelessly Devoted To You.* It was all the more impressive considering that she had only partaken in one dress-rehearsal with the rest of the cast. Most of her rehearsing had been done on her own in a prison holding cell, which must have been annoying for any other inmates.

The entire cast seemed to cope exceptionally well with the Baby situation.

'You know, this is much better than I expected,' Jackson whispered into Alexis Calhoon's ear.

The two of them were sitting at their own private dining table at the back of the hall. Calhoon was wearing a classy, black dinner dress that highlighted her femininity, which was something Jackson had never really seen before. He was wearing a traditional black dinner suit. He'd enjoyed the night right from the start when they arrived and walked down the red carpet. It had been an unexpected thrill and a taste of what it must be like to be famous.

On Jackson's only previous visit to the theatre he'd had to sit in one of the many rows of seats with barely any legroom. At Calhoon's request they had acquired the special table at the end of the aisle that ran down the middle of the theatre. There were fifty rows of seats in front of them and every seat was taken. The show's opening night was clearly a success.

'Baby's singing is impeccable,' Calhoon noted. 'She could have really made a career for herself as a singer.'

'Yeah. I think the girl playing Marty is better though. She's got an incredible set of lungs on her.'

'She's the one who will be playing the part of Sandy in all the remaining shows.'

'I might come again then,' said Jackson. 'She's awesome.'

A man in a black leather suit, who was sitting in an aisle seat on the back row turned his head to see who was talking through the performance. He was wearing sunglasses, which was kind of odd considering they were indoors, and he looked just like Elvis Presley. He peered over the top of his glasses and glared at Jackson.

'Would you shut the fuck up?' he grumbled. 'Some of us are trying to watch the show.'

When the man turned back to carry on watching the show, Jackson whispered in Calhoon's ear. 'He's touchy isn't he?'

Calhoon shushed him and pointed up at the stage. 'Watch what Baby does here with the cigarette. It's really cool.'

The show was nearing the end and Baby was wearing a black jacket and skin-tight black pants in readiness to perform the song *"You're The One That I Want"*. She had a pack of cigarettes in her hand. She pulled one out with her teeth and to the amazement of everyone watching, the cigarette lit up on its own when she sucked on it.

'Wow,' said Jackson, resisting the urge to burst into applause in case the Elvis lookalike got shitty again. 'That's good. I wonder how she did that?'

Calhoon whispered in his ear. 'One of my guys showed her how.'

'One of *your* guys? Which one?'

'Shush, they're about to start singing. I love this song.'

The cast began the performance of *You're The One That I Want.* The whole thing was very impressive, with great vocals from Baby and Danny Zuco and some well-choreographed dance sequences.

Halfway through the song, at the bidding of Danny Zuco, the entire audience began singing along and quite a few of them jumped up from their seats and started dancing. Blake Jackson was enjoying himself so much that he'd forgotten all about why he was there.

In fact he was so distracted that he didn't notice Joey Conrad was in the theatre until he walked right past him towards the stage. He was wearing his red leather jacket and even though he didn't have the yellow skull mask on his head, Jackson knew who he was right away. Joey ignored Jackson and Calhoon and headed down the centre aisle towards the stage.

'Holy shit!' said Jackson. 'Is that Joey Conrad?' He stood up from his seat with the intention of finding someone to arrest Joey.

'Sit down Blake,' said Calhoon.

'Huh?'

Elvis turned around again and leaned over the back of his chair. 'She said sit down, dipshit!'

Jackson reluctantly sat down in order to avoid an altercation with Elvis, who looked like he was itching for an excuse to thump him. Alexis Calhoon had stayed in her seat and seemed completely unfazed by the arrival of Joey Conrad.

'Alexis, what's going on?' Jackson asked.

'Just watch the show.'

Joey Conrad made his way down the aisle, until he reached the stage. He stopped a few yards short of it and looked up at Baby. No one else in the audience seemed to notice him, and if they did, they didn't seem to care because the performance of *You're The One That I Want* had them all captivated.

Baby didn't spot Joey straight away. It wasn't until she spun around in an intricate dance move that she saw him. She stopped singing right in the middle of a solo section. A broad smile gleamed across her face and she rushed towards the edge of the stage. Joey held out his arms beckoning her to make the jump. Baby didn't hesitate, she dived off the edge of the stage and he caught her in his arms. She wrapped her legs around his hips and the two of them kissed passionately to the bemusement of half of the audience, while the other half clapped and cheered assuming that it was a new twist on the original ending of Grease.

'This is just terrible,' said Jackson. 'It's more like *Dirty Dancing* than *Grease*. What a farce.'

'You haven't worked it out yet, have you?' said Calhoon, blithely.

Jackson was irate and not just because Joey Conrad had showed up and sneaked past security. The show had been ruined too and he'd been enjoying it.

'Seriously Alexis, what the fuck is going on?' he ranted, standing up again. 'How's he managed to get past all our people?'

He didn't wait for her to answer. It was time to go and find some of the undercover agents who were located around the theatre. He hurried towards the exit only to find his way blocked off by a big denim-clad Hell's Angel wearing a Stetson hat. Rodeo Rex had followed Joey into the theatre and he looked like he meant business. Jackson's gut instinct told him he was in trouble. He turned round to go back the other way only to see the Bourbon Kid blocking off any chance of escape via the other exit.

Confusion had started to break out everywhere. The cast of Grease were desperately trying to hold the show together without the female lead who was making out with Joey in the aisle. The audience were beginning to boo. And then to make matters worse for Jackson, Elvis got up from his seat and grabbed him by the arm, and he had a very firm grip.

'Come on buddy, let's take a walk,' Elvis said.

Jackson swallowed hard and looked across at Calhoon and asked her again. 'What's going on?'

'I know it was you, Blake,' Calhoon replied.

'What?'

Calhoon stood up and walked over to him. She patted him on the shoulder. 'You forgot about Dorothy,' she said.

'Who?'

'Mrs Landingham, remember her? She locked herself in a panic room when Frankenstein showed up at her house. I visited her the other day and she told me how you'd provided the champagne for the big day.'

Jackson felt a sudden urge to throw up. His stomach tightened and his mouth went dry with alarming haste. His heart was racing and his mind was working at a million miles an hour trying to think of a way to get out of the awkward predicament he found himself in.

He tried to shake Elvis off. 'You won't get out of here alive,' he threatened. 'I've got men everywhere outside. The building is surrounded.'

'No it ain't,' Elvis replied.

Calhoon seemed to be revelling in her triumph. She patted Jackson on the cheek in an extremely patronising manner. 'I sent all your people home,' she said, winking.

Jackson knew that his only hope was to make a run for it, but he wasn't strong enough to break free from Elvis's grip. Calling out for help wouldn't achieve anything either because his cries would be drowned out by the booing of the audience which was getting louder with each passing moment as they realised the show was ruined.

'Calm down,' said Calhoon. 'These guys aren't going to kill you.'

Jackson sucked in a huge breath of air. Even though he could tell he was in for some serious unpleasantness it was a huge relief to know his life wasn't in danger.

'Oh thank God,' he said, breathing a sigh of relief.

'I'm kidding,' said Calhoon, with a wry smile. 'Of course they're going to kill you.'

Elvis, Rodeo Rex and the Bourbon Kid escorted Jackson from the theatre. Baby and Joey left discreetly via a side exit. Calhoon knew she would never see any of *The Dead Hunters* again. And if she ever saw Blake Jackson again it would only be at his funeral. She had no idea what became of Baby and Joey Conrad, but she hoped they lived a happy life together, maybe in New Zealand.

Epilogue

Dr Jekyll's escape from Landingham Manor had gone perfectly, but the death of Solomon Bennett had left him with an unfortunate predicament. He was ecstatic about the fact that he had survived the massacre and even happier that he had gotten away with a trolley full of the precious Mistralyte. But without Solomon Bennett, Jekyll had to sell the Mistralyte himself. The deal had been arranged for months and was supposed to be a fairly simple transaction carried out in a public place. Jekyll had just never expected to be the person making the exchange.

After some nervous telephone conversations with a man that Bennett had negotiated the deal with months earlier, Jekyll agreed to provide one sample canister of the Mistralyte in exchange for five million dollars. If the exchange went well then a further deal for the bulk of the remaining Mistralyte would follow.

When he arrived at Rae's diner he was feeling more than a little nervous. Inventing and creating ground-breaking potions was his strength, not negotiating trades in poky little diners over breakfast and coffee. He'd done his best not to draw attention to himself by wearing a long grey raincoat, dark sunglasses and a trilby hat. He was carrying a slim black briefcase that contained one canister of Mistralyte. He hoped that he would look like a typical office worker. In truth he looked more like a shady Russian spy with a case full of international secrets. Dressing appropriately had never been one of his strengths. Self-preservation on the other hand, had always been a high priority, so he'd hired a pair of armed bodyguards named Frank and Kevin to watch his back during the exchange. He'd promised the buyer that he would come alone, so Frank and Kevin hung around on the opposite side of the street with instructions to charge in if anything looked like it was going wrong.

Jekyll was relieved to find that there was only one customer in the diner when he arrived. It was a burly black gentleman with greying hair who was probably in his fifties. He was sitting at a booth in the backroom where there were no windows. The man fitted the description of Jekyll's buyer perfectly. He'd been told to look for a big black dude in a red suit and a matching trilby hat, and that was exactly how this guy looked. He had a glass of tomato juice on the table in front of him and a briefcase by his feet, which hopefully contained five million dollars. Jekyll took a deep breath and headed for the table. The man in red stood up and greeted him with a warm smile.

'Good morning,' said Jekyll offering his hand. 'Are you Mr Legba?'

The man in red took his hand and shook it warmly. 'I am, but you can call me Scratch,' he said, grinning. 'It's a real pleasure to meet you Mr Jekyll. I'm a big fan of your work.'

'It's *Doctor* Jekyll, actually.'

'My apologies,' said Scratch, sitting back down. 'What kind of Doctor are you?'

'A creative one.'

'Excuse me?'

Jekyll kept a tight grip on the handle of his briefcase and sat down with it on his lap. 'What I mean to say is, there's currently no specific term for my skills. I'm unique.'

'Yes, I'm sensing that,' said Scratch eyeing up the briefcase. 'Can I order you a drink?'

'Just a water will be fine.'

'Of course.' Scratch shouted across the room. '*Waitress!* A glass of water for my friend, please!'

Jekyll could feel his palms sweating on the handle of his briefcase. The more Scratch stared at the case, the hotter Jekyll's hands seemed to get.

'Is that the merchandise?' Scratch asked.

'It is.' Jekyll nodded at the briefcase by the other man's feet. 'Is that for me?'

'Uh huh.'

'So what do we do now? Count to three and swap cases?'

Scratch grinned, showing off a set of impeccably white teeth. Instead of answering Jekyll's question he slid his case along the floor to Jekyll's side of the table.

'Feel free to count it,' he said. 'There's no one else in here.'

Jekyll picked up the case and laid it on the table in front of him. He took a quick look over his shoulder to make sure no one was behind him. The diner was still empty apart from the waitress behind the counter pouring his glass of water. Out of the corner of his eye he snatched a glimpse out of the front window to check if Frank and Kevin were still loitering across the street. To his relief they were still there, although they weren't particularly being discreet. They were staring into the diner like a couple of morons gazing into an empty fish tank.

'We're perfectly safe here,' said Scratch. 'No one will come in.'

Jekyll nodded and inwardly breathed a sigh of relief. So far everything was going smoothly and the atmosphere was very relaxed.

He flicked open the locks on the briefcase and opened it up. Inside was more money than he had ever seen. He picked out a thick wad of hundred dollar bills and flicked through them. It looked like all the notes were genuine. He lifted a few more wads out just to make sure that the money underneath wasn't made up of one-dollar bills. They all seemed to be okay and after flicking through a few of them he started to feel uneasy, like it might be considered bad etiquette to spend more than a few seconds checking the cash. And besides, even if there wasn't five million in the case, so what? There was enough there to last a lifetime.

'May I see what you've brought in your case?' Scratch asked.

'Of course.'

Jekyll lifted up his own briefcase and handed it across the table to Scratch. Scratch put it on his lap and flipped it open. His face lit up when he saw the canister of Mistralyte inside.

'So this is the stuff?' Scratch said with a broad smile. 'And there's more of it, yes?'

'If you've got more cases like *this one*,' said Jekyll, patting the money case. 'Then I've got plenty more like *that one*.'

'Good.'

The waitress finally appeared at Jekyll's shoulder with a tray carrying his glass of water. She was a slim young lady with short bobbed red hair and pointy blue-rimmed spectacles. Jekyll paid little attention to her face though because her body was to die for. She was just the sort of woman he was hoping to be able to attract with his newfound wealth. He would no longer have to worry about impressing women by being funny or interesting, which was a relief because he wasn't funny or interesting, not even when he was drunk.

The waitress placed his glass of water down on the table. While she wasn't looking he took a sneaky peek at her cleavage. Her pink uniform had a zip down the front and she hadn't zipped it up fully, *the tease*.

'Will there be anything else?' she asked.

Jekyll snapped out of his "tit-staring" trance and answered her. 'No, that's fine, thanks.'

She reached into a pouch on the front of her dress and pulled out a small white envelope. 'I think this is for you,' she said, placing it on the table next to the glass of water.

Jekyll picked up the envelope as the waitress walked away. Someone had written his name on it in black ink. He flipped it over and showed it to Scratch. 'Is this from you?' he asked.

'No,' said Scratch, frowning. 'What is it?'

'I don't know.'

Jekyll ripped the envelope open. There was a small slip of paper inside, folded in two. He pulled it out and unfolded it. Written in black handwriting was a message. It read –

One of the people in this diner is going to kill you.
Guess who?

Jekyll felt like someone had thrown a bucket of ice water over him. His veins turned cold and he felt a shiver down his spine. He had no idea who had written the note. It had to be either Scratch or the waitress. Unless there was someone else hiding nearby?

'Is everything okay? Scratch inquired.

Jekyll was afraid of what he might see when he looked over his shoulder. Maybe the waitress would be brandishing a kitchen knife, or perhaps someone else had snuck into the diner without him noticing? He grabbed the handle on his case full of money and swivelled around on his seat, ready to jump up and run for the door if the need arose.

Unfortunately there was no way he would make it to the door. Three people had stepped out from behind the counter and were blocking off his only escape route from the diner. He recognised them all. Rodeo Rex was wearing a denim outfit and a big brown Stetson hat. Elvis was kitted out in a white jumpsuit with a gold cape that hung down to his waist and an obligatory pair of gold-rimmed sunglasses. The third person was Jasmine. In a moment of feeble weakness, Jekyll forgot about his predicament and gawped at how hot she looked. She was wearing a skin-tight purple catsuit and the same black facemask she had worn when she was pretending to be Britney Spears.

He considered the situation for a moment and decided to remain calm. He had prepared for something like this. Any minute now, Kevin and Frank would burst into the diner and rescue him from these assholes. After all, that's what he was paying them for. In his head he counted to three, hoping to hear the bell above the front door chime as his two heavies stepped in to save the day.

One

Two

Three

The bell above the door chimed right on cue. *Perfect.*

Rex, Elvis and Jasmine didn't seem surprised by the sound of the door opening. They merely stepped aside and allowed Jekyll to see who had entered. Frank and Kevin poked their heads around the door. Well, actually the Bourbon Kid poked their heads around the door. He was wearing a long black coat with the hood up, and he was carrying Kevin's head in his right hand and Frank's in his left. Both their faces were gawping at Jekyll like a couple of imitation Scream masks. The Kid dropped them on the floor and kicked them across the room. They rolled across the floor until they came to a stop at Jekyll's feet.

He vomited at the sight of the two severed heads. The contents of his stomach raced up through his mouth and blasted out onto the ceramic floor. He coughed and spluttered, spitting out the last remnants of the puke, before straightening up and wiping his mouth clean. Another man had entered the diner behind the Bourbon Kid. A man in a mask.

The Red Mohawk.

He was holding a machete in his hand. It was dripping with dark red blood, most likely the blood of Kevin or Frank, or both. Was Dr Jekyll's blood going to be next on the blade? Was it the Red Mohawk who had written the letter? Or had it been written by one of the others?

In fact, it was none of them. The biggest threat was the waitress. She jumped up from behind the counter and slid over it to join the others. Jekyll hadn't looked closely enough at her face when she brought his water over. She had been wearing a bright red wig and glasses. And, well let's face it, he'd been staring at her cleavage more than her face anyway. But now, without the wig or the glasses he recognised her immediately. It was Devon Pincent's daughter, Baby.

She ignored Jekyll for a moment and instead walked up to the Red Mohawk. Without him removing his mask she kissed him on the mouth and her hand slid onto the handle of his machete. She took it from him and turned to face Dr Jekyll.

'You created the monster that killed my father,' she said, holding up the bloodied blade. She looked pissed.

Jekyll spun back round in the hope that Scratch might be able to help him. But Scratch wasn't the kind of guy who helped out people in need. On the contrary he liked a good gloat when someone was in trouble.

'Dr Jekyll,' he said, with a delightful level of smugness. 'Meet the Dead Hunters….'

THE END (probably…)

318

Printed in Great Britain
by Amazon

41759507R00189